Unholy Awakening

ALSO BY MICHAEL GREGORIO

Critique of Criminal Reason
Days of Atonement
A Visible Darkness

Unholy Awakening

Michael Gregorio

MINOTAUR BOOKS

A Thomas Dunne Book
New York

A THOMAS DUNNE BOOK FOR MINOTAUR BOOKS.
An imprint of St. Martin's Publishing Group.

UNHOLY AWAKENING. Copyright © 2010 by Michael Gregorio. All rights reserved. Printed in the United States of America. For information, address St. Martin's Press, 175 Fifth Avenue, New York, N.Y. 10010.

www.thomasdunnebooks.com
www.minotaurbooks.com

The Library of Congress has cataloged the hardcover edition as follows:

Gregorio, Michael.
    Unholy awakening / Michael Gregorio. — 1st U.S. ed.
        p. cm.
    ISBN 978-0-312-62502-3
    1. Stiffeniis, Hanno (Fictitious character)—Fiction. 2. Police magistrates—Germany—Prussia—Fiction. 3. Murder—Investigation—Fiction. 4. Superstition—Fiction. 5. Prussia (Germany)—Rural conditions—Fiction. I. Title.
    PR6107.R4447U65 2010
    823'.92—dc22

                                                                    2010030316

First published in Great Britain by Faber and Faber Limited

10 9 8 7 6 5 4 3 2

Many thanks to all of our readers.

A special thanks to Rita and Francesco Restani.

*'Non v'è pazzia, né dottrina contraddittoria che sia, che non
entri nel cervello dell'uomo.'*
Dissertazione Sopra I Vampiri, 1741
Giuseppe Davanzati, Archbishop of Trani

Translation:
'There is no madness, no doctrine so strange, but it finds its
place in the minds of men.'

Chapter 1

Fear is the price we pay for crime.

Did I read this aphorism in a book? Did someone recite it for me? Or was it an invention of my own making? I don't remember any more. So much happened during the two months when the epidemic was raging, that it was hard to be precise about anything. The fever carried off a third of the population of Lotingen. Like the rude cry of a hungry crow, those words echoed in my head whenever I saw the first signs of illness on faces that I knew and loved.

Lotte burst into the kitchen one morning, eyes wide with fright. The baby was in a dreadful sweat, she said. His eyes were open, but little Anders was unable to wake. Hour after hour we sat beside his cot, Helena and I, while Lotte kept the house and watched for signs of illness in the other children.

The doctor came and went, shaking his head. 'Nervous fever' was his diagnosis. He could offer no prognosis. The child was in the 'slow' phase, only time would tell what the outcome would be.

Anders responded to no-one. Not even to his mother. The fever was raging, it continued to rise while his pulse grew weaker. Within two days his face had altered beyond recognition. His once-blue eyes sank deep inside his skull, losing their colour and freshness. His pupils became opaque at last, his gaze fixed. Each bone in his body grew more pronounced. He had been a chubby baby, but now he was a rasping skeleton. His breathing was irregular, sometimes racing, at other times almost absent. He seemed to slowly fade away. 'Consumed' was the word I would have used, if only I had had the courage to pronounce it. The illness seemed to eat the baby up, and, when it had had its fill, his breathing stopped.

Fear took the place of every other emotion.

Fear for my wife, fear for my children, fear for our friends and neighbours.

… the price we pay for crime.

The phrase rang like a death-knell in my head. But what was the crime we were paying for? And who had committed it? The baby had been too young to sin, yet he had paid with his life. Nor were we the only parents to have lost a child. The fever carried off individuals of every age – from the youngest to the very oldest. Was Lotingen to blame, then? Had the town been condemned to pay for sins unknown and unconfessed?

We buried the baby on the second Thursday of July.

A week later, the worst of the epidemic was over.

But the crime, whatever it might have been, had not been paid in full. Fear persisted, death still knocked occasionally, it would not set us free. I was alarmed by every little upset. Nor could Helena be cured of it. And then, I heard the noise which would come to epitomise my fear that summer, though it had nothing to do with death, or with dying.

A long, low, whooping howl.

I was in my bed, but I was not asleep. I had been half-awake for a long time, lying still, trying not to disturb Helena. My wife needed sleep and the restoration of her spirits after the bereavement. All was quiet in the house, and in the garden, too, but then I heard that noise. I shifted my foot beneath the

4

sheet, searching for the foot of Helena. Her skin was warm and soft; she did not respond to my touch. She was fast asleep. No dream had frightened her that night, or driven her from our bed.

I laid my head flat upon the pillow, straining to hear.

All was silent and still.

Had one of the children made that noise?

I drew the sheet aside, slipped down off the high bed, and made my way barefoot onto the landing. I felt a choking in my throat, as if I could neither swallow nor breathe. Had one of the children caught the fever? They had seen their baby brother die, while they had been spared. Had the nightmare struck again? I would not wake Helena before I was absolutely certain.

I opened the nursery door. A glance was sufficient. All three were sleeping peacefully in their beds beneath the shaded nightlight. And it was in that instant that I heard the low, rumbling howl again. It was coming from the garden, not the mouths of my children. Nor from any human mouth.

I closed the door, darted down the staircase, keeping close to the wall, avoiding the third stair which cracks like a musket being fired.

In the entrance hall, I froze.

On either side of the stout oak door, there is a narrow honeycomb of tiny glass octagons set in a lead frame. I pressed up close to the honeycomb window, staring out.

There were five dogs in the garden.

Almost invisible in the dark, except for the shining red lights of their eyes, they were no more than a yard from my front door.

Seeing me, they bared their fangs and began to growl.

I had heard one voice before. Now, it was a chorus.

Wild dogs had taken possession of my garden, laid siege to my house. If hungry, why had they ignored the compost-heap on the kitchen side of the house? I had seen Lotte drop the remains of a boiled chicken out there that afternoon. Had something else drawn them to my front door? The gleaming panes of glass, perhaps? I had forgotten to close and lock the shutters.

Were they trying to enter?

As I pressed my nose to the glass, I could see the dogs more clearly. They leapt forward, snarling, saliva dripping from their tongues. Their fangs were yellow, pointed. The growl became a howl, as they jostled for position in front of the window. They were not afraid of me. They might have been baiting me, daring me to open the door and let them in.

My thoughts flew back to the epidemic.

Packs of stray dogs had been reported at the time. At first, the idea had been dismissed as nonsense. When we are subject to an enemy that we cannot see, we find an object which is evident to every man. All hate turns upon that object, all of our energy is consumed in condemning it. The fever was invisible, deadly; stray dogs were a visible threat. They could be shot. Then, Hans Hube was killed. Up at dawn to quarter a calf; they found the butcher's body several hours later. The doctor had been hard put to say which bones were his, and which belonged to the slaughtered calf.

These thoughts were dashed from my mind in an instant.

One of the dogs leapt at the window, breaking a pane of glass.

I jumped back, suppressing a cry that would have awakened the whole house. I had seen the dog rear back, but had not expected the attack which followed. Only the lead frame had repulsed it. I had never seen such aggression. A hungry hound is abject, eager to please. It will carry a pheasant to the hunter and accept a biscuit as a reward. This animal, instead, was bold. Savage. Its snout caught the moonlight as it smashed the glass. A spraying black fan of blood was torn from its nose, splattering and dripping on the remaining panes of glass.

The dog fell back, denied.

A moment later, it was charging for the gate. And in its wake the other dogs careered. It was as if the house had withstood the test. The dogs had tried to enter, and they had failed. Colliding in a pack at the narrow exit of the garden gate, they yelped and snapped among themselves, forming some predestined order of withdrawal.

In a matter of seconds, the danger was over.

A cloud passed from the face of the moon, silver light fell on the grass, dark shadows loomed from overhanging trees and bushes. The garden was empty, though I heard them in the distance howling, the sound diminishing as they charged away.

I stood there, unable to move or think until I heard them no more.

Nothing moved inside the house. Helena, Lotte and the children had slept through it. Suddenly, a gasp erupted from my throat. Sweat dripped from my forehead and ran down my back in rivulets, despite the night-time chill.

The dogs had returned to Lotingen.

When the fever was at its height, they had been drawn to town by the all-pervading smell of death. I stood guard by the broken window for quite some time, ears straining to catch the slightest sound, the smallest hint that the beasts had returned.

My bare feet ached with the cold.

Had the dogs smelt death that night in Lotingen?

7

Chapter 2

Winter would come early, everyone hoped.

There is nothing better than a cold snap to dispel foul summer air and ward off the perils of fever. Instead, the first week of September brought an Indian summer. The 7th was a Wednesday, the sun shone, the sky was sketchy blue. Clouds were massing on the horizon like an army clothed in grey, uncertain whether to engage the enemy that day, or wait until the morrow.

Gudjøn Knutzen came shambling into my office. He was minus his collar, and pigsty mud encrusted his boots. The news my secretary brought in – along with the smell of mulch – was as bland and inoffensive as the weather.

'I met one of the Schuettler brothers, Herr Procurator,' he began. 'He'd just stepped off the canal bank, and was in a bit of a puff. He asked me if I'd tell you something, sir. He had to get back home, and he told me that he would wait for you there.'

I put down my pen, and dried the ink.

'Wait for me where?' I asked.

Knutzen stepped close to my desk, and my stomach rolled over.

Carbolic crystals ...

I sat as far back in my seat as I could manage. Since the height of the epidemic, Knutzen, and many another citizen, had taken to carrying little sacks of the desiccated chemicals

8

around in their pockets. The penetrating odour was supposed to protect the carrier against infection. It certainly protected them from closer human contact with those like myself, whose eyes begin to smart profusely in the presence of the stuff.

'At the Prior's House, sir,' Knutzen replied, frowning thoughtfully. 'Have you got a cold, sir? Your eyes are watering like a broken pump. He asked if you would be so kind as to take a walk out that way.'

I wiped my eyes. 'Did he say why?'

Knutzen sniffed loudly. 'He did not, Herr Stiffeniis. Only that there was something there that you would wish to see.'

'He didn't tell you what it was?'

Knutzen shook his head.

Ten minutes later, I was striding out along the left bank of the Cut with Knutzen at my side, heading towards the Prior's House, which lies no more than a mile outside the western limit of the town. Knutzen held his peace for once, and I was grateful of it. No news of his potbellied pig. It had not littered, evidently. No complaints about the French requisitioning of his apples and plums. I set a good pace. Knutzen matched me in rhythm, and outdid me in vigour.

Halfway there, the sun was suddenly cancelled out as a cloud cast its vast shadow over the land. The evergreen woods were instantly tinged an opaque grey, the taller trees seemed stark and skeletal, having begun that week to lose their leaves. The fields, which had been recently harvested, changed in a flash from gleaming gold to dark russet brown. Sun or shade, the rippling waters of the canal were always black. The water erupted in a splash as a sizeable, silver-blue pike leapt out of the shallows, chasing sprats, or cannibalising its pickerel in the gluttony of autumn.

The ruined profile of the Prior's House stood out against the flat horizon.

Originally a Benedictine monastery, the church and cloister had both been demolished. The suppression dated back to the days of Luther, and only the dormitory wing had survived. Now, it was a ruin, too. Frederick the Great had requisitioned the building half a century before as a staging-post where troops on the march from Danzig to Königsberg could eat, sleep and smoke. And they had done just that, until one officer fell asleep, replete with food and wine, his pipe still burning, and the dormitory was burnt to the ground. Only the outer walls still stood, together with the Prior's House, which had been built four hundred years or more ago to house the head of the community.

Plovers whooped, and whimbrels whistled from the stubbly fields.

Two figures appeared in miniature on the gravel path ahead of us. One of them raised a hand in our direction.

'Gurt Schuettler,' Knutzen announced. 'And brother.'

'What's the brother's name?'

'No idea, sir. I've never been in his company. He'll not speak to any man, except his brother.'

The Schuettlers were as indistinguishable as twins. Both the same height – that is, below the level of my shoulder – they wore peasant-smocks which were grey and stiff with age and dirt. Their feet were encased in brown woollen socks and heavy wooden pattens. Matching baggy corduroy trousers were bundled tightly to their legs below the knee with twine cross-bindings. They were both on the downward slope of life, each year showing itself in a wrinkle, scar or mole.

'Gurt Schuettler?'

'And brother,' the man announced, stepping up to me, pointing over his shoulder with his thumb.

The other man looked away.

'What ...' I said, then paused. I had been about to insist on knowing the other man's name. Then again, I thought this was not an investigation. For the moment, it was nothing more than a formal presentation, a polite exchanging of names. 'My secretary tells me that you wish to show me something, Schuettler.' I spread my arms wide, and affected a smile. 'Well, here I am.'

Gurt Schuettler took a step closer, as if he felt the urge to confide.

I took a half-step backwards, assaulted by the heady brew of sweat that the man and his clothes gave off.

'I ... I don't know how to put it, sir. Then again, you'll judge for yourself.'

He turned away and began to walk towards a gate which gave access to the house and whatever else was contained inside the boundary walls. As he marched off, his silent brother fell into step at his side. Knutzen made to follow them.

'Where are you going?' I called, reluctant to join the party without some preliminary explanation.

Gurt Schuettler did not turn around. Nor did he halt. He pointed ahead, and called back over his shoulder. 'To the sunken garden, sir. And the dry well. That's where we are going.'

The boundary wall was long and high. The garden and the land must be extensive. And then there was the house itself. Peeping over the brick wall, I could see the top half of four mullioned windows and a mossy red-tiled roof. The dwelling appeared to be a sort of stately manor in the rustic style. It was three or four times grander than my own small house on the other side of Lotingen.

The brothers stopped by the gate, waiting for Knutzen and myself.

'Do you live alone here? You and your brother, I mean,' I asked.

'Not at the moment, sir,' Gurt Schuettler replied. 'A gentleman and a lady have come to stay. Recently arrived in town, I do believe. Been here a week. Rented the house from Lawyer Wellbach. He administers the estate on behalf of the Bishop of Lotingen. I am just the caretaker of the property.'

The gate was fifteen hands high, and almost as wide, divided in the centre, and closed by a latch. There was no lock to secure the gate, I noticed. Gurt Schuettler opened the right half of the gate, then went ahead, taking three broad stone steps down into what was evidently the sunken garden. I came next, and Knutzen followed on my heels. The silent brother trailed behind.

The garden was a large green square with well-kept borders full of flowers and shrubs. A gravel path like the one beside the canal ran close around the four walls and in a diagonal cross which intersected in the centre of the garden. At the meeting-point was a waist-high wall, built in a circle of rustic stone, surmounted by a cross-tree and a pulley. A wooden bucket black with age was resting on the ground beside it, while a partially rotted wooden cover had been thrown aside to reveal the well-shaft which was the centrepiece of the garden.

A woman was standing at the well.

White hands resting on the wall, she was staring down into the darkness.

All that I could see of her was a billowing black cloak and a hood of the same hue. She did not turn as we crunched over the gravel. It was as if she had not heard us. Her attention was focused on what lay inside the well.

'Mistress,' Gurt Schuettler called, as we approached her.

The woman turned her head. She looked to be no more than thirty years old. I am tall, but she was not much shorter. Her well-formed face was pale, her lips a muted and natural red. Curving eyebrows traced the line of her broad and handsome brow. Beneath, her eyes were brown like roasted hazelnuts. The pupils glinted as she watched our coming, raising her hands, throwing back her hood to reveal a mass of dark brown hair which fell in riotous curls upon her shoulders. Her aquiline nose, though prominent, was graceful, lending strength and purposefulness to a face which was immensely feminine.

'I am no man's mistress, sir,' she replied, her voice gentler than I expected. It was the cultured voice of a person who had lived in town. She was not rudely reprimanding the old man's mistake, but she was correcting it, and playfully, too, as if she had done so quite a number of times already.

Schuettler pointed at me. 'Here's the judge,' he announced.

For the sake of clarity, I, too, was obliged to correct him. 'I am a legal procurator. Hanno Stiffeniis,' I said, bowing slightly in the woman's direction. 'I am the magistrate of Lotingen. What is your name, ma'am?'

'Rimmele,' she said, rolling the m's, then rolling them again. 'Emma Rimmele.'

Her eyes glanced into mine, glanced away, glanced back again. She turned once more to peer down into the well. There was something feverish in her look. In some odd way, it reminded me of the look of Anders on the night that he had died. In his agony, his eyes had come to life again. Liquid, mercurial, darting here and there, never fixed or still for more

13

than an instant. She was afraid, I could see it clearly. But what was she afraid of?

'Here we are, sir.' Schuettler tapped the ancient wooden bucket with the side of his boot to attract my attention.

I glanced at the bucket, then at him.

The wood was rotten, the iron hoops were rusty. The vessel was of no use for carrying water, or anything else. It seemed to serve no more than an ornamental purpose, as if to say that a well without a bucket was no well at all.

Gurt Schuettler swept up the bucket, and he held it out for me to see.

I took a step forward, and peered into the bottom of the container. In the first instant, I did not recognise the thing for what it was. It might have been some small misshapen creature. The larva of some insect. Had he brought me all that way to show me some peculiar freak of nature?

'It is human, sir,' he explained. 'A tooth.'

Schuettler's voice and opinion took me by surprise.

I looked more closely. It was certainly a tooth. Bits of nerve and dried blood clung to the roots, which protruded as three stubby prongs of unequal length.

'Jus' like this one here,' Schuettler grunted, setting down the bucket.

He stood up, and I found myself peering into a gaping black hole. He was pulling at the side of his mouth with his left forefinger, exposing his own teeth, pointing with the filthy cracked nail of his right forefinger to a gap in the lower row of rotten, tobacco-stained tombstones.

'Wisdom tooth is what they calls it,' he gurgled.

He removed his finger, closed his mouth and stared at me.

'Whose tooth is it?' I asked him. 'Not yours, Herr Schuettler. Nor your brother's, I take it?'

Both men shook their heads.

I turned to the lady. 'I hardly think that it is yours, ma'am?'

'That is the point, Herr Procurator,' she said. 'We have no idea who that tooth may belong to. Nor can we guess what it is doing in the bucket.'

There was nothing horrifying in the spectacle, but it was certainly odd. And Emma Rimmele was right. How had it come to find its way into the bucket?

She was standing at my shoulder, peering down at the tooth.

'Might it belong to your husband?' I asked her.

A vein throbbed in her temple. 'I am not married,' she replied.

'So the gentleman …'

'My father, sir. No barber has been to pull a tooth from his mouth. And even if he had, my father could not walk so far as the well. Those three steps,' she said, pointing to the porch with its flat pediment and two slender columns, 'would quite defeat him. Herr Schuettler is correct. If it belongs to no-one here, then who does it belong to?'

I glanced into the bucket. 'Could it be a joke of some sort?'

There was no trace of amusement in the laugh which answered this suggestion.

'A joke, Herr Procurator? A threat, more like.'

'A threat, ma'am? A tooth in a bucket? What sort of a threat is that? If Schuettler had not found it, it might have gone undiscovered.' I turned to Schuettler, asking him: 'How did you come to find it?'

He rubbed his chin before he answered. 'It was not here yesterday,' he said. 'We was gathering up the dead leaves from

15

the garden with a rake in the afternoon. I moved the bucket twice to make the going easier. It was empty then. And as you can see, sir, someone has removed the cover from the well, too. Nobody's done such a thing these last five years.'

A short way from the well, the cover was lying on the grass.

I dropped down on one knee and examined it. The wood was black and rotten like the bucket, though stouter in its manufacture, five boards welded together by means of three cross-pieces, trimmed to form a circular lid which would have rested on the well-shaft.

'Why would anyone remove the cover?' I asked.

'That's the mystery,' said Schuettler. 'This well has not been used since they dug the canal, which was all of fifty years ago, sir. The well dried up very shortly afterwards.'

While he was speaking, I had placed my hands on the stone rim, and was looking down into the darkness. Emma Rimmele was doing the same thing on the other side. At the same instant, we both looked up. She held my gaze for some moments, as if she wanted to say something, but did not dare. Was she thinking what I had begun to think?

'Someone pulled it out of someone's mouth, sir,' Schuettler said.

'You think that there is ... something down there.'

'Aye, sir,' Schuettler seconded quickly. 'That's why I called for you.'

I was silent for a moment.

'What could this "something" be, do you think?'

The old man's face was brown and weather-beaten. White lines appeared as his expression changed. 'I ... I cannot say, sir,' he replied hesitantly.

I looked down into the darkness again. The light could

16

hardly penetrate more than ten or twelve feet, the shaft was narrow. And yet, it was solidly built, made of the same rough-hewn material as the section of the wall above the ground. I took up a fragment of a stone that must have shattered with last winter's frost, and I dropped it into the well, listening until I heard it clatter on solid ground.

'No water, as you said.'

'And deep, sir. That's why it is always covered.'

I turned my attention to a rope which was neatly coiled around the ratchet of the pulley. 'This rope is new,' I said. 'If the well's been dry so long, who changed the rope? And why?'

Gurt Schuettler swept his shapeless cap from his head, and ran a hand through his grey, uncombed hair. 'Herr Ludvig, sir. A gentleman who once rented the house. He had a new rope bought, and climbed down there to see what he could find. The old one was made of twisted straw. It was rotted through, and would have broke with the weight of any man who was bold enough to risk it.'

'When was this?' I asked him.

'Five or six years back, sir.'

'And what did he discover down there?'

Schuettler chuckled to himself before replying. 'Herr Ludvig had a theory, sir. He said the monks would rather throw out broken cups and plates than tell the Prior that they had broke his crockery.'

'You helped Herr Ludvig, did you?'

'Me and my brother pulled on the rope. He found no end of ancient bits and bobs.'

'You'll help us climb down in the same fashion,' I said. 'I'll go first. Knutzen, you will follow me.'

Knutzen gaped at me, his eyes wide with apprehension.

17

'Bring a lamp, Herr Schuettler.'

While Schuettler scurried off to find a lamp, his brother trailing behind him, Knutzen, Emma Rimmele and myself stood waiting by the well-shaft.

'What brings you to Lotingen, ma'am?' I asked.

Her lips pursed, but she did not answer immediately.

'I hoped ...'

She did not finish whatever thought was forming in her head.

'Hoped, Fraulein Rimmele? For what, ma'am?'

'To find some peace,' she said at last. 'My mother died quite recently. My father has still not managed to get over the tragedy.'

'I am sorry to hear it,' I said, thinking of my own dear son. 'Duty requires it, of course, I'll have to go down there and take a look. Still, I wouldn't worry, there may be nothing to find,' I assured her.

Her reply was a breathless whisper. 'I hope you are right.'

As the brothers reappeared through a wicket gate, each carrying a lamp, I began to prepare for the descent. I took off my jacket, detached the rope from the handle of the bucket, prepared a sliding noose with a safety-knot, then pulled it tight around my waist.

'Let me down slowly,' I instructed them. 'Release more rope as I call out for it. Then, lower a lamp. When I have reached the bottom, Knutzen, follow me down.'

I sat on the edge of the wall, and let my legs dangle into the shaft.

'Do not let out rope unless I call for it,' I warned Gurt Schuettler again.

'Be careful,' Emma Rimmele implored, concern written plainly on her face.

I turned about, resting my hands on the wall, taking the weight on my wrists, finding a sure grip with my toes, and began to slowly edge down into the void, moving carefully from stone to stone.

'Rope!' I shouted up whenever I needed more.

As slack rope came, I stretched further down and felt around for a toe-hold. It was easier than I had imagined. The walls were rough and irregular. The large blocks of stone had been hacked into cubes, then locked together by the downward thrust of their weight. They served as vertical stepping-stones, while the rope guaranteed my safety if my boots were to slip, which happened more than once as I moved down out of the light and into the penumbra, and finally into pitch darkness, proceeding ever deeper into the ground.

I took five or six more steps, and suddenly I was swinging wildly in space, feeling blindly for a wall that was no longer there. The sudden dead weight must have pulled the rope from the hands of the men above, and I began to fall. I had hardly opened my mouth to shout, when I hit the floor.

'Herr Stiffeniis?' Knutzen shouted.

I smiled, interpreting my secretary's anxiety in my own fashion. If I broke my neck, his wages would be slow in coming.

'Send down the lamp,' I shouted, slipping the rope from my waist, letting go of it, watching as it spun up above my head like a receding noose. The circle of light above me was no larger than a dull silver coin.

I stood in total darkness, waiting for the lantern to arrive.

My eyes were useless, but my nose was not. I could smell damp mustiness. And something else, a smell of putrefaction, as if an animal had fallen down the well and died there. Last

19

spring, I had been obliged to bury a rotting badger in my garden. This smell reminded me of it.

'Watch out, sir!'

The lamp came down, casting a circle of light on the mossy stone walls.

At last, I held it in my grasp, undoing the knot, calling for the rope to be pulled up, and for Knutzen to come down. I raised the lantern and looked around, surprised by what I found. I was in a sort of a cistern, a chamber built of solid stone, which opened out laterally at the bottom of the shaft. More spacious than the largest bedroom in my house, the ceiling was barely five feet high. I looked behind me, saw my shadow stretching out on the floor, bending sharply upwards as it struck the wall. I turned to the right, and that was when I saw it.

White. Clenched tightly in a fist. A human hand.

I drew in a deep breath, then took some steps towards it.

The hand was attached to the body of a woman, lying face-down.

I wondered how her corpse had come to rest in that precise spot, which was not directly at the bottom of the shaft, as one might have expected. Had she been alive after such a fall, and crawled to the corner of the cistern before she died?

I heard a curse above me.

Knutzen was dangling and swaying, kicking his legs like a swimmer in the disc of light above my head. He had lost his footing. Heavier and older than myself, he must have been a severe trial on the strength of the brothers up on the surface. With a whooping cry, he fell the last few feet, breaking his fall as he banged against me, knocking me sideways like a skittle.

'Are you in one piece?' I asked him, catching my breath.

As I bent to help him up, offering my hand, I saw his face.

His eyes were fixed on the sight which lay behind me. His mouth gaped open. He had seen the corpse, though the feeble lantern flame made only a slight impression in the gloom.

'Is she dead, sir?' he asked in a whisper.

I picked up the lantern, moved close to the body, knelt down beside it, and laid the flat of my palm on the woman's wrist. Her skin was very cold and damp. I felt her wrist, but there was no sensation of pulsing blood.

'Dead,' I confirmed.

There is nothing quite so awesome as a lifeless body. This corpse was slender, female, wider at the hips than at the shoulders. Her hair was long and black. It covered her neck, and hid her face. The exposed skin of her hands, arms and lower legs was pale and shadowy blue like glacier ice. She had lost one of her shoes. The sole of her left foot was lacerated. I took her hands in mine, one after the other, and examined the knuckles. They were scuffed and torn. She must have struck them against the rough stone wall as she fell.

'Help me turn her over,' I said.

Knutzen did not move.

'Come here and help me, Knutzen!' I ordered, hoping to shake him from his state of shocked and useless lethargy.

I slid my hands beneath her body, feeling the deadweight, the involuntary shifting of flesh as I began to prise her away from the ground, meaning to turn her onto her back. I wanted to see her face, hoping that I might be able to put a name to it – hoping, too, that I might not. She was unwieldy, as is every inanimate corpse.

Suddenly, she flipped over and slipped from my grasp.

Her body settled one way, and a sigh escaped from her lips. Her head rolled to the other side, lolling for a moment before it came to rest. I held the lantern up above her head. Her face was black with blood and damp earth. Fresh liquid like saliva began to ooze from the corners of her mouth and dribble down the sides of her face. Her nostrils were distended, flattened; the entire weight of her head had been resting on the tip of her nose. Her eyes were open wide, shimmering in the pale lantern-light like marrow-bone jelly.

Knutzen let out a whimper of fright.

'Do you recognise her?' I asked.

'It's … it's the seamstress, sir,' he whispered with a moan.

'Do you know her name?'

'Angela,' he murmured. 'Angela Enke of Krupeken …'

I checked to see if there was a wound, but I found none. The body seemed to be intact. Unharmed, apart from the fact that she was dead. I felt along her legs and arms for broken bones without result. I cradled her head in my hands – surprised at how heavy it was – shifting it gently this way and that, but I could find no evidence of any break in the neck. I pulled the matted hair away.

Two rivulets of blood were evident. Two wounds, half an inch apart, one above the other, along the line of the swollen artery in her neck. Like claw marks, they were deep where the incision had been made, shallower as the weapon had been ripped away. Her skin was blue, though the edges of the killing wounds were red and raw.

Two small circular holes …

Knutzen fell back. I heard the rasp of his breathing. He stared at the body, pushing himself frantically back against the wall, scrambling with his boots in the dust and dirt.

When he spoke, his voice was a hoarse growl.

'You *know* who killed her, don't you, sir?'

Chapter 3

Emma Rimmele was watching me with fixed intensity.

'There is a corpse down there,' I announced. 'A young woman.'

As I untied the rope from around my waist, her eyes flashed questioningly into mine. Her face was a mask of perplexity when she heard me ordering Knutzen to run to town for help.

'We'll need experienced men to bring the body up,' I explained.

I knew that I would face far greater difficulties when the corpse was on the surface, but for the moment I preferred not to dwell on that.

'You and I must talk,' she said, her voice raw-edged and low.

Her eyebrows met in an upward-sweeping frown. Her bottom lip was a bright and tender red, as if she had been chewing it in torment. She was afraid, I could clearly see. I was not surprised by her reaction, however, but by her forwardness.

'Very well,' I said. 'They won't be here for some time yet.'

I knew that I would have to question her in any case before the day was out.

'Inside the house, if you please,' she added, turning away, walking quickly back towards the porch.

'Wait here,' I told the Schuettler brothers. 'Call me as soon as Knutzen returns.'

Then, I turned away and followed her along the gravel path.

Emma Rimmele was standing on the front step, waiting for me. As I came up to her, she pushed with her hand against the door, and walked inside, closing the door behind me the instant that I had entered the hallway.

It was dark and chill, the hall undecorated, except for a sweeping flight of wooden stairs which led to the floor above. The staircase was old in style and rough in its making. The wood they had used was black, each step irregular in its shape, sagging at the centre, steep in profile like a quarry roughly cut in the side of a mountain. Again, I wondered what had brought her there. She was not like the Schuettlers, rough peasants who were used to living in a crumbling ruin. Was this the best accommodation that she could find in Lotingen? Why had she rented such a dreary place so far from town?

An aura seemed to emanate from her person. Indoors, it was more intense. It was not cloying and persistent like a perfume, nor flat and lifeless like a distiller's scent. It was more complex in its constituent parts than any chemist's artifice could produce. One part was made of the damp earth and crushed grass which clung to the hem of her cloak. The greater part was sweet and aromatic, like strawberries growing wild in the woods. She might have been a sylvan goddess, who dwelt beneath the sun and the stars, eating nothing but the riches of bounteous Nature.

I breathed in deeply, and a vital energy seemed to reinvigorate me.

'The day-room is upstairs,' she said, racing ahead with the grace of a cat.

I was swept along and carried up the flight of stairs in her wake. Her hair was now piled up tightly on her head, and held in place with a shining metal brooch which was embossed with

24

a figure – Medusa, as I later observed. She must have pulled her hair away from her face and clipped it up behind as she was staring into the depths of the well. As she passed before the leaded window on the staircase, it shimmered like a palette of autumn leaves – dark brown, auburn, gold, and every tint between.

At the top of the stairs there was a pale green door.

Though badly faded, it had once been decorated with golden garlands. Worms had left myriad holes in the wood. Pushing open the door with the heel of her hand, she strode to the centre of the room. I followed her in, hesitating on the threshold, looking around me, taking in my surroundings, noting the sober aspect of the grey stone floor, the vast emptiness of the room, the pretence of gentility in the powder-blue walls, a faded fresco on the ceiling – angels, pagan gods and birds in tangled flight together. The Prior's furniture had long since been removed, sold perhaps, replaced with the barest necessities.

She gave me little time to look around.

'Don't stand there, sir,' she said, a hint of raw impatience in her voice, glancing beyond my shoulder. 'Please, close the door. My father's sitting-room is on the other side of the corridor. I do not wish to disturb him, Procurator Stiffeniis.'

I turned away and closed the door with care.

'Come closer, sir. There is no reason for us to shout,' she said, taking a pace towards me, raising her hand to take me by the arm, stopping herself abruptly as she recalled who I was, and what I was doing there. 'I will not tell him what has happened here today. You can be sure of that, sir.'

The room was bare, except for a settle, and a matching cupboard of the same dark wood. It was dominated by a large open fireplace set around with pale Dutch tiles. Blue figures on a flour-coloured ground. They must have represented saints. The fury of the peasants had been unleashed against the monks, not against the symbols of the religion which sustained them. That brand of vandalism came later, when the buildings fell into the hands of the king's troops. There were bullet holes all over the room, pock-marks in the plaster, and all of the Dutch tiles were smashed and shattered. The soldiers had used the frescoes and the saints for target practice.

'The men will soon be here to bring up the corpse,' I warned her. 'It won't be easy to hide what has happened from your father, Fraulein Rimmele. I'll need to question him, 'in any case. He may have heard or seen something.'

While I was speaking, Emma Rimmele had taken a pace or two towards the mullioned windows which looked out over the lawn and the well. She turned on me in a flash, pointing her forefinger at me as if it were an arrow she was about to let fly. She stared at me in silence. The pearls which dangled from her ears were the only animated things in that room. 'Speak with him? What can my father tell you that I cannot?'

The windows in the room faced westwards. The incoming light should have been strong and bright, but two large trees had been planted close to the outer wall, and cast their leafy shadows into the room. It was not yet noon, but there it might have been late afternoon, or early evening. The patterns of the foliage fell on the grey stone floor like a shifting carpet.

I spread my arms wide, and appealed to her. 'It must be obvious,' I said. 'I am a magistrate. I'll have to question everyone who is living on the property. And that includes your father, unfortunately. There is a body at the bottom of your well, Fraulein Rimmele. The body of a young woman. She did not climb down there of her own free will.'

Her pointed forefinger sank down by her side. She covered her mouth with her left hand, closing her eyes, frowning as she said, 'She was murdered, then? There is no doubt of it, I suppose?'

I recalled the words of Knutzen at the bottom of the well. *You know who killed her …*

I had said nothing to contradict him. As I examined the wounds to her neck, had I seemed to share the truth of what he had said? Had my silence spoken louder than any words could, confirming what he believed?

'No doubt at all,' I said. 'The killer struck … a wound to the neck … with something sharp. Having mortally wounded her, he tried to hide the body by throwing it into the well-shaft. And there she bled to death …'

'Can you be so certain?' she challenged. 'Wouldn't you say that the killer left her there on purpose because he wanted her to be found? He could have thrown the body in the Cut. Why place that tooth in the bucket, and remove the well-cover?'

'We don't know how the tooth arrived there.'

'The tooth is hers, is it not?'

I did not reply. What could I say? I had not thought to open the dead girl's mouth and check while making a cursory inspection in the gloom. And how could I explain the omission to her, except by saying that I had been as shaken and confused as my secretary, Knutzen?

She seemed to want no explanation, however. In her opinion, no other possibility existed. 'It *must* be hers. It belongs to no-one here.'

With a rapid tug, she tore the clip from her hair, which

tumbled down in a mass upon her shoulders. Equally rapidly, she pulled at the bow which held her cloak in place, kicking away the garment as it slid to the floor. She was like a grass snake shrugging off an old skin. The cambric blouse she wore was dyed a dark, rusty red. It might have been a man's shirt, if not for the lace cuffs attached to the sleeves. She had turned the cuffs back at some point, exposing her forearms, perhaps to lean more easily on the rim and look down into the depths of the well. Her naked skin was the gold of Baltic amber. It contrasted sharply with the dark tint of her blouse, and even more so with the paler skin of her breasts, just visible where she had undone three or four buttons at the neckline. It was as if the sun had cut its way through the weave of her clothes and left its imprint on her body.

And yet, her face remained as pale as before.

Two seats had been cut into the stone on either side of the window. Perhaps the Catholic monks had sat there reading, taking advantage of the last rays of the sun in the failing light. They may have been sitting there, I thought, when the Lutheran hordes came to chase them from that place forever. Emma Rimmele let herself fall down on one of the stone benches, resting her back against the wall, gathering her gown in both hands, crushing it tightly in her joined fists. She looked out of the window, releasing her imprisoned dress, resting her elbows on her knees as she clasped her face in her hands.

She looked down, shook her hair out, and her profile was lost to my sight.

Beneath the gown, her legs appeared long. Her hands were nervous, energetic, constantly in movement. I could not find a trace of domesticity in her. Had those fingers ever sewn a hem, or darned a sock? The muscles of her hands and wrists suggested a life spent tugging at the reins, urging timid horses over stiles and fences. I had an impression of contained sensuality, and a tendency to dominate. This notion was re-inforced by all her gestures, which were somehow masculine and brusque.

'Sit here in front of me, Herr Magistrate,' she invited with a wave of her hand towards the other window-seat. 'I need to look into a human face, and feel compassion when you tell me what you saw down there. I saw no pity on the faces of the Schuettlers and that man of yours. I saw nothing at all,' she said, 'except for childish terror.'

I took my place on the opposite bench.

'Nor can I expect anything else if my father is to be told ...'

She looked up at me, her face a mask of concern.

'Let me tell you about my father, sir. He is ill. In the mind, I mean. No physician has been able to follow the pattern of his thoughts for a long time now. Every time that I look into his face, whenever I try to speak to him, I have no idea what he is thinking. Can you believe that? No idea *who* he has become.' She pressed her hands together, pushing them down between her knees once more, which caused the hem of her gown to rise. Her shoes were not the fashionable pumps that well-bred ladies generally favour. They were boot-like, tightly laced above her ankles. Except for the flat heel, they were the sort that a man might wear for walking in the country. And yet, her rapid steps had been quite silent on the tiled floor, while my metal-tipped shoes had set off an instant clicking and tapping as I followed her about. And even more oddly, I noticed that she wore no stockings. Her legs were as bare as the legs of a peasant woman who would rather work barefoot than consume her precious clogs.

'Can you understand the burdens brought by such an inconstant state of mind?'

I could have answered, but I did not. I knew the ravages of old age. I had seen dementia take possession of the most rational man that the kingdom of Prussia has ever produced. Professor Immanuel Kant, the metaphysician, had been immune to every idle mental caprice, critical of every human frailty, throughout his long and profitable life. And yet, before the end, even Kant had become the opposite of himself. He had been transformed into a different person. A creature lost in a world without rules, a world where rational thought no longer held dominion.

'What does your father do?' I asked.

'What *did* he do,' she corrected me gently. 'Seeing him today, you'd not believe his story. Erwin Rimmele was once the owner of four merchant banking houses along the coast between Danzig and Tallin. Not a thaler escaped his attention. Numerous clerks kept the accounts which shipowners and rich merchants entrusted to his care. But then a shadow fell upon his mind. Not all at once, but slowly, imperceptibly. He became forgetful of names, of people that he had known a lifetime, and, worst of all, of transactions that he ought to have been following attentively. Finally, even words began to fail him.' She flagged, and sighed out loud. 'As you know, sir, in Prussia these days it is the mode to blame everything on Napoleon, but even the French invasion washed clean over my father's head. He has lost his path in a mental fog, and there's no finding his way out of the wood. He no longer recognises what was once familiar. He does not always recognise *me*! And this uncertainty terrifies him more than anything.'

I gave her a moment to collect herself before I spoke.

'Why come to Lotingen, then? Why choose this house? This was a monastery once. Later, a military barracks. It … it hardly seems the sort of place to take up residence.'

Emma Rimmele looked up with dreadful seriousness, but she did not speak.

The leaves outside the window cast a greenish light across her features.

Suddenly, she shook her head and smiled.

I did not know where to look. If I expected demure femininity, she confounded me at every move. We might have been old friends. I could see quite clearly that she was upset, still frightened, though she would not resort to tears. Quite the opposite. She projected strength of character. There was nothing affected in her manner, no feigned timidity or manipulative use of a supposed female weakness. She did not appeal to masculine sympathy, nor seem to look for any grain of comprehension. She behaved towards me as one might towards a brother or a sister, confiding whatever came into her mind with candid directness.

'My great concern,' she went on, 'is to avoid change. I try to keep him on the old, familiar paths, hoping that his memory will come back to him. If only for a moment. Just one,' she said, holding up her index finger for emphasis. 'A normal day would be a miracle, sir, and yet I dare to hope that miracles are possible. I set out purposely to find a house like this one in Lotingen. That is, a house as similar as possible to the house that we were forced to leave.'

'Forced?'

She nodded. 'Our home was seized not long ago by the French. They lodged the officers of a cavalry regiment there. My father does not notice details; size and scale are everything

31

to him. If I could find a house of roughly the same layout and dimensions, I thought, it would be for the best. I had to remove him from our home, in any case. The rowdy behaviour of the French intruders made life impossible. And shortly after they arrived, my mother died. It was during the epidemic. Her death and the need to ensure a decent burial have done the rest ...'

I stared at her. 'Your mother?'

She held my gaze, and nodded.

'I am sorry to hear it,' I said.

'How many people died in Lotingen?' she asked. 'Was it half the population?'

'Not half the population,' I murmured. 'A third, almost.'

'In our house, apart from Father and myself, two serfs survived,' she said. 'There had been ten of them at the start of the month. But Mother was the first to succumb. In its way, it was a blessing in disguise. She was buried in a solid oak coffin, which was placed inside the family vault. The servants were bundled without much ceremony into holes in the ground. The spectacle drove my father out of his wits entirely.'

'Where were you living?' I asked.

She did not reply at once. I put her hesitation down to sorrow. She had lost her mother, her home and, in a certain sense, her father, too.

'To the north-west. In the country outside Marienburg,' she said at last.

I imagined that the burials in Marienburg had been like those in Lotingen. Hasty, lacking in religion and respect. Carried out by the employees of the sanitary inspector's office, whose haste hid fright as much as cruelty. Emma Rimmele must have walked the same dark road. I was tempted to tell her about the death of Anders. I would have liked to tell her about Helena's reaction to the tragedy, the high wall which had reared up between my wife and myself. It was folly, I realised. I was the investigating magistrate, and Emma Rimmele was a stranger to me. A corpse had been discovered in the garden of the house where she was living. That was all that mattered.

'Regarding the body in the well,' I said, seeking refuge in facts. 'My clerk was able to identify her. She lived not far from here, he says, in the village of Krupeken. Her name was Angela Enke.'

I did not think to ask her if she knew the victim. How long had they been living there? A week? She might recognise a few people from the neighbourhood by sight, perhaps, but she would know far fewer by name.

Emma jumped up. She turned towards the window, freeing her gown, which twirled around her figure. Her naked shins disappeared beneath the folds as if a shutter had been suddenly closed on a window that had been unexpectedly opened.

'Angela Enke?' she whispered, catching her breath, her right hand clutching at her throat. Then, she raised both hands to her head, pushing her curls back tightly over her forehead as if they were a troublesome veil. 'Is it Angela's body down there?'

'I'm afraid it is,' I said, surprised.

The pearls danced furiously in her ear-lobes as she shook her head.

'Oh, God!' she muttered softly.

'Did you know her?' I asked.

She shook her head uncertainly, then nodded. Her eyes filled with tears, her lips parted, sounds issued from her mouth. Moans of distress, but not one intelligible word.

She turned away, and stared out of the window.

I placed my hands on her shoulders. I felt the involuntary jerking of her frame beneath my palms as she fought to hold back sobs. Then she turned to face me, eyes staring into mine. Impulsively, she stepped towards me, crushing herself against my chest, pressing her hands against my shoulder blades, pulling me towards her.

I held her, and I felt the force of her emotions.

Her hair was in my face, crushing against my nose and mouth. I did not pull away, but breathed it in. I closed my eyes, and smelled the perfume of the woods, wild flowers, damp moss. I might have been walking in the forest after a rain shower.

She leant back in my arms, making no attempt to free herself, staring up into my eyes again. The tears were gone. Her eyes were wide with fear.

'Why would anyone want to murder her?' she asked.

'I do not know,' I admitted, but I was puzzled.

Why throw a body into a well, then leave a tooth in a bucket on the surface? Why leave the well-cover lying on the grass where it would be noticed? Why not put it back in its place, and hide the secret in the dark below? Had the killer been frightened off before he could finish the deed, or had he left those signs there purposely?

Down on the canal path, I heard the crunch of wheels, the sound of approaching hooves, the cry of the driver calling for the horse to halt. Knutzen had been quick. The men had arrived. I heard the voice of Schuettler calling to them to enter the garden.

I stepped back quickly.

'You must excuse me,' I said.

'For having held me, or for having let me go?' she murmured.

34

'I … I must go down. The body will have to be brought to the surface,' I explained, adding quietly: 'It might be better if you stay up here for the moment.'

She nodded her agreement. She seemed distracted as she raised her hands to her hair and began to twist and turn it into a manageable knot, which she fixed in place with the Medusa brooch. 'Father will call me if he hears them,' she said. 'I … I will have to deal with him.'

I felt abashed, the way one feels when leaving the presence of a person with whom we have shared something important, not knowing if we will see them again. Mentally, I cursed myself. What had got into me? I would have to speak with Emma Rimmele again. There was not one question – not one! – that I had asked the woman.

I ran quickly down the stairs and out into the garden.

Four men had returned with Gudjøn Knutzen. One of them had already pulled a black hood over his head and put on a pair of black gloves. With two slits for the eyes, he looked like a highway robber.

As I came upon them, he was leaning into the mouth of the well. He might have been gazing into the mouth of Hell.

'What if it stops me coming up again?' he was saying.

Chapter 4

Frederick the Great had tried to dignify them many years before with the honorary title of 'sanitation officers'. Despite the royal decree, the inhabitants of Lotingen persisted in calling them 'ghouls'.

As I stepped into the garden, I numbered myself as a Lotingener.

Each man was wrapped in a long black canvas cape and wore black leather boots. On their heads, they wore a sort of cap, which could be rolled down as a hood to cover their faces. With black-gloved hands on the rim of the well, heads bent forward, staring down into the darkness, they might have been waiting for the corpse of Angela Enke to come floating up of its own accord. They looked like huge black crows which had gathered in the hope of plundering rotting flesh.

They had frightened off the smaller birds, I noticed.

The Schuettler brothers had automatically relinquished the well, regrouping on the lawn some distance away, as if they might have liked to take themselves off home, remaining in the sunken garden only because I had told them specifically to wait for me there. Knutzen was standing close to them, but not too close.

One of the ghouls turned to meet me, throwing back his mask.

'What's all this about, Herr Procurator?'

It was Egon Tost, the senior officer. Black hair grew thickly on his chin and his cheeks like a parasite herb. Only his brow was free of it. His narrow eyes seemed to be peeping out of a thicket. There was such an air of sly mistrust about him that he seemed less menacing when his hood was down. Whatever I decided to tell him, I knew that he would only believe the half of it. And the other three would follow his lead.

'That man of yours was acting strange,' said Tost, glancing in the direction of Knutzen. 'Telling us to get a move on, saying that you had found a corpse, and that it had to be collected right away.'

'It is no more than the truth,' I said in Knutzen's defence.

'That wasn't all he said,' Tost replied. 'We met a man along the canal bank. A friend of his. I overheard them talking. He was saying something about strange wounds. Wounds to the neck ...'

'Bring the corpse up, Herr Tost. The sooner it is done, the better,' I said sharply, looking up at the large clouds racing overhead. 'A downpour will only make the task more troublesome.'

The other ghouls nodded, as if the thought of working in a well with mud and water creeping up around them was a good incentive to get the work finished and done with. They began to pull their masks down over their faces.

Tost's face remained defiantly uncovered. 'What's it doing down there, sir?'

I thought for an instant. 'That is for me to discover,' I said. 'You job is to bring it to the surface.'

'It's not fever, then? Nothing contagious?'

'Not fever,' I confirmed.

These men, and others like them, had retrieved and buried

hundreds of corpses during the epidemic. Some of their fellows had died, no doubt. Now, they seemed to be relieved by my denial, which was repeated, rough and muffled, among themselves.

'That's good news,' said Tost, turning to his men. 'We know what needs to be done, in that case. Me and Bruno will go down first,' he announced, pointing to one of his companions, tugging the mask down over his face. 'Let down the stretcher,' he instructed the others. 'Once we have got the body secured, you two haul it up to the top – these people here will give you a hand. Then, lay it out on the cart ready for leaving. Right?'

He waited for the other men to nod in agreement.

Tost was no fool, I realised. His instructions would make sure that they were all equally exposed to the risks. He and Bruno would touch the body when they lifted it onto the stretcher, but the men on the ground would be forced to do the same when they untied it and lifted it onto their cart.

'Come on! Let's get cracking,' he said.

As he and the other man disappeared down the well-shaft, I went to stand beside the men who were letting out the rope. Knutzen drifted across and stood by my side. He did not say a word, and I said nothing to him in return. If he was gathering his courage to speak to me, I would let him stew. As Tost had mentioned, Knutzen had spoken to someone on the canal bank. The ghouls had heard them muttering about 'strange wounds'. Now, the ghouls would see the wounds, too.

I realised that the investigation was going to be difficult.

I watched the operations, the ropes being paid out slowly, the climbers no longer visible, only their voices and their noisy grunts rising up into the light as they made their way into the darkness.

A cry arose from the bottom of the well. 'We're here!'

The loose rope was pulled up again, and a light was sent down to them.

Their voices rumbled to the surface as the light descended. The rope went slack while the lantern was being untied. I heard an oath from one of the men below. They had found the girl's body at the far end of the cistern, then. Snippets of their discussion drifted up, as if they were making efforts to finish the job without delay.

I leant out over the wall of the well, listening.

Their voices echoed up from the bowels of the earth, like the pronouncements of some mysterious Greek oracle. The depth of the tunnel, and its stone construction, seemed to amplify every sound that was made down below. I heard most of what they said.

'Better tie her mouth up ...'

One of them sighed like a whale spouting water from its blow-hole.

'Know what we should do before we lift her out?' This was said in a deep, snarling growl. 'That stick over there ... One blow ... That's all it takes ...'

'That magistrate has seen her, Bruno,' Egon Tost interrupted. 'He'd know!'

I stared down into the darkness and I shouted, 'Get a move on down there.'

'A couple of minutes, sir,' Tost's voice came back. 'Just making sure that the ropes are tight. Wouldn't want the lassie falling off now, would we?'

'Wouldn't we?' I heard the other man hiss.

I had to give them points for brazen courage. Still, I turned to Knutzen. 'You told them about the girl,' I said quietly.

'I told them what was necessary,' he murmured in reply.

'Concerning your suspicions. Or should I call them superstitions?'

Knutzen stared at me in silence.

'You told the Schuettlers, too,' I went on, nodding my head in their direction. The brothers were standing together by the garden wall, shoulder to shoulder, like trees which had been planted too close together. 'Who else did you tell along the way?' I was working myself up into a temper. 'I made myself plain, Knutzen. I instructed you to tell no-one!'

He stepped in front of me, blocking the Schuettlers from my view.

'I told them that there was a body at the bottom of the well ...'

'You told them how you think she was killed!' I snapped.

'I told them what they have a right to know,' Knutzen repeated stubbornly.

'A right?' My anger exploded. 'What *right*?'

As he began to speak, his voice was quivering, much like mine. At first, I thought that it was fear, but it was not. 'You ought to have warned everyone of the danger, sir. Not kept it a secret.' His eyes glistened with the passion of self-righteousness. 'When something like *this* happens, people have a right to know. They have a right to defend themselves, and protect their loved ones.'

He stared away in open defiance.

'Who else did you tell?' I insisted.

'A ... a friend,' he said at last. 'Selleck the saddler. He lives in the village where the girl was living. He has a wife, and children. They'll be the first to run the risk. He was going home from the market. I told him that Angela had died. And *how* she had died.'

Knutzen looked me squarely in the eye for the first time in the eleven years that we had worked together. We had never faced off against each other like equals. His head was always slightly bowed when he spoke to me. Now, his eyes blazed.

'They have the right to protect themselves until you find the killer, sir.'

I was stunned. I had never seen *this* Knutzen before.

'We're ready to haul her up, sir,' one of the ghouls called out.

Knutzen ran to help the man as he began to pull on the rope. I went to help the other fellow, glad of the distraction. It was no easy task. The stretcher bumped against the stone walls – the shaft was only inches wider than the stretcher was long. Once or twice, it stuck fast, and we were obliged to hold the ropes steady until one of the men below was able to release it from whatever was obstructing it.

It took some time before the stretcher came bobbing to the surface.

The corpse had been lashed around with a grey tarpaulin sheet. A hand had slipped from beneath the bindings. The right hand. In the light of day, it was plump, not much larger than the hand of a baby.

Thank God, they had covered the wounds in her neck.

The corpse and stretcher were set down on the grass, while the ghouls sent down the ropes to bring up Tost and Bruno. I did not help them. I could not take my eyes from the body. It might have been a land-mine primed to explode. It would bring terror and destruction if the fuse were lit. I considered the route that the ghouls would have to take with their funeral cart on the way to the medical examiner's office. They might be stopped by a French patrol before they got there. The French would want to know who had died. They would want to know *how* she had died. They would report the details to Colonel Claudet, who was commander of the garrison, and he would send for me.

What could I tell him, except her name?

If I told him about the puncture holes to her neck, the news would be on everyone's lips in no time. And they would all reach the same conclusion as Knutzen. A virulent new epidemic would sweep through the town. Provoked not by illness, but by fear.

I needed time.

The corpse of Angela Enke must be kept away from prying eyes. As few people as possible must see her. If I could find some explanation for her death, or lay my hands on the killer, all might yet be well in Lotingen.

'The body must be taken to the old cemetery,' I ordered the ghouls.

I ignored the looks of surprise on their faces, overriding their objections.

'Knutzen, you will go with them. Speak with Lars Merson,' I stepped close and hissed in his ear. 'Order him to lock the body in the chapel. You and he must make sure no-one enters. I'll be there as soon as I can.'

'What about the doctor?' Egon Tost objected. 'He should certify the death, sir. That's been the procedure since the epidemic …'

'This is *not* a case of fever,' I stated dogmatically.

Tost raised his chin in the direction of the corpse. He might have been indicating a dead dog lying in the street. 'What happened to her, anyway?'

'She is dead,' I said flatly. 'Now, do as you are told. Take her to the old cemetery. I will report her death to the French. Do your duty, Herr Tost. I will do mine.'

I watched like a hawk while they loaded the stretcher onto the cart.

Knutzen climbed up behind them, glancing back at me with the reproachful look of a man who had been condemned. Within minutes, the cart pulled away from the gate. I wiped my brow, praying to heaven that they would meet no-one else along the way. Before presenting myself to the French authorities, I would need to learn as much as I could about the victim. Where she came from. What she might have been doing in that part of the country. What sort of life she led. The people who had seen her recently. So far, I knew only her name and the name of the village that she came from.

I made my way over to the Schuettlers. They were standing by a stone arch on the far side of the garden. They looked up when they saw me coming, but they did not move. They might have been chained to the spot.

'Well, sirs,' I said, 'will you invite me into your house?'

The brothers exchanged a glance, then stood aside and waved me through the arch.

'We live in the kitchen garden. To keep the birds and thieves off,' Gurt Schuettler explained with a wave of his hand which took in cabbages, long beans, rows of green leaves which I thought might be turnips or potatoes, leading me along a path in the direction of a small building in the far corner of the walled compound. It was the only thing with four walls and a roof in that section of the property.

'This used to be the brother-apothecary's shop,' he said, as he slipped the latch and pushed open the door.

A billy-goat burst out through the narrow gap, and scampered off through the vegetable crops. Three hens came next, squawking loudly as they fought their way unceremoniously out of the door. An aged dog was asleep on the floor, but it did not bother to shift itself as we entered. The cramped room was furnished with a small table, two stools, and a cast-iron stove that was red with rust. The place was lit by a single window and the sun which came shining in through the open door. Two jute sacks stuffed with straw were laid along the wall for sleeping on. Bedroom, kitchen, henhouse, all in one. Was there no more spacious accommodation in what remained of the monastery?

'Would you like a stool, sir?'

'We can speak just as well outside,' I replied, returning the way I had come, opening my shoulder bag, taking out my pad, and the newfangled Faber-Castel wooden pencil which Helena had purchased for me from Durkheim's Emporium. It was like a sandwich – two slices of wood enclosed a slice of graphite.

'What is that, sir?' Schuettler asked me curiously.

I did not bother to answer him, writing down his name with the instrument.

'Did you hear anything unusual last night? A noise? A cry?' I began.

Gurt Schuettler turned to his brother, who shook his head.

'We heard nothing, sir,' the old man replied. 'Bit of a wind, that was all.'

'According to my secretary, the dead girl's name is Angela Enke. Did either of you know her?'

'Both of us did,' Gurt Schuettler said.

'Did you, now?' I asked. 'How come?'

'Angela was here this week, sir. Needles and buttons was her trade.'

'In this house?' I asked.

The brothers exchanged a smile, but it was always Gurt who spoke.

'You have spoken with the mistress, have you not, sir?'

Perhaps I should have summoned them to my office in town, and questioned them separately. 'Answer my questions directly,' I ordered him. 'Did Angela Enke work for you two?'

'Not for us. For Fraulein Rimmele, sir.'

'The lady has only recently arrived in Lotingen,' I said. 'How did she know of Angela Enke?'

'She came knocking on our door, sir, asking if we knew of anyone that was good with a needle. Well, I sent her to that place in town ... the one with the girls that sew and knit. Someone there must have given her Angela's name,' Gurt Schuettler replied. 'The mistress wanted someone who would come up to the house to work. Said she didn't want to leave her father on his own.'

I made a note of what he had just told me. *Check Frau Graube's.*

'What about the father?' I resumed. 'Have you seen him?'

Schuettler grimaced, tapping his right temple with his finger. 'Something wrong up here,' he said. 'She never lets him out on his own.'

'When Angela Enke came here to work, how long did she stay?'

The brothers' eyes met for a moment. The silent one nodded as if Gurt had asked him a question. I wondered how they communicated. Was a glance sufficient? Could they read each other's thoughts? There was a close tie between them, certainly, but I could not determine whether it was based on love, respect, or subjection.

'That's hard to say, sir. A couple of hours, I suppose. She worked in the kitchen, as a rule. It's that door over there,' he said, pointing through the archway to a narrow door on the ground floor of the house, which gave onto the garden.

The image flashed through my own mind as he spoke.

I saw the girl alone in the kitchen, the door open, her clever hands busy with her needles and thread, while those two strange Schuettler brothers stood watching her from beneath the archway which led into the sunken garden.

Spying on her.

Was that it? Two strong countrymen against a defenceless woman? An attempted rape: the girl screams; one of the men strikes her with the garden rake he is carrying: together they throw her body into the well before Fraulein Rimmele or her invalid father can appear on the scene ...

The objections to my hypothesis were all too evident: would they have put the tooth into the bucket? Would they have left the well-cover on the lawn, calling attention to the crime? And why would they have called the magistrate from town?

'Regarding the tooth you showed me,' I said. 'Did you call Fraulein Rimmele's attention to it?'

Gurt Schuettler shrugged his shoulders. 'One minute we're looking down the well. Next thing, so was she.'

'You did not call her?' I asked, surprised.

'She must have seen us from the window,' he said, glancing towards the broad façade of the house, 'and come down as the fancy took her.'

They had probably made a great deal of noise, I supposed. I could imagine the brothers, working in the garden, sweeping up leaves, finding the cover lifted off from the well, discovering what was hidden in the old bucket, shouting out loud,

46

expressing their surprise. Emma had heard them, of course. Her sitting-room overlooked the garden. Concerned for the peace of her father, she had come down, meaning to ask them to be quiet. Then, she had seen what they had seen.

'Was she afraid?' I asked.

'Frightened? Her, sir?' He seemed about to say something more. I stopped writing, and looked up at him. Gurt Schuettler scratched his chin, then winked at me. 'I got the impression she was furious, sir.'

'Furious? Why was that, do you think?'

He spread his arms in a gesture of helplessness. 'She said she was sure that there was something nasty in the well. She would have climbed down there on her own, if we had let her. Why, she even went and brought a lamp.'

'A reasonable reaction, I suppose.'

I remembered the fixed intensity with which she was staring down the well when I arrived in the garden of the Prior's House. Such curiosity was an understandable reaction in a man, more surprising in a woman. Then again, everything about Emma Rimmele had come as a surprise to me.

'Reasonable, Herr Procurator?'

The vehemence in these words struck me like a bolt of lightning.

It was not Gurt Schuettler who had spoken, but Benjamin, the silent one.

'Nothing about that woman's reasonable,' he said with all the passion of a misogynist. 'Is it reasonable to travel with your mother loaded on the carriage along with the baggage? In a coffin, I mean to say?'

He turned to his brother with a sneer.

'I told you she would bring us bad luck.'

Chapter 5

I had to go to Krupeken at once.

After what Knutzen had told Selleck the saddler, the villagers would be like sailors caught in a sudden squall.

The village was a half-mile walk along the Cut, a balancing act across a narrow lock-gate, a half-mile more along a beaten path which led across the empty fields. I felt vulnerable and alone in that vast landscape. The harvest was in, the fields were cut to a stubble, the prospect was as flat as a billiard-table. If anyone had tried to follow me, I could not have failed to see that person.

Was that why Angela Enke had been butchered close to where the Rimmeles lived?

Was the Prior's House the only spot where she could be taken by surprise?

Krupeken consisted of one street only, if it could be called a street at all. A dusty lane of hardened cart-ruts wound between one- and two-room cottages spaced higgledy-piggledy in a clearing in the centre of the wood. A dozen cottages of ancient, weather-washed wood and crumbling daub, each one crowned with a steep sloping roof of black thatch. There were wooden shutters in the place of doors and windows. Each house had a fenced-in garden and a lean-to shed where the villagers might lock up their animals for the night.

Everything seemed tranquil as I approached the village.

Suddenly, an old man in a brown smock began to shout and whistle, chasing ducks and geese out of a stagnant pond of emerald green, herding them quickly along the street before him with a stick. I might have been a poultry thief.

He did not acknowledge my presence, except by running away.

'I am looking for the family Enke,' I called after him.

'Oh, aye?' he said, hardly looking back.

'Where do they live?'

He pointed with his chin as he herded the fowl into a side lane. 'End house on the left,' he said.

As I walked past him, he did something that I did not expect. He held up his hands, forming a cross with his forefingers, as if to ward off evil. Selleck had done a good job, raising the alarm and putting his neighbours on their guard.

I glimpsed other persons as I moved along the road. That is, I saw them for a moment or two, then I saw them no more. A man was walking around his house with a basket on his arm, sprinkling thorn branches on the ground. I had seen this sort of ritual on my father's estate when I was a child. On the 30th of April, we celebrated the holy feast of Saint Walpurgis. Huge bonfires were lit, and thorn branches were thrown on the flames. On *Walpurgisnacht* the dead rose up from their tombs, it was said, and they went on the prowl, looking to sate their thirst on fresh human blood.

The man saw me, dropped his basket, and ran.

A woman in a linen bonnet was hanging something up above her door. Our eyes met for an instant. She blessed herself rapidly, then darted into the house, leaving behind her a cross made of straw bound up with long white ribbons. It dangled starkly fresh and new from the ancient thatch. Two boys were painting a cottage with lime, as if to change the appearance of the house in which they lived. A third was nailing dead rats up by their tails. Fresh blood dripped on the daub of the wall. If Angela Enke returned that night, she would hardly recognise what had once been her home.

Fear had laid its hand on Krupeken, and it would soon infect Lotingen, too. The panic would be multiplied a thousand times, and I would be unable to stop it. I would have to be careful when I spoke to the parents, I realised. I must impress on them that I was looking for a *real* killer, a murderer of flesh and blood, and not some troubled spirit of legend and myth.

I stopped at the gate, and looked at the last house at the end of the lane. I saw no straw crosses or bunches of ribbons hanging from the eaves; no nets or knotted ropes to confound and confuse the invader; no branches of thorns to wound and tempt the monster with the sight of her own blood; no freshly painted door to send her on her way; no rats' blood inviting her to sate her hunger before she knocked on the door. I felt a sense of relief, daring to hope that the grief of the parents and siblings of Angela Enke had taken more conventional forms.

The rapping of my knuckles on the door sounded loud.

'Reverend Pastor?' a female voice called out, though the door did not open.

The simple fact that they had sent for a priest comforted me further. The family had begun to make arrangements for a funeral service which would be performed in a church, according to the usual Christian rites of burial.

'It is I, Procurator Stiffeniis,' I replied. 'The magistrate in Lotingen. I wish to speak with you, ma'am.'

I heard a metal bolt being drawn. Then the heavy clunk of wood as a crossbar was removed from behind the door. Slowly, it opened a crack, and a sliver of a woman's face peered out at me. 'We don't need no magistrate,' she said. 'We need a holy pastor with the communion host!'

My heart sank as I pushed against the door and forced my way inside.

The woman backed off, holding up her hands, as if she thought that I was going to strike her.

'Are you the mother of Angela Enke?' I asked.

The woman nodded warily.

'I bring bad news,' I began to say.

A shrill laugh exploded from her lips, and she crossed herself three times.

'You've come too late, sir! What took you so bloody long?'

'Your daughter is dead ...'

'Dead ain't the word that *I* would use,' she snapped.

As my eyes grew accustomed to the gloom, I made out two other people who were cowering in a corner: an old man, and a young one. As my eye fell on them, they did as the woman had done, touching the tips of their right-hand fingers to their foreheads, midriffs and shoulders in the sign of the Cross.

'Who are you?' I asked, ignoring the woman.

The men stared sullenly back, but they did not answer.

'My husband, and my son,' the woman muttered gruffly at my side. 'For all the use they are! They're afraid to step outside the door. Not long now, and it'll be dark, I warned them. We'll need all the help that we can get. It ain't easy keeping *them* out!'

My hope of finding natural sorrow and Christian sentiment sank without a trace.

That explained the absence of charms, amulets and religious gewgaws outside the Enke house: the men were too scared to go out and arm the dwelling against the attack from infernal forces which the lady expected to arrive at any moment. I concentrated my attention on her. She had spirit. Tragedy had not put a gag on her tongue.

'Frau Enke.'

Her eyes flashed, weighing me up, looking defiantly from my hair down to my leather shoes and brass buckles.

'I am here about your daughter, Frau Enke. I only know that Angela was a seamstress. You must tell me more if I am to catch whoever killed her.'

The woman crossed herself again and stared at the beaten floor.

'She had a red mole,' she muttered, touching her skeletal cheekbone with her finger. 'Just here, sir. I should have known what *that* meant! The Dark One left his mark on her.'

I had noticed nothing of the sort, though that was not the issue. I pulled up sharply. I would need to be more pointed in my questioning. 'When did you last see Angela, Frau Enke?'

The woman's mouth was an ugly sneer, her skin a porous yellow. 'She went out yesterday,' she said. 'She didn't come back. Not *yet*, anyways …'

I ignored this provocation, pressing on. 'Did she tell you where she was going?'

The woman stared at me. 'What are all these questions for?'

It was clear that she did not trust me.

'Somebody has murdered Angela,' I said.

'Some *thing*,' she answered bitterly. 'Some creatures do not die, sir.'

'Some *person*,' I insisted. 'I intend to catch him.'

She mumbled a curse beneath her breath.

'When did Angela go out yesterday?' I asked her.

'Late afternoon,' the woman replied. 'She was going to Frau Graube's ...'

'That's where she works, I've been told.'

Everyone in Lotingen knew Frau Graube. The mother let out a sigh of exasperation, but at least she had begun to talk. By speaking, she may have hoped to free herself of me.

'My girl plied a pretty needle,' she said more quietly. 'She often went to see Frau Graube when she was looking for employment.'

'Perhaps you know already,' I said, 'that Angela's body was recovered from the well of the Prior's House. Angela had been working for a family that had rented the house.'

Frau Enke nodded. 'The mother recently dead?'

'Fraulein Rimmele and her widowed father,' I confirmed.

The woman raised her hand to her mouth. 'Angela had been there, though the work was finished,' she said. 'She had to go because the daughter couldn't leave the old man on his own. Domestic work pays best, sir, though my girl had to give up part of what she got to Frau Graube. Frau Graube doles out the work she doesn't want to girls like Angela.'

I began to wonder whether Angela had been robbed as well as murdered.

'Did Angela have any money on her person?' I asked.

'She wouldn't tell *me* if she did,' the woman answered sharply.

'Did she tell you anything about the Prior's House?' I pressed on pragmatically, ignoring her hostility.

'She did not like the place,' Frau Enke replied frostily. 'It was big and old, she said. Cold, too. Sometimes she sat out in the garden, working in the sun. But even then, she said, she had no peace, them Schuettlers watching her all the time. She told me they was ogling her while she was doing her sewing.'

I caught my breath. Had I chanced on something concrete?

'Angela did not like that, I suppose? Being spied on …'

'On the contrary,' the woman snapped. 'So long as those old men were watching her, she said, she felt quite safe. She knew that nothing bad would happen.'

'Bad, Frau Enke?' I cut in quickly. 'Why should Angela fear that anything bad would happen to her at the Prior's House?'

'That's where you should take your questions!' snapped the woman. 'The Prior's House. We don't know nothing here.'

Again, I ignored her rudeness. She had lost a daughter, after all.

'What else did she say about the house?'

Frau Enke folded her arms, and shook her shoulders. 'Not much about the house … She spoke about the mistress, though. A right strange creature *she* must be!'

'Strange?' I queried. 'What do you mean by that, ma'am?'

I thought I knew where the conversation was heading. A rich woman from another town, an educated lady with unusual and extravagant tastes, of marriageable age, but still unmarried, who travelled in the company of her ailing father. Angela Enke was a peasant girl. She would have judged them badly, no doubt. People of means, who chose, nevertheless, to take up residence in a spartan country house. The seamstress would have found them just as odd as her mother did.

'Angela told me of the dress she was making,' Frau Enke went on, adding in a sort of sneering exclamation: 'Supposed to be a mourning dress, puh!'

I jotted down what she was saying.

'Her mother died quite recently,' I explained, without going into detail, hoping to win some sympathy for Emma.

'I ask you, sir! What sort of a girl would have a mourning dress cobbled up from a cast-off, moth-eaten ball gown? And for her own dead mother! That's what she had my girl doing.' She bridled, and shook her head. 'She couldn't be bothered to waste good money. As if she had decided on the spur of the moment …'

'As if she had decided to do what?' I intervened. I wanted information, not slander and wild superstition.

'To wear a mourning dress, Herr Magistrate. If you want my opinion, sir, that woman grabbed the first black rag that came to hand.'

This was leading my investigation nowhere.

'Had anyone ever threatened your daughter, Frau Enke?'

'Why would they do that?' she spat back acidly. 'She ain't done harm to no-one. Not *yet*, at any rate.'

She looked directly into my eyes as she let fire this deadly bolt.

Again, I did not rise to the provocation, but I continued patiently to question her.

'Did Angela have a sweetheart? A man that she had refused, perhaps?'

The term 'lover' came more readily to my lips, but the girl was dead, and these people were her family.

'She had a lover once,' the mother said bluntly. 'They butchered him four years ago at Jena. He was forced into service with the Duke of Brunswick. Poor Pieter Guntzl's buried on the battlefield, they say. They never brought his body home.' The woman wrung her hands. 'That lad was a skilled cobbler, sir. Everyone needs shoes, or needs them fixing. They would have been wed by now, Instead, she's a … Well, you know … what she is …'

Tears flowed for the first time since I had entered the house, but not for long.

'Has there been no-one since?' I asked.

'No-one that *I* knew of,' the woman replied sharply with a shrug of her shoulder.

I glanced in turn at the two men, and they both shook their heads forlornly.

'What about her friends?' I tried.

The woman looked at me uncertainly, as if she feared to implicate anyone who had been a friend to Angela. 'Well, there … there was only the other girls at Frau Graube's institute,' she said at last.

I waited in silence. It is a trick that magistrates often use. If the witness has anything to add, something that we may not have taken into account, it may come out by means of silence and a moment to think.

'When Pieter died, she took it bad, sir,' the woman murmured. 'Angela wasn't a bad-looking girl. She was just twenty-three at that time. And as for other men, well, she never seemed to pay them any heed. Afterwards, I mean … She was a good girl, though very quiet.'

I was beginning to feel exasperated. Frau Enke had a way of couching everything in terms which were, to her way of thinking, obvious and conclusive. I could not quite picture a young woman who rejected all amorous advances in the noble remembrance of a childhood courtship which had died on the field of Jena. Especially in the countryside. In another year or two, Angela would have been too old to marry and bear a child. No man would have wanted her.

'Weren't you worried when she didn't come home last night?'

Frau Enke pursed her lips and frowned. 'It wasn't the first time,' she said. 'She often slept with the girls at Frau Graube's. At their homes, I mean. I'd always warned her never to stay out after dark. Only *they* go out at night.'

'They?' I asked, though I knew how she would answer me.

'Bad creatures,' she said. 'Whores, and ... and ...'

At her back, the two men moaned with fright.

'And who?' I insisted.

'You know who, Herr Magistrate,' she said, glaring at me. 'Them that never sleep.'

I immediately changed direction. 'Then, you heard that she was dead.'

She rubbed her nose with the back of her fist. 'Selleck brought the news from town this morning. He said how Angela had been killed, the wounds, and all her blood drained out. I started making ready. I sprinkled salt on the step and in the fireplace, and I placed a bucket of water hard inside the door. They won't cross water, don't like salt. She'll suffer if she tries to force her way in here.'

Silence hung heavily in the air.

She turned abruptly to face her husband and her son. 'Before the night comes on, them two will have to go outside and daub the walls. I don't intend doing any more for them. They'll have to help themselves for once!'

In a sort of frenzy, she swept a lighted candle from above the fireplace, and ran around the room, pointing. 'See here?' she cried. 'And here? And here?'

There were plates and saucers of blood that she had laid in every corner.

'I slaughtered our hens and rabbits while them two were sitting here feeling sorry for themselves!' she barked.

They were planning to barricade themselves in for the night in an attempt to keep their daughter out.

'I'll not let her enter the house!' the woman shouted, her shoulders shaking. 'No-one in Krupeken will let her in the cemetery if she does come back!'

That question still remained to be settled.

'About her burial, Frau Enke,' I said as gently as I could. 'As soon as I have completed my examination, I will let you have the body for ...'

The woman advanced upon me, fists raised.

'Do what must be done, Herr Magistrate,' she screeched. 'Make her safe, sir! Get someone to do it! I'll not have her here!'

As I left the house, I heard the door being closed and barred behind me.

The sky was a corrugated ripple of pearly blue and pink, darker purple on the horizon, still clear and bright above. A single star gleamed like a navigation light far out over the Baltic Sea. The day was drawing to an end. I did not return the way that I had come, however, but left Krupeken heading north-east, following another path through empty fields which would lead me to the Mildehaven coast road, and carry me back to the northern side of Lotingen more swiftly.

Along the way, I met no-one.

Not even the pastor. As the light began to fade, I wondered whether the holy man's courage had faded with it. Frau Enke was anxiously awaiting his arrival. He ought to have gone to Krupeken to bless the cottage and scatter protective crumbs of communion host inside and out, as tradition prescribed. If he did not go, the villagers would have a night of terror to look forward to.

Suddenly, I felt very cold.

I raised the collar of my jacket, and pushed my hands more deeply inside my pockets. My task was no longer simply to find whoever had murdered Angela Enke. First, I must find a place to hide her corpse. A place where she would be *safe*. Not in the sense that her mother intended, but safe from what her mother and the other villagers of Krupeken would do to her if they managed to lay their hands on her.

There was no-one to whom I could give the body.

Angela Enke was my problem.

Chapter 6

As I came over the brow of the hill, I spotted Knutzen.

He was standing in the middle of the narrow lane outside the cemetery gates, his back towards me, staring in the direction of town. Legs spread wide, feet firmly planted on the ground, his hands on his hips, he might have been a stone colossus guarding the entrance to a port, though he put me in mind of a farmer who was intent on stopping his cows from straying.

And there was Lars Merson, too.

The gravedigger emerged from the gate. He was wearing the 'uniform' that he always wore in the cemetery: a cut-off, moth-eaten cassock which he must have plundered from the chapel of rest, a black woollen helmet which covered his ears, and a pair of leather boots which some unwitting corpse had surrendered without a fight.

I was relieved to see that there was no-one else outside the cemetery.

I raised my arm and waved.

Merson waved back and said something to Knutzen, who turned towards the cemetery gate. My heart jumped into my mouth when I saw four French soldiers step into the lane. An officer in a leather shako and a tight-fitting frock-coat came striding out behind them. He stood, watching my approach, his baton jammed under his arm.

Major Glatigny.

During the epidemic, he had been in charge of the transport-ation of corpses to the fever cemetery which the French had hastily organised on the far side of the River Nogat. Evidently, they had still found nothing new for Major Glatigny to do. Death, and its registration, was still his business. My intention to keep the matter of the death of Angela Enke as quiet as possible was in danger of foundering on the sharp rock of French bureaucracy.

My first impulse was to slow down, if only to avoid his questions.

Instead, I strode on to meet my fate, knowing that it was better to get it over with.

The Frenchman stepped forward, touching the peak of his cap, slapping the seam of his riding-breeches with his baton. 'Procurator Stiffeniis,' he said, 'I have been waiting here for you for over an hour.'

'I had to ... start my investigation,' I apologised, short of breath after the long walk. I had been about to mention Krupeken – the fear of the inhabitants, the preparations they were making for the night – but I bit down hard on my tongue. I was as loath to send the French to the village as the inhabitants were to let Angela Enke enter it.

'Your secretary says that you have found a corpse, monsieur.' He looked at me sternly. 'You *know* where that corpse should be, according to the law. Do you not?'

Claude Glatigny pressed his narrow lips together and let out a loud sigh. His face was the colour of seasoned ivory, and equally inexpressive. His eyes were dark, bristling with rising impatience. 'Every death must be registered immediately with the French authorities, as you are aware. The sanitation men reported the finding of a woman's body, but they ... well, they

61

seemed to be confused about the manner of her death. As those men are Prussians, Colonel Claudet suspected, obviously, that the body had been …'

He paused, searching for a word.

'Stolen?' I suggested. I held up my hands in a gesture of surrender. 'That is exactly what I have done with the corpse of Angela Enke, Major Glatigny. I have stolen it.'

A frown furrowed Glatigny's brow. 'That corpse should be in my office. It is a question of French jurisdiction. She may have died as—'

'I held it back for a good reason,' I interrupted him.

He shifted his head towards his left shoulder, narrowing his eyes. 'Is that so?'

I took a step towards him. 'The girl had been murdered, and that is a fact. But how she died, that is, the nature of her wounds … If the news got out, I do believe that you'd have difficulty controlling the panic of the people in Lotingen.'

He stared thoughtfully at me for some moments.

'There was a small crowd here a short time ago,' he said. 'The people knew that a corpse had been found, and that it had not been taken into town. They tried to break into the cemetery, monsieur. My men had to chase them off with bayonets. I was obliged to report the facts to Colonel Claudet, of course. Is this the sort of panic that you are speaking of? In the colonel's opinion, this disorder suggests a fresh outbreak of the recent deadly fever.'

'He is not so far from the truth,' I replied with half a smile. 'Unless this fever is nipped in the bud, it will be far more dangerous than the last one, I assure you. We are not talking of a physical disease … When Colonel Claudet knows all of the facts, he will approve of my decision. However, this is a *criminal* case; I am investigating the murder of a Prussian girl. This is my responsibility. I will decide where the corpse should be taken, and what should be done with it.'

Glatigny rubbed his nose, then asked: 'How did she die?'

'She was found at the bottom of a well. I'm sure the sanitation officers told you that. But it is the way in which she was murdered which is the cause for concern. Wounds to the neck. Just here,' I indicated, touching the artery in my neck with my fore and middle fingers. 'She quickly bled to death. But in the village where she lived, they are saying that she has been attacked by one of those ... those infernal creatures[1] which feed on the blood of living people. Here in Lotingen, most of the inhabitants believe these tales. Do such legends exist in France?'

Glatigny's eyes gaped wide. Was it my impression, or did he look paler than before?

'Long ago,' he said. 'Not any more. We have sent our legends to speak with Madame Guillotine, monsieur. The supernatural...'

'There's nothing supernatural about it,' I hurried on. 'But until I can arrest the killer, the panic will spread. Especially if the corpse is brought into the centre of town. That's why I had it carried here. I need to examine the body with care. I need to explain to myself – and to everyone else in Lotingen – exactly what has happened. As soon as I have finished my investigation, Colonel Claudet will have my full report.'

His soldiers were standing some way off. They had not heard a word that we had said, and I was glad of it. The rank-and-file French trooper is an unschooled peasant for the most

---

[1] I chose purposely to avoid using the word 'vampire'. It had already been used too often.

part, and just as likely to be terrorised by the legends as our Prussian villagers. All the same, I knew that they would obey their officer.

'Major,' I proposed carefully, 'I would be grateful if you and your men remained here on guard. I cannot be inside and outside the chapel at the same time. The people must be kept back, by force of arms if necessary.'

I glanced towards the cemetery gates, and I saw the expression on the face of Merson. During the epidemic he had been supplanted by the French, and their new French cemetery beyond the river. With things getting slowly back to normal, it was evident that he resented their continuing presence in *his* cemetery.

'As a precaution,' I added for the gravedigger's sake. 'In case any Prussian hotheads return with more serious ideas about what ought to be done,' I specified loudly.

Glatigny glanced towards his men, then turned to me again. 'Are you asking me to prevent anyone from entering the cemetery, monsieur?'

I nodded quickly. 'As soon as I have finished with the body, they can carry it across the river, and bury it there. Would that be acceptable?'

Glatigny considered this proposal. I was issuing orders, asking him to put his men at my disposal. I was asking a lot, but I was hoping that the recent presence of the mob would convince him of the urgency of the case, and of the danger if precautions were not taken.

'I will follow your recommendations,' he said at last. 'The men will stay. I will have to report the matter, however.'

He turned to his soldiers, and told them to do as I instructed.

I watched Glatigny march off to town to speak to the colonel, while the troops took up their positions along the road. Now, I would have to exercise my powers of persuasion over the Prussians, too.

'Knutzen,' I said, calling him over, and placing my hand on my secretary's shoulder. For an instant, he shrank back from me, as if he feared that I might attack him. I smiled, instead, to set him at his ease. I needed him at that instant; his punishment could be meted out at any time. 'Go to my home and speak with my wife. Carry her this message, and say nothing more. Do you understand me?' I said, squeezing hard at his shoulder. 'Tell Helena that a body has been found, and that I must stay in town tonight. I do not know when I will be home.'

Knutzen opened his mouth to reply.

I held my finger up at him. 'Not a word, Knutzen. Not one!'

As Knutzen began to shuffle away, breaking into a half-trot, Merson and I were the only ones left outside the cemetery. I stood in front of the gravedigger, staring in silence into his eyes.

'I need your expert help,' I said. 'You and I will examine the body together, and you will tell me what you think.'

He closed his eyes, and nodded once.

Lars Merson is heavily built, with a large, ruddy face, and dark, leathery skin that has been tanned by the sun. He had laid her out in the sexton's office next door to the chapel. It was the coldest place in the cemetery, he said, the most secure. He kept the large key on a string around his neck. On my request, he took the key and opened the door of the long, low building which is just inside the cemetery gate. Made of rough-cut stone, it had been added to the chapel of rest at some time in the last couple of centuries. It looked new in comparison.

We stepped inside together.

'Lock the door,' I said. 'I don't want any interruptions.'

I glanced at the collection of tools which were hanging on the wall: shovels of various sizes, shapes and lengths; irons, pikes and chisels for prizing out and lifting tombstones; wedges, hammers, saws, and many other implements of unspecified use; a row of lanterns which were resting on the floor at the foot of the wall; old tombstones standing up against the wall.

A long, narrow table occupied the centre of the room.

Light rained down from the latticed skylight set in the roof. It played fitfully upon the table as clouds raced across the sky, throwing an ever-shifting chiaroscuro on the body of Angela Enke. The pattern of the window-leading covered her like a net; she might have been a large fish recently caught. Merson had pushed his pens and papers into a careless heap at the bottom end of the table, close to where the toe-cap of her right boot and the naked toes of her left foot pointed skywards. She lay on a sheet of canvas, her hands along her flanks, her head resting on what might have been a ragged curtain. The red velvet had been folded to make a pillow for her head. She could so easily have been a bereaved customer who had come to see the sexton, suddenly felt giddy, and asked him if she might be allowed to lie down for a moment to recover. Except that her skin was the colour of wet lime.

'What do you intend to do, sir?'

'I want you to cut that dress away. Do you have a suitable implement?'

Merson turned to the wall, and came back with a large pair of tailor's scissors.

'I have these, sir. They should do the job,' he said.

'Let me see,' I said.

His hand was shaking as he passed them over. I hefted the scissors in my palm, examined the blades, wondering why the points had been turned. Helena had scissors at home, but they were nothing like these strange things. 'Do they have some special use?' I asked him, as I handed them back.

'I use them to recover wedding-rings and suchlike before I close the coffin,' he explained. 'Mourners rarely have the nerve to take them off, and the finger-joints are the first thing to start swelling up and stiffening.'

In other circumstances, I might have been disturbed by the clinical coldness with which he described what he did. Then again, I thought, this was his job. He spoke of the details as thoughtlessly as I might speak of putting a man in jail.

I made a brief examination of her clothing.

The victim was wearing a plain brown blouse of coarse, heavy weave, and a light-blue taffeta gown with ribbed darker bands. Though worn and dirty, the gown seemed too good for her. Had one of her better-off customers passed it on to the seamstress, having no further use for it? The blouse was tightly caught inside the waist of the gown, except over her right hip, where it had come loose. I noted fine stitching along the seams – the victim's own work, I presumed – where the dress had been taken in to fit her figure. Over her breasts and thighs, the material was badly scuffed, stained here and there with streaks of moss. There was also a jagged rent between her knees. As the body fell down the well-shaft, it had evidently scraped and bumped against the rough stone walls.

Merson looked at me. 'Where do you want me to start, sir?'

I told him to cut through the centre of the lower hem of her gown and work his way up to the neck. 'Be careful not to mark the body,' I warned him, following the relentless progress of the cutters as the cloth fell loose between her legs. The snip with which he severed the heavy waistband of her gown, sounded obscenely loud in the silence. As Merson continued cutting through the blouse which covered her stomach and breasts, I told him again not to do any additional damage to the body. She had suffered enough without being carelessly mutilated.

He laid his scissors down on the table, and turned to me.

'Throw back the coverings,' I ordered.

He hesitated, looked at me.

'Surely you've done this sort of thing before?' I said with growing impatience.

He nodded grimly, laying his hands on the divided parts of the gown, and flicking them aside. His hands appeared very dark against the white flesh of the woman's legs.

'Remove the top, as well,' I added.

'I'll need to slice through the sleeves,' he said. 'Otherwise, they'll …'

'Do it,' I said.

From wrist to shoulder he managed the lower blade of the scissors like a knife, using the dead weight of the woman's arms to facilitate the operation. The sleeves fell away and slid to the floor like snakes. He set his hands just below her breasts and shifted the blouse and bodice, lifting them away like two perfect halves of a delicately hinged box.

Angela Enke lay on the table, naked except for a ragged pair of culottes the colour of mud which covered her sex. Her breasts sagged heavily upon her ribs. Her skin was so pasty and pale, it might have been rubbed with powdered chalk. Blood had flowed out in a torrent from the punctures in the left side of her neck, pooling in the deep crook of her shoulder bone, where it had hardened as a sticky cake, spilling over and thinning out onto her left breast, before running away in a narrower stream beneath her left armpit.

I had seen the wound at the bottom of the well, though not so clearly. I prayed silently that I would find some other injury which might explain her death, and put an end to the superstitious speculation which had spread like a raging fire through Krupeken, and which threatened now to engulf Lotingen, as well.

I began with the face.

The tip of her nose was ragged and bloody, broken perhaps. There were scratches and scrapes impressed on her temples and her forehead at different angles, as if she had been rubbed with a carpenter's rasp. I moved down, pressing my thumb against a large black bruise on her upper right arm. Some drops of blood seeped out of it. The arms and hands were scarified at numerous points. There was, indeed, a great deal of superficial damage to the skin, but that was easily explained. She must have bounced from wall to wall as she fell, and the well was as deep as two houses placed one on top of the other. From the quantity of blood which had issued from the cuts and scratches, it was evident that she had still been alive when she hit the bottom of the shaft. Her heart was pumping, she was bleeding copiously.

There was nothing fatal in those injuries.

The most notable damage to the upper part of her body was a large livid red-and-blue contusion on her left breast. The nipple had been torn away, the blood had flowed profusely, rolling away down the side of her ribs and underneath her back. I bent closer, looking more carefully. There was no sign of intrusion, or puncture, such as one might expect from a knife, a pike, or some other lethal weapon. Again, I concluded that the flesh had been ripped away on some sharp point – a nail, perhaps – as she fell. That wound alone had not caused her death.

I pointed at the rough culottes.

They hung down low on one hip, partially exposing her belly and the first trace of pubic hair. There were stains of blood which had soaked into the heavy material. I touched one spot with my forefinger. The blood was damp; it left a mark on my skin. Was the fatal injury concealed beneath her underwear? Had she been stabbed in the belly with some sharp blade which had robbed her life away?

My tongue was dry and pulled against my palate.

'Cut them away, Merson.'

He clicked his scissors together twice, then did as I had told him, cutting up one side-seam, then down the other, pulling the wool away, exposing the belly, womb and the dark bush of brown hair which covered her sexual organs.

There was a cut running almost parallel with the line where her left leg joined the trunk. It was long, and it was wide. I pushed at her left knee and the cut gaped open wide. It had bled abundantly, though it was not so deep. I put it down to a sharp stone or a jagged bit of metal which had ripped her body as she brushed against it, falling.

There was nothing else to go on.

That wound in her neck had signalled the beginning of the end. Her death had not been rapid, but it had been inevitable. Perhaps the vocal cords had been damaged during the attack, preventing her from shouting or screaming. Certainly, no-one at the Prior's House had heard her cry for help.

I examined the other side of her neck, but there were no bruises, no signs of any rough attempt at strangling.

I forced my fingers in between her teeth and prised open her mouth. As Schuettler had suspected, the tooth left in the bucket was a wisdom tooth, and it belonged to Angela Enke. There was a gaping black hole in the left side of her gum. It had bled copiously, staining her teeth and gums dark red.

'It looks as if she's been sucking blood,' murmured Merson.

'The blood is *hers*,' I said emphatically. 'Whoever killed her pulled that tooth out, then he threw her down the well. The tooth was found in a bucket ...'

'Where's the sense in that?' he quietly asked himself.

I felt the same perplexity. That tooth seemed to me to be the most obscene of all the indignities that Angela Enke had suffered. Her tongue was caught in a bulge in her gullet, as if she had begun to swallow it. I prised the organ out with my forefinger, pulling hard against the retracted muscles, pressing it flat upon her lower lip. It was grey like a boiled sausage, but there was no blistering or burning, no sign that she might have been poisoned.

'Help me to turn her over.'

Though rigor mortis had made the joints stiff, it was now beginning to pass off, which made the body difficult to manage. It gave with a series of sharp cracks as we held her up, rolling her onto her right hip, then placing her face down. The ruined clothes clung to her shoulders, back, buttocks and legs. They had been pressed flat by the dead weight of the corpse. It made external examination a matter of an instant. I noted some minor rips and ruptures – the jagged wall, I presumed again – but there was no evidence of wilful wounding. No external bleeding, anyway.

As I peeled the clothes away from her skin, I saw something that I will not easily forget, a condition which is often found in a corpse which has been abandoned, or which has lain undiscovered for any length of time. The skin, especially of her buttocks, was no longer white. It was a mottled red, blue and black carpet, the colours startlingly bright. This was what the onset of decomposition did to a body which had not been shifted. The blood settled to its lowest gravitational point in the human vessel which contained it, and there it pooled, slowly losing its familiar red colour as necrosis set in. On the basis of what I knew of her movements, I calculated that Angela Enke had been dead for almost twenty hours, and possibly more. Since the previous evening, that is, shortly after she had left her home to go to the Prior's House.

I looked up as Merson spoke.

'The blood's almost turned,' he grunted, confirming my guess with the expertise of a lifetime in the business. 'Been there all night, I'll warrant you that, sir. But it's that wound in the neck that did for her. It looks like a bite ...'

He pointed with his finger, but he did not touch the wounds.

'I do not think it is a bite,' I countered, but I could offer nothing better.

I bent forward, looking into the girl's face. Her left eye was badly bruised, swollen tightly shut. The right eye was wide open, the iris had once been dark, I guessed, from the colour of her hair, though now it was the neutral colour of dark slate, the eyeball itself a sickly jaundiced yellow.

'She sure looks dead,' Merson muttered.

'She is dead,' I said sharply, admitting no discussion.

'Maybe, falling, she has broken her neck,' he suggested.

I had checked the body in the cistern, of course. Even so, I placed my hands beneath her head, felt the weight of her head in my palms, and slowly moved the head to the left, and to the right. There was no sign of breakage. Which left only one possibility. That she had been damaged internally. We turned her over once again, and I laid my palms on her rib cage beneath her breasts. Her skin was cold, and damp, as if she had been sweating.

I pressed down hard again.

When nothing happened, I moved six inches further down and tried again.

The corpse shifted slightly, and made a sound.

I stepped back, pulled my hands away. Had I found the cause? The sound that issued was not the cracking of broken bone, but some indication of inner devastation, however. It sounded like the gurgling of water in a bottle, or the noisy rumbling of an empty stomach.

'She probably swallowed water in the well, sir,' Merson murmured.

'Water?' I echoed.

The well in Emma Rimmele's garden had been dry for half a century.

I placed my hands, one over the other, and pressed hard in the same spot.

The same noise came again. Far louder this time. I felt movement beneath my hands, as if whatever was trapped in there was fighting to find its way out. It seemed to vibrate up through her thorax, rushing upwards through her chest. Suddenly, her mouth fell open, and blood gushed out like molten lava. It welled up over her lips, then spilled out onto her chin, as if from the body of a living person, running out of the corners of her mouth, dribbling away down either side of her throat. It flowed for some moments. Just as quickly, it stopped.

Whatever had happened, it was over.

'Best get her in the ground, sir. Now. Tonight.'

'They won't have her in Krupeken,' I said. 'The mother refused to have her body in the house.'

Merson spoke, and his words ran through me like an electric current.

'She's suffered enough, sir. If the news gets out, God knows what the Prussians will try to do to her. If you give her to the French, she's lost forever. She'll be condemned to wander in the dark for all eternity. Let's bury her here, sir, in the old cemetery.'

Was that why Merson had helped me to bury my son?

Anders had died of the fever; the French would have thrown his corpse into a trench. No tomb, no stone, no name, no dates, no words to express our anguish for a child who had been cruelly taken from us. His soul, too, would have wandered in the dark for all eternity. Helena believed it. Merson, too.

That was what Merson had proposed to me that night two and a half months before.

'You're a magistrate,' he had said. 'Just tell the French that the baby died of a fall. Who'd dare to challenge your word, sir? Get the family doctor to sign it for you. He's a good friend of yours, no doubt. I'll come for him, sir. I have a covered basket. Trust me, sir, I'll put him under. The boy will sleep in Prussian soil. It will be the family plot …'

Merson had chosen the place. A plot which was no longer used, he swore. And he had placed an old wooden cross to mark the spot. My child was laid in a grave that might have been hundreds of years old, but anything was better than a

French pit. And I had paid the stonecutter, Ulrich Meyer, to carve a stone in memory of Anders. When the French left, I would have it erected. This was Merson's war, I thought, a personal war that he was waging against the French. They threw Prussians nameless into common pits, and doused them with quicklime. Lars Merson kept the bodies back whenever he could, and buried them in Prussian ground to spite the French invader. He was a rule unto himself in Lotingen cemetery.

'What are we to do, then, Merson?'

In this case, it was not a question of *if*, but of *how*.

Merson looked at me, then he nodded grimly. 'Glatigny has left his men here, sir. They're under your command. The crowd has gone, but they won't be far away, I'd bet. They'll be waiting to see her body carried off to the pits by the French squaddies.' He pointed to an ancient coffin propped against the wall. 'We'll give them a body to follow. Inside that coffin there.'

An hour later, the French soldiers loaded the wooden box onto a cart.

My instructions were clear and simple. They were to go to the new French cemetery on the far side of the river. 'Put the coffin into the trench, and get someone to fill it in,' I said. 'Ask Major Glatigny to make sure that the place is guarded over the next few days, and tell him that the guards must be armed and ready to shoot.'

'The area's a military zone,' said one of the soldiers. 'Our men are always armed.'

As they marched off into the night, two with their muskets on their shoulders, while the other two pushed the cart, I saw a contented smile on the face of Lars Merson.

'That's all they're good for,' he laughed. 'Heaving stones.'

The idea of four French soldiers carrying an old tombstone in a second-hand coffin was too much for him. Another Prussian corpse had been plundered from the French. He had won another battle.

'And now, sir, if you are ready, let's get down to work!'

Chapter 7

A cemetery is never silent, nor is it ever entirely still.

Life goes on quietly within its walls, and endlessly beneath the ground.

Merson laboured steadily, his spade slicing easily through the loose soil, while I froze at every possible announcement that we might have been discovered: the scampering of unseen creatures of the night; the rasp of a predator sharpening its beak or claws against a gravestone; a cry, a bark, or a howl; the endless orchestra of rustling and shifting which disturbed the darkness.

I prodded the blade of my long-handled spade into the yielding soil, and my lungs filled with the odour of vegetal decay. The deeper the hole became, the more intense the perfume grew. This was the wettest soil in the cemetery, according to Merson, the earth was full of worms. 'She'll rot far faster than normal here,' he announced, and that was what I wanted to hear.

The sooner Angela Enke became a harmless heap of bones, the better.

I winced as soil cascaded noisily into the trench. Something shifted in the canopy of trees above my head. I heard a soft hoot, the rustle of feathers, a swish of wings. Some moments later, the final squeal of a doomed mouse.

I leant on my shovel, catching my breath.

Helena feared the silence of the cemetery. She could not accept the fact that Anders was there. She thought that the child would be cloaked in silence for all Eternity, and the fixation tormented her. 'He hated silence,' she had said in tears. 'He seemed to be forever chattering from the day that he was born. Even when he was playing on his own. In his sleep, he burbled like a brook. How will he cope with the silence?'

Anders would be entertained by the unseen creatures moving in the darkness, I thought. The slow creeping of worms, the shifting of the soil. He would know those sounds by now, and they would keep him company. The child was not alone. Not there, among his fellows.

I shook my head and continued to dig. I suppose it was the strangeness of the situation in which I found myself. My mind seemed to fix on possibilities which had never occurred to me before. What stupefied me most was the similarity between the bizarre thoughts flitting through my imagination, and the superstitions that I had opposed so strongly in other people earlier in the day.

The dead do not hear what the living hear.

The dead do not lead the life that we lead.

The dead do not return to torment us.

Each sentence was a spadeful of earth, taken from deep down in the pit and thrown up into the pale sliver of light beyond my left shoulder. The moon was our only lantern – a clear silver disc with a bite out of the upper segment.

'As a rule, when digging down, the earth gets harder, more compact,' Merson grunted. 'There's clay, or shale grit hereabouts. But this soil's getting sloppier than mud. Can you feel it, sir? There's a spring just a few feet further down. That's what we are looking for. We're nearly done, I think.'

I stood up straight; the edge of the grave was level with my heart.

'It's time to bring her out,' Lars Merson muttered, rubbing his hands together, as if he were eager to get the business over.

We climbed up out of the trench, planted our shovels in the earth, and returned to the chapel, where a single lantern flickered. The corpse of the seamstress lay naked on the canvas. Merson positioned himself at her feet, leaving me no alternative but to stand where her head was. We covered her in an instant, wrapping her up inside that canvas shroud.

'Makes it easier to carry her,' Merson said, taking hold. 'Are you ready, sir? Lift when I give the word.'

She was heavy, but manageable.

I followed Merson out through the door and into the night.

Minutes later, the body fell with a dull thud into the bottom of the trench.

As he bent to pick up his shovel, I laid my hand on his arm and stopped him. We had acted too hastily. 'She must go naked into the ground,' I reminded him. 'You said so yourself. She'll decompose faster.'

'Aye, sir. You're right,' Merson growled defiantly, turning away, planting his shovel in the loose earth.

I did not wait for him. I skipped down into the trench, and began to pull the canvas roughly away from the corpse. It was no easy task. The dead weight of her body pressed down on the stiff material. As it came away, her arms and her breasts gleamed blue in the moonlight. The wounds on the side of her neck were two black holes, the traces of blood like a black, spidery web that ran across the upper half of her body.

'Do you need my help, sir?'

I did not answer, handing the canvas up to Merson, scrambling quickly out of the hole. I stood by the graveside, catching my breath, and I swore a solemn oath to the girl that I would find and punish the person who had murdered her. I would return by daylight to dig her up again when I had freed her of the superstition that had been attached to her name. I would take her home to her village and her parents. I would have her laid to rest by the pastor who had deserted them all.

I placed my hand on the shaft of the spade, preparing to cover her up.

'Hang on, sir!' Merson was standing by my side, looking down into the grave. 'There's something else that we have to do before we can fill her in.'

'Oh yes, of course,' I said.

The gravedigger was right. I felt ashamed of myself for my thoughtlessness. I looked down into the grave, made the sign of the Cross, and asked the Lord aloud to have mercy on the soul of Angela Enke.

'We don't have time for that, sir,' Merson growled.

'What do you mean?'

I could hear his laboured breathing. He laid his right hand on his heart and let out a groan, as if the work had robbed him of his strength. He was an old man, sixty years of age at the least. During the day he had a robust young lad to do the heavy work for him, Ludo Mittner by name.

'We have to bury her face-down,' he whispered.

'She is dead,' I protested. 'An inanimate corpse.'

Again I heard the heavy rumble of his breathing.

'It will not harm her, then,' he said flatly. 'Tradition demands it, sir. Face-down in the dark, she won't know which way is up.

If she should try to dig herself out, she'll dig herself deeper into the ground. That's what they always do in cases like this one.'

I did not oppose his whim.

We dropped down into the grave again. He chose the lower half of the body, leaving the head to me once more. I groped about in the darkness, struggling to turn her limp, naked body over, and lay her face down on the damp soil. What harm could it do, after all?

Dawn comes early on the Baltic coast in summer. The sky was glistening like a piece of mother-of-pearl. By the time that we had finished filling in the hole, the first cold rays of sunlight had broken over the far horizon.

'I am grateful for your help,' I said, as I watched him finishing off the job.

Before we began, Merson had removed the grass in large squares from the ground where we intended to dig with a scything motion of his spade, laying the pieces of turf aside in a fussy pile. Now, he replaced the squares of grass on the grave, pressing them down heavily with his boot.

'There!' he said, standing back. 'Who's to know?'

We were like a pair of thieves, I thought. Having ransacked the house, we were closing the doors and putting the cushions back in order. Though the grass was crushed, it would pass casual muster.

'No-one comes to this part of the cemetery much,' he murmured. 'But we must look to appearances, sir. The beadle comes and opens the gates at dawn. There'll be folk on the road from town already. If they see dirt on your clothes, they'll be curious … Hmm, it might be better if they see you praying by the grave of your son, sir.'

I felt exhausted, and confused. I wanted to go home and

sleep. 'Every bone and muscle in my body is sore,' I said with a shiver.

Merson eyed me critically. 'Come with me, sir,' he ordered.

I followed him between the tombs and vaults like a child. He strode on ahead, a shovel over each shoulder, making for the sexton's office. He closed the door behind me as I entered the room. I sat on one of his chairs for fear of falling down, my eyes drawn to the names chiselled on the old tombstones standing up against the wall.

'How long will it take?' I asked, as Merson handed me a stiff brush.

'Take?' he echoed, as I began to brush my trousers and my jacket.

'For the worms to do their work.'

'Within a day her mother won't recognise her,' he said, rubbing his face with the palms of his hands. 'No-one will know that she's been buried there.'

'No-one must ever know,' I said emphatically. 'Until I find the killer.'

Merson breathed in noisily through his nose. 'Do it quickly, Herr Stiffeniis,' he snorted. 'You know what people are. Someone will say that she has been to visit them, and next thing, they'll all be saying it. Then, the trouble will start.'

The gravedigger turned away, reaching for an earthenware bottle and two pewter chalices, which might once have held flowers. 'We need a good stiff drink. Bischoff's cordial,' he said with a smack of his lips, taking out the stopper and beginning to pour. 'The longer you leave it, the better it is.'

I raised the cup to my lips, grateful as I drank the cordial, and a fire burnt its way down my throat and deep into my intestines.

'You're beginning to look like one of the living again, sir,' Merson said, handing me a cloth, nodding down at my muddy boots, watching as I wiped them clean.

I pulled at the leather string, let my hair hang loose and ran my hands through it, pulling out the tangles before I knotted it up again.

I was ready to say good morning to Anders.

The rose petals were the hue of a baby's blushing cheek.

'These are for your child, Herr Stiffeniis,' Merson said, handing them to me.

He had cut the flowers from a bush which grew beside the door of the chapel of rest. I felt a lump in my throat as I took them from him, and walked out into the cemetery.

A number of women were bending over graves, brushing off tombstones, clearing away the windblown leaves, removing wilting blooms, changing the water in vases before filling them with fresh flowers that they had brought from home.

I hurried over to the spot where Anders had been buried.

A bunch of wild white crocuses lay next to the small wooden cross. The petals were huge, the pistils rigid, the green leaves waxed and shining. Helena had been there the day before, then. I had no idea how often she went to the cemetery. She did not tell me that she went at all. Whenever I visited the grave, I found the evidence, however: fresh flowers, or some other fruit of the season had been laid on the grass beside the ancient wooden cross. Even so, I had never met her there, not even by accident. Would she ever come to terms with her sorrow, I asked myself. Would repetition erode the hard stone of her pain, and smooth it into a smaller pebble of consolation?

I hoped that it would.

My wife and I had grown distant since the death of our youngest child.

I felt a flush of anger as I stood beside his grave. The stone was still not ready. There was nothing to read. No date of birth, or death. Ulrich Meyer, the stone-cutter, was notoriously slow. There was a shortage of quarried stone, he said, as a result of the epidemic, persuading us to choose an old stone which could be altered. It was still in Meyer's workshop, though Helena had insisted that I should pay him in advance to carve a cherub's pretty face, and a parchment scroll in bas relief with Anders' name, and a pair of angel's wings which would carry the note to the Gates of Heaven.

As I bent forward to lay my tiny spray of roses on the grass, I stopped dead.

Merson was standing some way off. His face was a mask of displeasure, as if he had just been nipped by a horse. His cheeks were pale and drawn, his eyes fixed on some point far beyond my shoulder.

'I might have guessed it,' he hissed, jerking forward, rushing up to me. 'After such a night as this, the she-devil's come a-calling!'

I turned to see what had provoked this change of humour.

My fingers parted, the roses fell on the ground.

Emma Rimmele was striding through the cemetery. A dense black cloud danced around her as she moved. I had never seen a garment like it. She moved rapidly forward as if she meant to leave behind the material in which she had so carelessly wrapped herself. Had Angela Enke had a hand in the making of it? Was this the mourning dress that Angela's mother had told me about? The material ballooned out around her knees and ankles. Her feet and legs seemed to thrust forward out of nothing, then slide back inside the dark cloud; she might have been slithering on marble, rather than walking on the ground. Above the waist, constricting whalebone pressed all too tight. A modesty cape of transparent black silk tried to hide, but succeeded only in revealing, acres of pale flesh – arms, shoulders, breasts. A gentleman's overcoat hung halfway down her back, trailing behind her on the ground.

There was nothing funereal in those clothes. On any other woman, they would have seemed ridiculous. Her hands held up her gown to facilitate her forward motion. She was wearing the same black boots that she had worn before, but she had forgotten to tie them up. The long laces whipped and played around her feet like twitching serpents. Her legs were bare, and visible almost to the knee. They were the colour of amber, as if they had been exposed to the burning rays of the summer heat. As if she had been walking, or running, in the sun …

Naked legs that the sun had warmed.

I felt embarrassed by the ideas which flashed through my mind.

She did not look like a woman in mourning. She did not wear a hat, or cover her face. Her hair was tied up on her head with that Medusa clasp, though loose swathes of it fell on her neck, cheeks and shoulders.

A gentleman was following her.

Though old enough to be her father, Herr Rimmele was not quite the invalid that she had led me to believe. White hair poked out in a stiff fringe from beneath his black top-hat. Now *that*, I assured myself, was a mourning hat. And the cape which flowed behind him as he shuffled in her wake was, unmistakeably, a black mourning cape. Black eyebrows sprouted in gentle arches above deep-set eyes. He was not unlike his daughter in that respect. In every other respect, he was totally different. Nothing reminded me of her. His receding chin, sunken cheeks, pronounced cheekbones, bony nose, lips so thin and grey that they were almost invisible. Her chin was bold, her cheeks were blooming, her lips were full and round. His eyes were pale, while hers were two dark mysterious pools.

She strode ahead, as if she were searching for something. In the determination of the moment, her father was forgotten. She lent no helping hand to steady his less certain steps along the gravel path. I saw how he struggled to keep pace with her, trotting almost, one leg taking longer steps, the other shuffling after it, as if such energetic exercise was not a regular item in his daily round. She did not look back to oversee his progress, nor wait to help him when the path turned sharply right.

I thought of Helena, her mourning dress buttoned up to the point of her chin, her veil coming down to meet it, her hair hidden beneath the black box-hat. Black leather gloves encasing the pale white skin of her hands. Not an inch of her flesh visible.

In that instant, her eyes met mine.

She stopped in her tracks, as if to ask herself what I was doing in that place. Her eyes shifted from me to the roses on the grass. Then, she stared at me again. I might have gulped another glass of Bischoff's cordial, such fire I felt in my stomach, the fumes rising to my head as she veered in my direction. Her father shuddered uncertainly to a halt, like a baby duck that had lost sight of its mother.

'Is this your child?' she asked me breathlessly, raising a hand, pushing back a curl that had fallen into her eyes. 'I will bring some flowers the next time.'

Instinctively, I glanced down at her empty hands.

She shook her head, her eyes fixed on mine. 'No flowers today,' she said. 'We are here to pray.' She looked back over her shoulder in the direction of her father. 'He is not at his best today, sir,' she murmured almost imperceptibly, as if those words were meant for my ears only.

'I must speak with you, Fraulein Rimmele,' I said.

She stared at me as if I had just said something odd.

'Here?' she murmured.

I looked down at the toes of my boots. There was a sardonic something in her voice, and I was instantly embarrassed by the playfulness of it. 'I will come to your house some time …'

'Your office might be better,' she offered. 'If it's all the same to you.'

She surprised me once again. No-one likes to be seen entering the Procurator's office. Most people fear the building. If any man is forced to enter there, his neighbours think that he has been summoned to appear before me to answer some charge.

'I'd prefer to leave my father at home first,' she explained.

'As you choose,' I replied. 'Some time later today, then.'

While we were speaking, her father had taken a step or two forward, as if he meant to reach his daughter. It was a feeble effort, like a child who had barely learnt to walk. He caught at her arm and managed to do little more than hang on awkwardly, almost bending double at her side. Emma turned and pulled him up with one hand by the lapel of his coat. As she did so, the heavy overcoat that she was wearing slipped from her shoulders and slid to the ground, carrying off the delicate modesty cape that had done something to conceal her breasts from public show. Her flesh was of the same amber hue as her legs.

'Very well,' she said, caught between holding her father up, and recovering her cape and her overcoat. 'I'll come to you the instant I am able.'

I dashed forward, and swept her garments from the ground, hurrying to cover her naked shoulders with the overcoat, while pressing the silk cape into her hands. A flash of static electricity passed between us.

She looked at me for one long silent moment, then slipped her father's lifeless arm into hers, and said: 'Come along, Papa. We'll walk the rest of the way together.'

As they made their way down the path, Lars Merson appeared at my side.

Erwin Rimmele looked back, peering around the protective arm of his daughter. His eyes flashed from Merson to me, and back again. His lips opened, as though he might be about to say something.

'Where is the Rimmele tomb?' I asked Merson.

'There is no Rimmele tomb,' he snapped. 'The mother's maiden name was Kassel. It's a vault, sir. One of the oldest in the cemetery. Until they returned, it was thought to have been abandoned. The dead lady has no living relatives left in Lotingen. Her daughter came with a coffin, insisting that it had to be buried with her forefathers. That had been Frau Rimmele's dying wish, the young lady said. She wanted it to be done at once, but these things take a while, sir. Permission had to be asked to have the old vault opened. Fraulein Rimmele was here the whole day to see that the work was properly done.'

'The whole day?' I queried.

He grunted audibly. 'We had her watching over us while we was working. We had to scrape out all the mortar, lever off the cap-stone, wash the dirt off. Then, clear out all the accumulated rubbish to make it fit to receive the coffin.'

'We, Merson?' I asked, turning to look at him.

'Me and my lad, Ludo,' he replied.

His eyes were fixed on the young woman and her father, as they made their way towards the Kassel family vault. There was nothing in his expression to indicate pity for their bereavement. Indeed, I thought I saw a look of disgust on his weather-worn face.

'Is there something odious in that?' I asked, surprised by his attitude. 'She has a perfect right to see that things are properly done. Is that why you spoke of her as a she-devil?'

'Ain't nothing odious in that, sir. But what I *did* find odious,' he said, repeating himself for emphasis, 'what I *do* find odious, is that no sooner did I slide the cap-stone on again – the mother was now inside the vault, if you understand me, Herr Stiffeniis – than that there lady went and … well, she wiped the mud off her boots on her mother's slab!'

'And you saw all this with your own eyes, I suppose?'

He shook his head, ignoring my sarcasm. 'Not three minutes after I had done the job. I took up my spade and crowbar, but I'd forgot my trowel and bucket. I had to go back for those, didn't I, sir? When I got there, she must have thought that she was all alone. I ain't never seen the like of it in all my days of working here. Would you clean your boots on any man's grave? On your own mother's grave, Herr Magistrate? It's a sacrilege, that's what it is! If I was looking for a vampire anywhere in Lotingen, sir, I would start in her front garden!'

If Emma Rimmele did not come to me that morning, I would go to her.

I had taken little notice of the fears that she had expressed the day before. The body *had* been found in her garden; men like Merson would say that the corpse 'belonged' to her. They would blame her for its being there. Emma Rimmele was a stranger in town. A beautiful and provocative one. She had brought a coffin with her. Her ways were not like ours. In the present circumstances, she was a danger to herself.

Suddenly, a shriek cut through the air.

It was human, loud, though some way off.

Startled rooks in the trees above my head took it up, cawing raucously, spreading their wings and flapping into the air like the circling buzzards I had read about in Africa when carrion is at hand.

I ran towards the sound, following the path that the Rimmeles had taken.

Merson's boots thumped the ground as he lumbered heavily after me. There was no-one else in that part of the burial-ground. 'Over there, sir,' he pointed. The gate of the vault was open, and I plunged down the worn steps, pulling up sharply as I cannoned into a human body. Erwin Rimmele was stumbling out of the dark interior as I charged into him. He fell to his knees before I could stop it from happening. As I bent to help him to his feet, I heard him mumbling. Sounds issued from his mouth in gasps, but I did not understand what he was trying to say.

Emma Rimmele was soon behind him, bending over him, too.

Her attention seemed more taken by her overcoat than by the sight of an old man kneeling on the damp stone floor. She clenched the garment to her throat, as if her whole demeanour might depend on it. Her blouse was torn, I realised. I caught a glimpse of bare flesh as she stretched her right arm out to assist him. Had there been a battle between them? Her hair had also been pulled loose, and it now covered the side of her face. As she pushed it carelessly away, I saw a gash and a drop of blood beneath her left eye.

'Heave him up, sir,' she said. 'He'll never shift on his own. I have the carriage waiting at the cemetery gate. We must get him home at once.'

It took a moment to make sense of what she had said, and what I must do. My hesitation was too much for her strained nerves. 'Lord above! Do as I say, Herr Stiffeniis. Can't you see that he is ill?'

I placed one arm behind the old man's shoulders, the other behind his knees. I had him up in an instant. Herr Rimmele was as light as a feather. Nor did he fight against me, as I thought he might. Instead, he clasped his arms around my neck, and held on tightly, as if to add what little strength he had to the endeavour.

'Stand back,' I ordered Merson, who was blocking the exit, carrying my burden up into the light. I shifted his weight a little, holding the old man in my arms as if he were a child, carrying him quickly back along the narrow path towards the cemetery gates.

Behind me, I heard Emma saying something to Merson. She might have been explaining what had happened as she locked the iron gate to the vault with the key. I was not listening to them. Herr Rimmele's head was inches from my right ear. I was listening to him. A single sentence, which he repeated, over and over again, in a small and distant voice.

'She is not my daughter … Not my daughter …'

As I bowed my head closer, urging him to be calm, the words changed, but not the insistent tone with which he pronounced them.

'A vampire has stolen her. A vampire ...'

His head fell heavily on my shoulder, and I realised that he had fainted.

I hurried forward, relieved to hear that monotonous sing-song no more.

Chapter 8

I had decided to interrogate Emma Rimmele immediately.

Instead of meeting her in my office, as she had suggested, I found myself sitting in the kitchen of her house, hat in hand, like a serf who had come to deliver fresh eggs. I had been awake all night, and was hungry, but I was obliged to wait while she was upstairs dealing with her father. The chair on which I sat was the only one in that vast room. A sliver of a tree-trunk formed the seat, four knobbly legs held it up, a vertical plank dug into my shoulders. It had been roughly hewn, and not by any skilled carpenter. Had the Schuettler brothers made it, I wondered. Then again, I thought, if Angela Enke had been sewing in the kitchen of the house, this was where she had sat.

I took a deep breath and looked around me.

It was the barest room that I had seen in quite some time. Much too large for a domestic kitchen, it had a high barrel-vaulted ceiling, and was almost unfurnished, except for a small larder cupboard pushed up against the far wall, and the ancient worm-eaten table on which I braced my elbow. The plastered walls had once been washed with lime, but the work had been done so long ago that they were stained uneven brown and yellow with grease and smoke and a century of cooking. Along the walls hung rough wooden frames and empty shelves which matched the rough rustic style of the chair. A range of pots and pans and ladles hung from bent nails driven into the wood.

The utensils might once have been shining bronze, but now they were black with age. Would anyone dare to set those pots upon the fire? Had Emma Rimmele done so?

In the corner was a stone sink and a hand-pump. Beside it, another waist-high tree-trunk was bristling with knives of different lengths and sizes. Generations of rabbits and hens had lost their heads on that gnarled block, which was black with ingrained blood. At my back, a huge fireplace took up almost the entire wall – the black metal cowl began at the height of my chin and rose to a point in the ceiling. Short lengths of wood had been stacked along the wall in an untidy pile, though the fire was out. When lit, I imagined, the choice was limited: either you sat in front of the fire and roasted, or you pulled your chair out into the room and you froze.

In that moment, it was so cold that my teeth began to chatter. Three narrow windows set low in the wall provided light. The rays of a pale sun could do nothing to combat the absence of warmth. Why in heaven's name had she chosen that place for herself and her father? She had mentioned that the Prior's House reminded him of the house that they had lived in before, the one which had now fallen into the hands of the French. Could the old man really find comfort in such austerity?

Above my head, I heard footsteps. They crossed the ceiling to the windows, then crossed back again. I could hear a voice, but only just – it was Emma, I supposed, though I could not make out what she was saying. She had taken her father up to his room the instant that we arrived. I had offered to help, of course.

'No, thank you, sir,' she said firmly, slipping her arm beneath her father's, carrying him forward. 'He must use his own legs.'

As his foot came up against the first step, Erwin Rimmele tilted forward, as if he might be about to fall. Emma steadied him, waiting while he raised his foot and searched uncertainly for a firm place on which to set it.

'You can rest for a little while upstairs, Papa,' she encouraged him, taking his weight on her hip, nimbly tucking her voluminous gown into her belt to facilitate her movements. 'Then, I will bring you something to eat.'

I had lunged forward to help her, thinking that he was going to fall.

Her head whipped round at the sound of my boots on the tiles. 'I know what must be done, Herr Stiffeniis,' she said. 'I am used to doing it alone.'

Like a practised nurse, she placed one arm behind her father's shoulders, and urged him on. Rimmele had no choice but to mount to the next stair. And the next. As I watched their slow progress, I wondered whether the manner in which she took control of him was the true source of the resentment that the old man had whispered in my ear as I was carrying him from the cemetery. Try as he might to fight against her, the force that she applied was irresistible. Herr Rimmele muttered angrily to himself, then turned his head in my direction.

Emma deftly raised her shoulder to prevent him, blocking me from his sight.

'You must go to bed, Papa. You'll have an ache in your head if you don't.'

Having witnessed the scene, I felt a deal of pity for her. How could an attractive young woman face such harrowing domestic duties every day? Alone, and without help. Her beauty would be stolen from her before she could put it to any use in her own cause. Her father might live for another ten or twenty years. And now her troubles had been multiplied by the discovery of the corpse in the well. And in a house not hers, in a town where no-one knew of the difficulties that she had had to face.

'Wait for me there,' she said, pointing to a door which led me into the kitchen.

I pressed my fingers hard against my eyelids.

Tiredness was catching up with me, and the kitchen was dim. I had not been home in twenty-four hours, and the little that I had instructed Knutzen to say to my wife would not suffice to reassure her. Anyone could have called to tell Helena that a body had been found, hoping to learn more from the magistrate's wife. Having discovered that Helena knew nothing, they might well tell her how the girl had been killed. There would be much gossip about the wounds. Word would spread in no time. I silently prayed that Lotte had managed to hold her tongue. If the maid began to speculate on the cause, there would be nothing left for me to tell the mistress. That is, my truth would seem pale and inadequate in comparison with the girl's imaginings.

I stood up quickly. My limbs were stiff after the labour of the night. I looked out of the kitchen window, resting my forehead against the grimy glass. In front of me was the well in the centre of the lawn. The bucket was in its proper place, as was the well-cover. The Schuettlers had evidently tidied up the garden after the ghouls departed. Over to the left, looking through the gate, I could see a slice of the canal, the stubbly fields beyond, and, farther off, the woods which hid the village of Krupeken.

'Angela came from over that way.'

Emma Rimmele was standing in the doorway.

She had cast off her overcoat-cum-cloak, but she had not

96

changed her dress. Though partially hidden by her undone hair, I could see that her right arm was bare, the material hanging down in tatters where her father had ripped at it. Her naked arm and bare shoulders seemed to glisten in the half-light. She reminded me of the girls who work out on the Baltic coast collecting amber on the shore in every weather.

'Why did Angela come here the other night?' I asked.

Emma Rimmele came towards me slowly, almost languidly. I stepped aside, thinking that she meant to show me something from the window. Instead, she stopped, and stared out at the world beyond my shoulder. A vein pulsed in her temple. Her brow furrowed. The nurse who had forced her father up the forbidding stairs was transformed into another person. The woman standing before me might have been the survivor of some terrible accident from which she had escaped with her life.

'I do not know,' she said. A moment later, she continued: 'Three days ago, the clothes were ready. Having paid Angela off, I never thought to see her again. There was nothing for her here … Except, I suppose, to end up dead at the bottom of our well,' she added with a sudden flash of irritation.

'Angela did not kill herself,' I said. 'She was murdered. Which is to say that someone killed her.'

While I was speaking, she pulled her hair away and threaded it behind her ear.

'Anyone could have done it,' she said. 'Angela told me that she often passed along the Cut on her way into town, or coming back.' Suddenly, her eyes flashed into mine. 'How was she killed, then?'

'A wound to the neck,' I said.

She seemed to think on this, twisting and turning her hair,

finally raising both her arms to clip it in place with the Medusa brooch that she held in her hand. She tugged gently at the damaged neckline of her dress, attempting to make it sit more comfortably on her shoulders. There was a studied carelessness about her, a reckless disdain for the state in which she found herself, which I had never met in a woman of her station. She was refined, but not affected. Extraordinarily natural, it seemed to me.

I was not immune to the sensual ambiguity of the situation.

'The Schuettlers asked me to return the keys,' she said quietly. 'I paid them two months' rent in advance the other week, and they seemed satisfied with the arrangement. Now, they wish to see the back of me, and my father. Something has upset them, and they appear to blame me for it. Why should that be? I suspect ... Tell me, sir. How was Angela *really* murdered?'

'Two deep punctures in the side of the neck,' I said, offering up my own neck, touching my own vein with the first two fingers of my right hand. 'They were more like holes than cuts.'

'God help me!' she murmured, placing her hands on the window ledge, staring into the garden. Suddenly, she turned to me, her voice low, almost accusatory. 'So, that was why I saw you at the cemetery so soon after dawn. You were not there to say a prayer for your child.'

I nodded, but she did not appear to see the gesture.

'There were traces of mud on your jacket and on your boots,' she continued. 'I wondered whether you might have been digging. I could not guess why ...' She looked boldly into my face. 'You buried the seamstress, did you not? In secret, because no-one must know where her body is.' She nodded slowly to herself. 'We all know what happens when country people take fright about ... well, for certain things. Am I right, sir?'

I answered her quietly. 'You must help me, Emma.'

She turned to face me. The speed of it surprised me. Like a cat when it hears a noise. One moment, she was staring out into the garden; the next, her face was close to mine.

'On the contrary, Magistrate Stiffeniis. You must help me,' she said, and her eyes were ablaze. 'A body is found with wounds to the neck in the well of a stranger who has recently arrived in town. I know who *I* would blame! So, that is why the Schuettlers have turned against me.'

I did not answer her directly. 'Tell me what you know about Angela Enke,' I said. 'Tell me everything, even things of no apparent importance ...'

The words froze on my lips. The concentration on her face was so intense, I seemed to be gazing into her soul.

'We hardly spoke,' she said, looking deep into my eyes. 'My father was in an agitated state of mind. You've seen this morning what he can be like. And she was here no more than half an hour on the first occasion. She was sent to me from a tailor's workshop in the town. She came, looked at the clothes which wanted altering, took some measurements, then went away, saying that she would return the very next day.'

'Surely you spoke to her the second time?' I insisted.

Emma shook her head. 'The only thing that Angela talked about was money. It would cost me more, she said, because I wanted her to come to the house, and she would have to walk to town to buy the materials. I realise that it is out of the way, of course, and I made no objection to her claim.'

'Did she seem to be afraid of the Schuettlers?' I asked.

'Is there anything to fear?' She shrugged her shoulders dismissively, which emphasised her collarbones. 'Angela spent two days working in this room. She was alone for all that time.

My father takes up every grain of my energy, as you know, sir. I hardly saw her.'

'Might the Schuettlers have come in while you were busy?'

She smiled and pursed her lips. 'I doubt it very much. I was upstairs most of the time, or out in the garden with my father. I would have seen them, or she would have called me if they had given her any offence. I left a bell in here for her. All Angela had to do was ring if she needed anything.'

'Did she ring?'

'Once or twice,' she murmured. 'To double-check a measurement of mine. My father's jacket, overcoat and hat needed funeral trimming, but nothing more.'

I glanced at her bare shoulders, and the corset which compressed her breasts.

'Is this the dress that the seamstress worked on?'

Emma looked down, as if to remind herself what she was wearing. She looked up, her head inclined to one side, as if I had just quizzed her. 'Of course, it is,' she said. Alarm flared in her eyes. 'Why do you ask, sir? Is it such an ugly thing?'

'I … I was wondering how much work she had had to do,' I said, recovering myself. 'She made you nothing new, then, working only to alter the clothes that you already had. Is that correct?'

I looked more closely at her dress. It was not black, but very dark blue, and it was made of satin. A floral pattern had been brought up by the fine stitching, though it could hardly be discerned. It was a ball gown, and it had been made by a practised hand. It was certainly not the work of Angela Enke. The shoulders had been pinched and puffed, and the lower hem, though taken up, was still a mite too long. Still, it was the expanse of bare flesh on display which caught and held my gaze.

Helena flashed before my eyes.

Her mourning clothes were plain, opaque, black.

'This dress is for Anders,' my wife declared solemnly, as I helped her with the buttons and the clasps, as if to ward off the thought that one of the other children might follow him prematurely to the grave. 'Until he has a monument, I shall wear this dress.'

Helena was crushed, while Emma Rimmele was not.

She had arrived in town with a coffin, insisting that Lars Merson should prepare an apparently abandoned vault to receive her mother's remains without delay. All for the sake of her father's peace of mind. Emma Rimmele, young and beautiful, a stranger, with a coffin as her baggage.

'Why did you not leave your mother where she was buried before?' I asked.

'I had to take my father away from there.'

'Eventually, you'll return to your home.'

Tears brimmed, but did not flow.

'They use our family graveyard for their target practice, Procurator Stiffeniis,' she whispered fiercely. 'They shoot at the crosses to calibrate their muskets.'

'Why did you come here, then?'

'Would my father have come away if I had not told him that we were taking my mother home? To her *real* home. She comes from Lotingen originally, you see. I knew that I would find a tomb here in the name of Kassel. It was her maiden name. My father's home is where my mother lies.' She glanced around the vast, empty kitchen. 'I searched for such a house as this one to put his mind at ease. To calm the fever in his brain. I hoped that he would recover something of the clarity that he once enjoyed.'

She crossed her arms over her breasts, and clenched her shoulders. 'Then this had to happen.' She nodded towards the garden and the well. 'I told you that the Schuettlers asked me to return the key to the house.' Her lower lip quivered for an instant. 'I … I had to give them money. More money. I had to *beg* them to let us stay! But what am I to do if they should ask for more?'

'What do you mean?' I asked.

'Blackmail is what I mean.'

The raw force of her feelings was evident. She looked disdainfully towards the garden, rage quivering in her eyes and on her lips. Then she gathered up her gown, pulled fitfully at the tatters of her shoulder puff, then marched the length of the kitchen to the lonely little cupboard.

'I must pay them, or leave the house,' she said, marching back towards me with a stone bottle in one hand, two green glass beakers in the other. She held them up for my inspection. 'I can offer you wine, if that will do you?'

I began to refuse, but she interrupted me.

'I do not like to drink alone,' she said, going over to the table, filling the beakers, pushing one towards me, inviting me to sit down on the stool, while she sat on the table-top. 'Those money-grabbers tried to justify their extortion. They said that they had had to chase intruders off last night. Why, sir, I saw them talking together! There were men with torches at the gate, though they did not have the courage to enter the garden, or attack the house.'

I felt a shiver of fright ripple down my spine. Members of the mob that Major Glatigny had thought to scatter outside the cemetery had made their way to the home of Emma Rimmele and her father.

'I'll ask the French to set a guard ...'

'Please, don't!' she spluttered. 'That would be the final straw. It would plunge my father into the nightmare from which I have been obliged to carry him off.'

I thought of calling for Prussian soldiers. But they might be more dangerous than the French. The people in the mob might be their friends or relatives. For all I knew, there could have been off-duty Prussian soldiers in their midst the night before.

'I barred the doors. I am used to it. We've been living under siege in our own house, surrounded by Frenchmen. I know how to defend my father and myself,' she said with a confident smile, closing one eye, sighting down her forefinger at me, thumb cocked vertically in an eloquent mime of a pistol.

'I hate to think how much the Schuettlers will charge me now,' she went on seriously, 'for bread and milk and wine. The eggs their scrawny chickens lay will be worth their weight in gold, I shouldn't wonder!'

She drank more wine. It seemed to drown her fear and fire her anger.

'The sum is bound to increase, but ... Well, I ... I cannot pay it ...'

She stared at me for some moments. Her brow creased, her lips appeared to tremble in supplication. 'Find the killer quickly, sir, or I'll be forced to beg on the streets to keep my father and myself alive.'

'I'll speak with Schuettler ...'

'I forbid you to do so.' The supplicant was gone in a flash. She had made a decision, and would not be shaken. 'They would only deny it, or send me on my way tonight. And where would I take my father, then?'

She raised her hands in a gesture of helplessness.

'Perhaps you are right,' I admitted.

She smiled ruefully. 'Help my father, if you can, sir. Which is to say, help him to remember how to release his money from the bank where it is deposited.' She placed her beaker on the table, and stood up. She rubbed at the wood of the table with the tip of her finger as if she meant to drill a hole in it. 'The cash that we had is running low,' she said. 'And as you've seen today, he is ever more demented.'

While speaking, she traced a line with her finger on the table-top. As she stood so close beside me, I thought I saw a hint of doubt on her face. It was as if she wished to ask me a question, but lacked the courage to put it into words.

'He has told you something, Herr Stiffeniis. It has shocked you. I can see it in your eyes. What did he say of me?'

'Who are you talking of?' I asked, playing for time.

'My father.'

I hesitated for a moment. 'What do *you* think he may have said?'

She smiled a glum smile. 'I know too well, sir. He's been telling everyone when he thinks that I am not listening. He says that I am not his daughter. That I am a … How did he describe me this time? As a demon? A changeling? Or has he now decided that I am a *vampire*?'

She hissed the final word as if to frighten the gullible.

'He did mention that possibility,' I replied, as lightly as I could manage.

I was sitting, she was standing. As a magistrate I am used to gazing down on those that I judge. Here the rules of interrogation were reversed. Even when she seated herself close beside me on the table-top again, I was forced to look up, while she looked down; we were both aware of the sudden change of role. She seemed to be waiting for me to say more, as I had often done before with a reluctant witness.

'A vampire who has taken his daughter's place,' I confirmed.

She placed her hands together on her knee, and leant towards me. 'Don't you believe him? Would any natural daughter care for such a troublesome father?' She was gently taunting me. Her attention to him was an obvious fact. She sat up straight. 'Now, Herr Stiffeniis, I must tell you the bitter truth,' she said very slowly. 'We have very little left. Money for a week, but not much more. That is, unless my father comes to his senses, which is out of the question, as anyone can see. Unless I find a person who will vouch for me to the extent that I may call upon our funds in the bank, I don't know what we'll do.'

I had not considered this necessity before. A daughter may manage, but a father or a husband generally pays. Money would certainly be a problem for her.

'By bringing him here, I had hoped to save the situation.' She raised her hand and pushed a curl from her forehead. 'But his mind is travelling downwards on a steep path. Faster and faster it goes. He no longer recognises *me*. He thinks that I am someone else.' A sob burst from her lips, but she smothered it with her hand. 'Can you imagine what that means, sir? A person you hold dear, who suddenly believes that you are his enemy!'

Her words set fire to the tinder in my own breast.

I thought of the change in Helena since Anders died. She had seemed, somehow, to accuse me of being responsible for his death, though she could find no way of putting it into words. She would not allow me to console her, and seemed to be unaware of my own pain.

'I think you *do* know,' Emma said, and her voice was hushed. The expression on my face had evidently been more eloquent than words. 'You understand what it means to be a stranger in your own home. In this house there are just the two of us. My father, and myself. I see the doubt in the eyes of others. Whom should they believe when he speaks against me? There is not much that I can do to convince them.' Suddenly, she clasped her right hand to her left breast. 'This is where they strike, is it not?'

'Strike?' I murmured.

She pressed her breast so hard it almost took her voice away.

'When they drive the stake into the heart.'

Was she mocking me again?

'What are you saying?' I asked dismissively.

'Isn't that what people do in such cases? Is it not what you have tried to stop them doing to poor Angela Enke?'

'Vampires do not exist,' I said with force. 'I know it, and so do you.'

'But what about the others ...'

As she spoke, her head drooped slowly until it rested on my shoulder.

I did not speak. Nor did I dare to move. I felt the weight of her leg on mine, her right breast crushing against my left arm. What could I do? Her breath seemed to scald my neck, her lips pressed urgently on my skin. They parted. Her tongue burnt hot against the vein beneath my ear. Her teeth nipped gently at my skin. Her wet mouth crushed my neck, and a delicious poison seemed to seep into my being. I felt as helpless as a fly caught in a spider's maw. She bit more hungrily against my flesh. I felt the sucking play of her lips. She might have been slaking an insatiable thirst from a chalice full of some narcotic liquid.

Just as suddenly, she pulled away.

I raised my hand and touched the spot. The skin was unbroken, though it was hot and wet. Her gentle laughter sounded in my ear.

'You are unharmed,' she said quietly. 'I do not want your blood.'

I stood up quickly, backing away until I struck the door which led into the garden. She sat watching me, her lower lip pinched between her teeth, an expression of puzzlement – or was it disappointment? – upon her lovely face. Clearly, she had expected some other reaction from me.

'I must go,' I said, fumbling with the door, which was locked.

I was in a panic, trying to run away, and I knew it. It was not so much that I wished to escape from her. It was what she wished me to do that shocked me. And the possibility that I might if I stayed.

'The Schuettlers will see you,' she said with an amused smile. 'That's not the door by which a magistrate would leave after having spoken to the lady of the house.'

'We have nothing to hide,' I said.

'You and I know that,' she said, never taking her eyes off me for an instant, 'but it is not enough. We both know that I am not a vampire, but nor is that sufficient. Leave by the front door, Herr Procurator Stiffeniis. And cover that red mark on your neck.'

I walked back to town beside the Cut.

What sort of relationship had I just established with my most important witness?

A witness, I reminded myself, that many people in Lotingen believed had thrown Angela Enke down the well after having sucked her dry of blood.

Chapter 9

The sign above the door had been painted by a fancy hand.

Scarlet letters on a creamy ground: *Frau Graube's School of Stitches – tailoring to order.*

Here, Emma Rimmele had found Angela Enke. The girl's mother had told me that her daughter often went to see Frau Graube in search of work, and that she sometimes slept at the homes of girls who worked there, too.

I lifted the latch and a bell tinkled.

A dozen ornate iron pillars held up a low ceiling above the bonnets of a score or more of young women who were sewing and stitching in the large room. An older dame, the proprietor of the place, was seated at the far end behind a desk which was raised on a high dais. Ruth Graube was a well-known figure in Lotingen. A half-blind widow in her sixties, she had been justly famed for making bridal gowns and christening smocks with exquisite stitching. Frau Graube herself had made the clothes in which my two eldest children had been carried to the Pietist chapel to be baptised. One of her girls had made the shift in which little Anders had recently been laid to rest.

'Is that the door I hear?' Frau Graube cried out.

Her shrill voice made an exclamation out of every question.

'Aye, Frau Graube,' a dozen voices chimed, breaking off the quiet chatter with which the room had been humming. The right-hand wall was made entirely of panes of glass set in lead frames which looked out onto an open courtyard stacked with carts. Sunlight flooded in, while the other side of the room was lit by overhead oil lamps with large glass bulbs. In the centre of the room stood three long tables around which the workers were perched on stools.

'Which friend has come to visit us this afternoon?'

The whole assembly looked at me, but no-one cared to answer. They all knew who I was, and had guessed why I was there. These girls knew Angela Enke better than her mother did.

'It is I, Frau Ruth,' I called, stepping into the room.

'Herr Procurator Stiffeniis,' the mistress's voice rang out. 'I've been expecting you since yesterday.'

I made my way towards her desk, passing between the long tables at which the girls and women were working. They were making uniforms, French and Prussian by the look of the rolls of blue, red and green material which were being cut into sections on the table to the right and nearest the windows, taking shape as sleeves, lapels and coat-tails as the pieces were carried off into the darker recesses of the room, where the youngest girls with the sharpest eyes were stitching them together beneath the oil-lamps.

'I need your help, Frau Ruth,' I said, taking her outstretched hand.

It was a pudgy hand, the fingers stiff, the joints knotted. Rheumatism had put an end to her needle-plying several years before. Now, she taught the young the secrets of her nimble-thimble generation, despite her failing sight, which she guarded behind a pair of metal spectacles framing two square lenses of thick black glass.

'I know why you are here,' she murmured.

'A dreadful business!' I exclaimed.

'How is Frau Helena now?' she asked me, her voice weighted with concern.

I had been there only months before to place the order, and collect the shroud.

'My wife is well enough,' I lied. 'She is still feeling the loss …'

She turned her head away from the light. 'And you, sir? I'm sure you feel it, too.'

I nodded, though I knew she could not see me. 'I am more fortunate,' I said. 'I have my work to distract me.'

'Such unhappy work, Herr Procurator,' she said with feeling. She turned her head the other way. 'I hear Gretel's footsteps!'

A girl in a dark dress and matching mob-cap placed a large tray on the table. It contained a small samovar and two porcelain cups and saucers with green floral designs. They were from the Dresden factory, I think.

'I used to detest the infusion made from nettles,' Frau Graube said, leaning close. 'But it is like the French. You get used to it, and them, by daily doses. They do provide a lot of work for us, it must be said. I don't know what they do with their underwear, shirts and uniforms! The stuff they use is stuff of the very poorest quality. They bring it with them. But you're not here to talk of stitches, are you?'

'Angela Enke,' I said without preliminaries.

'If she had stayed with me,' she said, 'it might never have happened. I have redeemed so many girls, you know – orphans from the workhouse, others from the prison. Angela wasn't one of those, of course. A poor home, but an honest one.'

She hesitated, thinking, leaning forward to sniff at the samovar.

'What was she like?' I asked.

Frau Graube pursed her lips. 'Headstrong, let's say. Had her own way of doing things. She worked quite regularly with us until … oh, it must be four or five years now, I suppose. She was quick and clever with a needle, but … you know the story, surely, sir? That boy of hers who went to fight the French, and never came back again? I caught her drinking,' she said, and her voice sank to a hoarse and very audible whisper. '*Drinking!* I won't allow it. Working on her own at home, or going out to houses, she was free to do whatever she liked, but I could not take her back.'

'And yet, she came to you occasionally,' her mother said.'

Frau Graube nodded. 'I've more work than I can handle, what with all the troops in the town. I could always give her something to tide her over. Our tea is surely ready by now,' she announced loudly, then added in a loud whisper: 'You know what idle hands get up to, sir.'

'Are you suggesting that she was a regular tippler?'

'No, no!' she answered quickly, waving her hand in protest. 'Once was enough for me. Angela Enke was a good girl, honest and Christian, but she had known tragedy. I like my stitches straight, sir, and so do my customers! You had do better to talk to one of her particular friends.'

She nodded her head dismissively in the direction of her employees.

This invitation was what I had been hoping for. 'Her mother mentioned a girl,' I said, as I sipped my nettle tea. It caused my lips to pucker and my tongue to fur, though I complimented her upon it, and I took another generous quaff, emptying my cup, which I set down with a rattle on the saucer.

'Would you care for more, Herr Procurator?'

'That's very kind, but no, thank you,' I said quickly. 'With whom would you suggest that I talk?'

Frau Graube finished her tea more slowly, savouring the sour taste, running her pale tongue over her grey lips. 'Kitti Raubel,' she called out loudly. 'Step up here to my desk, if you would be so kind. Make sure you leave your table neat and tidy.'

As the young woman put down what she was doing, a sort of stifled hubbub broke out among the rest of the assembly.

'Silence!' Frau Graube snapped, emphasising this order by slapping a large wooden ruler flat on the table-top. 'Get on with your work! Those jackets must be done before the day is out.'

I watched the approach of Kitti Raubel. She was tall, bony, her face long and thin, her hands bright red. 'Equine' was the word that I might have chosen to describe her. This impression was reinforced by her large bloodshot eyes, a long nose, large ears, and a receding chin. When she curtseyed, trying to smile at me – nervous at being called – and showed her large yellow teeth, the word etched itself upon my brain.

'Frau Graube?' she said, in a high-pitched, nervous whinny.

'This gentleman would like to ask you some questions,' the matron said. 'About that poor, unfortunate friend of yours. Don't pretend to be dumb, for I know that you are not. Do you hear me, Herr Procurator Stiffeniis? Do not take no for an answer!'

'I certainly won't,' I began to say.

'It might be better if you took her outside,' Frau Graube insisted. Before I had the time to wonder whether this delicate concern was for myself, or for the girl, she added: 'Otherwise there will be no work to be got out of any of them. Now, good day to you, Herr Stiffeniis.'

I walked down the room, the girl trailed after me, and the hectoring voice of the seamstress piped up again. 'Come along now, girls! Pick up your needles and threads! Back to the grindstone, I say. I'll only pay you for a full day's work. I cannot see so well, but these old hands will tell me who has been idling.'

I stepped out into the daylight, waited for the sewing-girl, then closed the door.

Kitti Raubel stood before me like a docile pony waiting to be saddled. She looked down, eyes wide, hands stretched stiffly down along her sides.

'You know what happened to Angela, don't you?'

The girl looked up. 'I know that she is dead, sir.'

'When did you see her last?'

Again, those brown eyes seemed to question what I meant.

'The last time she was here, do you mean?'

I nodded. 'Let's begin with that occasion.'

The girl pinched her lower lip between her thumb and forefinger. 'She came here last week, sir. Thursday … no, it must have been on Friday. We never work but Saturday morning, then Sunday's always free for church. The lady came that day …'

'Which lady?'

'The lady from the big house near our village …'

'Do you live in Krupeken, too?'

She blinked. 'I do, sir. That's how I know Angela Enke. Sometimes when she's coming to town in the morning, or going home again, we walk along the path together.'

I felt a sense of uplift and relief. Had I finally found a person who might be able to tell me something useful?

'Which path?' I asked. 'The canal path?'

The girl nodded again. 'It's longer, but we like it better.'

'You came to town that way together last Friday, did you?'

'Oh no, sir. I remember now. It was on Saturday morning. On Friday Frau Graube asked me if I could do the job, but I knew that I would be too busy. I had to spend that Saturday afternoon pickling onions with my mother. I had promised to help her, and I didn't dare go back on it. That was when I asked Angela ...'

'Let me get this straight,' I interrupted. 'Fraulein Rimmele spoke to Frau Graube on Friday. Is that correct?'

'It is, sir. She had a dress and some gentleman's clothes. She wanted them takin' in and takin' up, and dressing with black bunting. For a funeral, she said, but Frau Graube wouldn't do anything for her. Couldn't, really. Got to finish them uniforms by the end of this week, that was what she said. We'd been working on them last week, too, without a pause. A slight commission like that one, fixing up old clothes, Frau Graube said that one of us could do it out-of-hours, if that was what we wanted. But we was all tired out, sir,' she held up her hands, showing me the palms. 'Just look at my poor finger-tips!'

They were swollen, pricked and scratched.

'It's the needles, sir. They get so blunt, you see. An' that French material is rubbish, it's so stiff. I knew that Angela was looking for work, though. She'd told me so a day or two before. I went to their cottage that night, last Friday, as I said, and I told her. You come with me tomorrow, I said, Frau Graube'll give you something to work on. And that young lady was most insistent anyway. She said that the work would have to be done at her place. Said she had a sick parent to look after, what couldn't be left alone. Angela came to the school, got the address from Frau Graube, and that was that.'

The girl stared fixedly at me. Then she flicked her thumb loudly against her large upper teeth.

'Living in the same village, you must have seen Angela again,' I said.

She played with the fingernail between her teeth for a moment.

'I saw her two days ago,' she said.

'The day before her body was discovered,' I specified.

'That's right, sir. She'd been to the lady's house on Saturday afternoon. She'd started on the work. Almost finished it, she said, except for some hemming. She's very quick when she needs the money ...'

She dipped her head and looked down at her boots.

There was something else, I could see it. But the girl was reluctant to tell me for some reason or other.

'And?'

Silence.

'What else did Angela say? Come along now, Kati ...'

'Kitti,' she corrected me. 'Angela walked to town with me on Monday morning. She was supposed to be going to Durkheim's Emporium to buy black lace for trimming, she said. Fraulein Rimmele had given her some coins and told her to buy a yard of lace, sir, but it wasn't near enough ...'

All of this confirmed what I already knew. Emma Rimmele had told me earlier that morning, money was short, and she could not draw upon her father's bank funds.

'What did Angela do?'

Kitti Raubel cleared her throat, and glanced towards the closed door.

'I won't tell Frau Graube,' I went on. 'Is that what you are worried about?'

The girl nodded slowly. Her eyes remained fixed on mine, while her head bobbed up and down.

'Well?' I insisted.

'She took some old lace from the cast-offs box out in the yard,' she pointed. 'It wasn't nothing, sir. We'd never have used it, really. Not for nothing important, like. She took some of that old stuff, and said that it would do. The lady wouldn't notice ...'

'Frau Graube?' I interrupted.

Kitti Raubel shook her head from side to side. 'Fraulein Rimmele, sir. Angela said that she was a ... She used a word, sir. Said she was a flighty harringdon, and that she didn't care a nip. All she wanted was a frilly black dress. Not a real mourning dress, just something she could wear to visit her mother who'd been buried in the graveyard.'

A harridan? I had noted the oddity of Emma Rimmele's clothes, remarking to myself on the makeshift nature of her mourning outfit, the modesty cape of black lace, the heavy boots that she wore, her lack of stockings. Had Angela Enke been jealous of the lady?

'What else did Angela say?' I asked.

Kitti Raubel blushed bright red and hid her face by looking at the ground.

'Is something embarrassing you, Kitti?' I enquired.

She nodded solemnly, wiping her eyes with the back of her hand.

'I didn't know whether to believe her, sir,' she said at last. 'We spend all day closed up in the workshop. We talk a lot, us girls. 'Bout everything, really. 'Bout the ladies that come, and the clothes they make us make. Angela, too, of course. But she saw other things, sir. Going into people's homes, working there beside them, you see the lot. What they eat, what they drink. The things they say. To each other, and about other people, too. Angela was one for a bit of gossip. Half the time I didn't know whether to take her serious. Half the time I'm sure she made it up. It's true what Frau Graube said about her. Angela liked a drink, and she could tell a merry tale ...'

'What did she see or do in the house of the Rimmeles?' I asked.

'She didn't do nothing, sir. Nothing wrong, I mean. Not *her* ...'

'Who, then?'

'Fraulein Rimmele, sir.'

I felt like a man who is obliged to listen to an interminable joke.

'If Angela Enke told you something, I want to know what it is,' I said.

The girl nodded, but still she did not speak.

'Fraulein Rimmele?' I prompted.

'And her father,' the girl added in a hushed whisper.

I thought of the infirm old man that I had carried from the cemetery that morning, recalling the cruel words that he had whispered in my ear regarding his daughter. Emma was a changeling, a vampire. It was a ridiculous accusation. Had he said something of the same sort to Angela Enke? And had the girl believed him? Was this the gossip that she had passed on to Kitti Raubel?

The girl pulled out a rag and blew her nose.

'It isn't nice, sir,' she warned me.

'Let me be the judge of that,' I replied.

'The first time that she went there, she said she'd spent the morning fixing up the clothes that had to be altered. They were in a bit of a state what with bulging seams and buttons half-hanging off. If you have to alter clothes, sir, you need to mend them proper first. So, that was what she did.'

I listened carefully, doubting that this preamble would take me far.

'What happened then?' I encouraged her.

'Next thing, sir, you need to take the sitter's measurements, and make a note of what needs doing. An inch here, two inches there, snip this, cut that. By the time she'd finished working on the lady's clothes, it was late afternoon, she said. She knew what she would have to buy on Monday morn, and what she'd have to do that day. Well, it was the gentleman's turn to be fitted. She'd been working on her own down there in the kitchen, so she took her yardstick up, and went out into the hall. She looked around, but there wasn't no-one there. She called for Fraulein Rimmele, but the lady did not hear her. That is, she did not answer her. As Angela said, she may have been too busy …'

'Doing what?' I asked, unable to stem my impatience.

'The lady'd said her father had a room up on the first floor, so Angela went up there. The fraulein said she spent a lot of time with him, so Angela put her ear to one of the doors. Once she heard the voices, she thought, she'd knock and ask the young lady if she could take the old man's measurements. And that's exactly what she did, sir.'

She crossed her arms, and stared at me with a determined nod of the head.

'I don't follow you,' I said. 'Angela Enke listened at a door, heard a voice, knocked, and went in. What's so strange about that?'

Kitti Raubel pursed her lips and blew a hoarse whistle.

'The voice she heard was an old man's voice, sir. A moaning sound … Angela thought he might be ill, so in she went. That young lady was down on her knees, sir. She heard the door behind her open, tried to get up, and she couldn't. Her hand was caught inside his flap …'

Again she fixed me with that stare.

'His *trouser* flap. You know. *There.*'

She glanced down below my waist.

I was tempted to smile. I could think of a dozen reasons why a caring daughter might be found with her hands inside her ancient father's trousers. Two possibilities came to mind immediately: incontinence, or some physical discomfort. In either case, it would be a mercy to set the old man at his ease. Yet Angela Enke had put a malicious interpretation on the scene. And so had the friend in whom she had confided.

'What did Angela say about that?' I asked.

'What could she say?' Kitti shot back. 'She saw what she saw. Then, bold as brass that woman pulled her hand away, and said not a word.'

She blew out a loud sigh.

'And next thing, Angela's dead, sir! You know what all the town is saying about her, sir. That Fraulein Rimmele! They say that she's a *beast*, sir. One of them *creatures* that preys on folks at night …'

'Listen to me, Kitti Raubel,' I snapped. 'If you go telling stories like this, you'll get yourself into serious trouble. If the lady were to make a complaint to me, I'd be forced to hear it in the courtroom. You might get a whipping.'

Kitti Raubel's lips began to tremble, her shoulders began to heave.

'Pull yourself together,' I told her. 'Angela certainly

119

exaggerated what she thinks she saw. Tell no-one what you have just told me. Do you understand?'

She wiped her nose with the rag, then sniffled. 'Yes, sir.'

'Go back inside and do your work,' I said. 'I've taken up enough of your time.'

As I began to walk away, she called after me: 'I hope that I've been useful, sir.'

'Most helpful,' I replied, thinking that she had just put horns on the devil's head.

Chapter 10

I turned in to the narrow lane behind the market-square.

It was the quickest way to reach my house. I had not slept, nor had I eaten in twenty-four hours, and Helena needed to know more than the little that I had instructed Knutzen to tell her the night before.

The sound of snarling stopped me dead in my tracks.

Two black dogs, their pelts a mass of sores, were facing off in the centre of the cobbled alley. They were as high as my waist with blunt square heads. They might have been Irish hunters. Between them lay a bone so large it could have been the hind leg of a cow. It was red, raw, knotted with gristle. The curs growled and snapped at one another, hackles raised, fangs gaping, exposing mottled gums.

As they heard my boots on the stones, their bloodshot eyes turned in my direction.

I pressed my back against the stone wall.

Should I retreat, wait for the battle to end, or should I try to pass them?

That alley was notorious. Butchers, bakers, sausage-makers, fish-vendors, and just about everybody else in Lotingen dumped offal and innards there, hoping that scavengers – animal, or human – would clean up after them. Other bones and scraps were scattered on the ground, stripped clean of meat. Other battles had been fought and won that day, but I had chanced upon the rearguard.

At that moment, Helena turned the corner at the far end of the alley.

She was walking quickly, head down. A bunch of white flowers stood out starkly against her black clothes. The wind was blowing in her face, flattening her skirt against her thighs. She might have had the winged feet of a messenger of the gods. She went so swiftly that I thought she ought to have taken flight above the carpet of rubbish which had been abandoned there that day. That filthy lane was the quickest way from our home to the cemetery.

She had not seen the dogs. Nor had she seen me. But the hounds had spotted her. One began to bark, advancing on her, and she looked up. She saw the dogs, she saw me. Her lips formed my name, but no sound issued from her mouth.

'Stand hard against the wall!' I shouted, then did what I had hesitated to do just a moment before. I jumped into the middle of the alley, waving to attract the attention of the animals, rushing at them, arms out to make myself seem bigger, shouting at the top of my voice.

The hounds pulled up sharp, and turned to face me.

'Go back, Helena,' I shouted, pointing. 'Remember the old school.'

The Pietist schoolhouse had been abandoned for a year or more. The French had used it as a mapping-office, but the stench of the street by day, and the rats which nibbled at their maps by night, had taken them quickly elsewhere. It was the one Prussian victory of any substance in a long time.

Helena nodded, ran to the iron gate that was set in the wall. I saw her push it open, enter, disappear from sight.

I faced the hounds. But only for an instant.

To my surprise, seeing the road that Helena had opened up for them, the pair ran off in the direction from which my wife had come, rushing past the schoolhouse gate, howling, providing me with the opportunity to take refuge in the same walled garden where my wife had hidden.

I dashed to reach her.

As I laid my hands on the bars to push, Helena pulled hard, then pushed the gate closed behind me with a clang.

Relief spluttered out of me. 'You should know better than to come this way,' I said, sounding angrier than I intended.

'You should know better yourself,' she replied, and looked away. Her head was covered by a black woollen shawl, but curls had fallen loose on her forehead and in the hollows of her cheeks.

'Knutzen told you, I suppose?' I said awkwardly, by way of explanation for my absence the night before. My voice was gruff. I could only hope that she would attribute it to the agitation of the moment.

'Knutzen told me that a body had been found ...'

Her voice seemed to fade away like an invalid's. As she spoke, she rested her head upon her shoulder and let the scarf slide into her waiting hand. She had tied her curls up with a black velvet ribbon, but it had only half done the job. The locks had broken free on the left, clustering around her ear and covering her neck in great disorder. The fullness of her hair made a startling contrast with her pale complexion and drawn expression. While her hair seemed to thrive, my wife seemed to be fading away. Her cheeks, once full, were thin and hollow. Her mourning clothes enclosed her like constricting sorrow. Every nerve and muscle pushed and worked beneath her pale skin; blue veins pulsed along the edge of her temples; her lips were split and dry, white in colour, ridged with vertical lines the colour of blood.

My heart clenched at the sight.

Another face reared up suddenly in my thoughts. It was out of place, ungenerous, beside the harrowed figure of my wife.

Suddenly, there was a wolf-like howl from beyond the gate.

Helena folded her arms across her breasts as if to stop herself from quaking.

'They made such dreadful noises during the epidemic. The night that …'

She did not finish what she was saying. In truth, there was no need. We both recalled too well. We were sitting by candlelight at the bedside of our baby son, watching as the fever wore Anders down to the bone, waiting as it consumed him. And outside in the moonlight, stray dogs howled like wolves.

'Can animals sense that something's wrong?' she whispered, clinging to my arm.

All sorts of reasons had been given to explain the number of dogs on the loose in Lotingen. Their masters had died, the dogs were starving. They had eaten whatever they could and been driven wild by the taste of human blood. The devil had got into them, Pastor Röhl informed his bishop from the pulpit of the cathedral while preaching of the Gadarene swine. The explanation given by the mayor was more mundane, but probably the truest. Marcus Ziegler was dead, he said, and nobody had yet been appointed to take his place. Marcus Zeigler had been the dog-cat-and-rat catcher in Lotingen for more than fifty years. At last, French troops had been ordered into town to discharge their muskets at the beasts. I remembered going to my office the morning after, wending my way through the evidence of the slaughter. The market square had been carpeted with strays, not all of them as dead as I might have liked. For a long time afterwards, my sympathies were with the French. Every time I heard a musket crack, I took heart. One menace less, I thought.

'They are hungry,' I said, a mite too sharply. 'They'll wander off in no time once they've had their fill. We'll soon be free to leave.'

'They'll come back,' she murmured, staring into space. 'They always do.'

'If they become a nuisance, they'll be shot,' I protested.

'I was not talking of the dogs,' she said quietly.

'What, then?' I asked, perplexed.

'Frau Sauchen came to the house this morning selling apples.' Helena's voice was flat and low, without a trace of emotion in it. 'She said that something must have happened at the cemetery. She saw a crowd outside the gates with pikes and torches. A girl had been murdered ... She saw *you* there, Hanno. In the company of French soldiers, she says. And then, all night ... you did not come home. I didn't know what to do. Should I wait for you, or should I go to visit Anders?'

She was silent for some moments, the flowers still held tightly in her fist.

'What kept you away so long, Hanno?'

Silently, I cursed the tongue of the widow Sauchen who sold fruit from house to house. 'They will not let the body enter the village,' I began to say. 'The dead girl is from Krupeken ...'

Helena spoke, interrupting me. 'They think that she'll return to haunt them.'

'You know the superstitions,' I countered. 'They grow in Prussia like the apples on Frau Sauchen's trees.'

She appeared not to have heard me.

'Why do people believe that the dead come back?' she asked me, as if there might be a plausible answer. 'Why would they *want* to come back?'

I took her hand and held it in my own. It was as cold as ice.

'Folk tales tell us that when some people die, they are reluctant to leave the living. They wish to remain with their families and their loved ones,' I said, trying to explain it away, conscious of her fragile state after our recent loss.

'They are not damned souls,' she murmured. 'They cannot go away because they love us too much ...'

'You know these tales as well as I do, Helena,' I said, hoping to halt the flow.

She turned to me and she smiled. It seemed an age since she had smiled. 'Why should we fear them, in that case? Her parents ought to be glad.'

I was lost for words. She had found a logic in the legends and she seemed to be quite comfortable with it.

'Where did you bury her, Hanno?'

I let go of her hand.

'A temporary resting-place,' I said with a sigh. 'She won't be there for long. As soon as I have laid my hands upon the killer, I'll take her back to Krupeken ...'

'Is she lying close to Anders?'

Helena's intuition often confounded me. What should I say? The fact that they had both been laid in the same ground – this supposedly un-dead woman, and our child, who had died the most frightful of natural deaths – would frighten her, I thought.

I placed my hand on her shoulder, and gently pulled her to me, forcing her to turn around and look at me. We were so

126

close that the sigh which escaped from my lips caused the curls on her brow to flutter. I ran my tongue over my own lips to wet them, then gently touched my lips to hers. I wanted with all my heart to help her. I wanted to save her, repair the damage which the baby's death had brought upon us. Helena seemed to be physically tormented, unable to recover from the loss. Those wounds on her lips were a visible manifestation of her suffering. Did she bite her lips when she was alone with her sad thoughts?

Her shoulders stiffened beneath the pull of my fingers, but I held her close and urged her, lip to lip, to abandon herself to me, and let me comfort and console her. She gave herself to me for a minute, perhaps, then slid away, leaving a damp saliva trail on my cheek, settling her head into the cavity between my shoulder and my neck. I rocked her gently for some moments, as if she were a child who needed help before she could sleep. And as I cradled her, I told her where I had buried the body of Angela Enke the night before with the help of Lars Merson. In the same section of the cemetery, I said, though I was careful not to say that they were laid side by side.

'They don't come back,' I whispered. 'I am so sorry, Helena. Anders can't come back to comfort us.'

A sudden gulping sigh escaped from her lips. It might have been the start of a torrent of much-needed tears, but it stopped as quickly as it began. 'I wish he could,' she whispered. 'I'd welcome him in any form. I would open the door ...'

Something pushed hard enough to rattle the gate. Growling and yelping followed on. Helena drew herself up stiffly against me. I held her by the shoulders. We stared together at the gate, waiting to see if some more determined assault would follow on, but all we heard was silence.

'Are they lying in wait for us out there?' she whispered.

I held her close to my breast, making hushing sounds, urging her to be quiet. We stood that way for some more minutes, listening, but hearing nothing. On a sudden impulse, as if some signal had been given, we turned as one, still clinging to each other. I led her by the hand towards the gate, taking care not to make a sound. And there we stood for another minute.

No howl or bark was heard.

No cracking and chewing of bones.

Silence.

'They've gone,' I whispered.

I unlatched the gate without letting go of her hand. I inched it open, looking out for any danger, careful of Helena, knowing that she was still worried that the hounds might be lurking there, poised to attack us again.

But I was wrong.

I did not expect it. She withdrew her hand from mine, reached up, shifted the stock and pulled down upon my collar, exposing the spot where the lips of Emma Rimmele had pressed against my neck.

She studied it for an instant, knit her brows, but did not say a word.

Every possible explanation ran through my head. I had hurt myself while digging in the dark. I had burnt my skin on the lantern-glass. Lotte had put too much starch in my collar.

Helena removed her finger and pushed my collar back into place. 'I think we are free to leave,' she said very quietly.

Indeed, the lane was empty.

The dogs had gone, leaving the cow-bone of recent contention forgotten on the cobbles. I took Helena by the hand

and I led her home. We saw nothing of note until we reached our own front gate. As I closed the gate, I took a deep breath. At my back, I heard the voice of Helena.

'What in heaven's name is this?' she said.

She was staring up at the first floor of the house. Two rooms look out over the narrow front garden: the bedroom on the left, where the children sleep, and the other room, which has not been used since Anders died. That bedroom should have been used as a nursery for Edviga, but now the baby slept in the company of Manni and Süzi, her elder brother and sister. Three in a room, and one room empty. Helena would not allow a thing to be changed in there. The sheets and the mattress had been thrown on a bonfire, of course, but the medicine, glass and spoon which Anders had used throughout his illness still stand where they stood in that dark period.

Helena was shielding her eyes, looking up at the eaves above the windows. They poke out from the roof tiles like gibbets, or hoists. Blowing in the breeze, rattling and clinking together were the strangest collection of objects. I recognised a chicken leg, a pair of spiked hen's claws, a wish-bone, and some other bones that might have come from the chicken's wings and ribs.

'Silly girl,' I murmured, thinking of Lotte. 'She doesn't mind the ravens and the crows, if it keeps away the fantastic creatures of her own imagination.'

What Helena muttered through clenched teeth was not meant for my ears, I am certain of it. Even so, I heard what she said. For one instant, my heart, which had been beating rapidly with the exertions of the night and the excitements of the day, stopped still.

'She wants to keep Anders away!'

Helena ran for the house, crushing scattered grain and salt

beneath her feet, skipping over the tub of water which was blocking the doorway. As she ran up the stairs, her shawl and bonnet fell behind her. I picked them up as they cascaded into the hall, then carried them through to the kitchen.

Lotte was standing by the pump.

In her hands she held a rag, which she was wringing dry. She stared at me for a moment, then nodded. 'There's new cider, Herr Procurator, and fresh-baked flat cake. The children had an early supper. They're up above, playing.'

I said nothing of the clacking bones outside the windows. Helena would warn her not to frighten the children with her country superstitions. It would serve no purpose to tell the maid off twice. I sat down at the kitchen table, poured a little cider into a clay cup, broke off and ate a piece of the cake, then another, and drank the cider down.

Above my head, I heard the sound of Helena's voice. She was speaking sharply to Manni, my only surviving son, now seven years of age, who was speaking sharply back to her.

Then Helena's footsteps rattled down the stairway.

I retired to my study. I had a number of important things to do. I had to finish off the sketches in my album, notably the one that I had drawn from memory, showing the disposition of the corpse at the bottom of the well, and make final adjustments to the picture that I had made in the chapel of rest illustrating the wounds to Angela Enke's neck. I wrote up my notes, remembering the conversations I had had with the Schuettler brothers, with the family of the dead girl, and with the girl who had spoken to me about the victim at the School of Stitches. I would need to present a full report for the French at the earliest possible moment. Colonel Claudet would be expecting it. And I still needed to write an account of what had passed between myself and Emma Rimmele. That is, an account of what had been said between us.

How much should I include? Should I mention the turn her father had taken at the cemetery that morning? The strange things he had said when I accompanied them home? The oddity of the mourning dress that Emma Rimmele wore? The fact that it was made of cast-offs, and that she was short of money?

I was very perplexed, and sure of one thing only.

I would say nothing of the mark upon my neck. I had checked in the mirror, and seen that it had almost faded. The sharp pinch of her teeth was little more than a pink impression like a birth-mark on my own fair skin.

It was growing dark. I could have lit a lamp, of course, but I had a better idea. Overwhelmed by tiredness, I stretched out on the sofa, and fell fast asleep. And there I lay for quite some time, until a loud knock came at the front door. I jumped up from the sofa, stepped out into the hall and found that the door had been opened. Lotte was standing there, crumpling her apron in her fists, staring dumbfounded at two French soldiers who had taken off their caps, and appeared to be eyeing her up and down.

'Procurator Stiffeniis?' said one of the men with a smart salute. He wore two stripes on his green sleeve, while the other man wore a red cockade on his jacket, and no sign of rank.

'Can I help you?' I asked.

I spoke in French, and they replied in the same tongue.

Helena had appeared from the parlour door, lingering there, watching.

'You must come with us, sir. Orders of Major Glatigny.'

'What does the major want?' I asked.

'Something has happened,' he said glancing at from me to Lotte to Helena. 'That is … there is something he would like you to see, Monsieur Magistrate. A coach is waiting at the gate.'

'Where are you taking me?' I asked the corporal.

When I heard the reply, I reached at once for my jacket and my hat.

'The Prussian cemetery, monsieur.'

I followed them out of the house without saying a word, and with only one thought in my mind. Had the mob discovered the grave of Angela Enke? Had they tried to dig her up?

As I closed the gate, I looked back to the house.

Lotte was standing by the front door, peering through the crack. Helena was in the parlour. She had moved the curtain aside, and was looking out at me. Looking up, I saw Manni and Süzi at the nursery window.

I waved to the children.

As I held their gaze, I noticed the eaves above the nursery window. And above the other window, too. The tinkling amulets of chicken bones and hens' claws were gone. My waving hand froze in mid-air. Helena had removed the defences that Lotte had set around the house. She had said nothing to me, nor had she complained to Lotte.

What did it mean?

Had Helena dispensed with Lotte's charms because she thought them childish?

Or was she hoping that the baby might return?

Chapter 11

The corpse was lying on a flat rock.

An iron spike was poking skywards from his heart.

His head lolled back, rolling and shifting in the stream which runs inside the cemetery wall. He might have been shaking his head, trying to deny what had happened to him. His body looked as though it had been laid out on an altar, the chest offered up for the sacrifice. Only the high-priest was missing.

The scene was lit by two lamps. The first belonged to Ulrich Meyer, stone-cutter. Meyer was squatting on the ground, his back against a tree-trunk, his pale face cupped in the palms of his hands, mouth gaping open, as if he had just brought up the yellow mess that stained his apron. Joseph Meyer, his son, held the second lantern. Wide-eyed shock was written on the boy's face. He might have been a deer which had spotted the hunter, waiting for the musket-shot.

A small crowd was peering over the boundary wall on the far side of the stream. They were mute for the moment, almost invisible as dusk came on. They seemed to be watching, waiting for something to happen. On my way in through the main gate, I had ordered the French corporal-of-the-watch to let no-one enter on any account.

'Monsieur?' the man had bristled.

Clearly, he resented being given orders by a Prussian, especially one who was telling him to stand guard over a local cemetery as if it were a French munitions dump, and without the blessing of his superior officer.

'If there is a riot tonight, as there was last night,' I warned him, 'General Malaport will have your name in my report.'

The threat brought him into line. He ordered his troops to draw the bayonets from their scabbards and screw them to the muzzles of their muskets, while I shouted over to the crowd, telling them to stay well back if they did not wish to be stabbed or shot.

'What is happening in this town, monsieur?' the corporal growled. 'What the devil has got into them?'

'Ask Major Glatigny to come to me the instant he arrives,' I said.

I turned sharp right inside the gate, following the stream for thirty or forty paces. I spoke to Ulrich Meyer for a minute, confirming only that it was he who had made the discovery, then I scrambled down the bank of the stream towards the body. I had taken the lantern from the apprentice son, holding it in one hand, using the other to steady myself. I stepped down into the water and felt the cold as it seeped over the top of my boots. The stream was almost knee-deep at that spot.

I held the light above the body.

I had seen iron spikes of the same sort in the sexton's office the night before, never expecting to find one driven through the sexton's heart. Lars Merson's cassock had been ripped open, his chest was bare, shining dully in the lamplight.

They had tried three times before they struck the heart.

Two gaping holes, and that protruding spike. One blow had shattered the sternum and broken into the cavity of his chest, exposing bones and other things that I could not name. Another attempt had been made too far to the right; the iron point had skidded sideways, ripping and tearing crazily through the rib-cage. Shattered bones poked out through torn and mangled flesh. And then there was the final attempt to nail him to that rock. The spike had pierced his heart, but the most notable fact was how little blood all these wounds had provoked.

The blows had defiled the corpse, but they had not killed him.

I rested the lantern on the bank, then lifted his head from the water with both my hands, turning it to the right to examine his neck. The skin was puckered white around the wounds. There were two small punctures to the jugular vein, and longer rips below, where the instrument that had caused the fatal wounds had been roughly torn away. If not already dead, Merson must have fainted from the shock of the attack. His blood had flowed into the stream and been swept away. That was the cause of death – the wound to the neck. Angela Enke had died in the same manner. The spike through Merson's heart had come afterwards.

'Who found him?' I asked out loud, unable to look away.

'Me, Herr Stiffeniis. I found the body, sir.'

The face of Ulrich Meyer was paler than the face of Merson. He was standing stiffly on the riverbank, his boots hidden in the grass. He had no intention of stepping into the water, it seemed, though I noticed that his trousers were wet below the knees.

'Come here, Herr Meyer,' I ordered. 'Take a closer look.'

Meyer took a deep rasping breath before he splashed into the stream. He was shivering visibly as he stood beside me.

'What were you doing here?' I asked him.

He had come to deliver kerbing stones, and finished tombstones. 'The cemetery gates were open,' he said. 'I drove

135

straight in with the cart. I saw no sign of Merson, but it didn't really matter. I had work to do, and knew what was to be done. I left the tombstones in the office, then I worked over yonder for an hour or so on the tomb of the Böhm family.'

'Who did you see inside the cemetery?'

'Women,' he said.

'What were they doing?'

He shrugged and shook his head, as if the answer were obvious. 'Tidying up, sir. Planting winter bulbs, I think. A girl was working there by a grave,' he nodded over his shoulder. 'The other one was some way further off.'

'And you saw no-one else?'

Herr Meyer shook his head. 'No-one, sir. And no sign of Merson. When he comes, he comes, I thought. Me and Joseph left the finished slabs inside the sexton's office. The door was open. Then we got on with the kerbing.' He pointed off in a different direction. 'When we'd finished doing that – perhaps an hour later – we went to look for him.'

'And were the women busy all that time?'

'I've no idea, sir,' he said. 'I didn't see them again. I went to sit outside the office, and I sent Joseph to look for Merson. I wanted to be paid and get off home ...'

'How long was Joseph absent?'

Meyer shrugged. 'I've no idea, sir. Ten minutes. Maybe more. I must have dozed off. Next thing, Joseph came back. He woke me up.'

'And what did he say?' I asked.

'He couldn't find Merson anywhere, sir. That was ... worrying.'

'Worrying?' I repeated, rubbing my brow with the back of my hand.

'You know what Merson's like, Herr Stiffeniis. Dawn to dusk, he's here and nowhere else. If he'd had to go somewhere, he'd have left that lad of his behind. What's his name? Ludo? Lars Merson never leaves the cemetery unattended.'

I knew that he was right. Having buried the girl in secret last night, Lars Merson would never have wandered very far away from the spot. Indeed, his presence might have been too constant, too obvious, I told myself, especially if somebody had been watching him.

'In the end we went to look for him.' He pressed his fist against his chest as if the spike had been driven through his own heart. 'I saw him first. I must have shouted. Then, Joseph saw him, too.' He bent his head and examined the stain on his apron. 'That was when I was sick, sir.'

'And the body was in the water?'

He nodded, but he did not speak.

'On his back upon that rock?'

Meyer glanced sideways at the corpse for an instant.

'He ain't moved an inch, sir.'

'And there was no-one down here by the water?'

'No-one, sir. Not then, at any rate.' He glanced in the direction of the murmuring crowd. 'God knows where that lot came from.'

'What did you do, having found him?' I asked.

'Well, I was ... put out, sir. I mean to say, just look at him! His neck, those holes, that ... Like one of *them*, sir. Just like the girl they found the other day out Krupeken way.' As he spoke, his voice sank to a whisper, as if he feared that the corpse might hear him. 'I sent young Joseph running off to town to call the guards.'

And the guards had come to my house. The French had passed the problem on to me, and washed their hands of it. I studied Merson's face. His eyes were half-shut, his mouth gaped open. Had he been gasping for air while the blood flowed out of the wounds in his neck? Did the killer know what Merson and I had done together the night before? Was that why he had been murdered? Had he tried to defend himself with the spike? Or – my own heart clenched at the thought – had someone brought it there for no other purpose, having found the body, having seen the telltale wound that had caused his death, than to drive it through his heart?

In every treatise regarding vampirism, there is a description of what is to be done. There are only two ways to placate the monster's thirst for blood. I remembered reading an account which had been written by a Magyar scholar of the seventeenth century. A metal pin, a crucifix, or a wooden stake must be driven into the creature's heart. Or else, the head must be cut off from the body, and buried somewhere separately.

There have been many outbreaks of vampirism in Prussia, even in recent times. Fear drives people on a rampage. Burial grounds and funeral crypts are invaded, tombs opened, the dead removed from coffins, stakes and sticks driven through the heart of any corpse that does not look dead enough. Attempts had been made to stop such outrages, notably the edict issued by Maria Theresa of Austria in 1755, which had been widely adopted at the time in all the German states. The Empress had punished such crimes with death, but the practice had never been eradicated.

And there, before my eyes, was the evidence.

Lotingen was occupied by the French, Enlightened Reason held sway over the darker forces of Religion, yet someone had performed the *magia postuma* that very afternoon, and on that very spot.

My mind drifted back to Merson's office the night before. The girl's dead body lying on the table, the sexton's tools hanging on the wall. Had the killer taken the spike from there before he planted it in the gravedigger's breast?

What was the point?

The murderer had struck Merson's throat in the light of day, and seen him bleed to death. He knew that Merson was no vampire. Why perform the *magia postuma*, in that case? Clearly, there had been two separate attacks on Merson. The first had killed him; the second was meant to …

'You left new stones at the sexton's office, you say?'

'That's right, Herr Stiffeniis. Merson wants them there. When he's ready, he puts them up. Now, Ludo will have to decide, I suppose.'

'Which graves were the new ones meant for?' For an instant I was divided between my duties as a magistrate, and my duty as a husband and father. Was the memorial stone for Anders ready? 'Do you remember the names?'

Ulrich Meyer shook his head. 'I don't read them, sir. I just … well, I just copy the letters off the papers, sir.'

Was he unable to read? I asked myself. Was that the cause of his hesitation? I put the question aside, concentrating on the case before me. Ulrich Meyer knew the cemetery and Merson's workshop well. He must have been there hundreds of times. He had seen the iron stakes and bars that were hanging on the wall. I glanced once more at his apron. I could see the stains of vomit, but I saw no traces of blood. Then again, when that iron spike was hammered into Merson's chest, there must have been very little blood left in the body.

'You described the wounds, Herr Meyer,' I said, 'but you've said nothing of the stake that's poking from his chest.'

139

'What is there to say, sir?' Meyer objected.

'You didn't say you saw it.'

'Which doesn't mean I didn't see it,' he protested again. 'I didn't describe it, because there's nothing to describe. Anyone can see what's happened here. Everyone knows what it means. They should have done the same to that creature out in Krupeken!'

'Very good, Herr Meyer,' I said, cutting him short, stepping out of the water, and struggling up the bank. 'Let's see what your son can add to what you have told me.'

The stone-cutter came scuttling after me. Was he afraid of remaining alone with the corpse, or was he fearful of what the boy might say?

'You wait here,' I said, and I took some steps to separate myself from him. Then, I called to Joseph Meyer. 'Come over here. I wish to speak with you.'

The boy's eyes were huge with fright, his body rigid, his long arms stiffly aligned at his sides. Like an insect which freezes for fear of being eaten by a predator.

'How old are you?' I asked. This simple question seemed to disquiet him all the more.

'Twelve years old, sir.' His eyes were liquid mercury, never fixed or still. They glanced at me, they glanced away, they tried, but failed, to catch the eye of his father, but most of all they flashed in the direction of the stream and the body lying dead on the rock.

'I saw what my father saw,' he said before I had had the chance to ask him anything. 'But I was not so close, sir. He told me to stand well back.'

'How far away was that?'

'Ten paces, sir. A little more, or less.'

'And what exactly did you see from there?'

Joseph Meyer said what seemed obvious. 'I saw the blood, sir.'

'Blood?' I echoed. 'Where did you see this blood?'

Again, he tried and failed to catch a glimpse of his father. 'Why, sir, it was here, sir,' he said and touched the side of his neck. 'And here,' he added, patting his hand against his chest.

'How much blood did you see on the dead man's chest?'

Joseph glanced again towards the body, which was nothing more than a dark shape now, a silhouette against the rippling stream. 'I ... I cannot say exactly, sir.'

'A little, or a lot?' I insisted.

The lad looked to be in pain. He pursed his mouth, half-closed his eyes, rolled his head about on his neck, searching for the face of Ulrich Meyer in the thickening gloom.

'A ... a lot,' he managed to decide at last.

Joseph Meyer had not seen the body. There was hardly any blood to see. The stream had carried off the blood which flowed from Merson's neck; the spike through his heart had produced next to no blood at all. Joseph was telling me what he had been told to tell me, or what he thought his father expected of him. I had spoken of wounds. A wound in the neck, another in the chest. Wounds produce blood. Had Ulrich Meyer sent his son away while he did what remained to be done, believing that a boy so young should not see such things, and would not be capable of keeping them to himself? Why else would a child of twelve be lying?

'Did you notice anything else?' I insisted.

He hesitated, and I thought he might begin to cry. 'My father said that I must call the French soldiers. That I must run fast, sir. I didn't see no more 'til I came back.'

'Thank you, Joseph,' I said, 'you have been most helpful. Go now. Wait outside the cemetery gate, if you will.'

I watched him go, waiting before I turned again to face the father.

'What really happened, Meyer?' I asked quietly, standing very close beside him.

Ulrich Meyer glared at me defiantly, but he did not speak.

'I'll tell you how I see it,' I said. 'You found the body, you thought he had been bitten by a vampire. Is that correct? You sent your son to call the soldiers, and while he was away you did what … what had to be done. You took the opportunity to drive a metal spike through Merson's heart. It was not murder. He was dead already.'

I expected a fiery protestation of innocence, a feverish denial. Instead, the man squared up to me. 'Terrible things are happening in this town, Herr Procurator,' he said, his voice steady. 'First the fever, people dropping dead all over the place. Now this. A girl bitten to death, thrown down a well, and Krupeken in an uproar. Wild dogs in the market square this morning. Then, this death here … But I didn't do it. I couldn't do such a thing. I sent the boy to bring the authorities … the French … you, sir.' He pursed his lips, then bit hard on the lower one, as if he did not wish to say what followed. 'Send for the gypsies, Herr Stiffeniis. Let them enter the city. Let them find the creature. It's the only way to calm the people down, sir. They'll do it themselves, if you don't, sir.'

'Wait here,' I ordered him.

I looked at the crowd. The number had grown; they were watching silently. They hoped that I, their magistrate, would protect them. They trusted me for the moment, but what if I deluded them?

I walked a little way towards the gate and I made my voice heard. 'Take aim, soldiers,' I shouted. 'Fire upon the first man or woman who tries to enter here. Let no-one through, but Major Glatigny.'

I hurried on towards the sexton's office. The door was open. I entered, raising the lantern towards the end wall. The old gravestones were still there, and so were the new ones. The name of Anders was inscribed on one of the stones. Ulrich Meyer had finally completed it. Emotion took me by the throat. I fought against it. I could not give way in that moment. I turned away, concentrating all of my attention on Merson's tools. I had no idea what I was searching for. I had no idea how many iron bars I had seen there the night before. Even so, I took down one, and weighed it in my hands. They were used for opening graves and vaults. The point on this one would be pushed between two stones and used as a lever. There were a dozen bars of different lengths and thicknesses. Was one missing? Had Meyer removed it? If only hands could leave a permanent impression, I thought.

'What should be done with the new corpse, monsieur?'

Major Glatigny was standing in the shadows, a bitter smile set on his lips. 'It is happening, Procurator Stiffeniis. Just as you feared. A lethal epidemic, and far swifter than any illness. Have you no idea who is killing people in such a fashion?'

'A vampire,' I said. 'Who else? Have you seen the corpse?'

The Frenchman nodded. 'I saw the iron bar. Is that the way it's done?'

I nodded. 'It is supposed to stop them coming back.'

'Someone knows, then,' he said very calmly.

'Knows what?'

'That the girl is buried here in the cemetery.' Glatigny's pale face seemed to hover in the gloom above the dark cape that he was wearing. 'My men informed me of the trick you played last night, the stones that they found inside an otherwise empty box. I said that you were acting for the common good.'

'We buried her here together,' I admitted. 'Lars Merson and myself. But he was attacked in daylight. Vampires are forbidden to roam by the light of the sun, it is said. Whoever killed him took advantage of a moment when the cemetery was quiet. One grievous blow to the neck. It didn't take much.'

He was silent for some moments. 'How did he end up in the stream? Was he running away, do you think?'

I shook my head. 'Maybe he was working down there. Someone managed to approach without arousing his suspicions. Somebody who wants the world to think that Merson was slaughtered by a vampire, that the girl rose up from her grave, perhaps.'

My words echoed around the large room, and slowly died away.

'This corpse is more problematic than the last, is it not?' the Frenchman murmured. 'The people out there know very well what has happened. And, unfortunately for you, so does Colonel Claudet. He orders you to present yourself at the earliest opportunity, monsieur. I'd make your report as mild as you can. He is worried by the escalating situation. When the French allow themselves to be intimidated by the Prussians, there's trouble in store for all of us.'

I was obliged to smile. 'When the French are provoked, we Prussians pay the price.'

We exchanged a complicit glance.

'The crowd must not enter,' I said, pointing to the wall.

'Those iron spikes will be driven through every corpse in the cemetery.'

Glatigny raised his lantern and stared at me.

'Not if we carry him off exactly as he is!' There was a triumphant curl to his lip. 'Out through the crowd with that iron spike sticking out of his breast. We'll show them that the vampire Merson is truly dead.'

I was struck silent by what Glatigny had said. Lars Merson had worked long and hard to keep the city cemetery in order. Now, he would be thrown into a common pit in a French cemetery. It was a cruel fate for such a man. But what was the alternative?

'I'll let you know in which trench he has been laid,' Glatigny continued. 'It is a small price to pay for peace, but somebody must pay it.'

'The cemetery will need to be guarded,' I said.

'Leave that to me,' he replied. 'You must put an end to these blasphemies.'

Ten minutes later, Glatigny and his men marched out of the cemetery with Merson's body on a cart. I sent Ulrich and Joseph Meyer home, then I joined the parade.

Not a word was heard from the crowd. Not a shout.

They were wondering whether the spike had had the desired effect.

Chapter 12

'Lars always did his duty by the dead,' he protested dully.

'To the very end,' I said, pushing past, not waiting for him to shift his bulk.

Ludo Mittner ran his hand across his face as he followed me into the cramped room.

'Who'd have thought it?' he whispered. 'Killed by one of them he'd buried.'

I said nothing to oppose this notion.

Ludo had known Lars Merson well. Better than any other man, perhaps. He had been the under-sexton at the cemetery for as long as I had lived in Lotingen. Now, I had brought the news that his master was dead, and that he was the custodian of the cemetery.

'I need to check a number of things,' I said. 'Only you can help me.'

'Whatever I can do, sir,' Ludo said with a shake of his head.

He lived in one of the enclosures on the Rectory Close, a cobbled alley which stands in the eternal shadow of the cathedral. Built some centuries before as stabling for the horses of the clergy, the stalls had been converted into living quarters. The cells were high, too narrow to allow a horse to turn around. The French had talked of requisitioning them again as stables, until the officers of a lancer regiment rejected the accommodation as being 'cramped and unhealthy'. It was better that the Prussians living there should die of cold, they said, and not the Emperor's chargers.

In exchange for these lodgings, single men like Ludo were expected to scrub the cathedral floors, and carry the sick to the nearby Pietist congregation of Divine Love. When not at the cemetery, Ludo was generally to be found in one of those places. Merson had never offered to share the sexton's office with any man, not even Ludo Mittner. The cemetery was Lars Merson's kingdom. This is how the hierarchy works – every man in Prussia has his place, and he defends it to the bitter end. Ludo Mittner's turn to rule the cemetery had arrived.

I had followed the cart with Merson's uncovered body as far as the cathedral square. As the procession slowly wound its way through the town, more and more people came out of their houses to watch, bearing witness to the iron spike which poked from Merson's heart. 'Seeing is believing,' Major Glatigny confided to me. 'They'll see that there's no need for them to do anything. God above, what *more* needs to be done to him?'

On either side the watchers formed a solid wall, dividing left and right to let the cart pass. Hardly a word was said. No voice was raised in protest. It all went off with relative decorum. Had there been any breach of the peace, I would have recognised no-one. It was dark by then. Hoods, caps, hats had been pulled low to hide the identity of the wearer. If any man held a lantern, he closed the beam, or kept it low.

'I cannot say how long these pantomimes that you oblige me to invent will hold them back,' Glatigny murmured. 'This fear of the unknown is what the French hate most of all. Let me remind you again, monsieur, to report to Colonel Claudet without delay. He did insist upon it.'

As I stepped away from the procession, I cast a final look at the corpse. Had we done the right thing to display the body in public in that hideous manner? I shook my head, and cut across the cathedral square in the direction of the Rectory Close, wondering whether I would find Mittner at home. Almost everybody else was on the streets. Before presenting myself to Colonel Claudet, I hoped to have something in hand, something which would suggest that I was making progress in my investigation. So far, I had found nothing to placate his fright, except a bare chronicle of the events. For all the rest – suspects, lines of enquiry to follow, persons to interrogate – I was totally disorientated, my confusion compounded by the signs of mounting terror on the streets. I had nothing to offer Claudet which promised a swift end to the unrest and might lead to the solution of the murders.

Fortunately, Ludo Mittner was at home.

There was no furniture in the tiny room except for a pile of straw and some crumpled blankets in one corner, an unlit stove with a long rusty pipe poking out of a broken corner of the window high above the door, and a single three-legged stool. It looked more like the cell of a condemned man than a room provided by a Pietist charity.

'Have a seat, sir,' he invited me.

He was in his shirt-sleeves, while I felt frozen in my heavy ribbed jacket.

I sat down on the stool. Ludo set his heavy hip on the edge of the table. We were close, too close. The lingering perfume of burnt wood could not conquer the putrid smell of his unwashed flesh.

'Did you know Angela Enke, the girl from Krupeken?' I asked him.

He looked down on me from his higher perch. 'I'd never heard of her before today, sir,' he said with a shrug. 'Now no-one talks of anything else. I suppose I may have seen her in the town, but I couldn't put a face to the name.'

'Did Merson know her?'

'Not that I'm aware of. Why should he know her?'

'And when did you last see Merson?'

'Yesterday morning,' he replied. 'One of the vaults on the river side was filling up with water. We drained it out, then had a look at the old oak nearby. The heavy rain last month had uncovered the roots. We had to cut them back.'

'And what about today? Were you not at work?'

Ludo rubbed his hands together. 'It's my day off, sir. When I don't go to the cemetery, I go up to the Pietist hospice. I was there all the morning, swilling out the dormitories. I was there most of last night, too. One of the old men had his leg cut off. The surgeon will tell you, sir.'

'If need be, I will speak to him,' I said. I did not suspect Ludo of murdering his master, but I was hoping that he might tell me something that Lars Merson had failed to mention. 'Had Merson quarrelled with anyone recently?'

Ludo's blue eyes flashed a look of dull surprise. 'Merson? He don't fight with no-one, sir. Keeps himself to himself. He wouldn't tell me anyway. The sexton never told me nothing, 'cept for what I had to do. I've been his work-horse these twenty years ...'

'Not any more, you aren't.'

He nodded his head morosely. 'It wasn't meant to happen like this.'

I was silent for some moments.

Did Merson's death and the burial of Angela Enke have

149

anything in common? And if so, what could it be, apart from the fact that they had both been murdered in the same way, and probably by the same hand?

The name of Emma Rimmele loomed in my thoughts.

Angela had altered the mourning clothes of Emma and her father. Merson had opened up the Kassel vault and placed the coffin of Frau Gisela Rimmele inside the family tomb. Might Emma Rimmele be the connection?

'Were you and Merson working on the Kassel tomb?' I asked.

'It was in their well that the body of the girl was found, isn't that so, sir?' It was not a question. He seemed certain of the facts. 'Father and daughter came to live in Lotingen quite recently, so I've been told.'

'They are renting a house,' I corrected him. 'Did you meet the Rimmeles?'

Ludo nodded.

'One of them, or both of them?' I asked him.

Ludo swung his leg on the edge of the table. 'The daughter, sir. She spoke with Merson. I was there, but she didn't speak to me.' He shrugged in an exaggerated manner, raising his shoulders as high as his ear, and I wondered whether Emma Rimmele had made an impression on Ludo, as well.

'What did she want?' I asked him.

'It was most irregular, sir. She wanted him to open up a tomb that had been abandoned for many years.'

'Her mother was born in Lotingen,' I said. 'What's so odd about that?'

Like a butterfly emerging from a chrysalis, Ludo Mittner gave me a first glimpse of the new custodian of Lotingen cemetery. He shook his head disapprovingly. 'The law, sir. The law. Opening up a funeral vault's a serious business. You need the documents to prove descent. I'd have ...' He sniffed dismissively. 'That woman did have papers, but it was the Devil's job to read 'em.' He waved his finger in a circle in the air. 'The father's signature was like a fly that had fallen in an inkwell, and crawled its way out again. She said that he was ill and couldn't barely hold a pen, but Lars said the law's the law, miss, and he wouldn't touch that vault 'til things was straightened out.'

'He didn't hold out for long,' I objected. 'Evidently Fraulein Rimmele provided some further documentary proof.'

I knew Lars Merson well. He was a stickler for Prussian law, yet he had bent the French rules for Anders. And he had done the same in the case of Angela Enke. 'You're the magistrate, Procurator Stiffeniis,' he had said when I told him that my son had died. 'You're the law in Lotingen. The French won't last for ever. Tell me what's to be done for the child.'

Ludo was now the heir to the cemetery, which allowed him to criticise his erstwhile master, and probably for the very first time.

'That Fraulein Rimmele didn't need no document,' he sneered. 'She had a way about her. Tears was her strength. She had brought her poor mother's body to be buried in Lotingen cemetery, she said. She had her poor sick father to think of and what was she supposed to do? Take that body back to where it had come from?'

'She appealed to Merson's generosity. Is that what you are saying?'

Ludo ran his hand through his unruly blond hair. 'An' that's the truth of it, sir. Wrapped him round her middle finger, she did. Still, one thing surprised me.'

'What was that?'

'The way she handled it, sir,' he said. 'One minute, gentle as a kitten. The next, she's screaming like a fury. And having got what she wanted, all smiles and apologies. I thought that she was going to kiss him. No man had ever been so good to her. That's what she said, sir. I ain't never seen no-one get round Merson before. Not so fast, at any rate.'

I could imagine Emma's frustration. She had leapt from the frying pan into a pot of boiling water. She knew no-one in Lotingen. None of her relations was living; she had to bury the body. The sexton of the cemetery had raised objections to her plans. Merson had played with Emma as a cat plays with a mouse. But instead of eating her, he had thrown her a piece of cheese in the end.

Her wild behaviour had thrown Merson into confusion, it appeared, though once she got her way, she had rewarded him with charm and grace. She had done something similar with me that morning. I could not shake off the memory of her lips pressing hotly on my neck, her teeth against my skin, the wet heat of her tongue.

'When he took her to inspect the vault, he had to hold her up by the elbow,' Ludo added. 'She was almost fainting.'

'Where were you?'

'Following close behind them, sir,' Ludo said. 'When they reached the vault, she fell down on her knees and said a prayer. And when she'd finished, why, it was like she was transformed! She was all of a flurry, wild again. The coffin's on its way, she cries. 'Twill be arriving any minute. We have to do it straight away. Can't bring her father 'til her mother's safe inside the tomb. It don't matter if it is a mess ...'

I held up my hand to slow the torrent of his words. 'Was it in a mess?'

'It was abandoned, sir. No-one had done any work in thirty years. The vault was green with moss, the stones were chipped, the names hardly visible. It needed quite a lick of work, and Merson told her so. If it had been up to me ...'

I interrupted, asking, 'How did Fraulein Rimmele react to that?'

Mittner rubbed his nose with his forefinger, and smiled shyly. 'She put her hand on his arm, sir. Like this,' he showed me, gently laying his right hand on his left wrist. 'Me father's getting worse each day, sir! It won't be long a'fore he's in his grave! A week an' he'll be gone!' he trilled in a gruff sing-song falsetto which was as unlike the voice of Emma Rimmele as anything imaginable. 'I want to bring Papa tomorrow!'

The she-devil, Merson had called her afterwards.

But what had Emma done that was so terrible in his eyes? Wiping her dirty boots on an ancient tomb, he had said. On the other hand, might he have regretted making such generous concessions to a stranger?

Or was there something else?

Emma Rimmele had told him the truth. She had come to Lotingen to lay her mother's body at rest. Merson had fallen in with her request at last. But then, for some unknown reason, he had changed his mind. Perhaps he had seen her in the guise of a diabolical temptress, who had used her beauty and tears to get her way. And having obtained what she craved, she had wiped the mud from her boots on Merson's gift.

Whatever the truth of the matter, Emma Rimmele was right. Every step she took in Lotingen was fraught with misunderstanding. It had all begun *before* the seamstress was found dead at the bottom of the well at the Prior's House.

'Had anyone laid flowers on that tomb before the Rimmeles came?'

'Never, sir. Not since I've been working in the cemetery, anyway. Never a flower or a wreath. That's why Merson should have insisted on seeing the documents to prove that they had a right to use it.'

I frowned at his insistence. 'If the Lotingen branch of the family no longer exists,' I said, 'who else would be interested in that tomb?'

Ludo's limp foot began to swing back and forth again. He pushed his fingers beneath his collar, as if it were suffocating him. 'Lars himself said that it would be an intrusion, sir. So many other souls was resting peaceful there. You can't just put a body where it don't belong. It's the sort of thing that makes 'em come back!'

'They must have come to some sort of an agreement,' I objected.

Ludo pursed his lips, as if reluctant to continue. 'He put the coffin in the vault that very day,' he said suddenly. 'Just the way she wanted.'

I let out a deep breath, as if I had been present at the battle of wills between Emma Rimmele and Lars Merson. Ludo continued to stare at me. There might be more to say, but he seemed hesitant about saying it. 'You seem to think that Merson made a mistake, I take it?'

'We profaned the tomb, sir. I had no choice, he made me do it. We went in there and worked all morning, shifting things about, making room for someone who ... well, who may not belong. An intruder.'

He blew loudly upon his lips.

'What reason could Emma Rimmele have to lie?' I countered.

Ludo's voice was a low growl. 'Maybe you ain't seen her, sir. Lars Merson hadn't been himself since then. When she comes a-visiting with her father, it's, well, it's like he was seeing the devil waltzing through a holy place. The devil-of-the-tombs, he used to call her.'

I remembered the anger in Merson's voice, the dark look on his face as he saw Emma Rimmele and her father entering his cemetery that very morning.

'If she lied, Herr Procurator, if she put a corpse where it shouldn't be, no-one in Lotingen will rest in peace.' Ludo spoke in angry spurts, like water gushing from a pipe. 'I'll be in charge now,' he mused bitterly. 'Merson's things will fall to me. I'll sleep in the sexton's office, and get to do what he once did. The old tombs, and the new ones ... all my responsibility now. It's up to me to make my peace with them that lies beneath the ground.'

He stared at me in resentful silence.

'Might that be why he's dead?' he asked at last. 'The revenge of creatures that will never have eternal rest? We have set 'em loose, and now they've come back. I mean to say, sir, maybe me and him did something that ... well, that *they* didn't like.'

'Let there be no talk of vampires,' I admonished him. 'There is a murderer in Lotingen. He should be blamed for what is happening here. He'll be brought to justice, I promise you.'

I stood up, preparing to leave.

'Frau Stiffeniis comes there every day,' Ludo murmured. His eyes were downcast as he spoke, as if he were saying what he had to say, though he didn't like to say it. 'She ... she's always asking about the tombstone for your child, and when ...'

'Herr Meyer delivered it this afternoon,' I interrupted.

'She told me once,' he continued, apparently deaf to what I

had just said, 'she won't be easy 'til the child is properly settled, sir. Without a stone to mark the spot, she said, she thought the little one might be in danger. That is … you know, he might not sleep in peace, sir.'

I felt an ache in my breast, as if a hand had seized my own heart and squeezed it very hard. Was that what was going through Helena's mind? She had been going to the cemetery when we had taken refuge from the dogs. Was she standing guard over the grave of her child in the belief that a cross not his could do little to protect him? Did she think that a stone and a name would protect him better?

'I'll do your son's stone first thing tomorrow morning,' Ludo promised.

My nostrils filled with the smell of the man and his clothes, yet it was not the same stink that had repulsed me earlier. Now, I smelt damp freshly-turned earth, the perfumed odour of death. I had breathed the same odour the night before, burying Angela Enke, and that other night, too, when Merson and I had buried my youngest child.

I took a deep breath as I stepped out into the night.

What was I to tell Claudet?

Half an hour later, I stood in front of Colonel Claudet.

He glared at me suspiciously, one eye open and furious, the other one permanently closed and dead. Finally, he invited me to sit down. He had been appointed commander of the Lotingen garrison the year before, but those two eyes spoke of many years of peering down the length of a musket barrel. Perhaps a faulty powder-pan had once exploded in his face? He appeared to be taking aim at me. He would never shrug off the air of the peasant recruit and humble infantryman that

156

he had once been, though I knew that the all-seeing eye of his was waiting for me to bow my head with shame for being born a Prussian, expecting me to tremble in the presence of the conqueror.

Instead, I sat erect before his desk, and awaited his judgement.

In the end, he brought himself to use the word that I refused to pronounce.

'*Vampirism*,' he said, as if he was spitting out some vile phlegm that blocked his skinny throat. 'I have never heard such rubbish. Rest assured, monsieur, the French will not be taken in by these ridiculous tales. Your countrymen are plotting beneath the cloak of a mystery, Herr Stiffeniis.'

He thumped his forefinger on the broadsheet that he had thrust in front of my face the moment that I arrived in his office. It was a copy of *Le Bulletin Militaire*. I knew the news-sheet very well. The year before I had been sent to the Baltic coast to investigate the murders of the girls who were gathering amber there; the same newspaper had published a woodcut caricature of myself and a pregnant Helena, together with sarcastic suggestions that I would never solve the crime. They had never published anything to say that I had been successful.

He held the paper up to me.

'Read it, monsieur! We have become the laughing stock of the Empire.'

I read:

WILL WONDERS NEVER CEASE IN THIS STRANGE LAND CALLED PRUSSIA?
The summer sun shines bright at midnight. In winter, midday is as black as pitch. Whales sing aloud in the Baltic Sea, which yields up monsters of a miniature sort inside

157

the amber found upon the shores, and nowhere else in the whole wide world. And now a new word will be added to our national dictionary: vampirism!

When a girl is killed and thrown into a well in France, we speak of murder. When the same thing happens in a Prussian town, the devilish vampire is the villain in the case. This, it seems, is the line of investigation being followed by a Prussian magistrate, Hanno Stiffeniis, in the town of Lotingen, East Prussia. And all for the sake of two small holes in the victim's neck, wounds probably caused by a rusty nail or something similar.

There have also been reports of packs of stray hounds (werewolves?) of an equally ludicrous and superstitious nature in the same province. The terror is spreading, and we should be on our guard against it. It is common knowledge in the High Command that the Prussian people are a susceptible and irascible race …

'It is happening in other places in the north, too!' he cried, snatching the broadsheet from my hand. 'There is something going on, monsieur, some plot is being hatched, there can be no doubt of it. We must be on our guard, it says here, and I assure you, Procurator Stiffeniis, I am watching every move that you make.'

He waved his forefinger, circling behind me, forcing me to twist and turn in my chair to follow his menacing antics. 'And now, there is a second victim, which makes the situation all the more alarming. Where do we stand, Herr Magistrate Stiffeniis? What have you discovered? When can I expect to see the culprit in chains?'

'Major Glatigny and I have been working closely together

to contain the growing fear and unrest,' I replied, refusing to speculate further about the situation or its causes, fearing that he would act upon any hint that I might give him.

'You and Glatigny, indeed!' he snarled, resting his forearms on the back of my chair, leaning over my shoulder. 'I'll paint you in the blackest colours, Herr Magistrate, especially to General Malaport – you know him well enough, I think! – unless you bring this farce to a conclusion, and in the shortest space of time. Now, get out!'

I closed the door and stepped out into the corridor, congratulating myself that it had not gone quite so badly as I feared. Indeed, I thought, there was one bit of good news in what he had told me, and in what I had read.

I was not yet the Prussian butt of *Le Bulletin Militaire*.

For the moment, anyway.

Chapter 13

I walked in the direction of the Old Town Hall.

Abandoned after the invasion, the roof having been severely damaged by fire-bombs, the building had been put in order in the last two years, and many of the civic offices which had formerly been housed there were now in full and useful employment once again.

I made my way up the broad wooden staircase.

The Records Office of Lotingen was on the second floor. The ledger books of Births, Marriages and Deaths were kept up there. If I wanted information about the Kassel family into which the mother of Emma Rimmele had been born, that was where I would find it. As I pushed open the door, a youngish couple were on the point of coming out. I knew them well enough to acknowledge them. There was nothing remarkable about the pair, except that the woman was carrying a newborn baby wrapped up in a brown woollen quilt, while the man lacked his right leg below the knee, skipping sideways through the doorway with the help of crutches. Gregor Brandt's leg had been blown away by a chain-shot in the service of his king and country. There were a dozen other men who were missing a limb in town. They are, indeed, such a familiar sight in Prussia that one hardly thinks to comment on it any longer.

'Herr Stiffeniis, sir.'

'Good evening, Brandt.'

'Been to register the latest,' the man said with a broad smile.

'Congratulations,' I said, offering him my hand.

'It's a blessing after so many deaths,' he began to say enthusiastically, but then, remembering the fact that my youngest child had been one of the victims, his voice faded to a whisper.

I nodded glumly, and passed in through the door.

Another one of the mutilated was sitting behind the main desk in the Records Office. Otto Geisler had lost an arm at Eisenstadt to a sabre-cut. To my mind, he was one of Count Dittersdorf's rare mistakes. It is all very well to find public work for an invalid of war, but it should be the right kind of work, a job which will not be hampered by his disability. Geisler could write without any trouble – he had lost his left arm, after all, and he wrote in a bold and natural right hand. The problem was the ledgers. They were large, thick books in studded leather bindings, and they were exceedingly heavy. The room was almost full of them, and many of the older volumes were situated on shelves above head height.

'Procurator Stiffeniis, what can I do for you, sir?'

Geisler was on his feet the instant he saw me. His right hand shot up to salute.

'At ease, corporal,' I said.

There was something not quite right in Geisler's head. If you called him by his proper name, he might not respond. If you called him by his rank, and used the sort of language that a soldier understood, he would obey you instantly.

'I am looking for some line of attack,' I said carefully.

'In what direction, sir?'

I thought for a moment. I could start with the Deaths, of course, but I had no clear idea when Emma Rimmele's mother

161

had died. I was no nearer to knowing when she had been born either, but I thought that I could estimate it to within ten years or so. Having once dug out that information, the rest would follow on. I conjured up Emma Rimmele in my mind's eye – her dress was still torn, her shoulder still naked. She must be – what? – twenty-seven years old. A year or two younger? And how old had her mother been when her daughter was born? I added on another twenty-five years, which made a total of fifty, more or less.

'I am interested in a Birth,' I announced. 'Let's begin some time before 1760.'

'Glorious battle of Leuthen, 1757. Will that do you, sir?'

'It will do me admirably, corporal.'

The problem was that the volume with that date gold-chiselled on the spine was four shelves up on the far side of the room. As Geisler tried to carry his folding steps to the spot, and I tried to help him, the poor man tripped. It took a moment to help him to his feet, more time again to prevent him from mounting the steps and trying to extract the heavy volume from its place with just one hand. I ordered him to step aside in a brusque and manly fashion, as an officer might do, then I climbed up the wobbling wooden death-trap and pulled the volume out for myself.

'Thank you, Corporal Geisler,' I said. 'If I need to consult another volume, I'll see to it. I am certain you have more important duties to be getting on with.'

'That's very kind, sir.'

He saluted again and retired to his post, while I placed the volume directly under a lamp on a sloping reading-shelf. The volume was difficult to hold open; being generally closed, the covers and the boards were very stiff. Moreover, the turning of each page threw up a cloud of dust. I would have to breathe a great deal of it, I thought, before I had finished my research. For each single entry there was a wad of documentation – names and addresses of the father and the mother, a paper signed by a doctor or marked by a midwife to the effect that the child had been delivered that night by his/her hand, neither stolen from a neighbour, nor purchased from gypsies. The practice of careful registration had started with the reign of Frederick the Great: knowing exactly how many boys had been born in any single year, the king knew precisely how many men might be called up for military service sixteen years later.

It did not take me long to conclude that Gisela Kassel had not been born in Lotingen in 1757. Clapping the dust from my hands, I closed the book, climbed back up the ladder, replaced it on the correct shelf, and took down the volume for 1758. By the time I got to 1760, my hands were filthy, but I had found her.

Gisela Anne Alberta Kassel, born 2nd January, 1760, I read, *daughter of Alberta Frederika von Alfensstadt (mother), and Mikhail Erik Rupert Kassel, the Marquis von Trauss (father).* Gisela Kassel had been one of a pair of twins, though the other child had died on the night of their delivery. There had been an informal inquiry by a justice of the peace into the circumstances, though it did not amount to anything. The JP reported the testimony of an unidentified doctor, saying: *The un-named infant – a fully-formed male, posthumously baptised in the name of Jesus Christ – was strangled in the womb, or during parturition, by a fatal twisting of the umbilical cord, an accident which provoked a partial ripping of the placenta.*

In a word, the king had lost a potential soldier, and a girl-child had survived.

Among the documents which were attached to the page, I could expect to find a great deal more, and so it turned out. The next piece of paper that I opened was a stiff folded copy of the lady's marriage certificate. A copy had been sent to the Records Office in Lotingen, and it bore the stamps and the seals of the Municipality of Danzig. It was a magnificent document on a heavy sheet of parchment, despite the loss of brilliant colour which age had leached away. Floral decorations, garlands and drapes, surmounted by two winged angels, had been painted by a skilled artist, who had then inscribed the names of the parties involved in a swirling artistic hand. It was of some interest to me.

On this, the twelfth day in the month of October, in the year of the Lord 1780, in the family chapel of Saint Saviour in the canton of Danzig, on the private estate of Albert Peter Johann Rimmele, gentleman, [I read], *a wedding agreement was solemnly drawn up and contracted between the following parties: Erwin Oskar Rimmele, and Gisela Ann Alberta Kassel. Vows were sworn before Pastor Albrecht J. Kuster, who also celebrated the holy service on the same day.*

This same Erwin Rimmele was now in his dotage being cared for by his daughter, Emma, in the Prior's House. I turned to the next page, expecting to read of the birth of Emma herself. Instead, I found a sheet of paper, which ought to have preceded the one that I had just read. It was the letter of a lawyer, a man named Cornelius Haengel, and it had been written on the instructions of the father of the bride-to-be. Indeed, it pre-dated the wedding of Erwin and Gisela by six months, and was a copy of a copy which had been registered in the first instance at the town hall in Danzig. It was a proposal to withdraw from the marriage agreement 'at a sum to be agreed upon', and it was countersigned by Gisela Kassel's father. 'On the grounds of serious differences', the letter stated in couched and careful terms. No specific reason was given, though there must have been some infringement, or impediment which, in the watchful eyes of the young lady's father, had advised at least a temporary postponement, if not the definitive cancellation, of the wedding.

What could have caused the dispute? And why had the couple been married six months later, as if nothing at all had happened to compromise the match?

I wondered whether Emma Rimmele might know the reason. Then again, if she knew nothing, and if I brought up the matter, it might cause offence, and serve no useful purpose anyway. I turned to the next document in the sequence. It was a registered copy of the birth certificate of Emma Rimmele, and it was dated 14th April 1781.

I bit my lip and thought on that.

Though born within a recognised and legal marriage, Emma had been born only six months after the wedding of her mother and father. The child had been conceived illegitimately. Was this the cause of Gisela Kassel's father's opposition to the match? Had he realised that the wedding rites had been celebrated by the pair before their union had been rendered legal in a church? Had he tried to save his daughter's good name before it was too late?

I was just about to put the lawyer's letter back, when I noticed that the bottom of the page was folded upwards. Had I creased the letter while reading it? Had someone else at some time in the past? I turned back the fold, meaning to restore the letter to the ledger in the same condition in which I had found it, when I noticed two tiny sets of matching symbols at the foot of the page. They had not been printed on the paper by the papermaker, as had the lawyer's address. These signs had been added intentionally – by the lawyer, Cornelius Haengel, or by someone else – with a pen and ink. The first symbol represented three tiny green crowns placed one above the other. The cipher beside it was even more unusual; it featured what appeared to be three lines. It took some while for me to make it out, but even then it made no sense. The pen strokes were like a tiny, roughly-drawn kitchen-table. It was, I realised, the Greek letter *pi*, and it was written in blue ink. And, what was even more odd, the symbol of the three crowns had been heavily crossed out with a bold letter X in the same blue ink, and the word 'Agreed' had been written next to it.

What did it mean?

I turned to the next page, and I found no more regarding the Rimmeles or the Kassels. Emma Rimmele had told me why. Gisela Kassel had been the last of the family line. Emma had brought her mother home to Lotingen to lie beside her ancestors in the family vault which had been built for them in the old town cemetery. Indeed, I thought, with those documents she would have been able to satisfy any objection that Merson might have made.

'Finished, sir?' asked Geisler, as I came back down the ladder empty-handed, having returned the volume to its allotted place.

'Not quite, corporal,' I said. 'I need to check on a Death.'

'Death is hard by on the east flank, sir,' he said, pointing with his remaining hand to the far end of the room. 'In which year are you interested?'

'I do not know,' I admitted.

His face clouded over. 'Can I ask you something, Herr Procurator?'

'Certainly,' I said.

'Has this got something to do with what is happening in Lotingen, sir?'

'I am making enquiries of a general nature,' I said. I had no intention of taking the clerk into my confidence. Nor did I wish him to draw any conclusions from what he had seen me doing. 'There are many aspects of this case …'

'I want you to know, sir,' he interrupted me, pursing his lips, narrowing his eyes, glancing left and right as if the empty room were full of enemy spies, 'that you can count on me. I have an honourable service record to my credit, and I am ready to fight again in *this* battle.'

'Which battle, Corporal Geisler?'

I tried without success to swallow. I knew what he was going to tell me.

'The battle against these new invaders, sir,' he hissed. 'Hands don't come into it. You'll need brave hearts, strong wills, experienced soldiers who aren't afraid to rout out the infected ones among the tombs, sir. I'll not fail you, sir, I promise. I'll be ready when the battle comes.'

'There is no war to fight,' I said. 'Only a killer who must be found. I need to see the register of Deaths. The letter K,' I reminded him.

'Kassel again, sir?'

'Kassel again.'

'The letters J–K,' said Geisler, pointing to the middle shelf of three on the far side of the room.

'I'll get it, corporal,' I informed him quickly.

'Very good, sir. As you wish.'

He retired to his seat again, while I carried the volume over to the window.

Oddly enough, while Births were registered in volumes bound in dour black leather, Deaths were recorded in volumes that were a rich shade of red morocco. I soon found the page, and I began to read the information. Only one daughter had ever been buried in the vault – Paulina Erika Kassel in the early 1700s – and she had been unmarried. The fathers of the Kassel family seemed to have been extremely good at marrying off their daughters, who, when the time came, were buried by their husbands, or at the expense of the family into which the girl in question had been joined in marriage.

'Are there other documents relating to them?' I called to the corporal.

Geisler cocked his head at me.

'You have come too late, sir,' he called back. 'Lars Merson came scouting the other day. He withdrew a sheaf of documents, and he has not brought them back yet.'

I was not surprised. Certainly, Merson would have checked the relevant papers regarding Emma Rimmele's claim to bury her mother in the family vault. Probably, he had left them somewhere in the sexton's office jumbled up with all the other papers on his work-table.

'It doesn't matter, corporal,' I said as I returned the ledger to its place on the shelf. I had not expected to find anything out of the ordinary, and I doubted that Merson would have found anything either. Emma Rimmele's account of her mother and her family, and her right to use the Kassel tomb, was confirmed, so far as I could tell. 'I will ask Ludo Mittner about them. It is his responsibility now to bring those documents back.'

Corporal Otto Geisler snapped to attention and saluted as I walked out of the door, clattering down the wooden stairs, relieved to be out of that room, remembering what he had said, recalling the chill that I had felt as he said it.

I'll be ready when the battle comes.

Chapter 14

I stood like a stranger at my own gate.

The windows of the house were ablaze with light. Wood smoke drifted dreamily from the chimney directly above the sitting-room, and not from the kitchen chimney above the far gable end, as I had more recently come to expect.

My heart clenched.

Something was wrong.

I saw my home as I had not seen it for a long time. That is, as it used to be. The murders of Angela Enke and Lars Merson might not have happened. It was as if terror had not taken Lotingen by the throat. As if the population had not been ravaged by the fever epidemic. It was, indeed, as if my baby son were still alive.

The sitting-room had not been used since Anders died. As a rule, Lotte kept Helena close by her side in the kitchen. While the maid darned, patched, cooked and ironed, my wife would sit at the kitchen table, the children just a glance away. Helena did whatever Lotte told her to do. She peeled potatoes, diced vegetables, kneaded dough. She did it all without a word of protest, her face a mask of distant thoughtfulness. Sometimes, Lotte had confided to me, while they were working together in the kitchen, Helena would forget for a moment to be sad.

More rarely, I would see a weak light shining from our

bedroom window on the first floor. Helena was up there, and I knew that she was alone. I would find her sitting stiffly on the edge of the bed, her hands clasped tightly together, her gaze lost in the gloom beyond the range of the candlelight. On those occasions, the voices of the children – little more than whispers in recent months – were absent. The house seemed to suffocate any sound before it could be heard.

That evening, instead, I heard voices.

I was not in the mood for company. After what I had seen that day, I would gladly have returned to a house that was silent and sad. Instead, I could hear the babbling of little Edviga, and the excited cries of Süzi and Manni, while the front window blazed with light, and not merely from many candles. The fire was lit, and it was piled high with logs. And then I heard the voice of Helena, too. Not the lifeless murmur which had characterised her lately. Her voice was strong, and it was animated.

Something had definitely happened.

I rushed up the path, searching in my pocket for the key. Night was coming on, the garden was dark, the air chill and salty, blowing in off the Baltic Sea. That was what I had grown used to. Not the aroma of honey and freshly baked pastry which wafted out to meet me. As if some special treat had been prepared that evening.

Was it for the children, perhaps?

I stopped on the front step, and a sudden shiver shook me. It was as if my body registered the danger before my mind could fully grasp it. I placed the key in the lock, turned it slowly, then pushed open the door.

Lotte was crossing the hall in that instant, going from the kitchen to the sitting-room. In her hands she held a tray of biscuits just removed from the oven. The smell was irresistible.

I felt light-headed for an instant. Her skin glistened from the heat of the oven.

How long had it been since I had seen such a scene in my house?

'Lotte?' I breathed her name, and it came out as a question.

Lotte turned and looked at me for a moment in surprise. Evidently, she had not heard me open the door. I might have passed straight through it, if the expression on her face were anything to go by.

'Is it you, sir?' Lotte asked, as one might ask an unexpected guest. Her eyes twinkled in the direction of the sitting-room, then looked back at me. Her lips moved, but they made no sound. The shape of her words was clear enough. 'He's back,' they seemed to say. She trotted forward into the sitting-room, her spine as straight as a ramrod, the tray of biscuits held up before her, like a pert waitress who wants to make a good impression on a particularly favoured customer.

The children cried with glee. Hands were clapped.

Then, that voice. '*Et voilà, les bonbons!*'

I followed Lotte into the room.

The blazing hearth and wealth of candles made me blink. Helena was seated on the sofa on the far side of the fireplace. As my eyes grew accustomed to the light, they were drawn like magnets to her lips. Though dried and cracked, her lips were smiling as they had not done in many a month. And her hair, which she kept so tightly tied up behind her head in all that time, had fallen loose. And yet, I noted, it was not out of place. It was as if she had shifted *those* curls above her forehead, and bunched *these* behind her ears, all the better to show off what dangled from the lobes of her ears. Two chips of coral, as red as cherries, which I had never seen before.

172

Helena saw me, and the smile died on her lips.

'Hanno, you … you are just in time,' she said, recovering her composure. 'Did the aroma of baking entice you from your office?'

I was no longer looking at her lips, her hair, those pieces of coral.

My eyes were fixed on a head which poked up above the back of an armchair. It was the same armchair in which I often sat before the fire. I stared at the mass of curls which covered that head. They were of an unmistakeable silver hue with darker rivulets of black, unkempt, uncombed, as if they had been blown about by a fierce wind, or a long brisk ride.

The head turned, and two blue eyes regarded me beneath dark eyebrows, while an amused smile played about the corners of the mouth and eyes. The large misshapen nose seemed to sniff at the air. The well-formed lips murmured something that I did not catch, because in that instant the children called out with joy to see their father home. There was nothing in those features that I might have described as harmonious. Nothing that I could have called handsome. And yet that rugged face overwhelmed me with its strength and its intensity. He had not changed greatly in two years. If anything, his features were more deeply sculpted than they used to be.

He raised himself from the armchair, and turned to greet me.

He was as tall as I remembered him. A touch slimmer, perhaps, in a green cotton shirt beneath a waistcoat of heavy wool. The waistcoat was the sort of thing he always wore, the vivid plum colour and ivory buttons set off his silver curls and dark complexion to great advantage. His breeches were ribbed black velvet, his brown boots sewn by an expert hand, not military boots, though they were dusty and uncared for, as if on purpose to deny any accusation of dandyism. In all, there was a careless eccentricity about his clothes which proclaimed him to be elegant by nature.

He hesitated for a moment, then came rapidly forward, and I found myself being bear-hugged. Though I am tall, I felt his nose press flat against my forehead. 'Don't play the frosty Prussian with me,' he said. 'You're as glad to see me, as I to see you. It's been a long time, Hanno.'

His arms relaxed their grip enough to allow him to look into my face.

'Good God, Helena!' he exclaimed, turning slightly in the direction of my wife. 'This husband of yours is more handsome than ever. That pale poetic look. Those thin lips, straight nose, straight blond hair. A pair of nervous eyes which are never still.' His laughter exploded close to my ear. 'I told you once, my friend, and I will tell you again, you bring to mind those fearsome volcanoes in Iceland, which bubble and boil not far below the crust of ice. When they explode they are the most dangerous of all. It will happen sooner or later, I am certain.' He stepped back, narrowed his eyes, scrutinised me. 'Or has the explosion happened in my absence?' His strong arms gripped me around the shoulders like a crushing vice. 'Welcome me back, Hanno, and I will set you free to kiss your wife.'

As I pulled my face away, I caught a whiff of aromatic herbs from his clothes.

'Welcome to Lotingen, Lavedrine,' I said. 'You are the last person in the world that I expected to find here this evening.'

His hands still clasped me by the shoulders, holding me prisoner. Colonel Serge Lavedrine no longer smiled. 'It has not been an easy period, I know,' he murmured. 'Nor have the last few days been tranquil. For you, or for Lotingen.'

Lotte came running in with a jug of hot cider. She set it down on the hob, then called to the children. 'Kiss your father, then come along into the kitchen with me. I've got hot milk out there for the two of you.'

The children did not kiss me, as such. They rubbed against my legs and gave me playful little slaps as they marched out of the room. It was a new and most unusual way to demonstrate that they were happy. Then again, everything was new and unusual that evening.

The happiness, especially.

Out in the hall, we heard the voice of Manni protesting loudly: 'I want hot cider, too, Lotte. Like Papa and Colonel Lavedrine!'

This was something we had never heard before.

'We may have a problem there,' I said to Helena with a frown. 'Manni may take to drinking very soon.' More quietly, I answered Lavedrine. 'The last few days have been very … complicated. You are right, there.'

Among his other vagaries, Lavedrine always wore a ring in his left ear, like a common sailor who has rounded the Cape. The silver ring that I recalled was gone, and dangling in its place was something more exotic. A tiny mosaic picture of the church and the square of St Peter's in Rome.

He must have caught my glance because he set the earring dancing with his finger.

'Indeed, Hanno, I have recently been in Italy. Part of the time was spent in Roma,' he said, using the Italian. 'The Holy Roman Catholic Church is now but a bauble in my ear.'

Could any man but Lavedrine wear such a toy without

compromising his air of masculinity? As I was forced to admit to myself, it added something more which exalted all the rest. Like Scotsmen who wear a tartan skirt instead of trousers, yet seem to be all the rougher and ruder for doing so.

'The cider is growing *cold*,' Helena chided with fake severity.

This was more surprising than anything else. I had not heard Helena say a word in careless jest for longer than I dared to think.

'I hope you're well,' I said, going across to greet her.

She did not offer me her brow to kiss. Instead, she turned her head one way, and then the other, so that I might see her earrings. 'Colonel Lavedrine brought me these,' she said. 'They have come all the way from Italy, too.'

Seen close up, the earrings were lozenges of rich red coral on which a tiny female face had been cut in profile. Against Helena's pale ears and dark auburn curls, they might have been two brightly glowing lamps. Had he bought them for my wife, I asked myself, or had those trinkets first graced the ears of one of the creatures of uncertain sexuality that Lavedrine generally favoured? Such malign thoughts clearly did not trouble Helena. She moved her head rapidly from side to side, and took great pleasure in showing off the jewels.

I was tempted to announce that Lars Merson had been murdered, and tell them how he had died. My head was full of the difficulties of the investigation, the new dimension to the terror which had shaken the town. Had Helena not heard the news?

In silence, I sat beside my wife and wolfed down a biscuit.

Lavedrine relaxed once more in my chair, stretching his legs comfortably towards the fire. He appeared to feel at home, almost one of the family. Certainly not French, and decidedly not one of the enemy invaders who had occupied our land. He might have been a neighbour, and a friend.

'When did you return to Prussia?' I asked at last, crunching on another biscuit coated with honey. It was of the sort that Lotte generally made at Christmas time.

'Four months ago,' he said, his finger playing with his earring.

'You were visiting the Pope in Rome, I suppose?'

'As a matter of fact, Hanno, I did go to the Vatican. I went there to study the phenomenon of demonic possession at first hand. It seems that all the devils from Hell had gathered in Rome for a general council. I could not afford to miss the opportunity.'

'How did you and the devils get on?' I asked.

Lavedrine chuckled as he bit into another biscuit. 'I managed to calm a couple of them down by administering a potion of my own invention. As for the others … well, they remain without a rational explanation.' He gestured with the biscuit that he was holding. 'For the moment, anyway. I returned to quarters at dull old Bromberg in the spring,' he said with a heavy sigh, his eyes on the flames, 'and I was ordered recently to present myself in Marienburg.'

I nodded. 'They couldn't do without you, then?'

Lavedrine looked at me, his face suddenly serious. 'In the same way that Lotingen cannot do without *you*,' he said, sitting on the edge of the chair, leaning closer to Helena and myself. 'I've been catching up with recent events in Prussia by reading *Le Bulletin Militaire*. Helena was speaking of all that has happened just before you arrived.'

He sat back, brushing his silvery hair away from his face with his right hand, a look of concern on his face. As he lifted his hand away again, the curls sprang back into place like vegetation that had been battered flat by the wind.

'On a personal note, I wish to express my sorrow for your great loss, naturally.' He touched his hand to his heart. 'I cannot find the words. What can one say to two people who have looked into the bottom of the abyss?'

We had touched the bottom of the abyss.

Nor had we managed to climb out of it, no matter how normal we might have seemed to him that evening. I wondered whether he had chosen those words for Helena's sake. What else had he said to make her smile? Was this revival of her spirits occasioned by the gift of a pair of earrings? Or was his presence enough to transform her? I recalled her repugnance for him two years before. Lavedrine and I had been forced to co-operate when the Gottewald children were massacred. Helena had refused to let him enter our house on that occasion. In the end, however, when he left for Białystok, I remembered how warmly Helena had embraced him. Then, too, he had given her an exotic gift, a hair clasp made from whalebone from the Fiji Islands. Lionel the cat, his other gift to Helena, was still the lord and master of our domain.

'Your cat is well,' I said.

'I hope you do not want him back?' Helena put in. 'The children are so fond of him, and he of them.'

He smiled, but he never took his eyes off me. 'That's not why I am here,' he said. 'I'm more concerned about what is happening in town.'

This news took me by surprise. 'Our troubles interest you like the cases of those poor souls possessed by evil spirits in Italy, is that it?'

Lavedrine shrugged his shoulders. 'A member of the

Camera Segreta, a cardinal who is a treasured advisor to the Pope, defined me recently as a "scientist of the dark arts". I am curious about whatever affects human affairs, Stiffeniis. Nothing is sacred, if it helps me solve a mystery. What I was about to say is that something out of the ordinary is happening here in Lotingen. A girl ends up at the bottom of a well with mortal wounds to her neck, and the people immediately start to talk of vampires.' He held up his hands and he studied his nails. 'Cases of vampirism have occasionally been reported in the eastern parts of France – two centuries ago in Puy-de-Dôme, for instance – but we have nothing to match the stories which are circulating here in Prussia.'

'A vampire,' I specified. 'The people here believe that the creature carried the girl to the bottom of the well, there to gorge upon her blood. A similar attack has been made today on the jugular vein of Lars Merson, sexton and gravedigger. The victims now are two in number.'

'God in Heaven!' Helena stifled a cry, covering her mouth with her hands for fear of alarming the children, her eyes glistening with fright. 'That's why the soldiers came for you. Because of Merson. How did it happen, Hanno?'

I took a grim satisfaction in the thought that I had brought the shadows into the house. No candles could light them, no blazing hearth could warm them, no earrings of coral could conquer the power of terror. No French visitor could seduce our hearts with his facile charm and his evident self-satisfaction.

'The body was found by the stream which runs inside the cemetery wall,' I said. 'His neck had been ripped wide open. Every drop of blood had been drained from his body, which was left upon—'

'I heard something more, and would have mentioned it at a more … opportune moment,' Lavedrine murmured, his tone dry and distant. 'I was in the office of Colonel Claudet when a soldier came to report the news. The colonel is worried …'

'I wonder why?' I said, making no attempt to suppress my sarcasm. 'The victims are Prussians, after all. And these are Prussian superstitions.'

Lavedrine sat forward and stared into my eyes. 'Do not play the cynic with me,' he said. 'And don't ask questions when you know the answers. Everything that happens in Prussia interests France. We are trying to maintain some order in this country of yours. The safety of our soldiers is of paramount importance.'

'*Your* men are not in danger,' I said.

'Are you so sure?' he asked. 'Can we turn a blind eye if something out of the ordinary happens in Lotingen?' He sat back more comfortably. 'On the subject of strange events, I have some questions to put to you.'

Suddenly, the gloves were off. I saw the other side of Serge Lavedrine. No longer a welcome friend, he was now an unwelcome foe. Just like a vampire, I thought. He came into your home, and then he turned on you. A French officer, a high-ranking one, a man of power with influential friends, if he decided to question me about the case, I would have to answer him. I had been exposed before to his rapid changing of coats. He shifted from familiarity to command in a flash. Arrogance was only a short step away.

'Merson helped you bury the girl in the cemetery,' he said. 'Glatigny told me. People believe that you have hidden a vampire there, and that Merson …'

Helena leaned across and placed her hand on mine. Her palm was damp; I could feel that she was trembling. Those earrings quivered from the lobes of her ears again, though she had not caused them to move this time. The blue vein in her temple was pulsing furiously, as it always did when she was afraid.

Lavedrine's gaze shifted to Helena.

He must have seen how agitated she was. He clicked his tongue, as if to say that there was nothing to be afraid of, the way one might encourage a child while tying one end of a string to a tooth, and the other end to the door-knob. He sat forward, stretched out his hand towards her, but then withdrew it. Helena still held my hand. She would not be drawn. Nor would he presume too far. This I knew of him: he would never go beyond what was allowed.

'Forgive me, Helena,' he said quietly. 'Hanno raised the matter, and it cannot be avoided.' He turned to me once more. 'Now, tell me, Hanno. Why on earth did you and Merson bury her in the town cemetery?'

I told him everything. The parents' refusal to allow her to be buried in Krupeken. The need to bury Angela quickly. The need to put her in a place where she would not be found, where the corpse would decompose as soon as possible. The night spent digging.

'She had been murdered, but the corpse would have been defiled. That is what happens to a suspected vampire in Prussia. We were acting for the best.'

'And what do you make of the murder today?'

The discovery of Merson's body, the wound so like the one that had killed the girl. The iron spike that had been driven through his heart. The ritual which had inspired it.

It all came out.

'*Magia postuma*,' Lavedrine repeated, eyes wide, eyebrows

raised. 'I have never heard of anything quite so … ferocious. Nowhere in the civilised world.'

'The Empress of Austria issued an edict in 1755,' I corrected him. 'There had been outbreaks of vampirism in Moldavia and other places, cemeteries had been desecrated, tombs defiled, corpses had been treated in the same hideous manner as the rite performed on Lars Merson. The practice has never died out. When fear of the vampire takes hold of towns and villages, there is always someone who knows what must be done. They send for the gypsies, as a rule. The *magia postuma* is a childhood memory for any man who lives in Prussia.'

'And any woman, too,' Helena murmured. 'A living memory …'

'We are not so old,' I reminded him.

'Why must the heart be pierced, then?'

Helena answered him. 'All the blood must be drained from it. Otherwise, the creature will not die. It will rise again to feed on the living. They feed on nothing else. Human blood gives them sustenance. Each person bitten must feed on others. It goes on, and on. They live forever …'

As I listened, I cursed myself for having spoken of Merson's death. Helena had appeared, for a short time at least that evening, to be serene. Now, her voice was distant, melancholy, haunted by horror and uncertainty. Could I offer her no more than death and bloodshed? She had lost a child, and I spoke of nothing but murder.

'Why use gypsies?' he asked.

'They know what is to be done, and are not afraid to do it …'

'Did a gypsy drive the stake through Merson's heart?'

I shook my head. 'It was done by whoever found his dead body in the cemetery,' I said. Obviously, I was thinking of

Ulrich Meyer. The stonecutter knew where Merson's tools were kept. I could have arrested the man, of course, but that would only complicate the case, not solve the murder. 'That person evidently believed that Merson was not the victim of a killer, but of a vampire. He must have thought, when night came on, that Merson, too, would go out looking for human blood.'

Lavedrine nodded, apparently satisfied. 'Did Merson know the girl in the well?'

'Nothing has emerged. At least, for the moment.'

For an instant, I thought he was going to reproach me. 'Have you formed any idea who the murderer may be?' he asked instead.

My answer sounded weak to my own ears. 'I am almost persuaded to believe that there really is a vampire. That is ...'

Lavedrine ignored me. 'I have a theory, Stiffeniis,' he said, joining his hands, and touching his lower lip with the tips of his fingers. 'There is always something true, something real, in situations which are so apparently bizarre.'

'A *real* vampire?' Helena quizzed.

'Not in the literal sense, Helena.' He waved his hand dismissively in the air. 'During the *grande crainte*, as we call it in France, the peasants were terrified of ghosts, the walking dead, as they chose to call them. It was not a case of vampirism, but it was a general fear of the unknown. They were terrified of their own shadows, and everyone explained it away by speaking of superstition. I've always been convinced that there was more to it than that. Superstition is a cloak hiding something which is concrete. Someone saw something which was real, but it was mysterious, inexplicable, and it triggered a popular reaction, a communal terror. This was true in the cases of demonic possession which I witnessed in Rome. I saw a man vomit such a quantity of hair that it left me breathless. I knew there must be a rational explanation, but everyone around me was convinced that the man had been possessed by the Devil. A few days later, I made sense of the mystery. I caught him swallowing braids of hair which he had procured from God knows where. He had been summoned to appear that morning before a committee of exorcists. It was a case of controlled regurgitation. That man could swallow spoons and bring them up whenever he wanted to impress a crowd.'

'Why play such a trick?' asked Helena.

Lavedrine laughed lightly. 'They'd given him bed and board in one of the finest rooms in the Vatican palace. They treated him with all the respect that such an unusual phenomenon could inspire. I, and two other men, know the truth, having witnessed his deceit, but hundreds, nay thousands, of people had seen something that they could not explain: they saw him vomiting human hair in what appeared to be a demonic trance. Do you think the priests would reveal the truth to the faithful? Would they expose themselves as fools who had been taken in by a trickster? Most Catholics remain convinced that there were many cases of demonic possession in Rome in the months of January and February. The number of people going to church tripled in the same period. So did the offerings in the collection plate.'

'I have a similar theory,' I said. 'You did not allow me to finish what I was saying. Somebody wants to *persuade* us that there are vampires in Lotingen.'

'Frightening the population on purpose?' said Helena. 'If that is the case, there may well be no connection between Merson and the girl, except for the fact that they have both been murdered by the same person.'

Lavedrine jumped up, clapped his hands together, and smiled brightly at me. 'Hanno, you ought to enlist Helena's help in your enquiry. Can we ever forget the role that she played in the Gottewald case? Your wife swims more easily through these murky waters than you or I. You should take her with you whenever you go to question witnesses. Especially the female ones.'

My hand rose to my throat, as if to squash an insect which had tried to nip me. I touched the spot where the lips of a female witness had left their mark.

The Frenchman was watching me closely.

'Are you leaving, Lavedrine?' I asked to hide my embarrassment.

'This house, yes. At least for this evening,' he said, gesturing with his hand for Helena to remain where she was. 'But I will stay for some days yet in Lotingen.'

I went out into the hall with him.

He halted by the door, placed his hand on my shoulder, and smiled. It might have been a token of the warmest friendship. Instead, it was the prelude to an order. 'Let me have a report of what's been going on in Lotingen. By tomorrow. Is that all right?'

He was playing the French officer again. The authority to whom I must bow.

I nodded.

Suddenly, his hand shifted. Two fingers pulled at the stock of my collar, exposing the mark on my neck. If he had noticed my embarrassment before, he smiled at it now. Crow's-feet of amusement formed at the corners of his eyes.

I pushed his hand away, and pulled my collar back into place.

'Were you hiding that from Helena, or from me?' he said.

I opened the door and let him out without another word.

Later that night, lying in bed, I pretended to sleep when Helena came into the room, having been to check that the children were settled and well. Beneath half-closed eyelids, I watched her as she sat down on the bed and unclipped the coral earrings, placing them carefully on the bedside table, between the copy of the Bible and the candlestick. She intended to wear them the next day as well, it seemed.

She blew out the candle, then slipped into bed beside me. I heard her breathing, but I could not shake those earrings from my thoughts. It was as if Lavedrine were present in the room.

Just like a vampire.

Chapter 15

How many were there? Seventy? Eighty? A hundred?

A large crowd, by any count, and growing. It was still not eight o'clock, the town had not yet properly woken up for business, but the narrow lane was full of people, all of them rushing to see the spectacle.

A boy in rags had started the stampede.

He was standing on the cathedral corner, a stick in his hand, trousers cut short exposing dirty muscular calves, his feet hidden inside scraps of sheepskin that were tied around with twine. A skinny shepherd boy. He and I had reached the market square at more or less the moment that he began to shout. No-one could make out what he said at first, though the eyes that popped from his skull, and the spit that dribbled from his nose and mouth made an impression on everyone who saw him.

He took a deep gulp of air, then cried out more distinctly.

'Down that way,' he pointed. 'Outside the cemetery. There's soldiers. Frenchies. They've found something terrible.'

What it was, he did not say. He had said enough in any case. It was like throwing stones at pigeons. They took to the air. But unlike pigeons, they all went flying off in the direction he had indicated, and I was one of the number, my head filling with the worst imaginings. I joined the crowd, walking fast, then running down the slight hill that leads to the old cemetery, erstwhile kingdom of Lars Merson, now the domain of Ludo Mittner. People pushed and jostled, while the young men raced ahead, like rats in thrall to the Piper of Hamelin. The voices that I heard were muttered invocations to God, while any number of the women made the sign of the Cross. There were little children being pulled along by adults. No school for them that day. Some smiled, embracing freedom, while others cried for fear of the commotion. I went with the stream, less eager to arrive, fully expecting to find that the corpse of Angela Enke had been subjected to the same indignity as that inflicted on Lars Merson the day before. The sun was veiled by clouds, the restless air electric, promising rain before the morning was out.

I had left the house earlier than usual, intending to write the report that Lavedrine had imposed on me the previous evening. Catching sight of my office, I had taken the key from my pocket. I still held it clenched in my fist. Knutzen would not be there. His son was out of town that day, so there was no-one to tend to the pigs and fowl that they sold to the French. I had meant to take advantage of my secretary's absence and work for an hour without distraction. I wanted to put the evidence and the testimony that I had collected into some sort of order.

Then that shepherd boy appeared, and all my plans evaporated.

There was not a single uniform on the streets. It could mean only one thing. The French knew of what had happened. But were they gathering at the cemetery, or had they been recalled to their barracks?

No sooner did I reach the cemetery wall than my question was answered. A wall of blue uniforms formed a dam to hold back the river of onlookers.

And there, finally, voices were raised.

'Tell us what has happened.'

'If there's danger, we need to know …'

'They won't be happy 'til they've killed us all!'

I used my elbows, working my way forward through the crush, twisting this way and that until I came face to face with the barrier of armed French soldiers. 'I am the Procurator of Lotingen,' I said to one in French. 'Let me through.'

At my back I heard my name being passed around. Many of the Lotingeners persisted in asking the soldiers what the fuss was all about, while others tried to convince the French soldiers to let me pass beyond the barrier.

The Frenchmen might have been selected on account of their faces, which were guaranteed to scare. They stared at us in silence, their ferocious expressions intensified by waxed moustaches and ragged beards like rooks' nests. They bared tobacco-stained teeth, and jerked their bayonets to hold us back, as if we were wild animals bent on attacking them.

'I am a magistrate of the king,' I said again.

French eyes stared at me with the respect one might reserve for a fresh cow-pat found by chance in the middle of the street. Then, they looked elsewhere as someone made a move that seemed more menacing, and I was forgotten in the instant.

'Let no-one through, soldiers!'

The order came from behind the phalanx of blue serge.

Was it possible, *that* voice in that place?

The people all round made such a noise, shouting at the soldiers, shouting to each other, that I might have been mistaken. The wind was stronger now, it moved the trees, and roared through the leaves. I stretched up on my toes to see above the hats and pom-poms of the soldiers.

And there I saw him.

I might mistake the voice, but I could not mistake the man. His height for one thing, and the eccentricity of the long black leather coat that he was wearing. The wind played with his silver curls and whipped his unbuttoned coat around his legs. Lavedrine was in the company of two French officers beneath the shaded canopy of trees which fronts the main gate to the cemetery. A little wood of ash, sycamore and beech. I raised my arm and waved my hand to attract his attention, but he turned away without seeing me, all of his interest concentrated on something which I could not see for the soldiers and the laurel shrubs which blocked my view. As I watched, Lavedrine bent low to examine something on the ground. He turned his head, said a few words over his shoulder to his companions. Had the officers not been dressed in French uniform, I might have thought that the 'scientist of evil' was searching innocently for mushrooms with his friends.

I cupped my hands, shouting through them like a speaking-trumpet, hoping to project my voice in his direction and overcome the rumbling of the crowd. 'Colonel Lavedrine.'

The French soldier, who had snubbed me only a minute before, thrust his bayonet at my chest. The point quivered barely an inch or two from my heart. 'Keep to your place, Prussian!'

'My place is over there with Colonel Lavedrine,' I replied angrily.

'Do as he tells you, soldier. Let Procurator Stiffeniis through.'

While I was transfixed by the bayonet point, Lavedrine had come to my aid. We stared at each other, he on his side of the military barrier, I on mine. He looked as if he hadn't slept, and maybe he had not. He was a man of sexual appetite, a frequenter of bordellos, as I recalled. Then again, perhaps he was truly shaken by the 'terrible thing' that he had seen that morning.

'What's this commotion about?' I called to him.

'Come over here,' he shouted, making an impatient gesture with his hand. 'Soldier, let him pass.'

I pushed forward, but the barrier refused to yield, the bayonet now held up to my face.

'Are you deaf, man?' Lavedrine stormed, his hand falling heavily on the shoulder of the soldier who was puzzling over which order to obey: keep all Prussians back, or let one through because he was a magistrate. 'Stand aside!'

The man made a space, and I hurried through the gap in the French defence.

My own people saw it as a minor victory, and one or two let out triumphant cries.

'This way,' said Lavedrine, turning quickly, retracing his steps.

I asked myself again, what was he really doing in Lotingen? He had mentioned no official duties the night before, speaking only of vampirism with the natural curiosity which was his trademark. Whatever I was about to see, I thought, I was the only Prussian who would see it. Had it not been for a shepherd boy, even I might not have been so privileged.

We kept to the edge of the lane. Under the shade of the overhanging trees, the weak sun made little impression. The two French officers that I had seen at a distance turned to face him. They saw me coming, too. Neither man said anything, but they could not hide their surprise.

'This is Procurator Stiffeniis,' Lavedrine informed them. 'He represents the law in Lotingen.' More stiffly, he added: 'Take him forward, let him see what we have seen.'

Deference took the place of surprise on their faces. It was aimed at Lavedrine, of course. The two young adjutants hung on every word he spoke. With a nod that was at once a salute to him and an order for me to fall in and follow them, they stepped into the wood.

There was a small clearing, and we came to it obliquely. It faced the cemetery gate, which I could see from there with ease. With equal ease, any person coming out of the cemetery would have seen what was fixed to the trunk of the largest tree in the centre of the clearing. A stout rope had been strung on either side of a sturdy branch which was two or three feet higher than I am. Two nooses had been tied at either end of this short rope, and hanging from the nooses were the hands of a man, the wrists so limp that they must have been broken. His naked white arms and his shoulders were apparently untouched, though splashed with blood, which made what lay below seem all the more horrific.

I took a step closer.

The face was almost level with my own, but there was little of it left.

The eyes were two black holes. The ears were gone, and so was the nose. Huge gouges had been torn from the cheeks. The tongue had been pulled so fiercely before it gave that half of his gullet filled what remained of his mouth. Of the tongue itself there was no remaining trace. Shreds of flesh and muscle hung from the bones in streaks and tatters which were blackish red with coagulating gore. The chin was red-stained bone, the teeth and gums a clenched, naked grimace. Where the neck had been was a bloody knotted tangle of arteries and sinews.

I could go on, but what would be the use?

The body had been crucified, then flayed, then systematically ripped to pieces – from the face down to the knee-length boots. If any clothing there had been, it had been torn off. Indeed, there were scraps and strips of cloth caught up in the undergrowth and scattered on the ground. Below his twisted feet, there was a sodden muddy pool. His boots had sunk ankle-deep in it. So much blood had drained from the body that the earth could not absorb it all. As I examined the gaping crater where his stomach and his guts had been, I thought I saw impressions made by something sharp and pointed, which had caught and ripped along the bones of the ribcage and the pelvis.

'Do you know him?'

Lavedrine shook me by the shoulder, and repeated the question.

'I recognise the boots,' I replied in a daze. I had seen those boots the evening before, while he sat on the table in his room, swinging his legs and telling me about his master who was dead. 'His name was Ludo Mittner. This morning he ...' I caught my breath, and blew out loud. 'Ludo should have taken the place of Lars Merson today as the new custodian of the cemetery.'

Lavedrine ran his hand through his hair. The curls rebelled, cascading over his forehead, shading his eyes. He looked towards the gates of the cemetery, brushing his troublesome locks aside. 'Well, he was prevented from entering,' he said.

'Who found him?' I asked.

Lavedrine turned and spoke to the officers.

My gaze was lost on the ravaged face of Ludo Mittner. I did not hear what was being said. I was trying to understand whether Ludo had been murdered in the same manner as the other two victims.

'Not long after dawn, a patrol came by. Their attention was attracted by the baying of hounds. Their orders were to keep an eye on the cemetery during the night. I gather that there had been a riotous assembly ...'

'I was here last evening,' I said distractedly.

I could guess what Ludo had been doing there so early. Merson's job had fallen to him. He must have left his stinking cell in the Rectory Close while it was still night, eager to take up the position which was his by right without delay. I could see him hurrying towards the cemetery.

'What then?' I asked. 'After the soldiers found him.'

Lavedrine made a face. 'The officer-in-charge, a corporal probably, would have carried the news to his superior officer. The officer-of-the-watch would have written a brief report, which was passed to Colonel Claudet. And he sent for me.'

I wondered what my position was. Could I speak to the soldiers and read the officer's note in my capacity as the investigating magistrate? Or would I be refused in my capacity as a Prussian?

Perhaps Lavedrine understood what was passing through my mind. 'The soldiers saw what we have seen,' he said. 'They may have noticed a good deal less. The officer-of-the-watch who wrote the note saw nothing at all. Claudet knows the bare facts, but not much else.'

'Did anyone notice if the cemetery gates were locked?' I asked.

Lavedrine bunched up his cheeks, let out a sigh of impotence, then directed my question at the two officers. They spoke together in whispers which sounded like the angry buzzing of bees above the quieter hum of the invisible crowd.

'Colonel, tell your officers to hide nothing that they

know or have seen,' I appealed to Lavedrine. 'Every detail is important. As you know, the investigation here in Lotingen is my responsibility.' More coldly, I added: 'That is, it was my responsibility until this morning.'

I spoke in French. I wanted the junior officers to understand what I had said. But Lavedrine answered me in guttural German. He wanted them to gauge the sharpness of his reply, not the gist of what he said.

'If this is your investigation, Stiffeniis, tell me what is happening in this cemetery. This is the second body that's been found here.'

'I need to know whether this man was killed before he entered the burial ground,' I insisted, taking a step towards him, clenching my fists.

Lavedrine's blue eyes peered into mine. 'What will that establish?'

'The sequence of events.'

He frowned and tapped his fist against his lips. 'You don't believe that he was killed by dogs, then?'

'He was murdered first, then left to the dogs,' I replied. 'That is, the dogs probably chanced upon the body. There are packs of strays in Lotingen. My own house was attacked not long ago.'

I recalled the dogs outside my door, the violence with which the leader had thrown itself against the glass, the blood it left upon the window-pane. Had there been no glass, my own throat would have been at risk.

Lavedrine thrust his hands deep into his pockets and sucked in air, breathing out noisily as he stared up at the sky through the trees. 'This homeland of yours never fails to amaze me, Stiffeniis,' he said. 'The Church of Rome is more sober in its storytelling than any Prussian. First, vampires. Now, a man tied to a tree and consumed by dogs!' He turned to the officers. 'Herr Stiffeniis wants to know whether the cemetery gates were open, or closed.'

The two men exchanged a glance.

The older man nodded; the younger must speak.

He told me what I had already heard. Two hours earlier, a French patrol had come by the cemetery, and found that dreadful spectacle in the clearing on the opposite side of the lane. The gate appeared to be closed, he said, as it was at that moment. Perhaps the key was one of those on the ring, he added.

'Which ring?' I asked.

He looked with disgust at the pool of blood at the corpse's feet.

'Perhaps it has sunk into the gore, monsieur,' he said.

For one instant, I was tempted to fall down on my knees and thrust my hand into the awful mess. 'Neither of you has been inside to check?' I asked.

I saw the perplexity on his face. 'Inside, monsieur?'

Lavedrine spoke out. 'Inside the cemetery, Remy. That's what he means.'

Remy stared wide-eyed at Lavedrine. 'Why would we do that, Monsieur le Colonel? We were busy enough out here without going to see whether the graveyard is in order.'

Lavedrine turned to me, and a thin smile pulled at the corners of his mouth. 'A good question,' he said. 'What would they have been looking for inside the cemetery?'

I did not reply, but walked rapidly out of the clearing and across the lane. I placed my hands on the metal gates and shook them hard. They were securely locked. I grabbed hold of the spikes which were intended to repel trespassers, braced my foot on the lock, and pulled myself up. From that position I could see the spot where Merson and I had buried Angela Enke. The grass still grew; the earth had not been disturbed. No-one had attempted to disinter her.

Lavedrine had followed me. 'If you wish, I'll have them find the keys,' he said. 'Sooner or later, people will start arriving. They'll need to be able to enter the precincts of the burial ground.'

As I stepped down off the gate, Lavedrine rested his shoulder there, folded his arms, and peered at me through half-closed eyes. 'Helena will be coming to tend to the child's grave, I suppose?'

Was that what he thought I had been looking at? The grave of Anders?

'I think she comes here every day,' I said.

Lavedrine tilted his head the other way. 'You *think*? Don't you know?'

He shook his head and turned away.

'Find the keys, Remy,' he called to the officer. 'Do what needs to be done. These gates must be opened. The soldiers can stay here on guard until the town decides who will take the place of the dead man.'

He took three steps away from them, then called me to him by waving his finger.

'Do you believe all three were murdered for the same reason?' he asked.

I recalled the strange paths his mind could take when trying to get to the root of a mystery, but I did not offer him an answer. 'Can there be three different reasons for three such similar deaths in the space of three days?'

The din of the crowd seemed to have died away, as if they

were trying to listen to the conversation that we were holding animatedly in the middle of the lane. We were too far away for them to hear, of course, but the two French officers, who were so much closer, seemed equally preoccupied.

'I would guess that the man killed yesterday, and the one killed over there in the wood, were meant to be found. They were supposed to terrify the life out of those people down there,' he said, nodding towards the crowd. 'An iron spike through the heart. What did you say the rite was called?'

'*Magia postuma.*'

'And now, a man torn to shreds by dogs.' He raised his left hand and counted off on his fingers as he spoke. 'Vampires, cemeteries, wild dogs. Somebody wants to bring your fearsome Prussian legends to life.'

I nodded in agreement.

'And yet, there is the question of the girl who was found at the bottom of the well. It would seem as though our "vampire" did not want her to be found.' Lavedrine took a step closer, bowing his head to meet my eye. 'I ask you again, Hanno. Are you sure that these three victims have all been killed by the *same* vampire?'

'Was that death any less horrid?' I asked him. 'The killer certainly intended that the corpse of Angela Enke should be found.'

'Can you be sure?'

'Terror has been the aim from the start,' I reasoned. 'Throwing the corpse into a well was a calculated move. No-one wants to die alone, and in darkness. And there are other details that you are not aware of. The well-cover, a tooth …'

Lavedrine's curls brushed against my forehead, he came so close. 'I want to know those details. I want a written report this morning. A complete report, leaving nothing out. Two copies, please. One will be for Colonel Claudet.'

He took two paces back, his authority established.

'A report for you, Lavedrine?' I snapped. 'This is *my* investigation.'

Lavedrine and I stood toe to toe, like dogs shaping up for a fight. There was not a sound in the lane – not from the Prussian crowd, nor from the French officers. It was as if everyone were waiting to see who would throw the first blow.

'Investigating? Is that what you call it?' His voice was cold, sarcastic. 'Where are your witnesses? Where is the evidence? I don't believe that you have found a thing which will help you solve the mystery. You are blundering in the dark. Three murders, and nothing to show for them.'

'You do not understand the complexity ...'

'I'll give you two hours,' he said. 'We'll meet in the office of Colonel Claudet to compare notes. Before you go, speak to your people down there. Send them about their business, so that we can get on with ours!'

Lavedrine turned up his collar and began to fasten the buttons of his coat. The wind was cold, but it seemed to me that he was doing up his armour ready for a battle. 'We are hunting criminals together once more, Stiffeniis,' he said. 'Try and pretend that you are happy about it. I tell you sincerely, I am glad to be working with you.'

I walked down the lane, and stood before the crowd. What I told them was no lie, though it must have seemed no more than a half-truth. I announced that Ludo Mittner had been savaged to death by a pack of wild dogs. I told them that I would petition the French to send out sharpshooters to massacre the animals, as they had done during the epidemic.

No-one seemed particularly convinced. They had seen the spiked corpse of Merson the night before – it was too much of a coincidence for any man to swallow. I asked if there were any questions, and I did my best to answer the few that were raised. When there was nothing left to say, I announced that I would be returning to my business. I advised them to do the same, and I warned them that the French might choose to disperse them if they did not.

As I walked back the way that I had run an hour earlier, heading towards the Procurator's office, one of the questions that I had been asked was ringing in my head. It had come from the mouth of Daniel Winterhalter, a man from whom I occasionally rent a horse if I am obliged to go out of town about my business.

'Procurator Stiffeniis,' the stable-keeper asked, 'are you still in charge of the investigation into these murders?'

Chapter 16

I took refuge in my office.

I stood at the window, looking out on the market square below.

What should I put in my report regarding the murders in Lotingen?

Colonel Claudet had built his career on licking the boots of his superior officers. He had always avoided creating problems, according to Lavedrine. Indeed, he had sought to distinguish himself as an officer who solved problems. He would look to me to solve *his* problems. And three unexplained murders in three days in a small Prussian town under his command was a huge problem. Claudet would be called to account by General Louis-George Malaport, who governed the coastal provinces from Königsberg to Danzig.

There were, I reasoned, two possible lines of approach.

The first would be to make a great deal of what the people in Lotingen believed: that the murders were the work of vampires. I could try to convince Claudet that when the wild fantasies of Prussian folklore take shape in reality, the French would do well to leave the business in the hands of a local magistrate who might know how to deal with such arcane matters.

The alternative would be to persuade him that I held in my hand the connecting thread which would enable me to solve the question of the murders, and put an end to the irrational fears of my fellow citizens by providing a concrete explanation for what was, apparently, supernatural.

I could not ignore the fact that Lavedrine was in Lotingen.

As we stood before the corpse of Ludo Mittner, he had said that we were 'hunting criminals together once more'. Was he being ironic at my expense? I was still unsure what he was really doing in Lotingen. The evening before, he had talked of demonic possession in Rome and vampirism in Prussia as if they were two sides of the same dark coin.

'I am curious about whatever affects human affairs,' he had explained.

The truth might well be different. Especially if Claudet had convinced himself that a Prussian magistrate was not the right man to conduct the investigation. Had he sent for Lavedrine? Had he decided that it was easier to trust a French investigator to bring things to a rapid conclusion? And if so, what could I write which would show Claudet that I had discovered more than Lavedrine ever could, and persuade him that I would soon uncover the rest, if left to get on with the job in peace?

The real impediment was Emma Rimmele.

Everything that I knew led in her direction.

Could I tell Claudet that the first victim had been working for her? That the murdered girl had told Kitti Raubel that she had witnessed what she presumed to be incestuous goings-on between Emma and her father? That Erwin Rimmele, whose mind was sinking into a morass of confusion, had suggested to me that Emma was a changeling who had taken the place of his real daughter? If I then informed him that the body of the girl that everyone in Lotingen thought to be a vampire had been discovered at the bottom of the well in her garden, he would have her arrested on the spot.

Which left me with only one possibility. I must tell Claudet what I truthfully believed. That Emma Rimmele was in grave danger. Everyone was speaking openly of her as the cause of every evil in the town. Whoever had killed Lars Merson and murdered Ludo Mittner might well attempt to do the same thing to her.

I sat down at my desk, and I reached for my *nécessaire*.

Helena had bought it from a pedlar as a birthday gift for me. It was an ingenious writing-case: a hard leather tube with a hinged lid in which to store quills, ink, and a bottle of pounce. Attached to the tube was a sheet of softer leather, which could be rolled around it when travelling, or pulled out to form a smooth surface on which to write, or blot what I had written with unsized paper. Whenever I went out of town on official business, I took up this leather scroll as if I were a Roman senator, and it were my staff-of-office.

What should I tell them?

I must frighten the life out of Claudet and confound the ambitions of Serge Lavedrine. I would portray the affair in Lotingen as being of such an obscure and mysterious nature that the French would prefer not to touch it. If anyone were to take the blame for failing to get to the bottom of it, I would be the scapegoat.

I heard the door of the outer office click open, then quietly close.

I had not heard a knock. Knutzen must have finished feeding his pigs, I concluded, and decided to present himself for work, perhaps having heard the news about Ludo Mittner.

'You did well to come, Knutzen,' I called out. 'I'll need your help in a while. The French authorities are as nervous as the Prussians over this dreadful business.'

I had heard his footsteps on the creaking boards. Now, all was silent. He would be lingering outside, changing his muddy gardener's smock for the worn black jacket that he wears when he is in attendance on me. Generally, he makes audible grunting noises as he prepares himself for a morning's work.

Today, he was silent.

'Colonel Claudet wants a report regarding the murders, but I will need a second copy, too.'

'Have you mentioned me in that report?'

I raised my head, and the pen dropped from my fingers.

I struggled to control my racing heart. Sweat broke out on my forehead. I did not recognise my own voice.

'Fraulein Rimmele?'

I felt like an eel caught in a trap. I glanced towards the door, hoping that Knutzen would follow hard on her heels, so that I would not be forced to remain alone with her.

'I hoped that you would come to me again, Herr Stiffeniis,' she said. 'The French came, instead. A French officer, that is. He said he wished to speak with me, and with my father. My father, as you know, is terrified of the French. Can you imagine what he might say of me to that Frenchman?'

She was wearing the mourning outfit which had shocked the people of Lotingen. And yet, it was not exactly as it had been the day before. If the lower half were a sombre ball-gown with some minor adjustments, the bodice was composed of the most eccentric elements that I had ever seen a bereaved woman wear. Her blouse was a peasant smock of dark red, which formed a V, revealing the dark skin of her throat and the darker cleave of her breasts. Over this she wore a heavy waistcoat of brown wool, which negated any pretence of elegance, and seemed, indeed, the sort of thing that a man might wear for work, or for a stroll through the country. And over this, she wore a short black velvet jacket, whi. clung to the contours of her body, modelling her form and leaving nothing to the imagination. It might have been an old smoking jacket which had once belonged to her father. Her ensemble was, at the same time, strange to behold, yet not without refinement.

'Please, sit down,' I said, incapable of saying anything else.

She looked at the chair in which the persons I interrogate usually sit. Then, she shifted it, placing it at the side of my desk, removing in a sense the obstacle between us. We were face to face, as we had been the day before in the kitchen of the Prior's House, though not so very close as then.

She had piled the mass of curls on top of her head by gathering them up from the neck, and securing them with the large silver clasp that I had already noticed that she favoured. The engraved face of Medusa, the Gorgon, peered out of the forest of her hair as if it meant to turn me to stone.

Was her appearance the result of careless unconcern, or an effect that she aimed at? She gave the impression from one moment to the next that she might simply shrug off the clothes in which she happened to have enclosed her body, and remain completely naked. Quite at ease, she did not seem to fear the consequences.

I could think of nothing else; my mind was in a whirl.

'Which French officer were you speaking of?'

I knew the answer before it came.

'He calls himself Lavedrine, it seems. I was not there. I was walking my father along the canal bank. He'd been very odd all the day, refusing to eat, refusing to drink. Then, suddenly, he wanted to walk. I took his hand, and led him into the garden, but he insisted on walking out beside the water. He walked so far along the Cut, I thought that he would never manage to walk back again. And yet, he did so.' She shrugged. 'At a certain point, he said, "We must go home." I knew *which* home he was referring to …'

She was staring into space, overcome by the heaviness of her thoughts. She was paler than she had seemed the day before. Or was it that her lips were redder?

'Go on,' I prompted her.

'I took it as a good sign,' she said. 'His memory was better than it has been for quite some time.' She looked up, and she smiled. 'He called me by my name as we were walking back. I dared to hope … He'd been lost in such dark ruminations all the morning, but suddenly, he was himself again.' Emma sat back and let out a deep sigh. 'Gurt Schuettler was waiting at the gate. He told me that a French officer had been there, and that he had been asking questions. Schuettler said the soldier would be back. He thought the Frenchman meant to carry us off to town. Father heard every word that he said.'

'Was Schuettler certain?' I asked.

'He wants to be rid of us by any means. Papa was very frightened,' she said, changing tack. 'He began to shout and cry. I had to put him to bed, and give him a potion to calm him down. He did not wish to stay there a moment longer. We must recover my mother's coffin from the tomb, he said, and take her home. You can imagine the fuss.'

'What did this Frenchman ask Schuettler?'

Emma bit her lip, and shrugged again. A button of her blouse slipped loose. 'How long had we been living there. What was wrong with my father. Why had we rented that particular house. The same questions that you asked me, Herr Stiffeniis.'

She stared at me for some moments, then a smile appeared on her lips. 'Can you imagine the tales that Schuettler told him? About us? About me?'

I did not smile. I felt a sense of rage building up within me.

What had Lavedrinc been doing there? And why go to the Prior's House the previous afternoon before he came to visit me? Then again, why had he said nothing to me?

'Did Schuettler describe him?'

'Very tall with silver hair. Schuettler was puzzled by the fact that he was not in uniform. And yet he claimed that he was an officer. Schuettler seemed to think that he had taken on the investigation of Angela's murder. "It is all in French hands now," he said.' She leant towards me. As she looked down at the clenched hands in her lap, the silver Medusa stared out at me from the forest of her hair. 'Is it true?' she asked. 'Are the French involved?'

We are hunting criminals together, Stiffeniis.

Was *that* true?

I let out a resounding breath, as if to free my lungs of foul air. 'I am still in charge of the investigation,' I said. 'But I know who the Frenchman is. Herr Schuettler is right in thinking that he will return to question you and your father.'

'Stop him.'

It was not a request, it was an order. As she spoke, she laid her left hand on the sleeve of my jacket. Suddenly, her fingers caught my wrist and held it tight.

I was stunned by the ease with which she touched me for the second time. She showed no fear, no thought of having gone too far. Was she aware of the reactions that she provoked in me? Was she blind to the dangers of intimacy? The memory of her lips on my neck was so intense that I could barely stand it. A part of me wanted her to do it again. But that is not the dominant part of Hanno Stiffeniis, thank God. Had she tried to do so, I might have risen from my seat and fled.

'I cannot,' I said.

'You are still the magistrate, are you not?'

'A magistrate who must bow to the French,' I said.

Her eye fell upon the paper on my desk. 'You could say nothing about my father and me in what you are writing.' Her words came in gasps. 'We just happen to be here in town. By chance. It is the truth, after all.'

'I have written nothing yet,' I said, 'though … well, it is inevitable, you must see that. Everyone in Lotingen knows where Angela Enke's corpse was found.'

'At the bottom of a well not mine,' she protested. 'Near a house that I chose on account of a father who is ill. To avoid all contact with the French who robbed us of our estate.' Her voice was taut with anger. 'A house which is overseen by those two brothers. A house with an unlocked gate on the banks of a canal. Anyone could have entered the garden at night and thrown the corpse of Angela into the well. Indeed, they did!' she said emphatically. 'I can understand that you must point an accusing finger at someone. The French expect it, and I am the obvious choice. Is that your reasoning, sir?'

Her fingers let go of my wrist, but she did not pull away. Her hand fell open in supplication, her fingers resting on my hand. They were as light as leaves which had been carried there on a breath of wind.

'Everyone speaks of me as a vampire. Even my father.'

She smiled ironically and shook her head. Two curls came free and settled lightly on her shoulders. 'Surely you remember what he said at the cemetery? I am the devil's daughter, not his

own. He'll say something of the sort to anyone who
His mind cannot be relied on. I thought his memory
back, 'til Schuettler put an end to my hopes.' She p
curls away. 'You may as well name me in that report of yours,
Herr Stiffeniis. Tell the French everything, and let them close
the case.'

Of a sudden, she seemed weary and detached, as if the whole
thing bored her.

'I know Serge Lavedrine,' I said. 'He'll not be impressed by
superstitions. And as for vampires, you will not hear that word
from his lips.'

Her nails lightly raked the skin on the back of my hand.
'Serge? Is that his name?' Her gaze was so attentive, I believed
I could guess what was passing through her mind. Was the
Frenchman the door by which she might escape from the
situation in which she found herself?

She might be right, I thought. Lavedrine would laugh out
loud to hear the bizarre tales circulating on her account. He
would give no credit to Schuettler, whatever the man might
have said to Emma's detriment. Nor would he pay attention
to the scandals voiced by Kitti Raubel, friend and confidante
of Angela Enke. To say nothing of the blasphemy of Angela's
mother, who now regarded her daughter as a vampire.
Lavedrine might be the only man who *could* rescue Emma
from the trap into which she had been dragged. He would only
need to speak with her.

In my mind, I saw them standing toe to toe. They might
have been in the room before me, the impression was so
vivid. In that instant, I understood how similar they were.
Even physically. They were matching eccentrics, quick in
their enthusiasms, equal in their unpredictability. Both were

sensual. Both were narcissists, careless of the effect that they had on other people, so taken up with themselves that they did not see how easily they shocked the world around them. Like Emma Rimmele, Lavedrine could enter easily into intimate proximity with strangers. His frankness left the object of his interest bedazzled.

He had often laid his hand on my shoulder, or taken me by the arm and gazed into my eyes. And then there was the famous 'kiss' – the mad impulse with which he had embraced my wife the day he left for Białystok two years before. He had almost knocked Helena off her feet as he planted his lips on hers – there, before her husband's eyes! – and then, a moment later, he had stepped into a carriage, where the androgynous Neapolitan creature of whom he was enamoured was waiting to carry him off forever.

In that instant, I felt the sting of jealousy.

I did not want him ever to meet Emma Rimmele. What impudent questions he would ask – about herself, her family, and her history. I would set him loose on Frau Enke or Kitti Raubel, but I would not let Emma be subjected to the insinuations and the gossip that he would throw in her face. Nor would I constrain her to submit to his French arrogance, no matter how much she might yearn to escape from her present difficulties. I knew how easily Lavedrine could draw people out. He must not trifle rudely with her thoughts, sensations and fears.

'Two years ago, there was a massacre in Lotingen,' I said distractedly. 'Lavedrine and I were forced to work together. The authorities were frightened. On both the French and Prussian sides. If he is here, it is because the French have sent for him.'

'Everyone is frightened,' Emma murmured, bo[w]ing her head dejectedly.

I was reminded uncomfortably of a picture I had seen while still a boy. Perhaps the delicate curve of her neck and the twisting ringlet of hair which fell on her breast brought the memory back. My father had an edition of Shakespeare with exquisite steel engravings, which I was permitted to look at. A languorous image of the Egyptian queen, Cleopatra, with a coiled serpent nipping at her naked breast, had provoked my first sexual awakening.

And in that instant, as I was fighting to suppress the embarrassing recollection of my youthful indiscretion, she arched her spine and inclined herself towards me. Like a cat stretching. I could see nothing beyond her face. I sat back as far as the confines of my chair would allow. Her lips were on a level with the point of my chin. She raised her eyes, stared at me, and a gentle sigh issued from her parted lips.

'Despite everything,' she said, 'today has brought me one ray of hope. It may be possible to redeem my father and myself, Herr Procurator Stiffeniis.'

'Do not trust Lavedrine,' I protested.

The point of her finger rested on my lip.

'This Frenchman may have come too late,' she said.

'What … what makes you say that?'

She purred with amusement.

'I began to tell you,' she said shyly. 'My father called me by my name. For the very first time in, oh, I dare not say how long. And then, you'll never guess! He produced a note from the bank in which our funds are kept. That really was a miracle, believe me. At last I know where it is! God has lit a lamp, I told myself. He will lead us out of this wilderness. Money is a wondrous thing. I can pay the Schuettlers off. We can stay in Lotingen. I can send for a physician who may help my father. We can eat as we used to, and not depend on the vegetables and eggs that those abominable Schuettler brothers charge the earth for. I can … well, my clothes, you see …'

She stopped and ran her hand over her forehead.

'I was doomed to disappointment. My father cannot take the final, all-important step. He cannot confer on me the power of attorney. He would have done it, too. I wrote it out, and I asked if he could copy it, but his hand shakes so. He tires before he can even manage to write two words. He must declare that I am Emma Rimmele, his only heir and daughter, and that I have the authority to manage his funds. I put the pen in his hand, then took his hand in mine, intending to help him, then, suddenly, I realised what I was doing. It would not be legal, would it?' Her voice broke for a moment, and when she spoke again, she seemed to be drained of strength. 'If only the French would leave him alone, and let him live out the rest of his days in peace! If only he could regain the strength to sign the affidavit.'

She was whispering close beside my ear like a penitent Catholic sinner in the confessional. As if the fact of being near to me gave her the strength to say what had to be said. Her final gasping declaration spilled with intimate warmth upon my ear – so warm that I felt my left ear burn with blushing. No woman had ever pressed herself so forcefully upon me since my marriage.

Emma Rimmele wished to share these thoughts with me.

I could understand why she was afraid of Lavedrine, intimidated by the possibility that he would appear at the house and upset her father. Erwin Rimmele had found the needed

document, he had shown it to her, and then he had frustr
the hopes that he had raised, by his incapacity to write.

What delusion she had suffered!

I suppose I had been conscious of it from the first moment
that I saw her. That morning at the Prior's House, as she stood
staring down into the depths of the well. Her preoccupations
went beyond the normal cares of a woman. Her hair and clothes
revealed that she was careless of all formal considerations. She
wore her passions on her sleeve, so to speak. She was a creature
of light and shade, mutable beneath the pressure of circumstances. And yet, there was one constant which she could never
throw off. She was unashamedly herself. Her spirit permeated
the atmosphere around her. Like blood flowing from an open
wound.

'A signature would save me from disaster,' she announced.

'Does no-one know you at the bank?' I asked. 'Can no-one
testify to the fact that you are his legitimate daughter?'

She closed her eyes, bowed and shook her head. The face of
the Medusa seemed more tragic than before. 'My father was
always secretive. The tendency grew worse as he grew older. He
never told my mother of his business, nor did he mention it to
me. I have the document upon my person, but what use is it
now? What can I do with it?'

'A doctor could examine your father and certify his state
of ...'

'A magistrate,' she gasped, her eyes wide open now. 'If only
you would do it.'

'I?'

A sad smile impressed itself upon her face. 'You do not wish
to help me. Is that not so, Herr Procurator Stiffeniis?'

'I am not qualified to assess your father's state of mind ...'

Her finger touched my lips, and stopped my voice.

She nodded slowly. 'There's no need to explain. I may be a vampire, after all, as everyone here in Lotingen has told you. You know of the suspicion hanging over me, and that the money would allow me to flee, even before this Colonel Serge Lavedrine decides to arrest me. And my father, too. The Schuettler brothers will stand witness to whatever the Frenchman decides to accuse me of.'

Her lips trembled, as if each word had burnt her tongue.

'I'll not ask you to put your signature to the document,' she said.

Here was another turn-about. I looked at her in confusion. Her fingers no longer touched my lips, but gently rubbed against the point of my chin. They seemed far colder than before. 'I thought you needed me to testify that you are Emma Rimmele,' I said, wondering what had caused this change of heart. 'That, I can do. Why refuse the little help that I am able to offer?'

'It is better that I never see the money,' she said.

'I do not understand ...'

Her hand began to stroke my cheek, the expression in her eyes tender and ironic in the same instant. 'Why must you always play the magistrate with me?' she said softly. 'Things can never stay the same. Circumstances alter everything in a trice. Some roads divide, while other roads unite. The future cannot always be what we would wish it to be. A few days ago, I would have given anything to lay my hands upon the money. But now ... I might ... well, having money, I might be tempted to leave Lotingen forever. And that is not what I want to do. Not now. Don't you understand me, Hanno Stiffeniis? Do I have to say it?'

'Say ... what?'

She looked down, and spoke like a priest pronouncing a litany.

'Not an instant passes, but I feel your mouth against my flesh. I taste your skin upon my tongue, sir. I try to crush the memory, but I cannot. An instant later, it possesses me again. It is like the urge to drink when we are far from water. I think of nothing else. Water, water, water. Ah, it is intolerable!' A stifled moan escaped from her lips. 'I know that this is not what one should think of a man one hardly knows. A magistrate who is investigating murder. A man who belongs to another. But this is what I think when I am with you. And when I am far away, I can do nothing to help myself. I need you, Hanno. My need is … It is greater even than my need to help my father. Or myself. In time, the cruel things they say of me will be forgotten. You'll solve the case, and rescue my good name. I believe in justice, and am not afraid to wait. I'm not afraid to work by the sweat of my brow. I'll earn the money I need. I'll pay the Schuettlers for their complaisance. A doctor will be engaged to cure my father. If Father sees a change in me, it may bring him the tranquillity he craves. Then, perhaps, he will recognise me as the daughter that he has forgotten.'

My gaze wandered over the table, noting my writing-case, my pen, the inkwell. I looked around the room, where everything was known to me. My books, law codes and registers, my jacket hanging on its hook behind the door. I stared at it all, and it all looked strangely unfamiliar.

'What a pretty object!' Emma murmured, her fingers shifting my writing-case aside.

I was searching for something to hang on to.

I was the Procurator of Lotingen. I was married to Helena Jordaenssen, with whom I had had four children. The younger

o boys, Anders, had died of the fever just a short while
. Helena's heart had been broken, and so had my own.

I was all of *this*.

I did not recognise the man who was listening to this
stranger, quaking with excitement at the bewitching words she
spoke. And yet, I wished to hear her say those things. Again
and again. Over and over.

'Emma, I do not know …'

'I do,' she interrupted gently, laying her hand on mine,
pressing her forehead against my cheek. 'Is it not strange how
quickly the world may change? I came here, wanting only to be
certain of my father's money. Now, I wonder, what use would
money be, if it divided me from you? I have a confession to
make. I am in a turmoil. When you came to the house and
found that girl at the bottom of the well, I … that is, I believe
I may have fallen into quite another sort of bottomless pit
myself. I would have done anything to climb out of it at first.
But now, having fallen down, I do not *wish* to escape. I want
to remain in Lotingen. With you. In spite of Serge Lavedrine!'

Her hand let go of mine. With tantalising slowness, I felt
it sliding over the cotton of my shirt, until it reached the
topmost button at my neck. Her fingers eased it open, then slid
downwards, opening the next, and the next, while I continued
to cast my eye around the room like a shipwrecked sailor in
the middle of the ocean, searching for the tiniest bit of flotsam
which might save my life.

I closed my eyes. The sensations were too strong. Those
searching fingers slipped between the partings of my shirt, and
began to play upon my flesh with the lightness of a spider. And
then her lips, which had briefly grazed my neck, slid slowly
down the vein, and caressingly kissed my chest, stopping every

moment to whisper my name. Spasms began to envelop my body like the widening circles when a stone is thrown into a pond. Emma paused for a moment, pushing aside my shirt in a more determined fashion, then planted her lips upon the spot where my heart was beating.

It beat so furiously, it threatened to burst out from my body.

She spoke directly to the heart that sought to flee, her voice so low and vibrant that I had to strain to catch it.

'If anyone must hunt for me, Herr Procurator, I hope it will be you.'

Chapter 17

The air was foul inside the courtyard.

The building towered above on all four sides, cutting out the sunlight.

The yard was empty, except for a black calash which was standing in a corner with two black horses munching in their nosebags. There were fresh horse-droppings on the cobbles, but that was not the cause of the stench.

As I passed beneath the low arch, my stomach surged up towards my throat.

There was no understanding the French. This was the main administration building, the General Quarters, where the commanding officer lived and worked, and the officers' mess was situated, yet a heap of rotting meat had been dumped against the walls in one of the corners. Blood trickled in a sticky stream towards an iron grid in the centre of the courtyard, the cobbles sloping down in four triangular segments to converge on it.

Had someone left a cold room open, I wondered, and had the beef gone off?

Just then, a soldier came into the yard, trundling a wheelbarrow. His nose and his mouth were covered with a grey neckerchief. Despite the mask, he was whistling a tune to himself. There were bloody tails hanging out over the side of his cart. He reached the pile, and tipped the carcases of four or five dogs onto the cobbles along with the rest.

As he turned away, he spotted me.

I was standing at the foot of the staircase, watching silently, one hand covering my nose and mouth. The heads, legs and tails of the animals were covered in fur, though the bodies had been rigorously skinned from the ears to the hind quarters, the pelts peeled away, revealing raw blue muscles. Dead eyes glistened like wet glass. Jaws hung open, revealing long teeth and drooping, pink-grey tongues.

Even dead, those dogs looked menacing.

'Bet you won't find a live hound within ten leagues of town,' the soldier called to me. He spoke French, of course. Anyone who entered the General Quarters was obliged to do so. We were, so to speak, in France, not Prussia. He lowered his neckerchief and spat theatrically on the heap of bloody corpses. 'This should stop the Prussians shitting themselves every time they hear a barking stray. Our lads are still out hunting, though game is thin on the ground now. Jesus Christ, the folks in this town are more afraid of a few starving dogs than they are of us! God knows why we had to do the hunting. I'd have left the killing to the locals.'

He let out a string of curses on the heads of the Prussian people.

'What would the Prussians kill them with?' The words were out of my mouth before I could stop them. 'They have no weapons.'

'They got vampires,' he said and smirked. 'Vampires got teeth.'

He must have taken me for a Frenchman. Certainly, my French was grammatically more correct than his. My hand still covered my mouth and nose, which did something to distort my German intonation.

I nodded towards the dogs. 'Why skin them?'

'The pelts have gone to the company tanner. Be a waste to throw the good ones out, monsieur. Winter's cold in this damned country. It'll soon be on us. Make good mittens, these will,' he said, aiming a kick at the nearest carcase, raising a skittering spray of blood with his boot. 'Many a trooper will pay well for a decent pair of gloves. You got to stand guard all bleeding night in this town! This should be the last lot. I'll give it half an hour, then burn the meat before the rats get wind of the feast.'

I turned away, making for the stairs which would take me to the first floor, and the offices of Colonel Claudet. I met no-one as I mounted the stairs. Were all the officers out hunting? Nor did I meet any person as I made way along the wide corridor of the *piano nobile* with its ivy-frescoed ceilings and coats of arms of all the Prussian families who had offered up their services to the State and the town in the last three hundred years. All the office doors were closed. Perhaps the French officers were huddled there together, plotting further campaigns against the packs of strays which were creating problems for the garrison?

Was that the best way for us to defeat Napoleon and the *Grande Armée*? Not with weapons and rebellions which were destined to fail, but with the wildest fantasies of our lugubrious tradition? Vampires and wild dogs had done more to upset French dominance in recent days than any Prussian plot or uprising had ever managed to do.

I stopped at the door of Colonel Claudet's office.

Had Lavedrine got there before me? I was curious to see how far Antoine Claudet, the commanding officer in Lotingen, was prepared to bend to a man who was his superior in wit and

220

intelligence, though his equal in rank. Equally, I wondered how Lavedrine would react to a man that he would consider hardly fit to lick the Prussian mud from the hand-stitched boots that he had recently brought back from Italy.

I knocked.

'*Entrez!*'

I recognised the voice of Lavedrine.

I opened the door, advanced, and my eyes fell on the bald pate of Colonel Claudet. He was sitting behind a massive writing-desk, reading a sheet of paper, the mud-and-blood-stained standard of the regiment draped like an ornamental tapestry on the wall behind him. Lavedrine was standing by the window, silver hair cascading over his forehead, arms folded, shoulders square to the glass, blocking out the light that ought to have fallen directly onto the city governor's desk. For once, I was on Lavedrine's side.

Claudet glanced up.

'Is it you, Herr Procurator Stiffeniis?'

Clearly, he was not expecting me. Had Lavedrine forgotten to mention that I would be bringing my report? This idea was confirmed by the fact that Claudet held out his hand uncertainly, as if to shake mine. Awkward and aggressive as he generally was, I seemed to have caught him in an unguarded moment.

I glanced towards Lavedrine.

No word of welcome escaped from his lips, no show of interest. His gaze was fixed on something that only he could see. It was as if the person standing by the window was some lookalike that I had never met before.

'I have come to submit my report, Colonel Claudet,' I began. 'Regarding the murders.'

He glanced in the direction of Lavedrine, who was now staring fixedly at the sharp toe of his Italian boots. 'Colonel Lavedrine mentioned something of the sort.' He picked up a piece of paper, shook it out, laid it flat on the desk, smoothing it out with the palm of his right hand. He glanced again at Lavedrine, then looked at me. 'Sit down, Stiffeniis,' he said with a loud sigh, pointing to the visitor's chair as if he had no alternative.

Still, Lavedrine remained in silence.

'Have you any idea what's going on?' Claudet asked me at last.

I opened my shoulder bag and took out my *nécessaire*, slipping the bow, rolling out the leather writing-mat on my knee to reveal the report.

'A handsome object, Hanno. Too pretty for the horror story you have to tell us.'

Though Lavedrine spoke, his comment was said for the want of saying something, I thought. I had never seen him so lacking in animation. In that moment, from my point of view, this sullen humour was totally unexpected.

'I know your skill as an artist,' he said. 'I remember the drawings that you made during the Gottewald investigation. Do you still use that method of recording facts?'

'I do.' I stopped short. 'I did not think to bring my album and drawings.'

Lavedrine raised his hand. 'Words will do for now,' he said sharply. 'Well? Go on, read it.' Suddenly, he seemed impatient. Not to hear what I had to say, but rather to get it over with, and out of the way.

I began to read what I had written, occasionally commenting on a passage which needed clarification. Neither man said anything. There seemed to be no way that Claudet could be drawn into the argument, no way of shifting Lavedrine from the leaden humour which had laid its hand on him.

I spoke of the well, the tooth, the recovery of Angela Enke's corpse. I described the Prior's House, and reported what Gurt Schuettler had told me, being careful to limit myself to what I imagined he had told Lavedrine, placing emphasis on the fact that the dead seamstress had been working at the house for a short time only, altering the mourning clothes of Fraulein Emma Rimmele and her father, both of whom had recently arrived in town.

I spoke briefly of Emma and Erwin Rimmele. A sick old man, a loving daughter, who was caught up in duties which must have been distressing. I stated unequivocally that almost every person with whom I had spoken had voiced suspicions regarding Emma Rimmele and her father.

'It always happens when irrational fear gives way to superstition,' I was careful to specify, looking from Claudet to Lavedrine. 'The blame is inevitably thrown onto the shoulders of innocent strangers.'

As I explained each aspect of the affair to the Frenchmen, it became another solid brick in the high wall of prejudice which had been constructed against her. Add to which, I conceded, there was the question of her character, her dress, her eccentric mode of doing things, and the way these elements were interpreted by her neighbours and those who had been thrown into contact with her.

'She would appear to be a most unusual woman,' murmured Lavedrine.

I gave him no opportunity to ask more questions on her account, but continued by speaking of the victims. Angela

Enke, Lars Merson, Ludo Mittner. I went into detail in the first two cases, which Lavedrine had not seen for himself, describing their lives and characters, the nature of their work, the manner of their deaths. In particular, I dwelt on the specific circumstances in which the two corpses had been found at the cemetery. The similarities, and the differences.

At this point, I began to quote the edict of Maria Theresa of Austria aimed at curbing the profanation of tombs and cemeteries which had taken place on so many other occasions in other towns and cities, not in Austria alone, but also in Prussia half a century before.

'The royal edict did not put an end to the gruesome practice of what is generally known as the *magia postuma*,' I admitted, 'given that almost any Prussian of my own age would be in a position to recall at least one episode of vampire-hunting from his own youth.'

Neither man interrupted me.

Claudet listened with his head bent over his papers, hands clasped tightly together as if to hold the documents in place on the table-top in case a sudden wind should come along and carry them off.

Lavedrine remained by the window, never changing his position, or his stance.

I came to my conclusion by reading out the date which I had affixed to the bottom of the report. Then, I shuffled the sheets, lined up the edges, placed the manuscript on the desk-top, and pushed it towards Colonel Claudet. This was my official version of the events in town. Facts as they had happened. The names of the victims. A description of the bodies. No-one had, as yet, been arrested. For the simple fact that all my conclusions led to what everyone else in Lotingen was saying.

A vampire…

Claudet looked up at me as if I had just that minute entered the room. Had he heard a word that I had said? And then there was the silence of Lavedrine. He had said nothing then. He said nothing now.

What was wrong with the pair of them?

Suddenly, the voice of Lavedrine broke the uncomfortable silence. 'You say that the Schuettler brothers spied on Angela Enke while she was sewing in the kitchen of the Rimmeles?'

I had made more of this point than it merited, noting that it was a distance of less than fifty paces from the front door of the Schuettlers' cottage to the garden door of the kitchen where Angela was working, and that the well was just a short distance away in the sunken garden.

'Do you think they may know more than they have told you?'

'They may know more than they've admitted to either of us, Colonel Lavedrine.'

I wanted him to understand that I was aware that he had been to the Prior's House the day before and that he had spoken to the brothers. 'It is a fact that the Schuettlers are curious. And equally, it may be significant that they were watching Angela Enke.'

'No-one was watching when she was pitched into the well,' he countered.

'If it happened at night, or shortly before dawn, the fact that no-one saw her is not surprising. Equally, the fact that no-one heard a thing. The walls of the house are thick, and the bedrooms are situated on the other side from the garden where the well stands. It is probable that she was murdered while the house was sleeping.'

Claudet seemed to be watching the movement of my lips.

Did he know what Lavedrine and I were talking about? He was miles away. At the same time, there was something odd about the voice of Lavedrine, something that was flat and mechanical. What had happened to the energy which had galvanised him earlier that morning as we stood before the massacred corpse of Ludo Mittner?

The Frenchmen were tensed and strained, like archers as they flex their bows in the instant before they release the string. Were their arrows already pointing in the direction of Emma Rimmele?

Like a desperate man, I stepped onto thin ice and named the thing I feared.

'Emma Rimmele reports that the Schuettlers spy on herself and her father, too.'

I studied Lavedrine as I said this, hoping to read the expression on his face when I pronounced her name. At the same time, I did not wish to lose sight of Claudet. The fixed expression of perplexity on his face must refer to something, after all.

Lavedrine relieved me of my uncertainty. He shrugged his shoulders and waved his hand, as if to say that the matter was of little interest so far as he was concerned. 'It is not so surprising, Stiffeniis. A single woman – a beautiful woman, I believe – and an aged father whose mind is disturbed. They are bound to provoke a degree of prying malevolence wherever they go. Especially if they decide to live in a run-down country house where the body of a girl is found in a well a short time after they arrive.'

I sat back in my chair, and the tension drained out of me.

The worst was past.

'One thing remains unclear to me, Stiffeniis, despite our little talk this morning. These three murders. Are they all so similar as you make out in your report?'

'I did not say very much of Ludo Mittner,' I replied defensively. 'I thought that you would report the facts in that case to Colonel Claudet, seeing as you were present at the scene of the discovery this morning. Still, I would assume that the three deaths are related in some way. The wounds are similar. In Ludo's case, it is difficult to be more precise, given the manner in which his corpse had been ravaged by animals. But it is possible that he died by a wound to the neck ...'

'*That* is not the death which interests me.'

As Lavedrine quickly stepped away from the window, Claudet rose, as if to surrender his privileged position to the interloper. But Lavedrine held up his hand, and Claudet settled back uncomfortably in his comfortable chair. It was clear to me who was in command in that room.

'I was thinking of the circumstances in which the first victim was found, Stiffeniis. The bodies of the gravedigger and his assistant were left on public view to horrify, as you suggest. After what I saw this morning, I have no doubt that the killer, or killers, intended to terrify the inhabitants of Lotingen. But what about the girl? Why hide her body in a well, but leave a human tooth in a bucket where it was bound to be discovered? It was only a matter of time. What does that enigma signify?'

I shrugged my shoulders. 'The investigation has only just begun.'

Lavedrine placed his hands flat on the desk.

'Colonel Claudet,' he said, his eyes fixed on mine, 'please read out the despatch which I received shortly before Procurator Stiffeniis arrived.'

Claudet's mouth gaped open, and he mumbled something to himself.

'Read it, Colonel Claudet,' said Lavedrine, slamming his right hand impatiently down on the desk, never taking his eyes away from mine. 'It is addressed to me. I take full responsibility for making it public now.'

'As you wish,' Claudet conceded, holding up the despatch. '*There can be little doubt that the body found last night in a cottage outside Marienburg belongs to 2nd Lieutenant Sebastien Grangé who was posted missing as a deserter thirteen days ago. Respecting your orders, Monsieur le Colonel, the lodging has been closed up, and a guard has been mounted at the door. Nothing has been moved, or touched. However, given the great length of time in which the body appears to have remained there undiscovered, your presence here is urgently required. Problems of hygiene may otherwise arise.*

'The despatch is signed by Major-General Olivier Layard, commander-in-chief of the General Quarters in Marienburg,' Claudet concluded.

He let the paper drop from his hand, and turned to look at Lavedrine.

'What does it mean, Lavedrine?' I asked.

Claudet stood up from behind the desk. 'Colonel Lavedrine, I'll leave you to deal with this matter. When you've decided what you intend to do, I will do everything in my power to assist you.'

Lavedrine nodded, but he did not speak. Nor did he make any move to occupy the seat which Claudet had vacated. He remained in the same position, palms pressing down on the edge of the desk, staring fixedly into my eyes.

At my back, I heard Claudet open the door, then close it as he left the room.

'I am investigating the murder of a French officer in the town of Marienburg, a vicious attack on a second officer, and the disappearance of a third.' He pointed to the paper which Claudet had left on the desk-top. 'That note arrived this morning while you and I were at the cemetery. The third officer has now been found. Dead, as you heard.'

I stared at the despatch on the desk. What had his investigation in Marienburg to do with me? 'I don't follow you,' I said.

Lavedrine stood up straight, moved behind the desk, and sat down in Claudet's place. 'It isn't easy to comprehend,' he said. 'I was called to Marienburg a week ago when the first body was found. Second-Lieutenant Gaspard was living in private quarters in the town. The Eleventh Hussars are stationed there. The man had bled to death. Two days before, an officer in the same regiment, a man named Lecompte, had been attacked in the town while passing along a dark street at night. The men were sharing quarters. As a result of his wounds, he is hardly able to speak. In both cases, the blow was aimed at the neck. The wounds were peculiar. A ripping of the neck with an unknown weapon, a severing of the jugular vein with two small punctures, massive bleeding. You have seen something similar in Lotingen. So, Hanno, the question is this: is there also a vampire in Marienburg? And could it be the same vampire which has claimed three victims here?'

'It isn't possible,' I said. 'It's hard enough to find any rational connection between the victims in Lotingen ...'

'What link can there be between the Prussian victims here, and French officers in Marienburg?' Lavedrine took the despatch in his hands and looked at it. 'While trying to understand what was happening in the ranks of the French army in Marienburg, I chanced to read in *Le Bulletin Militaire* of the finding of the girl's body in the well. The wounds to her neck, the fear of vampires which spread like a forest fire through Lotingen. And of the great difficulty in which the investigating magistrate – you, Hanno Stiffeniis – suddenly found himself. I had been contacted by a Prussian scholar, who spoke to me of vampires. I dismissed his opinion at the time as being worthless. Now, I am not so sure. Indeed, I don't know what to believe.'

Lavedrine rubbed his forehead with the tips of his fingers.

'Lotingen and Marienburg are close enough. Two hours or so at a gentle trot. I had that pair of earrings in my bag as a gift for Helena. I took the opportunity to see what was going on.' He sat forward, bracing his elbows on the table, rubbing his palms together. 'I don't believe in vampires, Stiffeniis. I told you so last night. Nobody returns to suck the life from the living. But if these stories persist, there must be a reason behind them. There must be somebody who keeps the myth alive. Otherwise, why have people believed it for so long?'

We sat in silence, face to face across the table, but our eyes did not meet. I stared out of the window, while Lavedrine examined the despatch on the desk-top, as if he had never seen it before that moment.

'I believe that the victims in Lotingen and in Marienburg are definitely connected, Stiffeniis.' He raised his hand before I could protest. 'You and I have been giving chase to the same malefactor without knowing it. The latest victim in Marienburg is as much a concern of yours as he is of mine. From this moment onward, you are charged by me to interest yourself in the murders of the French officers, as well as the murders in Lotingen. I will explain to Helena that you are acting under an order which you cannot refuse to obey.'

'Which order are you speaking of?' I asked.

'The order to accompany me to Marienburg. A coach is waiting in the yard.'

Chapter 18

Evening was fading as the coach rattled into Marienburg.

We entered town by the east gate, and left it again by a different gate on the other side of town which gives onto the River Nogat. As we passed beneath this gate, the coach slowed down for a moment, and a man in uniform jumped up and took his place on the box beside the driver. He saluted Lavedrine, who introduced him to me as Alain Coin, colour-sergeant of the Eleventh Hussars. The driver whipped his horses, and the carriage wheels began to rumble noisily over the wooden slats and braces of the bridge which crossed the river.

Lavedrine resumed what he had been saying. Marienburg was an important military centre, he explained, not only on account of its vital strategic position close to the east–west highway between Berlin and Königsberg, and on the road which runs north–south from Danzig to Warsaw, but also because of the officer who had recently been appointed commander of the garrison.

'Major-General Olivier Layard is a soldier to be reckoned with,' he said.

'Isn't the town within the governance of General Malaport?' I asked.

'Malaport is supreme commander of the northern plain,' Lavedrine replied, 'but Layard is a specialist. He has Napoleon's ear, it is said, in matters of military intelligence, advance strategy and campaign planning. Since he arrived in Marienburg, the fortress has become …' He broke off suddenly. 'Let's just say that the town is important.'

I was not reassured by what I had heard. How would General Layard react to the news that a Prussian magistrate had been seconded to the investigation of the murders of officers under his command? If Layard decided to send me home again, I would have been happy. I had been spirited away from Lotingen. I had work to do there, and I was still very dubious that there was any connection with what had happened in Marienburg.

'Where are we going?' I asked him.

'Over to the far bank,' he said vaguely, slapping his hand loudly, calling out to the sergeant. 'Coin, what can you tell us about this place?'

'Not much, sir,' the sergeant called back. His face was round and red, his large nose and bulging cheeks pitted and scarred with pimples and warts. 'I was over there this morning for the first time. Our lot steer clear of the area. Patrols go past, of course, but they keep to the road and they travel fast. This place is down by the riverbank, monsieur, well away from the road. That's Prussian territory, though the General says it falls under our jurisdiction.'

'What was Grangé doing there?'

The sergeant blew on his lips. 'That's anyone's guess, monsieur. There's only one thing certain. That's where he was found. There's an inn over yonder, and the news came from there. I'm surprised they even bothered to bring it to our attention. It's a low dive, a Prussian drinking-den used by river-rats, smugglers, wherry-men, eel-fishers – characters that steer wide of the law, sir.'

Lavedrine thanked him for the information.

'I don't set much store by Layard's claim to control the area,' he said to me more quietly. 'The major-general is a desk soldier, a forward planner. He gives orders to his underlings, and records their reports in statistics and fractions. I place my trust in men like this fellow,' he said, nodding at the broad back of Sergeant Coin. 'They tell you what they know for sure, and nothing more.'

We carried on along the road which ran parallel with the river for ten minutes more, and then the carriage pulled up. Lavedrine threw open the door, pushed hard at the folding step with his boot, jumped down, and invited me to follow him out onto the high road.

While he and Coin were speaking with the driver, I looked around. A large painted sign swung above my head affixed to a gallows: The Black Bull – fine ales. It creaked and shifted in the breeze as if a hanging felon had been left on public display. Off the road to the left was a tumbledown cottage. There was no light, no sign of any person, no sign of any other house.

The sergeant was pointing towards the inn, muttering something to Lavedrine. He took the carriage lamp from the calash, and lit it with a flint.

'Wait for us here,' Lavedrine called up to the driver.

I followed him and Sergeant Coin as they turned onto the sloping path that led down towards the river. They were walking at a brisk pace. By the time I caught up with them, Lavedrine was snorting at something that the sergeant had said.

'When was the body found?' Lavedrine was asking him.

'Some time unspecified this morning. We got word of it at eleven, sir. I came out here with my men, saw what there was to see, and carried the news straight back to town. General

Layard ordered this carriage to go to Lotingen, and bring you back, monsieur.' He shook his head. 'Everyone in the regiment was saying that Grangé had run off with the hares. They had branded him as a deserter, sir. There's none more hated.'

'A deserter?' Lavedrine echoed sarcastically. 'With a fellow lieutenant already dead, and another seriously wounded? Do you hussars tell each other fairy tales to calm your fears?'

Coin made no reply to this attack.

'How was he found?' asked Lavedrine.

'Someone from the tavern reported it. That is, he told the landlord, then skipped. This man was drunk last night, the tavern-keeper said. He must have followed this path that we are on. He may have been going to throw up in the river, that's my guess. He ended up near a place that they call the old slaughter-house. There's a little cottage close by. This piss-face fell asleep on the steps, and when he woke up this morning, he could smell that something wasn't right. He thought an animal had been locked in a stall, and forgotten there. There are pig-sties, kennels and suchlike, though they're all empty. Eventually, he looked in at the window, and he saw the uniform.'

'So, who identified the body?'

'I did, sir. That is, I recognised the regimental jacket of a second lieutenant. There's no missing the epaulettes and the silver braiding, the regimental clip on his collar. Who else could it be? Grangé is the only second lieutenant who is missing.'

'How did he die?'

'I … I cannot say, sir. I saw that he was dead, but I didn't go inside.'

'That's what I wanted to hear,' said Lavedrine.

'I left strict instructions with my squad to wait outside the gate.'

'Have they been standing here all day?'

'*Oui, monsieur.*'

'And nothing has been touched?'

'The door has not been opened.'

Lavedrine clapped his hands together gently. 'Well done, Sergeant Coin. You and your men will be commended for your work when you return to the fort. A double ration of cognac, I should say.'

I could just make out a large dark building silhouetted against the sky.

'What's that place?' asked Lavedrine, pointing ahead, walking towards it.

'The old Prussian slaughter-house, monsieur. It is empty now, except for flies.'

The building was constructed like a fortress: four high walls, two towers. As we drew closer, I saw that there were three large windows along the wall, each covered with a rusty iron grating. The tall double doors facing the river were neither closed, nor open. Anyone could have entered the place, though I doubted that any man would want to. The air was ripe with the musty smell of animals, stale blood, old meat.

Lavedrine stopped by one of the gratings. Covering his nose, he peered into the dark interior. 'How long has it been closed, sergeant?'

Coin held up his lantern, illuminating the grimace of disgust on his face. 'Since we came to Marienburg, sir. All livestock destined for the butcher-shops must pass through the register-ed French abattoir outside the town gate. It's the law, sir.'

It may have been the law, but there were other important considerations also. The French controlled the slaughtering of beasts. The commissars and cooks of the *Grande Armée* got to select the very best meat, and they paid as little as possible for it.

'How far off is the house?' asked Lavedrine.

'We're almost there, sir.'

We went on, Lavedrine and Coin walking side by side, while I trailed after them.

'Did you speak to the people at the inn?' asked Lavedrine.

'I did, monsieur,' the sergeant replied.

'And?'

'Nothing, sir. I couldn't get a whisper out of them. No-one admits to seeing anything. They are a close lot, sir, all Prussians, and not to be trusted.'

'Your informant didn't tell the locals what he'd found?' I asked.

Sergeant Coin stopped in his tracks. He held up the lantern, staring hard at me. Until that moment, he must have thought that I was French. 'Informant? What the ...' he muttered, turning uncertainly to Lavedrine.

Lavedrine stepped between me and the sergeant. 'You can answer a simple question, can you not, Coin? Magistrate Stiffeniis is helping me in this investigation. He, and you, will answer to me,' he said, stepping back.

Alain Coin's throat bobbed nervously. He was confused, and it showed. 'We ... well, we are talking about a dead French officer, monsieur,' he mumbled.

Lavedrine nodded. 'That's true, sergeant. It is also true that we are in Prussia. It takes a Prussian to know his fellows, and the magistrate's question is a fair one. So, did this "informant" tell the others at the tavern what he had discovered?'

'He said he hadn't spoken to anyone, but all the people at the tavern seemed to know what was going on. He looked inside the cottage, saw the uniform, came straight to us, or so he said. I reckon he went and had a drink there first for the sake of his courage, sir. No doubt he'll want something for the favour.'

Lavedrine ignored this parting shot. 'I'd be most grateful if you would question the people at the inn first thing tomorrow morning, Stiffeniis.'

I nodded. Lavedrine had given me an order without asking whether I was agreeable. He treated me as if I were his helper, not his equal. At the same time, I realised, he was telling Sergeant Coin that he considered my assistance to be invaluable, especially regarding the native population.

Lavedrine raised his head, and sniffed aloud.

'Can you smell it, Stiffeniis?' he said. 'Ah, French tobacco. And I can see cross-belts glimmering in the gloom ahead.'

As we approached, a pipe-smoking soldier turned to meet us, bringing up his musket. *'Qui en va là-bas?'*

'At ease,' said Coin, and the man raised a whistle to his lips and let out a wail as we filed past him. 'He is telling the others that we are coming through.'

We passed two more soldiers as we made our way towards the house. Each one saluted, then turned to whistle on ahead. I could imagine how the Prussians felt, the ones who habitually used the nearby tavern. If that part of the country was generally held to be Prussian territory, and of no particular interest to the French, they must have felt as if they were under siege that day. Anyone moving on the river would have seen the foreign troops. Lavedrine was right, of course. The owner and customers of the inn would react far better to me than they would to a French sergeant waving his fist, or a naked bayonet in their faces.

'Who does the house belong to?' I asked.

Lavedrine did not reply. He was waiting for the sergeant. When Coin said nothing, Lavedrine growled sharply: 'Answer Procurator Stiffeniis, damn you! Whose house is this?'

'The house has been abandoned. It was closed along with the slaughter-house. It used to be the cottage of the man who killed the beasts. Now, it's under French dominion, monsieur.'

'What is *that* supposed to mean?' Lavedrine guffawed.

'It means that any Prussian wishing to enter it must ask permission.'

'I can see them forming a queue,' said Lavedrine sarcastically. 'And what about Grangé? Did he ask permission before he came here?'

'No, monsieur. I don't believe that he did,' Sergeant Coin replied, turning off the riverside path and leading us along a narrower path which led inland between tall grass. Fifty paces ahead, there was a small dwelling.

We passed in through a low arch, and found ourselves in an enclosed yard.

A soldier was sitting on the steps that led up to a covered walkway on the first floor. He jumped up in surprise, whipping a pipe from his mouth, holding out his musket, pointing his bayonet at us.

'At ease,' snapped Coin. 'It's me. And Colonel Lavedrine.'

He did not refer to me.

'Holy saints,' the man replied, raising his left hand to his heart. 'That was near the end of me, sergeant. I did not hear the signal of your approach.'

'I did not whistle. Whistle or not, you're supposed to be on your toes!'

'French troopers of the line,' Lavedrine murmured ironically for my benefit. 'They know no fear.' He raised his voice and said to the soldier, 'Go and smoke your pipe out in the yard. You are killing off whatever smells this place once held, damaging the scene of the crime. Sergeant Coin?'

The sergeant stood to attention.

'Which window did you look through?' Lavedrine asked him.

'The windows are all upstairs, monsieur.'

A worm-eaten wooden staircase climbed up the wall to a covered walkway, which was open to the elements and ran the entire length of the building. I followed them to the top of the stairs, where Lavedrine and Coin huddled together, blocking the way. On this landing, there were two windows, and a door in the middle between them.

'The stink is strongest down there, sir, at the far end of the balcony. And if you care to glance in through the second window pane ...'

'Wait here.'

Lavedrine snatched the lantern from his hand and was gone.

I squeezed past Sergeant Coin, who did not budge, and followed Lavedrine past the first window and the door, and on to the farthest window.

'It must have been a decent little cottage,' I observed.

'Apart from the smell,' he murmured, holding up his nose, inhaling the air.

'The man living here was used it,' I said. 'The more animals he killed, the more blood spilled, the more money he made.'

'I can understand the butcher,' Lavedrine replied, 'but not Lieutenant Grangé of the Eleventh Hussars, Stiffeniis. What in heaven's name was he doing here?'

Lavedrine held up the lantern, pressing his nose against the glass, narrowing his eyes as he attempted to see what was lost inside the darkness of the room.

'What's this filth?' he grumbled angrily, rubbing his leather sleeve in a circular motion on the glass pane in the hope of improving the poor visibility. 'It must be on the inside of the window.'

It may have been the angle at which I came upon him, or the way that the lantern flame reflected off the glass surface. It may have been that I was concentrating less on what might lie beyond the window. I saw the hint of a brownish-orange colour that Italian artists call *sanguinaccio*.

'It is blood,' I said. 'Dried blood. A great deal of it.'

The window looked like a map which shows the lie of the land, indicating the gradations in height by marking them with a different intensity of colour. Indeed, where the residue of blood was thickest, the colour was the rich dark brown of melted chocolate.

Lavedrine held the lantern closer to the glass.

'Oh, for God's sake,' he murmured, pulling back in disgust.

I briefly saw the shadow of a black lump which was lying on the floor beneath the window. Only the red jacket, dark trousers and glistening leather boots declared that this was a man. His epaulettes, cuffs and other markings indicated to Lavedrine that he was a French hussar. I looked closer, and saw a shako which had rolled onto the floor. Above the peak in silver figures, the number '11' gleamed in the lantern light. Only then – I don't know whether it was because of what I had seen, or because the sharp odour of tobacco in the courtyard had been dispersed – my nose rebelled against the fetid odour of human decomposition.

'The body's been there for a week at least,' said Lavedrine.

'A few more days, and there would have been little left of him, except the uniform. Rats have started chewing at it. And at him, of course.'

He shifted the lantern, making space for me.

The body was stretched out on what might have been a black carpet.

'I saw the other corpse in Marienburg,' he said. 'You have seen the bodies found in Lotingen. We must look for anything … familiar.' He turned to face me. 'Are you ready to go in?'

I nodded without speaking. We had come there for no other reason.

Lavedrine stood back, preparing to put his shoulder to the door. Instead, he thought again, stretching out his hand to touch the wood. He pushed hard with the flat of his hand, and the door swung open with a painful creak.

He held up the lantern, looked at me, then crossed the threshold.

Cobwebs caught at my mouth and clung to my nose as I went in through the door. But it was the terrible smell in that enclosed space which was so oppressive. The stench of human decay is unmistakeable. There was something mouldy and unwholesome, too, as if the smell had once been many times more pungent.

Lavedrine stepped closer to the body, holding up the light, pulling a kerchief from his pocket, pressing it to his nose. Carefully he shifted the jacket of the uniform with his foot. Dust erupted into the lantern beam like smoke spouting from a volcano. The candle flared, then settled again.

'Hold this,' he said, passing the lantern to me.

He knelt down beside the corpse, the soles of his boots leaving clear imprints in what I had thought to be a dark carpet. A vast amount of blood had dried out on the floor, slowly turning to powdered, red dust. The body was stretched out on the floor beneath the window. The face was pressed up hard against the wall. The flesh on the back of his neck and the right side of the face was black where it had been exposed to the air. Patches of the skin had liquefied. His blond hair was tied up tightly in a neat waxed tail, though the whole thing seemed to have slipped sideways on his scalp, like a wig gone astray.

And yet, I noted, it was his natural hair.

Lavedrine let out a sigh and squared his shoulders.

'He was reported missing five days before the other man was murdered,' he said. 'And two days before Gaspard was killed, a third man had been attacked inside the town, while returning to his lodgings. Ten days, give or take a day or two. He's been lying here for almost two weeks. Indeed, I think we can say that he was probably murdered the day that he disappeared. That is why he never returned to his regiment, or reported again for duty.'

He looked at me, then back at the body.

'The neck. We need to look more closely at his neck and his throat,' I said. 'This is how he fell, but it is not clear how he may have died. Nor if he was murdered. If we are to make useful comparison with the other murders ...'

'Give me a hand,' said Lavedrine, taking the kerchief from his nose and mouth, stuffing it away in his pocket. Together, we rolled the body onto its back, shying away as it slowly settled onto the shoulders. The cheeks had disappeared, the gaping jaw revealed an empty mouth, no lips, good teeth. The ears were like black flaps of withered leather, the eyes two empty blood-dark pits. In places, especially around the forehead and nose, the skin was white and brittle, pulled tight. It looked as thin as writing-paper of the finest quality with many little rips and tears.

'Maggots,' said Lavedrine.

I could see no moving worms, but the floor was carpeted with chrysalises, which we squashed beneath our feet as we moved about.

'We must turn the head,' said Lavedrine, dropping down on his haunches, holding out his hands, hovering close, but still not touching the body.

'Let me. I'm closer. One moment,' I said, opening my bag, taking out a pair of black leather gloves, slipping them on. 'I'll turn the skull. You lean over and see what there is to be seen.'

I placed my hands on the head, and slowly turned it.

Bones cracked, resisting. It was not so easy as I had foreseen.

'A little more,' ordered Lavedrine, and I obeyed him, forcing the unwilling parts to move at my command.

We seemed to breathe in the essence of the dead man. It was cloying, horrid.

And as I turned the head, I saw what Lavedrine saw. The skin which covered the throat and neck was like stiff dark card, where blood had drained, coagulated and dried. There was a wound, and it was vividly evident. Two small holes, one above the other, in the neck below the line of the jaw, following what had once been the artery. Shallow lacerations appeared in two channels etched as two darker lines into the skin, running from just beneath his ear towards his gullet.

The wounds to Angela Enke, Lars Merson, and, probably, Ludo Mittner, too, would have looked like this if I had been called to examine their corpses ten days or more after they had been murdered.

'It is the same vampire, is it not?' he said.

I nodded.

'You can let him go, Stiffeniis. We've seen enough.'

I released the head, which rolled away and hit against the wall with a sickening crack which caused my heart to jar.

Lavedrine was on his feet. 'I imagine that you have your drawing album in your bag,' he said. He did not wait for me to reply. 'Make a sketch of the body, together with a closer study of the fatal wounds. I want Layard to see what we have seen.'

I would have done so whether he had suggested it or not. I took up my position in the corner of the room, sitting at the table on one of the chairs, sketching the disposition of the corpse as I observed it, and the general layout of the room as it was. I did not need to examine the wounds again to remember what I had seen so shortly before. In cases such as this, I make an outline only, intending to finish off the drawings in greater detail in a more congenial and less macabre place.

Within ten minutes, I had done two adequate drawings

While I was working, I heard Lavedrine moving about in the next room, opening drawers, shifting furniture. He went up into the roof by means of a ladder in the corner, and came clattering down it again a minute later. He had examined the house and returned to my side before I had finished, standing at my shoulder, watching the movement of the graphite on the paper.

I found his constant presence a trifle intimidating.

'What have you discovered?' I asked him, rubbing with my finger on the paper, soothing the graphite into the weave to achieve the effect that I required to suggest the extent and the nature of the dried lake of blood in which the body lay.

I flicked the page, and worked on the drawing of the neck in a similar manner.

'Next to nothing,' he said. 'This is it. There is a loft up there, but it is practically empty. Certainly, it has not been recently used. Anyone living here would be restricted to this room and the bedchamber. This room was used for eating too.' He pointed to a small alcove which contained an open fireplace, and a bricked-in hob. 'The bedroom is tiny. The man who used to live here – the one who worked down there in the slaughter-house – he lived alone, I think. It is hardly big enough for two people.' He was quiet for some moments. 'Unless, that is, Grangé was happy with the crush.'

I raised my eyes and looked at him. 'What do you mean by that?'

'Come and see,' he said.

The bedroom was even smaller than the living-room. A single window looked onto a wood, beyond which the river gleamed in the light of a rising moon. There was a single wooden bed which had been dismantled, the pieces resting up against the wall. Another, larger sleeping place had been fashioned on the floor by spreading reeds and cut grass, and on this base was laid a twisted bed-sheet and a pile of blankets. They appeared to be clean, if one discounted the dust which had gathered on the bedding since the last time anyone had slept there. On the floor was an oil-lamp which had burnt down to the wick before extinguishing itself.

'The single bed belonged to the workman,' I began to say. 'Before they sent him on his way.'

'So who left this?' said Lavedrine, dropping down on his haunches, and flicking the bedding to one side. The under-side of the bottom sheet was stained dark brown in large patches.

'This is blood,' he said. And when he shifted the rest of the bedding out of the way, I could see that there was more red dust on the wooden floor. It appeared to have soaked into the boards. 'And here there's more of it.'

'Was he still alive?' I asked. 'Did he try to crawl to the door before he died?'

Lavedrine did not reply immediately. 'I doubt it,' he said at last.

'In that case, from whose throat did *this* blood come?'

'I've no idea,' he said.

'And where is the body?'

Chapter 19

I felt like a prisoner in a cell.

I heard soldiers marching past the door. Sometimes the sharp intonation of a Gallic voice, or the sounding of a distant trumpet, disturbed the heavy silence. I was surrounded by Frenchmen, enclosed on all sides by the enemy.

Yet this was not the true measure of my confinement.

Before they would allow me into that room in the heart of Marienburg Castle – a stronghold of the Teutonic Knights for centuries, a barracks of the Prussian army until the siege of January 1807 – I had been forced to wait outside a closed door while Lavedrine attempted to convince General Olivier Layard that my presence inside the castle was a necessary part of an ongoing investigation into the deaths of two French cavalry officers, and the grievous wounding of a third. That was what galled me. Finally, I had been allowed to enter the castle, but not because I was a Prussian magistrate with power to investigate any crime committed in my country.

I was held to be the drudge of Serge Lavedrine, and nothing more.

I looked around the room. A French soldier had led me there in silence, passing along dark, lofty corridors which were lit with nothing more than the lantern that he held in his hand. Now and then he glanced behind, as if he feared the worst of a Prussian. The fact that I had been admitted to the castle on the orders of the governor himself seemed to make no difference. Lavedrine might have eased my way more gently into the place, but he had remained behind with General Layard, who had given the order that I was to be 'escorted to the zone which will be occupied by Procurator Stiffeniis'.

The 'zone' was neither big, nor small. While no smaller than I expected, I was surprised to think that it was probably larger than the private quarters reserved for many of the French officers. The towering ramparts and stark exterior of the castle gave no hint of the welcoming aspect of the interior. The room, I reluctantly conceded, was pleasant beyond my hopes. The walls were painted a pale shade of blue; a ceramic stove of darker blue stood in one corner beside a bucket filled with logs. The Gothic arches of the door and window were decorated with alternating edging tiles of bright red and green, while the wooden fittings had been recently painted bright green.

I wondered what the room had been used for in the five centuries before the French arrived. Too small for any military gathering, it could have been an office, where some accountant worked at his ledgers. He might have been concerned with grain, or any one of a hundred products passing up and down the river, with shipbuilding, pine wood imported from the Scandinavian countries, furs from the east, or even amber from the Baltic coast.

As we were coming back to town by carriage, crossing the bridge, Lavedrine had responded to my proud Prussian praise of the history, the size and the noble architecture of Marienburg Castle as we saw it from the water, with a single word.

'Dreary,' he said. A minute later, he added: 'It's too large, too draughty, much too Prussian for my simple Gallic tastes.'

He had been explaining to me the role that the castle played in the case which he was investigating. The entire French garrison had been housed inside the castle precincts immediately after its capture, though restrictions had recently been lifted, he said. Junior and middle-ranking officers, who did not have a role to play in the day-to-day running of the three regiments, gathered there and had been allowed to take up residence in the town at their own expense, if that was what they wished to do.

'As three second lieutenants in different companies of the Eleventh Hussars made haste to do,' he explained. 'It is a risk when soldiers live among the civilian population, and yet it is an essential part of any military occupation. We must mix if we hope to win their sympathy. We cannot live forever behind high walls and barricades. But what we must ask ourselves, Stiffeniis, is what Sebastien Grangé was doing in that lonely place on the other side of the river. He was not registered as living there. What could he do over there that he could not do better here in the regimental barracks, or in a private apartment in the town?'

I kicked at the stout wooden frame of the bed.

The straw mattress was provided with a lumpy pillow and a thick woollen blanket. Moths had eaten a hole or two in the off-white wool, but that would hardly spoil my sleep. And beneath the bed within easy reach there was a large ceramic chamber-pot with a ribbon of small red flowers painted on the rim and handle. Even better, it had a lid, which meant that I would sleep without the smell of piss to foul the night air. I looked towards the corner and the window. There was a triangular wooden table on which stood an ample, matching flowered bowl and a jug which was filled to the brim with water. Beside it, on an iron frame hung a folded cotton cloth with blue stripes. I would be able to wash in private without the need to mix with French soldiers.

Was privacy what Grangé had been looking for?

If the room in which I found myself was typical of the castle as a whole, then Sebastien Grangé was either a Spartan or a fool.

I thought of Lionel, the large grey cat that Lavedrine had entrusted to the care of Helena before he left for Białystok two years before. When Lavedrine first brought him to the house, the animal had crowned himself sovereign of our home the very next day by urinating in every corner of every room. Unbuttoning the flap of my trousers, I decided that I would mark my 'territory' by using the ceramic night-bowl.

Cautiously I lifted the lid.

It was not only empty, it had been freshly rinsed.

I imagined that some poor soldier had been told to wash it out as a punishment. How much more of a punishment, I thought, if he ever learnt that he had washed it out for a visiting Prussian.

I emptied my bladder, emitting a sigh of pleasure as I did so. I had just conquered my own little square of French-occupied territory. I closed the lid and placed the bowl in the corner furthest from the bed. Even so, a nauseating stink seemed to hang upon me, or on my clothes. I had not been conscious of it while we were crossing the water, but in the confines of that room, I could smell the decomposition of human tissue, as if I had been infected by the foul air in the cottage where we had found the corpse.

I opened the window, leant out and breathed in deeply. The night air was cold, lightly scented with wood smoke. I looked up at the stars for some minutes. But as I closed the window, I was aware of that sweet, revolting smell coming from my person. I threw the window open again, preferring the chill. At the same time, I decided to use the basin and the jug of water which French hospitality had provided for my comfort. I poured water into the bowl, then went to search in my bag for the small Meissen jar filled with liquid lye soap. Lotte makes it once a month by mixing lard and wood-ash. I unscrewed the lid, closed my eyes, and I was at home again. I could almost have been in the kitchen, watching her prepare the concoction. As I dreamt of home, I stripped off my clothes, letting my shirt, my trousers and under-hose slip to the tiles. I stood naked for a moment by the window, exposed to the cold night air, immediately feeling a little cleaner for it. And yet, that smell was with me in the room.

Like the ghost of Sebastien Grangé.

I stepped over to the bowl and began to wash myself from head to toe, careless of the water which splattered onto the tiles and ran away to the centre of the room. I went to work with the soap, concentrating on the parts which were most likely to have suffered from the journey and the fatigues of that long day.

Suddenly, I felt a rush of air at my back. Then, I heard the click of the door.

No-one had knocked, but I realised that I was no longer alone.

'What a sight, Stiffeniis! A Nordic god from Valhalla!'

I turned around, pulling the towel from the stand as if it were a sword with which I might defend my honour. I felt exposed, ridiculous. I had made a mistake. I was not in my own home. I had forgotten to lock the door.

Lavedrine was standing there.

He was groomed to perfection. He had already washed and changed his soiled clothes. He had brushed his silvery mop of hair, and tied it tightly in a pigtail at the nape of his neck, exposing his ears and the dangling mosaic earring. He was wearing a blue military half-cape on one shoulder, a mess-jacket of the same colour, a pair of light-grey riding breeches and black leather boots. Even so, it could not be said that he was wearing anything so bland as a uniform. A colonel's wide gold chevrons emblazoned the sleeves of his short jacket, though he had left it carelessly unbuttoned, showing off a most unmilitary waistcoat of green silk worked with embroidered flowers along the line of brass buttons. He looked like a man who had put on whatever conveniently came to hand in his wardrobe. And luck had clearly guided his choice, because the ensemble was excellent.

He was, as always, elegant, though not in any conventional way.

In his right hand he held a roll of papers.

It was a strange, intimate moment. *Intimidating*, I should say. My first thought was that no woman could resist such a look from a man like Lavedrine. His gaze was fixed on me, slowly moving down from my face, seeming to appraise the form of my chest, which rose and fell in response to my intense embarrassment, lingering a moment longer than was polite on my sex, running down my legs to my bare feet and the water that was pooling on the tiles. Having sunk so low, his bright eyes began to work their way back up again to meet my own. In silence. I felt the blood rush to my face, and I was tempted to cover my nudity with the striped cloth which I still held in my hand.

And yet, I did not.

I knew that he would consider such an action to be infantile.

I forced myself to face him, letting my hand and the cloth fall along my flank, setting my feet more squarely on the floor, bracing myself to meet his challenge. Indeed, I managed to fold my arms, and even raised my chin in the hope of appearing nonchalant and disdainful.

'I did not hear you knock,' I said.

'Nor did I,' Lavedrine replied with a smile, shifting his head slightly, his eyes still on me, as if to alter or improve the perspective of what he saw from the doorway.

'Because we are in French territory, I suppose?' I could hear the venom in my voice.

Lavedrine took two steps forward, lowered his head to one side and peered at the fading marks the lips of Emma Rimmele had left on the right side of my neck without saying a word.

Instinctively, I took a step backwards, bumping my hip against the basin, spilling water onto the floor.

He raised his hand and waved the tube of rolled papers at me.

'This report regards the finding of the corpse of Philippe Gaspard, the first victim in Marienburg,' he announced. 'I doubt that the general would be happy if he saw me handing it to you, as if you were a Frenchman and privy to our secrets.'

'You could persuade him with your supernatural powers,' I replied.

He shrugged, and looked away. 'That's why I crept in without knocking,' he said. 'It might be thought that I was playing the traitor. If news got back to the general …'

'A different explanation comes to my mind,' I interrupted him.

254

'What might that be?'

'You will keep a constant check on what I do. As, and when, you wish. Without bothering to knock. I am your prisoner.'

He rested his fist upon his hip, pursed his lips, and exhaled loudly. 'I do not understand you, Stiffeniis,' he said, shaking his head. 'I'm very tired, and you appear to be in a foul humour. You seem to be engaged in some sort of private debate, and I have no time for it. I brought these papers to share the information with you. I happen to have read them first, of course. The same thing happened to me when I arrived in Lotingen. I read your reports *after* the events that they described.'

'I did not know you were in Lotingen,' I objected.

He stepped across to the bed, and dropped the roll of papers on it.

'If I were you,' he said, 'I'd get dressed quickly. This damned fortress is worse than the Arctic north, not some glorious château on the sunny banks of the River Loire. Helena would not approve of your decision to wash beside an open window. Then again,' he added with a smirk, 'it may be that you wished to be found in this state of undress. Did you think to impress me with the fact that a Prussian body may be closer to the Greek ideal of harmony than some flabby Mediterranean peasant with a pot belly and dirty fingernails?'

I felt my cheeks begin to burn again, and hid my reaction by vigorously towelling off my body, intending to get dressed at once.

'There'll be no mention of vampires in those papers,' I murmured, wiping the damp from my upper arms and chest. 'I must forget all that I have heard and seen in Lotingen if we are to get to the bottom of what's going on here.'

Lavedrine stepped close. His hand grasped my wrist.

'Forget nothing!' he snapped. 'It is part of the same story. Get that idea straight in your head. Vampires go wherever they wish, and do whatever they like. If they can kill in Lotingen, they can kill in Marienburg, too. They are diabolical creatures, Stiffeniis, whatever else they are. But we will catch them!'

His hand let go of my arm, hovering for a moment close to my chest.

Like a diving hawk, his finger jabbed at my breast-bone. His fingernail pressed against my skin, running quickly up to my chest, coming to rest on my throat. 'From these strange signs, I would say that you had met a vampire recently,' he said with a harsh staccato laugh, his face very close to mine, his eyes half-closing as he stared at me. 'Lips … Teeth … Tongue … Hmm, a female vampire, I would say.' He pulled his finger away, and took two paces back. 'And not an unpleasant experience. Am I wrong, Hanno Stiffeniis?'

He had entered the room on a draught of cold air.

He went away on another.

'I told Layard that I would return those papers first thing tomorrow morning. See if you can make some sense of the fact that the vampire who killed two French lieutenants and attacked a third in Marienburg, was just as keen to gorge on Prussian blood. We have seen too much blood tonight, more than one man could lose, yet the general says that no-one else under his command is now missing. Grangé makes up his tally. Think on that.'

The door closed with another click.

I stood for some minutes with my hand on my neck. There was no mirror in the room. Had Lavedrine really seen a mark there? Had it not faded away by now? I dressed quickly, changing my linen and my shirt, then set the lantern on a table by the narrow bed, sat down, and began to examine the papers that he had left behind. He had told me not to dismiss the idea of the vampire from my thoughts.

What did he mean by that? And could he be correct when he said that Grangé had not been the only victim of a murder in the cottage?

<u>Report concerning the death of PHILIPPE GASPARD, 2nd September, 1810</u>

<u>Preliminary observations:</u>
a) The dead body of a man was found last night at the hour of 2 a.m. in the dock area of Marienburg.
b) Subsequent investigation revealed his identity several hours later as a French officer. Captain La Maurice, surgeon to the sixth company of the eleventh hussars, was on duty last night in the infirmary. Having washed and cleaned the corpse, he identified the unknown man as Second Lieutenant Philippe Gaspard of the sixth company.
(See death cert. attached.)

<u>Log:</u>
We were patrolling the district on the western side of town (I, Corporal Didier Auguste, and three privates under my command), where a number of narrow alleys lead down to the quay on the right bank of the River Nogat. The area is densely populated, there are many drinking dens, gambling houses, taverns, brothels, and so on. It is a well-known fact that the area is plagued by drunken lewdness and brawling. Indeed, General Layard has declared the zone to be off-limits after midnight to all ranks lodging in the Castle.

For this reason, it was not immediately apparent that the victim was a French officer. He was wearing civilian clothes; his shirt, neckerchief and jacket were soaked in blood. The man had died – it was clearly evident – by a serious blow to the neck, a gouge or rip on the right-hand side, which had severed an artery, causing the loss of life in a very short time. The body was lying in a pool of blood which had gathered in the street.

We attempted to ascertain whether there had been a fight, but no witness could be found. The reluctance of the Prussian population to assist the French army is notorious. However, it seems impossible to believe that such a violent attack, and the consequent agony of the victim, went unobserved.

The sixth company records reveal that Second Lieutenant Gaspard had been granted permission to lodge in a private apartment in Edmundsgasse number 9. The door of the lodging has since been sealed and a guard will be maintained there until further orders.

Respectfully,
Didier Auguste, Corporal, 4th Chasseurs, 1st brigade.

One thing that Lavedrine had said was clear. The description of the fatal wound to the dead man's neck was too similar to the injuries suffered by the victims in Lotingen to be ignored. I closed my eyes and I recalled the horrid tearing at the necks of Lars Merson and Angela Enke.

There was something disquieting about all of the attacks.

How could someone strike the fatal blow before the chosen victim realised what was happening? How had the killer got so close, and why had the victims not tried to defend themselves?

This was the stuff of legend, particularly those concerning Prussian vampires. The victim often recognised the killer, sometimes kissing him or her in a sign of welcome, failing to realise that the creature was interested in one thing only: sucking the life-blood from whomever had invited it to cross the threshold.

The doctor's medical report was terse: *a fatal incision to the artery in the right side of the neck causing irreparable loss of blood.* But then the doctor had added a short note. Second Lieutenant Gaspard was known to him personally, he said.

Philippe Gaspard was of an excellent reputation, neither a dicer, nor a duellist. He was not remarked upon as a drinker, but was widely known as a courageous officer, fearless in battle, of indomitable will and most remarkable physical strength. Within the brigade, he is known to be of an amiable disposition, a good companion, a regimental stalwart, trustworthy, a loyal friend ...

Who *were* his particular friends?

I turned to the second report, and I found a partial answer to my question.

Henri Lecompte, second lieutenant of the Fifth Company, Eleventh Hussars, was lodging in a private apartment in Edmundsgasse number 9 when he was attacked and almost killed ...

Lavedrine had added a signed note in his own hand in the left-hand margin:

He was a friend and fellow-lodger of Second Lieutenant Philippe Gaspard, the man who was murdered on the night of …

The two young officers had shared an apartment in town, and Lecompte had been attacked in the same manner, and in the same street, as his friend. The only difference was that Henri Lecompte had survived the violence, which had taken place two nights before the murder of Philippe Gaspard, and in the very same alley.

Was something illegal going on there, and had the two young men discovered it?

I turned to the final page of the sheaf, and I read that a third young officer had been registered as living in the same suite of apartments. Again, he was a second lieutenant. Again, he was a hussar. He had been reported missing a week or so before the other two were attacked. In his case, for some reason that was not clear to me, it was suspected that he had deserted his post and fled from Marienburg.

Sebastien Grangé, second lieutenant, Fourth Company, Eleventh Hussars …

If he had run away, Lavedrine and I would have been spared the sight of his corpse.

Chapter 20

A trumpet reveille called me from my sleep.

I waited for an hour or more, but Lavedrine did not come. The night before, however, he had told me what he wanted me to do. I must go to the tavern on the other bank of the river, and question the landlord. I opened the door, intending to leave, and I found that a piece of bread and honey and a shot of cognac had been left on a wooden tray outside my door. This was a welcome surprise. I carried the tray inside the room, satisfied my hunger, then went in search of the main gate.

I passed from one courtyard to another.

Blacksmiths were shoeing cavalry chargers in one yard, saddle-makers were beating out leather in another, wheelwrights and carpenters were making wagons here, while soldiers were marching and training everywhere else. No-one asked me my business, not even the sentries on the main gate, who were resting idly on their muskets. It was early morning, and the long day had hardly begun. They let me out of the fortress on the simple assurance that I was going to meet Colonel Lavedrine. Their lips hardly moved as they muttered a gruff, 'Va bien.'

I passed from shade to muted light.

Inside the fortress, the high walls, soaring towers and covered walkways created deep shadows everywhere, a sort of permanent evening, while on the riverbank, the sky was a rippling sheet of mother-of-pearl, the sun still struggling to make its first appearance, but casting a shimmering, blinding light on everything. Without Lavedrine, I had no access to a carriage. Still, the thought of walking across the river and the bridge was not unpleasant, and in ten minutes or so, having passed a score of men who were smoking and fishing, I had reached the far bank. It was a mile or so to the tavern standing off the high road where Lavedrine and I had stopped the night before.

As I turned off the road at the Black Bull, I lingered for some moments.

The view across the river was impressive, the fortress in the distance, its red-brick walls and tiled roofs gleaming in the morning light. And despite the unkempt character of the countryside, the long grass, the trees and bushes, the looming bulk of the slaughter-house to the right, and the knowledge that the cottage lay beyond it, I could not help but feel a warm regard for my homeland. Even the fetid smell of the river was acceptable to me that day. And so was the appearance of the lonely tavern. It was more attractive in the light of day. It was made of wattle, the timbers grey with age, the plaster dirty white, but the moss-covered tiles of the roof and the lead bow-windows gave an impression of being welcoming. It was no more than fifty paces from the river, though it had seemed a longer walk the previous night in the dark. As I approached, I saw a board beside the entrance indicating that pies and cuts of meat would be available all day.

I pushed on the wooden door, and entered.

'I hope you haven't come to eat? We're closed.'

The man who blocked my way was a mass of blubber, his

hair an uncombed white tangle, the dark skin of his face and bare arms spotted pink and white, as if he was suffering from ringworm.

'I've come to talk,' I said. Frankly, having seen him, I would not have dared to eat a thing in the house. 'I am a Prussian magistrate. My name is Hanno Stiffeniis. If you are the landlord, I must ask you some questions.'

'Questions, sir? There's none of them on the menu. Not today, as I said.'

I took a step forward, but he did not step back.

'What do you know about the French officer whose corpse was discovered yesterday in the little house down by the river?' I asked him.

The landlord looked beyond my shoulder. 'Are you alone, sir?'

'What's your name?' I countered.

The man blinked. 'It's Voigt, sir. Wilhelm Voigt. Can I ask you a question in return?'

'Certainly,' I said. I had no desire to alienate him before we had begun.

He pulled a face and crossed his mottled arms, which were the size of hams. 'Since when have Prussian magistrates been chasing men who kill the Frenchies? Shouldn't we be trying to slaughter the whole damned lot of them?'

As he spoke, he stepped aside, waving me to come in. It was a tight passage. As I brushed against him, I realised that there was nothing recently washed about landlord Voigt. Neither his body nor his clothes had been touched by soap or water in a very long time. He smelled, indeed, like the River Nogat, especially those eddying bays and forgotten basins where every sort of putrefying filth can gather.

Had the French avoided the Black Bull for the sake of their noses?

The interior was perfectly suited to the owner. The atmosphere was mephitic, noxious, a compound of stale tobacco, stale ale and, of course, stale landlord. Did he keep the windows closed to keep his own smell in, or to avoid compounding it with the smells that the river might add to it?

I sat down at the nearest table, and I waved to Herr Voigt to sit on the other side of it. Then, I took my album from my shoulder-bag, laid it flat on the table-top, taking out the silver tube in which I carried my pencil. In the rush of departure, I had forgotten my *nécessaire* in Lotingen. Herr Voigt stared at what I was doing, then looked at me. He opened his mouth to say something, and I had to turn my head away. It was like sniffing at a pig's bladder full of rancid grease and lard.

'How long have you been at the Black Bull?' I asked him.

He joined his hands together, pressed them against his nose, and leant across the table. I had to force myself to remain where I was, and neither pull back, nor pinch my nostrils tightly closed. 'First, let me tell you about the tavern, sir. It's been here since the slaughter-house was built. That's more than a hundred years ago. My grandfather built that place, and he built this one, too, around the same time. My father took on the place when he came of age, and I took it over when my old man died. I've been here since the day that I was born.'

I made note of what he said.

'How long ago was that, Herr Voigt?'

'Fifty and seven years, sir. It was doing good business in all those years, but since the Frenchies came, it's dropped off dead, more or less. They closed the slaughter-house, didn't they? We'd be heaving here from dawn to dusk back in the old days. You wouldn't think so now. There was farmers and their boys from the country, butchers and their lads coming out from town, housewives that liked to get in first and pay the lowest prices, old folks looking for hooves and tails and ears and giveaway bones. They was here because of the slaughter-house. They all came in for a drink or five. In them days, it wasn't pies that we were selling, it was plates of fresh meat grilled over the fire down there.'

He nodded into the dim interior, where a girl was raking ashes from the grate.

'Who are your customers now?' I asked him, keeping my head low as I spoke, staring fixedly at my album on the table. When Voigt did not reply at once, I glanced up. 'Well, sir?' I prompted with my pencil.

Voigt was chewing on his fat bottom lip.

'You'd do better to speak with me than with the French,' I warned him. 'Does it have something to do with the death of the Frenchman? They'll find out soon enough, I tell you. They'll come crashing through here like a slaughter-man's hammer. You are lucky for the moment, Voigt. They sent me.'

He considered this prospect for some moments. 'We've had bad luck these last few years, sir, but that damned officer coming out here to get himself murdered was the worst that's happened yet,' he said.

'Just five minutes ago you were talking of butchering the whole French army,' I reminded him.

He reared up suddenly like a bear, pushing his chair back noisily on the tiles, and marched across to the bar. He groaned as he ducked beneath the counter, grabbing two large earthenware mugs from a shelf and setting them beneath the tap of a large barrel.

'It's time for a warmer,' he muttered, coming back a minute later, carrying the mugs which slopped and spilled over the brim as he rolled from side to side. He set them down on the table, one for himself, the other in front of me. 'Marienburg's best,' he cried, as if it were a toast, and downed a huge gulp of the stuff. 'Drink up, sir.'

I raised the mug towards my mouth, and sniffed.

It was as stale as last night's piss. The reddish brown colour seemed to declare that it was beer, but it was flat and dank-looking. I had never smelled anything like it. Added to which, I had my doubts that those drinking-vessels had ever been rinsed. In the meanwhile, he had taken another gulp, and he fixed me with a smile of immense satisfaction. I might have been watching a Friesian cow enjoy a tankard of ale, and those white patches on his face reinforced the impression.

'This is why they keep on coming here, sir,' he said, tapping the side of the mug with his finger. 'The customers, I mean. Of course, they come to do a bit of business, too. It's better here than other places. At least, it was until that Frenchie went and got himself done in. They've been all over the place since yesterday morning. Who's going to stop along the river if they see that lot marching up and down the bank armed to the teeth? I ask you! And now they've come, it won't be easy to be rid of them. Nothing will be the same for quite some time.'

The beer had made him talkative, and I took a sip to fortify the atmosphere of camaraderie. I had some trouble swallowing, of course. It was like acid on my tongue. French soldiers would have thrown it back in his face, I am sure. And I found it hard to imagine any Prussian taking kindly to the stuff, even if he was dying of thirst. Yet men went there to drink, and, as Voigt said, to do business.

'What type of business?' I asked.

'Meat,' he said, and took another drink. 'That's always been our staple here. Not just the slaughtering, but the sale of meat. Here the prices are cheaper. A lot of it comes down the river by boat. Still mooing when it gets here. Once cattle get to town, once the French get their claws on them for the killing, it passes from hand to hand, and every time the price goes up. Here, you get a fair deal.'

They were smuggling meat, avoiding French taxation. I finished the note that I was writing. I did not see any connection with what had happened to Grangé. He could have had all the meat that he wanted in Marienburg fortress.

'And so, the slaughter-house was closed ...'

Voigt took another swig of ale, wiping his mouth with the back of his hand. There was nothing forced or false about his pleasure. Might other local Prussians come for the ale, and no other reason? But as he caught my eye over the rim of his mug, I realised that there was something else he wished to tell me.

'There's other trade, as well,' he said. 'There's the river, here's the tavern. When it's dark ... it's always dark at night down here ... sometimes a boat stops by. Sometimes, like I said, it's on the hoof. Other times, like I'm saying now, it could be ... other things. Amber, for a start. Now, that's a nice commodity for you. Small, doesn't smell or make a noise, and worth a mint. The French have put a whacking load of tax on that, all the way along the coast from Königsberg down to Danzig. You'd be surprised how much of that gets through.'

I had a good idea, having recently investigated murders on the coast where amber was collected, stolen and smuggled, but I said nothing of that.

'Was that what the Frenchman was doing here?' I asked him.

'Who'd have trusted him not to give the game away?'

'Might he have been spying, then?'

Voigt shook his head. 'If they wanted to close us down, sir, they would do it in force. One man? Now, it's my belief …'

He said no more, staring at me suspiciously.

I put my elbow on the table and leant over it, hoping to say what I had to say before the fumes of ale and Voigt did for me. 'Continue,' was all that I could manage.

He came to meet me, and I was forced to breathe. I opened my lungs and took it in like a drowning man who hopes to hasten his own end. 'When Frenchies go a-thieving,' he said with a wink, 'they call it the spoils of war. When they get billeted on us, they are instantly the masters in the house. They'd take a widow's wedding ring, and boast of it to their pals. Each and every one of them is running a race to see who gets rich the quickest. They'll ask you for your last penny in exchange for not robbing it. That's the Frenchies for you!'

Voigt was telling me nothing that I had not heard a hundred times before. When the French invaded Lotingen after Jena, I had hidden out in the woods with Helena, Lotte and the children, expecting the worst. Many of our neighbours were in the same uncomfortable situation. Everyone had brought his most precious portable possessions. When the fighting was finished, and we returned home, French soldiers had installed themselves in our house. They had already sold off the greater part of our furniture. For food, they said, but we found many empty bottles of expensive wine which had been thrown into the long grass in the garden when we finally repossessed our home, and only then because the baby was barely two months old.

'Sometimes, one of them gets his throat slit 'cos he's said too much about his booty,' Voigt continued. 'It's his mates that do it. No love's lost between thieves, they say. There, that's what I think happened in that cottage. That soldier was over here to do a bit of dirty business, and he was killed for it. By his mates, I mean. Something mighty precious, if you ask me. Maybe they argued over the transaction … Greed's a curse, sir. In any case, the smell of blood has filled the air again in these parts. That's my idea of what has happened.'

It was certainly possible. The cottage was close to town, yet far enough away, in Prussian territory. It could be easily reached by road, or by boat, and without being seen by the French or the Prussians. It might have seemed to Grangé the perfect place to meet with other conspirators and conduct their business.

Then again, if amber was at the heart of it, it was far enough from the coast to evade the surveillance of the French officials who rigorously controlled the amber trade. I knew the sort of greed and violence that amber could engender, especially among the French who were actively seeking the most precious specimens in the interests of science.

'How have you managed to avoid the French, Herr Voigt?'

The landlord took a deep draught of beer and shrugged. 'I reckon that they feel vulnerable outside the city walls. They are … well, they're afraid of being seen alone in places like this, sir.'

'Afraid?' I echoed, bravely sipping at the ale again. 'Why would they be afraid?'

He drank deeply, as if it were the finest beer that had ever passed his lips. 'They don't like the slaughter-house, if you ask me, sir.'

'They've closed down everything that they consider unhygienic ...'

He laughed and shook his head. 'They can't close off the smell of blood. Folks hereabouts have never stopped telling stories about the slaughter-house. Maybe that's what scared them off.'

'Stories?' I asked, forcing myself to take another sip.

He ran the tip of a finger around the rim of his glass.

'Stories,' he said.

'What kind of stories?' Lavedrine had been right to send me here. Voigt would never have told a Frenchman what he was telling me. The important thing was to decide what was relevant, and what was not.

'They've been slaughtering beasts down here for centuries, sir. Where there's blood,' he added, holding his ale-mug up to the light as if it were the finest crystal glass, then taking another large swig, 'there's creatures that drink nothing else.'

The tension which had been building up inside me melted away like ice thrown onto a blazing fire. I had fallen into the same dark pit that had almost swallowed me in Lotingen. Speak to a Prussian, and demons leapt out at you in every shape and form. Was this what Lavedrine had meant when he told me that the fact that French soldiers were the victims changed nothing?

'Vampires, Herr Voigt?'

The landlord nodded vigorously. 'Some say that they were drawn here at night when animals were being killed in such large numbers. Now, that river of blood don't flow like it did, but still ... There are people that leave carcasses there at night for the creatures to feed on. Dead dogs, sick animals, what have you. That way, the vampires come down here to quaff, and they stay away from the villages along the river.'

And one of them had taken the coach to Lotingen, I thought ruefully.

'Are you suggesting that a vampire may have attacked the French officer?' I asked with a smirk.

Voigt raised his mug, and winked again. 'To the good health of the vampire, if that's the case. I wish we'd had a few at Jena.' He shook his head. 'I don't believe in that supernatural stuff. I told you what I thought had happened in that cottage, sir. That man had enemies in *this* world, sir. Forget the creatures of the night! There's something down-to-earth behind it. Still, little Elsie thinks the vampires got him.'

I stopped writing and looked up. 'Elsie?'

'When the slaughter-house was up and running, sir, we had five servants working here. Now, we've just got little Elsie, Elspeth. Good girl, she is, an' does the lot, dusting, clearing, cooking if there's any call for it. She was here before, sir, brushing out the fireplace.' He looked around him, then pointed over his shoulder with his thumb towards the far end of the dark room. 'Down there, she is. Silent as a mouse is that girl. She got a real fright when she saw the soldiers milling about.' He leant across the table. 'Thought that they was going to rape her,' he confided. 'Some chance of that! We was watching at the curtains when we saw you coming, sir. I guessed that someone would come in here asking questions sooner or later.'

I stood up, looking over the massive shoulders of the tavern-keeper.

A girl no more than fourteen or fifteen years old was shovelling ashes up with her hands, pouring them into a large black pot, tamping them down. She lifted up some dirty clothes from a pile at her feet, dropped them into the pot, then threw in another handful of ashes. She glanced up, and realised that she had been found out. Her face was very pale, and she was very slight of build. I would have sworn that that work was too heavy for her.

'May I speak with her?' I asked.

Voigt's chair scraped loudly as he got to his feet. 'Elsie, come over here,' he shouted. 'Let that bucket alone. Herr Magistrate wants to ask you a few questions.' He set his beer-mug down on the table with a thump. 'You can finish drinking that, if you like,' he said as the waif approached. 'I've seen you at it often enough when you think that no-one's looking. You answer the gentleman's questions now,' he warned, 'or he'll set the Frenchies on you.'

The girl stood dithering in front of me.

'Sit down,' I said.

She did so, taking the mug, looking inside. 'Here, this is empty!' she cried.

Voigt waddled away, laughing.

I pushed my beer towards her. 'Drink that,' I said. 'I've had my fill.'

No sooner said than done. The child drank more deeply than the landlord had. As she put the mug down, and made herself comfortable, her pale tongue flickered over her lips like that of a tiny lizard. The girl enjoyed her ale. Indeed, I began to wonder whether I was the truly delicate one.

'Now, tell me. Why do you think the Frenchman was killed by a vampire?'

Her brown eyes had a pinkish, bloodshot cast. Her blonde hair was lank and hung in uncombed tails which spiralled around pale, sunken cheeks. She had no eyebrows, eyelashes so pale that they were almost invisible, thin grey lips. There was no distinguishing feature to her face, nowhere to look, except into her eyes. She might have been a ghost on the point of disappearing.

'Because I saw it.'

Her voice was like the voice of a young boy breaking into maturity. Maybe the foul liquid that she liked to drink and the smell inside the tavern had got into her throat and corroded it, I thought. Then again, it took no great quantity of ale to conjure up creatures in her head.

'What exactly did you see?'

Elspeth shrugged her shoulders and looked at the bottom of the ale mug. 'It must have been a week ago,' she answered indirectly.

'Can you describe it?'

Voigt was leaning on the bar, a grin on his face as he watched us.

'A woman, more or less.'

'Was it, or wasn't it, a woman?' I snapped.

She exhaled audibly. 'Looked like a kind of woman to me, sir.'

I held up my stick of graphite, and indicated my drawing album. 'Good. If you describe exactly what you saw, then I will try to draw it.'

'Dark,' she said.

I looked sharply at her. 'Dark. And?'

'Dark,' she repeated stubbornly.

'In heaven's name, child, can you say no more than that?' I said with exasperation. 'How many times did you see this dark creature?'

'Twice. Wearing a black shawl on her head. A kind of hood that hid the face.'

'How can you be sure it was a woman?'

'A man don't move like that.'

'What time of day was this?'

'It was practically night, sir. I went down to the river to chuck out scraps. That was when I saw her. Walking on the river path. Well, not *walking* … not exactly. She was bent over, like, as if she didn't wish to be seen. I chucked the rubbish in the water, and she must have heard the splash. She turned and looked in my direction.'

'Was she old, young, ugly, pretty?' I suggested.

'She was strange, sir.'

'What do you mean by that?'

'Her eyes, sir. They were evil. She looked around her like a wild thing. Lucky it was dark. She didn't see me. And then she carried on towards the slaughter-house.'

'And the second occasion?'

'It was two nights after, sir. This time she was coming back from there. Then I knew that she was one of *them*!'

'Them?'

The girl shuddered. 'Them creatures that drinks blood, sir. Vampires. That's why she had gone down to the slaughter-house. She knew what she would find there. Fresh blood, and others like herself. I could see it on her hands. They was black and shining 'til she washed them in the water, sir. Then, she ran off like a fury.'

If she had told that story to a French soldier, I had no doubt she would have got a slap for her trouble. I glanced at Voigt, who rolled his eyes to heaven.

'Can I see what you have drawn, sir?'

I turned the album towards her. It was little more than a blur of black. Vertical lines at the bottom representing grass, a sort of dark hooded cloud of a figure filling the middle ground, the black of night behind her. The sort of illustration one might find in a book for children. I had no illusions about where my inspiration lay.

The girl's mouth fell open. 'Have you seen her, then, Herr Magistrate?'

'Is this a fair picture?'

The girl nodded. 'Except for the sliver of moon, sir. Just here,' she pointed.

I added a slender slice of moon, then I closed the album. 'If any Frenchman asks you what you saw, say nothing of this,' I said. 'He'd think that you were lying.'

As I replaced the graphite in its tube, and put my album in my bag, I wondered whether there was anything in what she had told me which might relate to what had happened in that house near the slaughter-house.

I stood up, thanked the girl, who went back to her work, then I turned to Voigt, who had already poured himself another mug of ale. 'Did the girl mention to you that she had seen someone on the riverbank a week ago?' I asked him.

He wiped his mouth on his arm. 'Elsie's full of stories, sir. Came back here one night – she'd been down to the river for a bucket of water – saying that she'd seen a wolf down there.' Some private amusement caused him to laugh.

'Is it so unlikely?' I asked.

He laughed again. 'Seeing a wolf, no, but she said that it had spoken to her!'

'And what had the wolf told her?' I asked, amused despite myself.

Herr Voigt grinned from ear to ear. 'That wolf said that the Frenchies would all die in the snow, and he'd make a damned fine meal of 'em. So, what do you make of that, sir?'

I left the tavern a minute later, and turned in the direction of the river.

I saw no sign of the French soldiers who had been standing guard the night before. Then again, the body of Grangé would have been taken away. There was nothing there for the soldiers to do. I reached the riverbank, and stood there for a while considering the prospect. Despite the shimmering vision of the town and the fortress on the other bank, despite Herr Voigt's tavern two hundred paces behind me, despite the nearness of the abandoned slaughter-house, it really was an isolated spot.

I heard the distant whistling of a plover, the hissing of the breeze through the long lush grass, the gentle flow and lapping of the water. At night, it must be a frightening place for a young girl all alone. Especially a girl with such a colourful imagination as the maid from the inn. Mysterious figures that might have been female, a dark and menacing creature seeking blood, a ravenous wolf that saw a defeated French army in the snow. In that spot anything seemed possible. Even that a French officer might have been attacked and murdered by a vampire.

I made my way along the narrow path towards the slaughter-house.

It was a big old barn of a place. The ribbed planks that protected the stone walls were black with age, stained, split with ingrained moisture, yellowish-green with moss, and yet it was solid and massive. It was closed on the river side by a big double entrance-door. One of the halves hung open on enormous rusty hinges. I paused outside the door for a moment, listening in case anyone else was in there. Except for the shrill cries of the swallows which darted in the air, all was silent.

I stepped into the gloom.

The smell of putrefaction and rotting meat was strong. The buzz of flies was loud.

I glanced around, noting the large iron gratings, three on either wall, which let in light and air. Once, I supposed, they had also kept out thieves. In the centre of the room there was a large stone trough, six or seven feet long and three feet wide, like a Roman sarcophagus without a lid, a runnel cut down the centre of the tub. It was raised above the level of the ground on a base made of bricks, higher at the far end, sloping down towards a small hole and a run-off channel just where I was standing. At the upper end, this bath – 'blood-bath' was the word that first occurred to me – was two feet higher, and there was a stone block raised above the level of the trough.

It was stained and dark with encrusted blood.

I could see how the operation was organised: a cow, pig or sheep would be led in through the far door. It would be tethered to the block, its head pulled forward over the chopping-block with a rope. One sure blow with an axe and the head would be off, the animal dead.

I looked up into the air.

Beams of light crisscrossed, entering through holes in the roof and walls. A rusty pulley, chain and hook were hanging from a crossbeam rafter of the ceiling. When the carcass was hauled up, the blood would run away to the bottom of the trough and out through the runnel, where it was collected in buckets. Then, the blood would be used in any one of a hundred different ways. The smell of black pudding and blood sausage filled my mind for an instant. Or it would be dried and used to make medications. Closed in bottles as sustenance for the sick, locked in amulets to protect the living. Blood was energy, life, renewal.

I bent and looked more closely at the chopping-block. The stone was blacker than the trough, though trough and block appeared to be made of the same rough, granite-like material. How much blood had been necessary to effect that change of tint? How many animals had been butchered and bled there? How many barrels of blood had the local butchers and the herders harvested in a hundred years?

I ran my fingers over the top of the stone. It was slick and almost warm; the thick black film had not entirely impregnated the stone. I examined my fingertip, and saw that it was stained a dirty brown.

The slaughter-house was still being used.

Did they slay beasts there to avoid paying French taxes, as Voigt suggested, or, as Elsie had said, to placate the blood-lust of the supernatural creatures who frequented the place, and stop them wandering farther afield? Dark female figures, who washed blood from their hands in the river, while looking all around with piercing eyes …

It was the stuff of wild superstition.

I stepped closer to the left-hand wall, and looked through the grating.

I should have guessed, of course, though still it took me by surprise to see it there before my eyes. Fifty paces away was the gateway to the cottage where Grangé had been slaughtered. Had the killer been inspired to murder the French officer by imitating the methods that the butchers used to put down animals? Or had he purposely intended to feed the fires of superstition, exploiting the local belief in supernatural creatures which attacked the throats of their victims?

Sunlight flooded into the building from those windows set in the wall, forming bright rectangular pools beneath the windows, leaving a great deal in darkness in the centre of the room. It was a trick of the sun, which was almost directly overhead at that time of day, I supposed, combined with the position of the building and the windows in relation to the direction of the rays. As I stepped into the light, I noticed the footprints in the dust.

It was impossible to say how recently they had been left there. The only certainty was that the cottage was visible from that position. It would be an easy matter to spy on the house, to see whoever came, and went. To know when he arrived, and when he left. And whether he was armed, or not.

I recalled something that I had read in one of the reports the night before. It was not about Sebastien Grangé, but concerned the second man who had been murdered, Philippe Gaspard: ... *a courageous officer, fearless in battle, of indomitable will and most remarkable physical strength ...*

These men were no easy prey.

I knelt down and touched the footprints as if they could tell me more. I traced them with my fingers and they almost disappeared, like brittle figures made in dry sand. The ground was too dusty to conserve the marks. At the same time, my eyes wandered to the wall beneath the grating. There, the shadowy darkness was almost impenetrable. And yet there was something pressed up against the foot of the wall. A lump of some sort, a stone perhaps. I touched it, prised it away from the wall. It was a piece of rag, and it had caught or stuck against the rough surface of the wall. I lifted it into the light, where the

279

sun came in as a solid beam at an acute angle, and saw that it was a strip of cloth which had been ripped from a larger cloth. It was pale in colour, streaked with darker stains. Again, the words of Elspeth returned to my mind. *Blood, sir. I could see it on her hands. They was black and shining 'til she washed them in the water.*

I let the filthy rag drop to the floor, and kicked it away.

As it fell beside the stone trough, I saw something beneath.

A large black dog was hidden in the shadows. It was dead, its throat cut, wriggling with maggots …

I ran for the door, and charged out onto the river path, taking deep breaths.

I walked away quickly, heading back towards the tavern and the road.

I knew that I would say very little to Lavedrine about what I had managed to 'discover' that morning. The Black Bull tavern and the old slaughter-house were grim places for the spinning of stories about ghosts and other supernatural beings. He would not be interested in such things.

I might tell him that the place was sinister, and even a little frightening.

And yet, if I did so, I knew that he would laugh at me.

Chapter 21

'No-one enters without a pass. Not even the Emperor.'

The sentries leapt from their boxes as if they had been fired from a cannon. The muskets which had been resting on their shoulders now pointed at me.

'I am a Prussian magistrate,' I explained. 'I walked out of this gate no more than two hours ago. Surely you saw me then? I am working with Colonel Lavedrine.'

The two men exchanged a glance.

'What was the name of the officer again?' one of them asked.

'Lavedrine. Colonel Serge Lavedrine.'

'Never heard of him,' the sentry said.

'You cannot have failed to notice him,' I insisted. 'He wears a full-length leather coat, and has curly silver hair …'

'Fancy earring hanging from his lug?'

I blessed Lavedrine for wearing things in public that very few men would dare to wear in the privacy of their own homes. 'That's him,' I said with relief.

The soldier's eyes were small and round like brown chick-peas. They opened wide with surprise. 'I saw him walking out first thing this morning,' he said. He turned away and spoke to the other man with a hiss. 'Was he a *colonel*?'

I began to answer this question with renewed vigour. 'Colonel Lavedrine has been ordered …'

'Don't waste your breath, Stiffeniis! I must see Layard. And so must you.'

Lavedrine had appeared like a genie from a lamp. He looked even wilder than usual, his hair a silvery tangle, his trench-coat slung over his left shoulder like a cloak. He placed his right hand on his hip and scrutinised the sentries, who stared ahead as if he were a basilisk who had threatened to kill them with a glance. 'Do you need to see *my* pass?'

It was quite a spectacle. The men snapped to attention, shouldered arms, clicked their heels, and saluted in perfect synchronism as Lavedrine and I strode in through a gate which Napoleon himself could not enter without a pass. We walked quickly across the parade-ground in silence, then Lavedrine ducked through an arch. We were in a long, wide corridor with columns on one side like a cloister, opening onto a garden.

Marienburg is unlike any Prussian castle that I have seen. Not merely an impregnable fortress, it has all the pretensions of a princely palace. Seen from the outside, everything is solid and stern: stone walls, brick keeps, tall watchtowers. But on the inside, Gothic traceries and coloured ceramic tiles lend grace and elegance to the austere architectural forms. On the walls and ceiling there were frescoed garlands, fruit, flowers, and here and there, a bold heraldic device.

From the pace which Lavedrine set, I realised that there was something urgent which he needed to discuss with General Layard. I would be a witness to it, of course, but I seethed at the thought. Lavedrine would speak, while I would have to listen.

I laid my hand on his arm, and pulled up sharply. 'Before we go any further, can I know at least what you intend to say to the general?'

At that moment, a squad of soldiers came marching in our direction.

The corridor was wide enough, but suddenly it seemed very narrow. There was a rugged determination in their advance, a disciplined pounding of their boots on the stone flags. Lavedrine stepped back, pressing himself to the wall, and I was forced to do the same. Shoulder to shoulder, a dozen men swept past in files of three. They held muskets across their chests, their bayonets fixed.

'I hope that they are not going where I think,' Lavedrine muttered.

The boots moved on like an avalanche.

'Where might that be?' I asked him.

'The Black Bull,' he said. 'They'll make a clean sweep of it.'

'Why go over there? I questioned them an hour ago. They know nothing which can help us. They are steeped in superstition ...'

'General Layard wanted to raid the place last night. I persuaded him to wait. I did not tell him why, but I wanted to give you the chance to speak with them.' He was angry as he continued: 'I warned him. It will do more harm than good, if we blame the murders on Prussians who just happen to live there. We need proof of guilt. If our men even begin to think that the locals have been killing officers of the *Grande Armée*, anything could happen. Unfortunately, General Layard is not a patient man.'

'Neither am I,' I said. 'You insist that we must work together to solve these crimes. Then, you disappear without a word. I have done exactly as you asked me. But what have you been doing in the meantime?'

His laughter greeted my complaints, ringing along the corridor.

'You'd have been a hindrance, not a help,' he said. 'I have been in places that you'd do better to avoid, Stiffeniis. If you have learnt anything useful at the tavern this morning, tell me now. Before we speak to the general.'

'We?' I echoed.

'Tell me what the Prussians said,' he insisted.

I stared at him for some moments, concluding that the best way to help the people from the Black Bull was to tell Lavedrine the unadorned truth. 'The landlord had no idea that Grangé was even in that house. He believes that Grangé is, or was, a smuggler, and that he was purposely trying to avoid any contact with the French.'

'A smuggler?' said Lavedrine with a frown. 'Not a bad guess, though there are a thousand other possibilities. I gather that when the slaughter-house was closed down, the toll-collector's cottage passed into our hands. The keys were here in the fortress. No-one had taken any notice of the place, of course. It's in Prussian territory, and out of the way. Yet that's where Grangé's body was found. He may well have stolen the key. If there was any danger over there, he chose to ignore it. Did the people at the tavern tell you nothing else?'

'Nothing,' I said, though it was not entirely true.

French troops had been sent to the inn. If they spoke to Elsie, the maid might tell them everything that she had told me. Then again, I thought, perhaps it was all for the best. If she said that she had met a wolf, and that the wolf had told her that it intended to eat the entire French army when it perished in the snow, they would certainly believe that she was mad.

Suddenly, I felt the weight of Lavedrine's hand upon my shoulder.

'Let me talk to Layard, will you? Don't say a word unless you are called to do so. There'll be no mention of the fact that we were out on separate errands this morning. I want the general to believe that we are constantly together, that I know what you know, and vice versa.'

'In other words, Layard must not be told that I have been to the tavern on my own,' I said bluntly. 'I'll go along with it, but I still want to know where you have been while I was over there, Lavedrine.'

He removed his hand from my shoulder, staring at the palm as if it were a document, and he were reading it. 'I've been making enquiries about the recent history of the *Grande Armée*. Just remember, let *me* speak with General Layard.'

'Very well,' I said.

'Now, for God's sake, let's get out of this doorway. It must look as though you're trying to seduce me!' he said, pulling back with a laugh. 'Then again, Hanno, after what I saw last night, I don't believe that I'd hold out for long.'

He turned and strode away down the corridor, while I followed, speechless and blushing. Two guards were standing at the far end of the corridor, which branched off to the left and the right.

'Where is General Layard?' he growled.

'He's in the East Wing, sir. Topography room …' The man stopped short. 'Have you got a pass?' he growled back.

'What do you think, private?' Lavedrine snapped.

He turned right, marching away with long strides, his leather coat flapping out behind him. His mouth was set in a stiff smile. His lips moved only when some unfortunate soldier had the temerity to ask him where he might be going. Then, he was abrupt to the point of arrogance.

Our wandering ended before a set of large double doors

which were made of the very finest mahogany, so brightly polished that they seemed to glow. On the wall above the lintel was a bright blue enamel plaque inscribed in white.

REALM OF THE UNIVERSAL INTELLECT

The uniform of the sentry in front of the door was truly immaculate. He was even taller than Lavedrine, broad enough to match an Imperial Guard. This man nodded to Lavedrine and stepped aside

'We are about to enter the territory of Laplace,' Lavedrine announced. 'For a follower of Immanuel Kant like yourself, it will be like stepping into the enemy's camp.'

'Pierre-Simon Laplace?'

Lavedrine nodded, and smiled grimly.

I knew of the controversy which had linked the Frenchman's name with that of my master. The Prussian philosopher and the French astronomer had never met, which was fortunate. They were of different generations, and when the young correct the old, there is an inevitable clash and a loss of dignity on both sides. Professor Kant had proposed a theory regarding the formation of the galaxies in the 1750s. Two decades later, Laplace had reformulated the theory on modified principles. Who had the primacy? More to the point, as Kant contended, would Laplace have formulated a theory at all, if all the hard work had not been done for him?

The mahogany doors were thrown open and we entered a large ballroom. A truly magnificent ballroom. The room was panelled with wood which was painted a pale shade of green. Darker green frames outlined many large mirrors which had been fitted into all the walls. The infinite reflections made the room seem limitless. Immense silver-painted carvings like dripping ice provided the dominant motif for the decoration.

The room seemed to be melting in the rays of the sun which illuminated the ceiling, where St Cecilia was strumming a harp in the company of a group of red-faced cherubs who were playing fiddles, lutes and flageolets.

Beneath this metaphorical scene was hurly-burly itself, a barrage of syncopated sounds, though it had nothing to do with music. On the right were a dozen men in brown aprons, each armed with a fretsaw – some large, some small, like the string sections of an orchestra. They were cutting slices of white wood into complicated outlines like jigsaw pieces. Next to them were four men wielding large brushes, thrusting them into buckets, applying a layer of glue to the pieces of wood which the carpenters passed on to them. These oddly-shaped wafers were passed on to others in the far corner of the room, who appeared to be placing them one on top of another, like orchestra-masters putting away the sheets of music at the end of the concert. Other men began to hammer them into place like glockenspiel players.

'What are they doing?' I whispered involuntarily.

'Fashioning Prussia from wood and plaster,' Lavedrine replied.

As we proceeded to the far end of the room, I began to see what he meant. In the centre of the room there were tables covered with maps, some relating to the road system, others to rivers, lakes and woodlands, still more containing written data which gave the relative heights of points upon the land. From all of this a huge three-dimensional model of Prussia in relief was being made.

'What is it for?' I whispered.

Lavedrine turned to me. 'Laplace says something to the effect that the present state of the world foretells its future.

If we condense all the relevant data into a single model, he believes that the future will unfold before our eyes.'

'What do you think of the idea?' I asked him.

He edged close to my ear, and said: 'It is what General Layard and the Emperor think that is important. They hope to predict every source of rebellion in the whole of Prussia, and crush it before it happens.'

As he spoke, two messengers came rushing into the room, carrying reports and notes, handing them over to a team of secretaries who seemed to be co-ordinating what was going on. And in the place of honour at the head of the secretaries' table sat General Layard himself. He was, I thought, like a spider building his web. His intention was to catch a million Prussian flies in it.

'General Layard.' Lavedrine's voice recalled me from the trance into which I had fallen. 'I need to speak with you, sir.'

I took him at his word. They would speak; I would remain in silence.

Major-General Olivier Layard was small, thin, altogether unimpressive, except for the magnificent uniform that he was wearing. I admired the quality and cut of the dark-blue material, his chest weighed down with bars of medals, while his shoulders, sleeves and collar were richly embroidered with thick gold braid, a figure of the most imposing grandeur. He had imposed smartness on his men, he had imposed it on the fortress of Marienburg, and, as I could see in the Realm of Universal Intellect, he intended to enforce it on the whole of Prussia.

General Layard's eyes fixed on me like those of a famished hawk.

Those eyes were small, black, close together, divided by a

narrow beak of a nose which was short and hooked. He seemed to have no lips, his mouth a thin line drawn across his face. His skin was wrinkled like ancient parchment, yet he looked to be no more than fifty years of age. His brown hair was combed flat over his forehead in a style favoured by the Emperor, though it was longer at the back, tied up with a little blue bow, waxed and twisted. There was not a single hair out of place.

'This is remarkable, Lavedrine,' he said at last, and he sounded shocked. 'A Prussian in this room ... Well, it is unthinkable!'

'What is happening in Marienburg is unthinkable, Monsieur le Général,' Lavedrine corrected him suavely. 'And if the Prussian is a magistrate who can help us understand what's going on, then you must make an exception. I am convinced that the quickest way to solve this case is with the help of Procurator Stiffeniis. You may not know it, General Layard, but Stiffeniis was sent to the Baltic coast by General Malaport last year. Women who collected amber on the shore had been murdered. In just a week ...'

Layard started up from his seat.

'Those were Prussian women,' the General said stiffly. 'This case concerns the killing of French officers. Correct me if—'

'You are wrong, Monsieur le Général.'

If Layard was stunned, I was amazed. Lavedrine might have been setting a servant straight for having forgotten to light the fire. He set his fists upon the table, leant forward and stared down at his superior. Was there any authority that Lavedrine respected more than his own?

'The victims here in Marienburg are French officers,' he conceded lightly, 'but the trail of victims continues to the nearby town of Lotingen. There, monsieur, the corpses are Prussians.'

General Layard cleared his throat, as if words failed him.

'I have just sent a patrol across to the tavern that you mentioned,' he said. 'To be on the safe side, Colonel Lavedrine. One of my men was butchered there. I reversed my judgement of last night. I cannot afford to wait until you reach your conclusions.'

Lavedrine pursed his mouth and shook his head. 'Another officer was attacked in town, sir, in a street frequented by men of every description – Frenchmen, Prussians, and many another nation. An officer was murdered in the same street two days later, where all three men had been lodging together in a private apartment.'

A man came up with a map in his hands.

'Not now,' hissed General Layard with a wave of his hand. He stared at Lavedrine as though he were the captured Duke of Wellington. 'Are you suggesting that three of my men have been attacked and murdered by Frenchmen?'

'That is exactly what I am saying.'

No doubt my own expression matched the surprise which registered on the general's face. Lavedrine had spoken with measured determination.

'I hope that you can prove the consistency of this theory, colonel.'

Lavedrine seemed to relax. His fingers caught at the slight red ribbon which was holding his hair in place. He pulled hard on the knot, and his curls fell loose. He let out a sigh, as if some charade were over, and he might now revert to his own true self. He had tried to play the part of a subservient officer, apparently, and he had failed. So, he seemed to say, why continue to act? He shook his head, then vigorously ruffled his curls with his right hand.

'These things have already happened in the *Grande Armée*, sir. As you well know, Monsieur le Général. There is too much proof. I consulted the statistics this morning. The fortress is provided with the most recent information, as you well know. There have been feuds involving rival groups of officers in the garrison of Arles. Five men died. Duelling incidents in Venice. There were four victims, in that instance. Then, in Utrecht, Limburg, Essling … Shall I go on, sir? The list is all too long. Cliques form up wherever men are thrown together. Freemasonry represents just one of these groups.' Lavedrine shrugged and let out a sigh. 'Something similar has happened here, I think, and for some reason, these vendettas have involved people living in Lotingen, not thirty miles away. Prussians. The killings are physically identical—'

'Are you certain, Lavedrine?' I spoke without thinking, forgetting what I had agreed with him, that is, to give General Layard the impression that we had arrived at these conclusions together.

Lavedrine's eyes blazed angrily into mine. The hand with which he had been combing out his hair clasped suddenly into a closed fist. For a moment, I thought he was about to plant it in my face.

'Procurator Stiffeniis is right to doubt,' murmured General Layard with barely concealed sarcasm. 'Where is your evidence for these accusations, Lavedrine?'

'Evidence is too strong a word, sir. I would talk of hints, suggestions …'

'Hints?' Layard repeated, and a smile traced itself at the corners of his mouth.

Lavedrine renewed his assault with fury. 'In the first place, sir, why is Lieutenant Lecompte so reticent to tell us what he knows? He was wounded in the same manner as the other two, and he escaped with his life by a miracle. Yet his account of the attack is totally unconvincing. And he was talking to *me*, sir, a French soldier talking to a superior French officer. This morning I informed him that the corpse of Grangé had been found. I saw the terror in his eyes, but it makes no difference. He stubbornly repeats the tale that he told me when I was investigating the murder of Philippe Gaspard. He is not telling the whole truth. He is hiding something. If a Prussian had attacked him, don't you think that he would have told us? Why would a French soldier defend his Prussian aggressors? If he will not denounce his attackers, General Layard, I must conclude that something strange is going on within the ranks of the French army. Before we start arresting Prussians who just happen to live close to the place where only *one* of the three attacks occurred, I must have more precise information from you, sir. That is, if we are to avoid the outrages which are taking place in Lotingen.'

'Lotingen? What has Lotingen to do with Marienburg, Procurator Stiffeniis?' Layard turned on me, his face stern with anger.

I was about to answer, but I did not. This was a French duel. It was between Lavedrine and Layard. I would leave them to sort it out.

'You will have read of the recent murders in Lotingen, sir. The news was reported in some detail in *Le Bulletin Militaire*,' Lavedrine replied. He turned to me. 'Stiffeniis, please tell the general what has happened, and what may happen next if other people die in Lotingen. Tell him what could happen in the cemeteries. Regarding *vampires*.'

He sounded the final word with particular emphasis.

I did as I was told, and measured the effect of my words in the expression on the general's face. It passed from sarcasm to incredulity, and, finally, to concern, as I began to describe the violated tombs and graves that I had seen, corpses torn from their resting places, subjected to the final indignity of a pointed stake driven through the heart. As I recalled the violated corpse of Lars Merson, I felt the fright rise up in me once more. If another corpse were found, I said, and if a vampire were invoked again as the cause of death, no French bayonet would be able to keep the Prussians in check.

'Not one corpse will remain beneath the ground,' I concluded.

'Naturally,' Lavedrine picked up the tale, and he accentuated the catastrophic consequences, 'the fear will spread to other towns and villages. Cities will be overrun. You will be faced with a rebellion of enormous proportions, General Layard. You won't have time for any of this,' he said, indicating the room and its contents. 'Your plans will all dissolve into dust. Did you not foresee this danger, monsieur?'

Lavedrine's sarcasm faded into silence.

General Layard's hawkish eyes flashed from Lavedrine to me, then back again. Then, he looked beyond us at the workforce in that room, the cartographers, carpenters, model-makers, and all the rest.

'What do you want from me, Lavedrine?'

'Some files are not available to me, sir. I want to examine your regimental lists, sir. The lists which relate to the officers in the companies of Gaspard, Lecompte and Grangé. I want to see your confidential files regarding these men.'

Layard nodded stiffly, and gave the order for the files to be brought.

Lavedrine turned away to watch the work going on in the Realm of Universal Intellect. I stared down at the floor, examining the exquisite grain of the parquet beneath my feet, fearing to look at General Layard in case he changed his mind.

The messenger returned, and a sheet of paper was duly placed in the hands of Lavedrine. He studied it attentively for some moments.

'Thank you, Monsieur le Général,' he said, handing back the paper, staring into the eyes of the superior officer, on whose account he appeared to have scored a sort of victory. 'Believe me, I understand the difficulty in which you find yourself. Just as you have understood the delicacy of my position. Where can I find these men?'

'You'll find them in the *longue paume* room at this time of day,' he said.

Lavedrine saluted, and we turned away.

As we made for the door, I threw a sideways glance at the relief map they were modelling and shaping on the other side of the room. I saw the snaking blue of rivers, the raised heights of a vast plateau, ranges of hills and mountains, the names of a hundred towns and villages written in bright red ink. To my surprise the entire map was painted white.

Was it snow?

It was not a three-dimensional map of Prussia, that was for certain.

The Realm of Universal Intellect was looking to the future, attempting to predict events and mould them into a crushing victory, I gathered. Pierre-Simon Laplace would have been proud to see his ideas taking shape in reality.

One word was written large in red capital letters.

MOSCOW

This was the threat that Lavedrine had used.

Vampires, cemeteries, uprooted corpses, riots.

Nothing must happen in Prussia to compromise the Emperor's future plans.

Chapter 22

The *longue paume* room was situated on the northern flank of the castle.

Light flooded in through windows set high up in the walls. And above our heads there were three large latticed skylights as well. Given the length and vastness of the hall, and the beaten earth floor, I guessed that it had once been designated by the governors of Marienburg fortress as an indoor school where horses could be exercised when the winter winds brought snow and ice that would prevent any man or beast from venturing out for more than minutes at a time.

Evidently, the French had found some other solution to the problem.

The room had been set aside for a form of exercise which was more congenial to the officers lodging in the fortress than the breaking-in of horses. I was surprised to think that General Layard had taken so much care of the physical well-being of his men as to provide them with an entertainment which was, I believe, available to them nowhere else in Prussia. The room had been laid out for playing *longue paume*, as Lavedrine was quick to tell me. It was a game which I had never seen before.

A net was stretched tightly from side-wall to side-wall, dividing the playing area into two equal rectangles. Along the left-hand wall a seating area had been laid out for spectators in the form of a raised balcony containing rows of benches –

the pavilion, as I soon learnt to call it – in which we could sit and watch the game protected by netting in front, and a high sloping roof above our heads. Dozens of iron braziers hung high upon the walls. They would provide light and heat, and allow the game to go on when the sun had faded, or on days when it did not shine at all.

When Lavedrine and I ducked in through one of the narrow doors which led to the pavilion, a game was in progress between four young men, two on either side of the net. The players were armed with what appeared to be large fly-swatters made of a wooden frame and latticed gut – '*raquettes*', as Lavedrine called them, '"long palms", the traditional name, is out of fashion now,' he added – with which they were hitting a small cork ball from one side of the playing area to the other with unrestrained ferocity. There was a large crowd of spectators in the pavilion, together with an individual seated on a high stool, a judge or referee, who called out the score whenever a point was scored.

'*Trente–trente*,' he cried, as we sat down.

One of the players picked up the ball, called out, '*Tenez!*' and struck it very hard, aiming at the pavilion roof, which resounded with the violent force of the blow. The ball flew off at a wild angle, bouncing high off the ground on the far side of the net. I watched in bewilderment as the game went on, then came to an abrupt end for no reason I could easily divine, and the third round of the fourth set of six games began with only a short pause for refreshments in the form of fluted glasses of wine. The more that Lavedrine attempted to explain to me what was going on – he spoke of chases, forces, hazards, bobbling volleys, and *piqué* long shots – the less I understood of what I saw.

The other people in the pavilion were better informed.

They followed what seemed to be the vagaries of the game with loud excited whoops, or grunts of fierce disappointment, egging on one side, or the other. No-one down in the playing arena wore military uniform, though they were all dressed in like manner. The players wore long white linen shirts which hung loose, their sleeves rolled up to the shoulder, baring their arms, while trousers of the same light colour and material ended just below the knee. Their riding-boots had been replaced with leather-soled shoes made of stuff that looked like jute, and they were tied with long ribbons strapped around their calves.

'The pair on the right are winning,' Lavedrine informed me. 'Now, they are coming up to serve for the set, defending *dedans*.'

I did not ask him what he meant. There was a pervading smell of sweat and warm bodies, and the shouts of the players and the watchers echoed and rebounded all around the playing-hall, but I did not find it unpleasant.

'They'll be at it for some time yet,' said Lavedrine. 'Wait here for me, Stiffeniis. I want to find the fellows that we are looking for.'

I watched him go towards the centre of the balcony, directly above the net, where the majority of the spectators were sitting tightly packed, ignoring the empty spaces on either side of them. He tapped one man on the shoulder, and spoke to him. I saw the puzzled faces of the soldier and his neighbour turn unwillingly away from the game. Then, a fellow next to them leapt to attention, having recognised the presence of a superior officer. The other two made haste to follow their companion's example, but Lavedrine held up his hand, indicating that they should remain where they were. And even while he spoke to them, I could see that their attention was torn between what was happening on the court in front of them, and what the eccentric colonel in civilian clothes was saying, as he nodded to the left and to the right of the net, indicating the players.

Lavedrine waved his hand in thanks, and made his way back to me.

'The men we are interested in are losing badly,' he murmured. He sat down at my side, leant close and said, 'I would have abolished the game forever after what happened on the twentieth of June, 1789.'

'The twentieth of June?' I asked, uncertain of what he was getting at.

'Versailles. Our national assembly. Mirabeau's confrontation with the king. The revolution began on a *longue paume* court, remember. I'm in favour of the revolution, you understand, but I hold a less favourable view of many of the hotheads who seized power in the name of the people, and exercised it in their own miserable interests. Now, of course, the Emperor has put an end to all that nonsense.' He puffed out loud and shook his head. 'If they lose, they'll be in no mood to speak to us. Can you be patient a little longer, Stiffeniis? We ought to encourage them to put their hearts into the game.'

No sooner said, than he had done it, standing to his feet, cupping his hands to his mouth, letting out a sporting cry in French which was beyond my comprehension.

'I have never seen this game before,' I said as he sat down, 'and probably never will again. I am told that the French are fanatics.'

Lavedrine watched the ball fly and spin and thump around the walls. 'I played a lot when I was young,' he said, 'but now I find it boring. I have never enjoyed the passive role of the spectator. I cannot watch other men doing something, while I sit idle.' In that instant he sprang to his feet with a curse. 'There! They've have lost another point. God in Heaven, what lying compliments we'll be obliged to pay to induce them to talk. *Merde alors!* Can they not pull off a single chase?'

Although I did not understand it, I was beginning to enjoy the ritual of the game. The server hitting the ball towards the pavilion roof, the thumping noise that it made as it bounced away, the strange trajectories that the sphere took, the desperate attempts that our two fellows made to return it.

'Any idiot could read the under-spin on that shot,' Lavedrine muttered angrily, as yet another point was lost.

'What do you intend to ask them?' I said, hoping to distract him.

My eyes were on the two young men who interested us. They glistened with sweat, their faces tense. They were speaking together in whispers, one of them having gone to retrieve the ball from the far corner where it had landed as they lost another point.

'The same thing that I asked Lecompte,' he replied. 'He refused to answer me ... Damnation, another point! I went to see him this morning, and told him of the finding of the corpse of Grangé, but I couldn't get a word out of him. His throat may be damaged, but his hearing is not. He can say yes and no. You read those reports last night, I take it? They all belong to the same regiment. They were friends. I cannot believe that Lecompte knew nothing of what Grangé may have been up to on the other bank of the river, and why he ended up in that abandoned house.'

'A closing of the ranks,' I said, my eyes moving left, right, then left again, as a cry of momentary victory exploded from the throats of the two men that Lavedrine intended to interrogate, and a burst of applause erupted from a section of the spectators.

'If that is the case, there may be others involved.'

'Is that why they are not telling you the truth? Do you include Layard in the conspiracy?'

Another burst of applause greeted a spectacular parry.

'I include everyone. Even you, Stiffeniis. You've told me very little about this woman, Emma Rimmele.'

Had I been struck in the chest by the cork ball, the effect could hardly have been more painful: I gasped for breath, my heart seemed to stop. I had not expected to hear the name of Emma Rimmele. Not in that moment, nor in that place. In Marienburg, I had made a conscious effort to put her out of my mind. As if, by doing so, I could hide her away from everyone else, especially Serge Lavedrine. Then again, we were deep inside Marienburg Castle. Two officers had been killed, another had been wounded. Lavedrine had voiced his suspicion that there might be a feud going on within the ranks of the army. He had mentioned personal vendettas which had left a trail of blood in Arles, Venice, and many other places. Now, suddenly, he raised the name of Emma Rimmele, as if she had some role in the conspiracy.

'I've told you everything,' I said, my tongue as rough as sandpaper.

'It is very little, given that the first victim was found in the well of her garden. Don't you think you ought to have unearthed a great deal more on her account?'

'It is not her house,' I said, instinctively rising to Emma's defence. 'She arrived in Lotingen a short time ago ...'

'I was thinking of the stories that people tell about her.'

I forced myself to look at him. He was watching the game as if it concerned him more than any strange Prussian story possibly could. 'Superstition is a terrible thing,' I said. 'It turns the tongues of ignorant people into slashing blades and piercing nails. No-one is safe against it. Fraulein Rimmele is a stranger in Lotingen; her ways are not *their* ways. Her appearance is … eccentric. The accusations I have heard are nothing more than slander. Her arrival in town with a coffin on the roof of the coach did not win her friends. But I see nothing which would induce me to accuse her of not one, but *three* murders.'

He turned and looked at me. His clear blue eyes held mine for a moment, then they shifted to my neck, as if he were looking for some remaining sign of the fading marks in the vicinity of my collar. His left eyebrow curved upwards in an ironic fashion which was characteristic of him.

'You know nothing. Not even where she comes from. Did she tell where this country estate of theirs is located? When you were reporting to Claudet, I remember thinking that you had barely scratched the surface. Did she avoid your questions, or did she employ some other … strategy?' He tilted his head and peered more closely at my neck.

'Why are you asking me now?'

'I am whistling in the wind, Stiffeniis. The investigation of the murders in Lotingen was in your hands in that moment.' He waved his hand emptily in the air. 'Who can say why we wish to know so little of the people who perturb us most? Perhaps we are afraid to think that they hold us, somehow, in their power.'

I turned back to the game, as if it truly interested me. 'I thought you said that the reason for these killings would be found within the ranks of the French army? Isn't that what you told General Layard? Now, instead, you harp on about Lotingen, pointing an accusing finger at Emma Rimmele.'

'We'll sit through the tedium of this dull game,' he growled, 'until the time is ripe to ask these men what they know about the behaviour of officers in their regiment. But I can never forget that we are also looking for a link connecting Marienburg to Lotingen.'

My temper broke forth in a rush. 'You wish to lay your hands on my investigation in my town.'

I felt his breath hot upon my cheek. His face was so close to mine that I could not turn to face him and retain my dignity. I froze in profile, eyes fixed on the players on the right of the net, while he hissed into my ear. 'Having seen the corpse of Grangé and read those reports, don't try to tell me that there is no connection. The wounds are identical. There is a link, Stiffeniis, and I will find it!'

I stared ahead, the game forgotten.

There would be no shifting him. And yet, I believed more strongly than ever that Lotingen and Marienburg were two distinct and separate cases, and that the victims were equally distinct and different.

'To sustain your theory,' I said, 'you've got nothing but vulgar superstition in the form of vampires.'

He chuckled softly. 'Don't give me that, Hanno Stiffeniis. I will exclude no possibility from this investigation. No person either, no matter how embarrassing you may find it. I am breaking all the rules, as I hope you realise. A Prussian magistrate in a French barracks? It will be the end of me if I fail. That's how far *I* am prepared to go. You, instead, have backed down, failing to make exhaustive enquiries about a witness for reasons that I prefer not to speculate about. Damn your embarrassment! You are not impartial, and it clouds your judgement. You guard your secrets as if you were the subject of the investigation. I …'

The rest of what he had to say was drowned by cheering. The game was over, the men he wished to speak with had been defeated. He punched me lightly on the arm and leapt to his feet. 'Come, Stiffeniis, the waiting is over. See if you can find something positive to say about the way that they were playing. We must unglue the tongues in this place.'

He had spoken in the plural. As if together we might enter into the confidence of those young men by means of shallow compliments. Frankly, I did not understand what he expected of me. A moment before, he had been critical of how I had conducted the murder investigation in Lotingen. Now, he wanted to involve me in the interrogation of French soldiers. If the wounded officer had refused to answer him, what could he expect from these two? How would the presence of a Prussian magistrate enable him to penetrate a barrier of French silence?

In the pavilion, discussion of the merits of the game continued passionately as money changed hands. The players disappeared from view by means of a small door at the far end of the hall. Lavedrine opened a gate and led me down onto the playing area. As I took in the immensity of the space, he laid his hand on my arm. 'Let's give them a minute or two,' he said, walking slowly towards the door. 'It is the players' dressing-room, where they wash and change.'

Lavedrine burst into the place a few minutes later, and I had no choice except to follow him. Two large brass basins were bubbling over a charcoal stove, giving off a lot of steam. Lavedrine pushed me forward with his elbow, calling out as we advanced into the steam-filled room: 'Congratulations to you all! The victors obviously, but also the losers, lieutenants Carnet and de Blaine, who worked so hard and gave the winners such a splendid game. I am certain that they'll have their sweet revenge in the very near future.'

The four players were naked, more or less. One still wore his drawers, another had a towel draped around his waist. The other two wore nothing. They were standing beside the basins, washing the sweat from their bodies, soaping their torsos and legs, massaging their stiff muscles. Their pale skins glistened in the half-light. Their faces were drawn and tired after the exertions of the game. They stared at us, then glanced among themselves.

'Who are you, monsieur?' one of the winners asked, wrinkling his brow as he took in Lavedrine's unusual garb and dangling earring. 'What are you doing in here?'

'Colonel Lavedrine,' he said lightly, looking around him with a smile, as if his name was a sufficient explanation of his presence there.

The players exchanged another look, but not a word was said. Clearly, they were surprised, whether by his name or his rank. Even so, despite their state of undress and the steamy atmosphere, they pulled themselves up and stiffened their backs, attempting to assume some semblance of military respect. Sweat trickled in gleaming trails down their faces, necks and chests.

'At ease, messieurs,' murmured Lavedrine, sitting down on a wooden bench hard up against the wall. 'I wish I could say that sporting sentiment brings me here, but that would not be the whole truth. The losers are about to be subjected to a second match of hard serves and difficult parries. You'll have to answer the questions that this Prussian magistrate, Procurator

Hanno Stiffeniis, and I would like to ask you.' He nodded his head in my direction, but he never took his eyes from those men for a single instant. 'We are investigating the murders of members of the Eleventh Hussars. Which of you belong to that regiment?'

The eyes of all four men flashed with alarm.

'We are with the Third Fusiliers, Monsieur le Colonel. Does that mean we can go?' one of the winners asked uncertainly.

'It means that you *must* go,' Lavedrine replied.

His casual dress, the rank that he claimed, the supreme disdain with which he ordered them about, had an effect on those men which was almost hypnotic. The ones who had been dismissed turned away, slipping on their trousers without worrying to dry themselves.

'Go on, get out,' he added gently.

The two men ran, picking up their boots, socks and shirts, throwing their jackets over their shoulders, bumping into one another in their hurry, stopping only to salute Lavedrine, knocking their naked heels together, before they rushed out of the door.

The other two did not move.

They were naked, clasping the cloths with which they had been cleansing their bodies to cover themselves. Water dripped and gathered in puddles around their feet. Their eyes followed Lavedrine as he stood up, stretched himself, then moved to another bench, which was just a short way away from the pair of them. I knew exactly how they felt. He had played a similar trick on me the night before. I saw the muscles tighten in their jaws, the uncomfortable bobbing of their Adam's apples.

The situation was made all the more alarming by the stiffening penis of the fellow on the right, and his useless attempts to hide it beneath the flannel that he was holding. He flushed bright red, covering his face with one hand, his sex with the other.

Lavedrine said nothing.

He sat back comfortably with his shoulders against the wall, crossing his arms as if expecting to be entertained. He was purposely intimidating the men, and his tactics were formidable. He would get what he wanted without much ado, I thought. My presence was an intentional part of his strategy. I was blocking the doorway, which was the only way in and out of that room.

'Messieurs,' he began calmly, letting the word echo around the room. 'Philippe Gaspard was murdered the other week. Henri Lecompte was attacked and almost lost his life in similar circumstances. You knew them both, of course. They are fellow officers, and you all belong to the same regiment. Another corpse was found last night. Another officer from the same regiment. Another officer that you both know. Sebastien Grangé.'

He paused, studying the reactions on their faces.

'I see you are not shocked. The news is out, as I imagined. I wonder whether you will be surprised, then, if I tell you where his body was found? Do you know the other side of the river?'

The two men stared at one another, one still clutching his genitals, though his embarrassment seemed to have collapsed. They shook their heads in unison.

'Have you never been inside the Black Bull tavern? The ale is excellent, I believe.'

Again, they moved their heads from side to side.

'Grangé's body was discovered in a small cottage close by.' He sniffed theatrically. 'You would not believe the horror of his wounds. It was not a pleasant sight. There was blood, messieurs. A river of blood. From here,' he said, touching two fingers to his neck. 'Just like Gaspard and Lecompte. And like you all, messieurs, Grangé belonged to the Eleventh Hussars. Other officers of the Eleventh will certainly die.'

He paused, and turned his gaze on me.

'That's why we are here. Myself, and Procurator Stiffeniis. It is our job to stop these killings. That's why I was sent for by your commanding officer. To save others in the regiment from the same fate. But that will depend on you, messieurs.'

He placed his hands on his knees and he sat forward.

'So, what might Grangé have been doing in a house on the wrong side of the river? And why would anyone wish to murder the officers of your regiment?'

Lavedrine joined his hands like a priest at prayer, and waited for them to speak.

The two men exchanged a look, and the man on the right spoke up. 'Grangé disappeared some time ago, Monsieur le Colonel, but no-one knew where he might have gone. Everyone in the mess believed that he had deserted, sir.'

Lavedrine half-closed his eyes. 'Carnet and de Blaine. Which one are you?'

'Alphonse Carnet, Monsieur le Colonel,' the man replied, standing stiffly to attention. This was the same man who had suffered an involuntary erection. Now, his member was limp, while his face was pale and anxious.

Lavedrine's expression was impassive, apparently indifferent, as if they were both in full dress-uniform. And yet, I thought, it could not be pleasant to stand naked, answering awkward questions, before a French colonel and a Prussian magistrate who were there to investigate the murders of your comrades-at-arms. Again, I recalled my own embarrassment the night before. Shame and subjection were evident in their readiness to answer him. They were in his power, there was no question of it.

'Desertion? Was there any reason to suspect such a thing?'

'In truth, there was,' Carnet replied without a moment's hesitation.

'Is that so?'

'De Blaine and I knew the victims,' Carnet went on. 'We also know Lecompte, though we've not seen much of him or them in the past couple of months. This fortress is not suitable for military exercises. It's too close to the town, and though there are many rooms, they are all small and cramped. Except for the *longue paume* court, of course. We move out into the country-side when it's time for military training. And yet, the fort must always be manned. Each brigade goes out in turn for three weeks. Here in Marienburg ...'

He stopped in mid-sentence and looked pointedly at me.

'You can speak freely, Lieutenant Carnet. Procurator Stiffeniis is here on the orders of General Layard,' Lavedrine lied.

Carnet nodded. 'In Marienburg, we are working on the maps, sir. Drawing up the battle plans. Here, we are collecting and collating strategic information for ... for future campaigns.'

'Go on, Carnet,' Lavedrine encouraged him. 'You had not seen much of your fellow officers before the killing started, you said. Why was that?'

'De Blaine and I came back from training a month ago, sir. Gaspard, Grangé and Lecompte were preparing to leave the fort. It was their turn—'

'Did you not see them when they returned to Marienburg?'

'Officers returning from the country are given a week's leave, monsieur. Many remain in the fortress, but others do not. We did not see them …'

He paused, and threw a sly glance towards his tennis partner.

'But?' Lavedrine put in sharply.

Carnet took a deep breath. 'But we did hear something. There was gossip in the regiment.'

'About the three of them?' Lavedrine asked quickly, leaning forward.

Carnet jerked his head in the direction of his companion. 'De Blaine told me, monsieur. I did not hear it myself.'

Lavedrine nodded. 'Good. De Blaine?'

De Blaine made a loud noise, blowing out a raspberry through his lips.

'There was talk in the mess, colonel. While they were out in the country, there was trouble in the house where they were lodging …'

'Trouble?'

'Between one of the lieutenants and the people living in the house …'

'Do you know which officer it concerned?'

De Blaine shook his head. 'No-one uses names for fear of being called to account.'

'Challenged to a duel,' added Lavedrine for my benefit.

'Might that be the cause?' I asked. If duelling had led to the deaths of two men and the wounding of a third, I would be free to return to Lotingen.

De Blaine shook his head again, and this time he laughed. 'Oh no, Herr Procurator. The one thing you can't keep secret in a regiment is a duel.'

'Who was living in that house in the country?' Lavedrine asked quickly.

De Blaine looked at me before he answered Lavedrine. 'Prussians, monsieur.'

'Their house had been requisitioned, then?'

Both men nodded, then Carnet spoke. 'Like many other houses in that area. As I told you, monsieur, the officers are sent to that area for special training. They lodge with the local people, or they camp on the land. When we heard that Philippe Gaspard had been murdered, we thought it was the work of Prussians, monsieur. And the news that Grangé's corpse was found on the other side of the river, in a place where the Prussians live, seemed to confirm what we had feared.'

Lavedrine stood up, walked across to one of the brass pots, and plunged his hand deep into the water. 'The water is now getting cold, I'm afraid,' he said, beckoning for de Blaine's towel, examining the man's naked body while drying off his hand. 'It won't do much to ease your aches and pains. You are not in pain, I hope?'

Both men opened their mouths to reply, but he was too quick for them.

'So, *if* the killers are Prussians, and *if* they had it in for those three officers, the second lieutenants of the fourth, fifth and sixth brigades, then you and the other officers have naught to fear, though you all belong to the same regiment. Is that what you think?'

Carnet and de Blaine shifted uncomfortably.

'Well?' insisted Lavedrine, rubbing his hands together as if he were cold.

The room was definitely chillier, like the water, and they were naked still. The sooner they told Lavedrine what he

311

wanted to know, the sooner their suffering would be ended. In the manual for Prussian magistrates, this sort of interrogation is known as 'goading'.

'Sh ... should we be afraid, sir?' Carnet's lips were quivering as he spoke.

Lavedrine did not reply immediately.

He stretched again, massaging the back of his neck with his fingers, closing his eyes as he did it, shifting his head, as if to demonstrate to those two men the pleasure that he took in it, while the muscles in their arms and legs were growing stiffer and stiffer. 'I think you should be very careful,' he said at last. 'I mean to say, if a Prussian attacked Lecompte, I can make no sense of the fact that he refuses to admit it. They are, Herr Procurator,' – he bowed his head to me and smiled – 'the enemy, after all. Instead, he tells me nothing of the sort. He was attacked at night, in a dark and deserted alley, by an unseen assailant. What harm would there be in saying that the attacker was a Prussian? He would win my sympathy! His reticence leads me to conclude that you should all be afraid. If there is a murderous conspiracy within the ranks, any officer who offends will pay with his life. Did those officers belong to a secret clique? A duelling or drinking club? A Masonic lodge? A group of religious fanatics? I've been doing some research this morning. More than three hundred French soldiers have died for all those reasons, and in similar mysterious circumstances.'

The two young men were shivering now, perhaps with fright. Like Lecompte, I thought, they might have been too frightened to admit what they knew.

'I suppose that it is possible, Monsieur le Colonel,' murmured Carnet.

'Gentlemen, this is not the time for tergiversation. Do you know the word?' he peered closely at them. 'I came across it first in the Italian form. According to the Great Dictionary it means "a state of being evasive". Danger hovers over you. Especially if the source of that danger is French. I will repeat the question. Do you know if those three men belonged to any military group in particular? And is it a group to which you, and the other officers in your regiment, subscribe?'

'No, monsieur. There are many groups and many different loyalties within the army. One joins or not, belongs or not, as one desires. Many men belong to a dining or a drinking circle, and quite often the members of these clubs are considered to be rivals,' de Blaine admitted in a voice which was trembling.

'This leads to scuffles, does it not?'

Neither man would answer.

Lavedrine began to laugh. 'I have served for almost twenty years in the army,' he said. 'I have no unit, no brigade, no regiment. I go wherever I am required, whenever some crime has been committed which involves the army. I am a colonel as a result of my achievements. Is there *anything* you can tell me that I have not heard already?'

'This person is a Prussian magistrate,' de Blaine protested.

'Does that prevent you from speaking? Are you afraid of him?'

Lavedrine's temper was up, or so he wanted it to appear.

I was tempted to remind them all that three Prussians had also died, and that the threat was as great on one side as it was on the other. I waited, wondering whether either man had read the newspapers, whether they would mention the murders in Lotingen.

'There are rival groups, monsieur,' de Blaine admitted at last. 'There are sometimes fights within the different groups belonging to the same regiment.'

'Fights to the death?'

I happened to be staring at their feet. I saw their toes curl inwards with the tension. Lavedrine must have seen it too. He was standing over them, almost a head taller than the shorter of the two. Was that the reason for the expression of triumph which I saw in his eyes? They were trapped, caught.

De Blaine nodded.

'There have been … accidents. When fights break out between groups, or within a regiment, that is what they call them. Accidents, colonel. You have to defend yourself with any means at hand to obtain what you want …'

'And what is that, de Blaine? What do you wish to obtain, for example?'

He strode close to the man, peering into his face.

'Well?' he said. 'What are you after?'

'A position, monsieur. Power over others. A commission, or a transfer to a … well, to a better regiment. The possibility of fighting in the Emperor's guards, rapid promotion and the spoils of war. No man advances, but he buys his way ahead. With cash, or with favours.'

In the silence, I could hear the breathing of de Blaine, the crackling of the spent wood beneath the brass tubs full of water. When the voice of Lavedrine sounded, it caused them both to jump, and I was not immune to it. 'Very good, gentlemen,' he said. 'You can get dressed now. And if it's any compensation to you, I'd say that your defeat today was a question of bad luck, rather than the superiority of your opponents. You'll have your revenge, I imagine, one way or the other.'

Lavedrine strode out of the room.

I followed him onto the playing court, which was empty now and silent.

'What do you call that technique of questioning,' I called after him, 'making them stand naked and in a position of physical discomfort until they tell you what you want to hear? As you did to me last night.'

He turned on me, and greeted me with a challenging smile.

'That was different, Stiffeniis. Last night was an accident, but this was intimidation. Then again, do you know what the greatest torture was for those two, Stiffeniis?'

I shook my head.

'Your presence,' he said. 'Standing naked before a Prussian. That's what brought them down. Now, let's see if you can work another miracle.'

Chapter 23

The hospital was a long low building in the most remote corner of the fortress.

It was more like an abandoned shed than a hospice. There was dirt, dust, and much unnecessary clutter, as if the place were rarely used. We were obliged to pass through an empty dormitory – there must have been sixty beds, each one with a bed-mat rolled on top of it, as if they expected a rush of wounded men at any moment – before we reached the room where Henri Lecompte had been confined.

Lavedrine stopped me outside the door. 'I want him to see you, Stiffeniis. I want him to feel the full weight of your presence. But I do not want him to be distracted by your voice. Unless you notice anything that I do not ...'

We entered without knocking.

'Good morning, Lecompte,' Lavedrine said brightly. 'How are you today? Found your voice, have you?'

I leant my back against the wall near the door, watching the man on the bed.

He wore a sort of bonnet made of bandages. The dressings were stained with blood, bulging out on the left-hand side where a poultice had been pressed against the wound in his neck and throat. His left eye was red, black and bloodshot. His right eye was bright blue. The tiny room stank of flesh and tar.

Somewhere, a shriek broke the silence.

It sounded very close. A moment later, there was a second cry, then a third, as if several teeth were being pulled at once. At every cry, the eyes of Henri Lecompte darted towards the door.

When Lavedrine began speaking, telling Lecompte who I was, he hardly spoke above a whisper. His look was hard, cold, menacing. I observed the effect that it had on the young man. His face was a whirling kaleidoscope of expressions. Some were due, no doubt, to pain and the discomfort of the unseen wound beneath the linen dressing; others reflected what was passing through his mind. As the interview progressed, he often stared in my direction, as if to avoid the onslaught of Lavedrine's questioning. It was clear to me that he was trying to gauge where the real danger lay. Was the greatest threat this Frenchman who looked anything but a colonel, or the silent Prussian who Lavedrine told him was a magistrate? He may have thought that I was Lavedrine's mastiff, a bulldog on a short leash, waiting for the order to attack. Or was some greater threat hanging over him, something more frightening than the danger that Lavedrine and I represented, something that Henri Lecompte had refused to confess up until that moment?

His eyes darted around the room like globules of quicksilver on a porcelain dish.

If Lavedrine's intention was to frighten the man, he had succeeded. He had begun the interrogation in classical fashion, and might have been following the guidelines of a manual written by Robespierre for the Committee of Public Safety: if the witness retreats into silence, prise him out of it, frighten the life out of him. Terrorise him. If you lack the means to make him talk, persuade the witness that you can hurt him more than whoever has convinced him to play the part of a mute in the conspiracy.

'I told you this morning,' Lavedrine snapped. 'The body of Grangé has been found. You are the only one who is still alive. Can you believe that they will leave you in peace, Lecompte? Are you sure they won't come back tonight to finish off the job?'

Lavedrine paused, tenderly massaging his throat with his hand.

It might have seemed as though the gesture was unthinking – provoked by an itch, perhaps, not meant to scare – yet Lavedrine's manner had been purposeful, contrived and callous from the moment that we entered the room. Lecompte was alone in a cell which would have seemed cramped to a Franciscan friar. Now he had to share the space with us, and Lavedrine crowded in on him.

'Sit up,' he commanded. 'This Prussian magistrate wants to hear the story from your own lips. Every word of it. And damn your throat!'

Lecompte raised himself up on his elbow, his head on one side as if his neck was painful, not saying a word, as if it were a soldier's duty to a higher rank. He must suffer the unwanted visit of a colonel, who would, eventually, talk himself to a halt, give up, go away and leave the sufferer in peace.

I slid onto a wooden chair beside the door.

There was a tiny window high up in the wall above my head, and it was open. A draught of cold air struck the top of my head, but it was not enough to dissipate the cloying smell of coal-tar in that room. The lieutenant's wounds had certainly been dressed with it, but that was not the reason for my sense of suffocation. The smell reminded me of the

318

death-room of my child. Lotte had insisted on swabbing out the nursery with coal-tar water every day for a week. I avoided going in there any more. The smell persisted in the house, as did the memories that I associated with it. I looked around me, noting the graffiti on the wall above the bed – scribbles, drawings, words both rude and desperate – made by injured men to pass the time, and leave a bit of themselves behind.

My eyes met those of Henri Lecompte.

The left side of his face was a map of jaundiced skin and dark bruises. Burst veins had drawn a delta of red lines across his cheek. And yet, the form of his face was square-cut, a well-designed chin, his nose long and straight, black hair cut short, bristling on his head. Had he celebrated his thirtieth birthday? His hands were those of an old man. They were dark with fuzzy hair, the nails cut short or broken off, with calluses on both thumbs, which he had chewed at. My impression was of a big, strong country lad who had been carried off from a prosperous French farm and deposited in the military hospice in Marien-burg. No doubt he had found opportunities in the *Grande Armée* which had not existed before the guillotine carried off half the nobles of the officer corps. He was a grasping child of the Revolution. Boys like him had risen to the top. They had defeated hardened Prussian warriors who had been trained to fight from childhood. Our men wore their hair in long plaits in the fashion favoured by Frederick the Great. This man, like many of his fellows, had no doubt hacked off those Prussian plaits as gruesome souvenirs in the calm after the battles of Valmy and Jena.

The face of a boy, but the bloodstained hands of a man.

'We have spoken with other officers,' Lavedrine went on.

'They told us of the cliques which form in the officers' mess. They spoke of duelling, jealousy, death. Can this behaviour go unpunished? French officers slaughtered like beasts by their fellows! General Layard is determined to stop whatever is going on between the men under his command.'

Lavedrine sat down on the bed next to Lecompte. 'Your first concern should be for yourself,' he said. 'You may be able to smash the enemy on the battlefield, but what can you do when the enemy wears the very same uniform? You can't always be awake. You cannot always be on your guard. They'll do to you what they have done to Grangé and Gaspard. They'll attack you when you least suspect it.'

Silence hung heavily in the room.

I watched, Lavedrine waited, but no-one said a thing.

My eyes darted instinctively towards the window and the door. It was as if a shrill wind had begun to blow. The sound was coming from the man's throat, I realised. His vocal cords had been damaged. The noise seemed to bubble and hiss before it formed itself into words.

'What did they say?' he wheezed.

'What did *who* say?' Lavedrine fired back.

'The other officers,' the wind was forced to whisper.

Lavedrine's head jerked up, and he looked hard at Lecompte, his face a pantomime of irritation. 'I am not here to report to you, lieutenant,' he sneered. 'I'm waiting for you to answer *my* questions.'

Lecompte looked at me for an instant, then his eyes lashed back to Lavedrine. Eventually, they settled on the wall. There were drawings and scrapings on the plaster, as I mentioned before. Until that moment, I had not paid much attention to them. They had been done with a bit of charcoal, and they looked like the sort of thing that a condemned man might scrawl the night before his execution.

I shifted my position to have a better view of them.

I was reminded of a chapel I had seen in a church outside Milan. There the walls were covered with *ex-voti*, which are little paintings illustrating accidents. I remembered a picture of a man crushed beneath a heavy wagon, another of a child being savaged by a wolf. Most of all, I was impressed by the miniature silver limbs which were hanging all over the chapel. Arms, legs, ears, noses. Every bit of the human anatomy. A friar had told me that the faithful left them there when they were cured of some malady through the intercession of the Virgin Mary. In the military hospital of Marienburg, the patients had left their amputated arms and legs behind them in the form of drawings.

Lecompte was staring at one image in particular.

I saw that it bore a legend: *Lec. et la bête*. A man was lying on the ground, blood spurting from his throat like a spouting whale. Over him a swirling, dark cloud floated, and what seemed to be an arm and a ripping talon emerged from it. It was not precise in any respect, and might well have been a fantasy, except for two large eyes which stared out from this malignant cloud.

Had he tried to draw his impression of the attack?

Meanwhile, Lavedrine continued with his assault.

'Have you nothing more to say?' he demanded.

Lecompte shook his head from side to side; he appeared to shudder.

'You have only recently returned to the fortress,' Lavedrine went on. 'You were at some sort of training camp in the country. Is that correct?'

Lecompte nodded, but he added nothing to the bare information.

'You, Gaspard, Grangé, and who else?'

'There were twelve of us. Not just the Eleventh. From the Fourth, as well ...'

'How long have you known Gaspard and Grangé?'

Lecompte cleared his throat, then he spat blood into a rag. 'We are Bretons. From Quimper. I ... Philippe and I were at the same school. He knew Sebastien.'

'And what of the men in the Fourth?'

'Gone, monsieur. We are cavalry. They are grenadiers. We did not mix.'

His words were mangled, not always easy to comprehend. Blood and mucus filled his mouth as he spoke, causing him to spit frequently into the rag in his hand. Lavedrine made a gesture, as if to suggest that he should speak more slowly.

'*Merci*,' Lecompte murmured.

'Do you belong to a Masonic lodge, Lecompte?'

The man managed a smile, then wiped away spittle with his rag. 'No, monsieur.'

'To a group, then?'

'My friends ...' Lecompte said slowly. 'You are an officer, monsieur, you know these things.' He clutched his hand to his throat, though it was not pain which inspired the move. The sound which issued from his mouth was stronger when he pressed. 'When the recruiters come to a town, they prefer a group of friends, a school class, brothers. One man joins, another follows. Some are forced ...' He coughed and spat again. 'Anything can happen on campaign. For good, or for bad. When a Breton bites the bullet, he bites it with his friends. We look out for each other ...'

His voice broke, and he brought up blood again.

Lavedrine turned to me. 'Have you ever been in the army, Stiffeniis?'

I shook my head.

'Living through a battle depends on many things,' he said. 'Apart from your sabre. It depends on who the commander is, the name and strength of the regiment, who gets the best tent, the thickest blanket. If you sleep well, you're ready for the battle. If you don't, you may die. Am I right, Lecompte?' He waited for the man to nod, then he went on: 'If you know one of the cooks, you'll eat more and better. Life is made of these little things on campaign. The more of those that you have, the better life is. Then again, if you are an officer, there's your career to think of.'

Lavedrine was speaking from experience, and I saw Lecompte nod his head occasionally as he listened.

'Fighting's not the only thing,' he went on. 'You could die tomorrow. You want the best of everything. If towns are being sacked, you want to be the first man entering the richest town, not bringing up the rear in some forgotten village out in the middle of nowhere. If you've got money, you can buy a place near to the general if you want to be noticed and be promoted to his staff. If the group that you belong to has power, you have power, too.'

The same tale might have been heard from the mouth of any Prussian officer. Any officer in any army in the whole of Europe. Lavedrine knew it from experience, and so did General Layard. 'Tell me about the training, Henri.'

Lecompte looked at Lavedrine uncertainly. His eyes were the bluish-grey of unpolished gunmetal.

'We were there together,' he murmured.

'And you were sent away together,' Lavedrine said quickly.

Lecompte looked away again.

'You were sent back early to Marienburg. In a word, you three were cashiered. What happened out in the country?'

Lecompte shook his head, but it did not prevent him from speaking. 'We were lodging in a big house. General Layard had chosen the place ...' His eyes turned in my direction.

'Go on,' Lavedrine encouraged him. 'Procurator Stiffeniis was in the Realm of Universal Intellect not half an hour ago. General Layard was present.'

Lecompte studied my face before he answered. 'We were sent there to learn new methods, monsieur. Methods which have come from Spain. There was a colonel there to teach us. But then ... Well, there were Prussians living in the house, monsieur. Women. And Grangé ...'

'What about him?'

'He was like a cat at night. He was onto something ...'

His eyelids flickered nervously, as if he regretted having said so much.

'Sebastien Grangé and a woman from the house?'

Lecompte was silent. Then, he seemed to come to some decision. 'We wanted to know who she was, but he just laughed. Cover for me, he said, there might be something in it for us all.'

Lecompte was showing signs of growing discomfort, growling deep in his throat, turning his head from side to side. Lavedrine jabbed his forefinger into the man's ribs.

'Something?' he asked. 'Was he talking of the woman? Of money? What?'

'He did not say, Monsieur le Colonel.' His cheeks flushed as he spoke. 'Sebastien Grangé was always a sly dog. He said that we would all gain if we played along.'

'But then he was caught,' Lavedrine put in.

'We shared a room. The commander came one night, and Grangé's bed was empty. We refused to admit where he was. The three of us were sent back to Marienburg the following morning. After we got back, he disappeared for good. I don't know where he went.'

Lavedrine looked at me with an interrogative air, as if he expected me to supply the answers to the questions which continued to puzzle him. I stared back, miming my own state of confusion and ignorance.

'Was no-one punished?' Lavedrine asked him.

Lecompte raised his hand to touch his wound. 'I got this,' he said. 'Gaspard got killed. And now, Grangé ...'

Lavedrine stared at him for some time in silence.

'Who attacked you, Lecompte?' His voice was a low hiss, not unlike the damaged voice of the officer.

Lecompte leant forward, pointing to the drawing I had previously noticed on the wall. 'You won't believe me,' he complained. 'I've told you twice. I tried to draw what I had seen after you spoke to me the first time.'

I took my album from my shoulder-bag, slipped the stick of graphite from its silver tube, and began to make a copy of the drawing which Henri Lecompte had made. He was no artist. For myself, it was the work of but a minute or two. And while I was drawing, I heard the voice of Lavedrine.

'What *is* it, Lecompte? That's what I want to know. This *thing* ... The person who attacked you has a name. I want to know if it belongs to someone in this regiment.'

Phlegm bubbled in Lecompte's throat, causing him to cough and spit more blood. 'The regiment of Hell!' he spluttered. 'That fury struck so fast. It was like a canister of chain-shot. It hit me in an instant, going at my throat. I am a trained soldier, Monsieur le Colonel, but it hit me before I knew it.'

'You've told me this before,' Lavedrine said flatly.

As I rubbed my finger over the figure of the assailant, blurring what must have been a large black cloak and hood into a voluminous black cloud from which a hand emerged, I wondered why Lecompte was insisting on repeating a version of the facts which Lavedrine refused to believe.

I stopped drawing, and I looked from one to the other. Lavedrine was peering at the soldier, while Lecompte's eyes remained fixed on the image on the wall. What had this to do with Lotingen? What had attacks on a bunch of scheming French soldiers to do with the murders of innocent Prussian civilians? And why, the instant that Lavedrine insisted on naming names, did Prussian demons rise up to complicate everything? Lecompte was French, and probably had no idea what a vampire was, yet he spoke of furies and devils.

In that instant, my sketch-book began to slide from my knee.

I looked up from the page. Lecompte was leaning out of the bed, his hand stretched out, grasping at the album. I glanced questioningly at Lavedrine, but he was watching the witness like a hawk. Lecompte's fingers just managed to reach the page, though he could not wrest the album from my hands.

'What is it?' I asked him.

Lecompte did not reply.

Suddenly, Lavedrine stood up, tore the album from my hands, and passed it to Lecompte. He turned the album around as he did so, showing Lecompte a sketch which I had made some days before. That was what had Lecompte's attention, not the copy that I was making of his drawing on the wall.

'Who is she?' Lavedrine asked me.

'One of the witnesses,' I replied.

Lavedrine grunted something, turning back to the soldier. 'Is this what you wanted to see, Lecompte?' he asked, glancing from the picture in the man's hand to the drawing that Lecompte had made upon the wall.

The soldier was staring at my drawing, so absorbed in it that saliva dribbled from the side of his mouth again. With a loud and violent suck, he tried to halt the flow, then pulled on the dressing which covered his wound, using it to wipe the side of his mouth before it dripped onto my picture.

'If I had been able to draw like you, monsieur, I would have been able to help the colonel. Those eyes remind me of the face I saw that night.'

'May I see it?' Lavedrine asked, taking my album from the lieutenant's hands, studying it attentively for a moment, turning it around, holding the drawing up for me to see.

I stared into the eyes of Emma Rimmele.

'Don't say a word, Stiffeniis,' he warned me.

Minutes later, we left Henri Lecompte.

I stepped into the corridor first, while Lavedrine was closing the door of the room.

As he turned, I raised my left elbow, pushing it hard into his chest, forcing him back against the wall, grasping with my right hand at his throat. I began to squeeze, while he cried out in surprise. I pressed in upon him all the more.

'What was that supposed to mean?' I hissed. 'You are mad, Lavedrine. Do you hope to clear the name of French conspirators at the expense of a Prussian woman? She has been falsely accused in Lotingen, and now you think you can take advantage of the fact. Is this the result of your criminal science? Tales, stories, superstition? Anything, so long as it keeps the French general happy?'

I pressed harder at his throat and felt elation, though I saw no panic in his eyes.

'God help you, Stiffeniis,' he seethed. 'She has pierced your heart, and sucked out your soul.'

I relaxed my grip a fraction.

'I accuse no-one,' he said. 'I simply passed your album to Lecompte. That picture caught his eye. I make nothing of his words, vague as they were. It was a stratagem to make him talk, and nothing more. Better than the vague uncertainties that he has told me up to now.'

I stared into his eyes. 'Lecompte has seen what you wanted him to see. A woman. Had you shown him a picture of his mother, he'd have sworn that she was his attacker. Don't make the mistake of passing on that information to Layard. I'll not forgive it.'

'You let Emma Rimmele tell you what she wanted,' he hissed. 'She left her mark on you, and you are no more than her branded slave. Let go of me, damn you!'

I took my hand away from his throat, but I did not release him.

'Legend says that vampires hypnotise their victims,' he went on. 'Is that what Emma Rimmele has done to you? I told you once that you conceal the abyss within yourself. Not even Helena has seen the real you, Hanno Stiffeniis. Do not let your demon out, I warn you. It will be the end of you, and anyone who is close to you.'

We stood face-to-face in open defiance.

'Next time you try to strangle me,' he said, 'I will not hesitate to defend myself.'

328

I dropped my hands, and took a step back.

'I do not hide from the dark side of my soul,' he said, and stepped towards me with a smile, thrusting a small pistol into my face. 'I will shoot you. It would not trouble me in the least. I could have shot you a moment ago, or at any time since you laid your hands on me. I will do as any Frenchman would, if some fool Prussian dares to assault him.'

He lowered the pistol, then slipped it back into his pocket.

'Enough of this nonsense, Stiffeniis! We must push hard on the door that Henri Lecompte has partly opened up for us.'

Chapter 24

The officers in the fortress had been sent to Kirchenfeld.

The country estate was about ten miles out of Marienburg. A tall gate marked the entrance from the high road. A tree-lined avenue ran through fields which lay fallow, or had been given over to grazing. No cows or sheep were evident, which did not surprise me. The French have eaten everything in Prussia since they invaded it. The countryside is in a miserable state as a result.

Lavedrine jumped down from the carriage, and shaded his eyes from the sun.

'Every building in this Prussia of yours, be it a cathedral or a pig-sty, looks as if it was made to withstand a full-pitch battle,' he observed.

I was looking at the house, and did not answer him.

Built originally as a fortified farmhouse, the moat surrounding it was now dry and lush with long grass. A narrow bridge led across to an entrance gate, above which a coat of arms had been sculpted in stone. Two storeys high, the interior was lit by tall latticed windows on the ground floor, smaller windows on the floor above. The roof slates were green with moss, and swathes of darker ivy climbed over the red-brick façade. At some point in its history, square towers had been added to the four corners of the edifice. The architecture spoke of compromise: a desire to amass the produce of the country on the one hand, the need to defend the contents against marauders on the other. The genteel pretensions of the owners – I assumed that they had been *Junkers* – was expressed in the form of a white clock-tower which stood above the gate. The clock had stopped at five twenty-five. A year ago, perhaps, or a hundred years before that.

It was not yet midday as Lavedrine and I began to cross the bridge.

'General Layard appreciates our obsession with defence,' I replied. 'French is spoken here nowadays, I believe.'

Lavedrine chuckled, though I had meant no joke. 'The general thought you might be critical,' he said.

'He was upset at the idea of a Prussian seeing French troops preparing for their next important campaign,' I replied.

Lavedrine laughed aloud. 'He's more concerned about the fact that *I* am here,' he said. 'Two of his men have been murdered. He fears that I'll create more problems than I am able to resolve.'

As he spoke, I rubbed the lobe of my left ear between my finger and thumb.

'No earrings today?' I asked him. 'Is that to avoid upsetting the troops?'

He nodded. 'I know how French soldiers think,' he said. 'They are the most superstitious men alive. They see omens of disaster in everything. If questioned by an officer sporting the image of St Peter's church, they would think immediately of the Inquisition, and clam up!'

'Will the sight of a Prussian make them happier?'

'They'll be on their guard in any case, take my word for it.' He stopped and sniffed the air like a hare. 'What is this?'

Looking back along the length of the bridge, a troop of men

were approaching quickly along the gravel road. They formed a tight formation running four abreast, a column of five rows, twenty men in all, their boots thudding on the pebbles. They were naked from the waist up. No, not quite naked, I saw, as they drew closer. They were wearing cross-belts, each man was hugging a musket to his chest. Bayonets, trench-tools, water-bottles, powder horns clashed and dangled from their waists, and on his back each man was carrying a pack which may have weighed a ton. Their faces were twisted masks of pain. They streamed with sweat as if they had just come out of a river. They sucked in air, and gasped it out again, as if each breath would be their last.

Lavedrine and I stood back to let them charge through.

The last man passed. He carried no pack or musket, and wore a vest and braces. Lavedrine caught him by the arm and spun him around, holding him fast. 'I am here on the orders of General Layard,' he said. 'I need to speak to the commanding officer. Are you the man?'

The officer gasped and gulped for air.

'I wish … I were, monsieur. You'll find … him … in the inner court.'

Lavedrine let him go, and the officer ran off, accelerating to catch up with his men.

We followed after them, passing through the gate.

'Oh no!' muttered Lavedrine under his breath.

The half-naked men were stacking their muskets, putting aside their bayonets and their equipment, emptying out the rucksacks, which contained large stones. The pile of stones was quickly growing. Each man had been forced to run with a dozen of these heavy weights on his back. In the far corner, a group of men were watching a demonstration which involved two of the soldiers, one of whom was evidently trying to slit his fellow's throat. It would not take much, I thought, to convert the exercise into a tragedy. On the right, a dozen men had formed up a circle surrounding two of their number, who were wrestling, pushing and pulling, backwards and forwards, as each man tried to gain some advantage over his opponent. Such things seen in a street or at a fair would have caused furore and excitement. Here, instead, everything was solemn, serious. Silent, too, except for the stones crashing down on the cobbles.

'What's wrong?' I murmured.

Lavedrine raised his chin in the direction of a man standing on a covered dais who was watching everything that was going on. Legs apart, arms folded across his chest, he was not in uniform. He wore a jacket of cream-coloured jute, the roughness of the weave contrasting with the elegant cut and closeness of the fit, which adhered to his body like a tight sheath. His shoulders seemed immense, while his chest and abdomen were as narrow as a girl's at court confined inside a whalebone corset.

A stern, forbidding look was accentuated by a square chin and a prominent nose. His hair was as white as snow, cut short on his head, a forward quiff sitting up as stiff as a brush. His eyes were black and piercing, darting glances here and there as he watched what was happening in the courtyard. Once, he must have been strikingly handsome. Now, his features had hardened into granite. His bony brow and hollow cheeks were a mass of scar tissue and bulging folds where some approximating surgeon on a battlefield had stitched him back together.

'I should have guessed we'd meet again,' Lavedrine said.

His voice was low and aimed in my direction, yet I would have sworn that the strange fellow's ears pricked up at the sound of it. His eyes slid round to take us in, though he did not shift his head an inch. His gaze settled on Lavedrine like a cat before it pounces.

'Colonel Jacques Massur,' Lavedrine called out loud, pacing forward to meet him. 'I thought that you'd be lying on a hot rock somewhere, laying clever ambushes for Spanish rebels!'

Jacques Massur opened his mouth in what may have been a smile, or a sneer. His upper lip had been slit in the centre, almost to the base of his nose, exposing too much of his yellow teeth. The wound had healed before it could be decently sewn up.

'Lavedrine! Still sticking your tongue up criminals' arses, are you?'

He spoke in staccato bursts, as if the damage done to his lip had been inflicted on his tongue as well, some words poorly formed, some too long, others too short. And as I followed Lavedrine across the courtyard, I saw the reason for the fixity of Massur's gaze. His upper eyelids had been cut away, and had healed as strips of lumpy gristle which barely managed to hold his eyeballs in place.

Lavedrine jumped onto the dais and held up his hand. There was nothing tender in the gesture. He might have been warning a wild beast not to come any closer.

'Someone is poking holes in the throats of the officers in Marienburg. It happened shortly after they left here. You've heard the news, I suppose?'

Massur's head jerked in my direction. 'Who's your friend?'

Lavedrine told him, and I was subjected to rude scrutiny.

'Only a heathen such as you would mix with men who've killed our comrades,' was Massur's acid comment.

Lavedrine nodded. 'I don't give a toss,' he said. 'I'll mix with anyone who can help me solve a crime. Even you, Massur.'

Colonel Massur let out a sigh. 'I hate to think that we are equals, Lavedrine. I've been chopped to pieces in the service of my country, while you have never held a sword, I think. You're as pretty as ever!'

Lavedrine stepped close. 'I tried my sword at Aboukir,' he said quietly. 'Once was enough for me. Since then, I've used my brains.'

'I place my faith in my balls,' the other replied, taking a step forward.

Standing face to face, I could see that they were equals, and not in height alone. They both wore fashionable clothes, though Lavedrine was the dandy of the pair. The originality of their dress was as much a coded ensign as the uniform that they both chose not to wear. They poked sharp words at each other the way that duellists probed with rapiers.

All around them the wrestling and the throat-slitting went on without interruption, while I stood beneath the dais wondering what to do with myself. Did they hate one another? Was their rivalry inspired by mutual admiration? Was it a combination of those two things?

I waited for a moment of silence.

'Who is your friend, Lavedrine?' I said, trying to ape the disdain which Colonel Massur had directed at me.

Lavedrine turned to me, eyebrows raised in surprise. With a smile, he turned back to Massur. 'That's a pair of Prussian balls for you, Jacques! I do not judge a man by his birth or nationality. I count the vital organs that he has, or does not have, as the case may be. Brain, liver, heart, balls. Some Prussians have them in the right place, too.'

'Jacques Massur is a living legend,' he said, turning his eyes to me. 'He has trained more men to survive than you have eaten apples. Equally, he has killed more Frenchmen by his training methods than he has butchered enemies on the battlefield. He has frightened the life out of every man who has ever passed through his hands. With one or two exceptions, anyway. We are here ...'

Massur's shoulder cannoned into Lavedrine's back as he leapt down from the dais and charged at the soldiers. I don't believe that he had heard a word of Lavedrine's panegyric. His gaze had never shifted from the soldiers. He charged across the cobbles, shrugging off his jacket, letting it fall to the ground as he burst through the ring of watchers. One man was on the ground, another leaning over him, holding a bayonet at the first man's throat.

'You,' he growled at the man who was evidently the victor.

The man looked up, eyes bright with anticipation, expecting praise from his commanding officer.

'Let him go,' Massur growled. 'Now, try it on me, and let's see the colour of your stuffing. Get back,' he ordered the man at his shoulder, jabbing with his elbow, sending the man coughing and spewing to the ground. 'Well, rabbit, what are you waiting for?'

The man on the floor scuttled out of the way as Massur began to circle like a crab around the man who was armed with the bayonet. The standard-issue blade is three feet long. While not the most manageable of weapons, it is the most effective in holding an enemy at bay. Massur feinted to the left, took two steps forward, wrapped his forearm around his opponent's throat, and had him on the ground in a flash. The blade was ripped from the man's hand in an instant, and, a moment later, Massur was drawing it slowly across his opponent's throat. The soldier's eyes were wide with terror and surprise.

'What is he expecting?' Massur asked the watching soldiers. His mouth came close to the ear of the fellow on the ground. 'He thinks I'm going to slit his gullet. Right?' He shook his head, looking around slowly, totally in control of all of them. 'Wrong! It's a total waste of time. You want to make him scream so much, he terrifies the life out of his mates. Like this,' he said, moving the blade slowly, pressing the point down into the man's flesh, scraping it over his chin until it reached his mouth. If Massur's expression was any indication, there was a definite possibility that this man was going to end up with a scar. 'You can open him up from here,' he said, pressing the point down near the mouth, then moving it up towards the eye, 'to here. Then again, you can start from the nose ...' the bayonet point was now inside the fellow's nostril. 'Just slide it in, the slower the better, and keep on pushing 'til the point tickles his brain. Or you can go from ear,' he moved the blade again, '... to ear. The opportunities are endless.'

Had he been subjected to some similar torture? His face bore all the traces. Then again, I thought, he had survived. And having freed himself, what had he done to the man who had attacked him?

'You kill one, but you tell the rest what they are in for.'

In a single movement, he was on his feet. He tossed the bayonet to the soldier who had won the tussle, and was now as terrified as the man who had lost it. 'Five minutes to catch your breath, then we start again,' he said, dismissing them.

As Massur turned to Lavedrine, I saw that his chest was

heaving up and down, in and out, in rapid movements. His pale face was bright red. He may have felt hot, for he pulled at the ribbons on his shirt, which fell open.

I looked once, and could not look away.

The right side of his chest was encaged inside a wicker corset. I could see the straps which held it to his body. He appeared to have lost half of his chest and ribcage. Beneath his shoulder blade, a dark chasm disappeared inside the wicker basket. It was like red wine against his pale skin.

Massur looked at me, and he grimaced. 'The Spaniards taught me much about the knife and its uses,' he said. 'I had to pay for the lesson, though.' He beat the flat of his hand against the wicker cage. 'He carried off one of my lungs, that dago did. He won't be carrying off any more.'

He turned to Lavedrine. 'What are you two doing here?'

'Two officers are dead in Marienburg. Their throats were slit. A third man got away with his life. Those three men had been here recently—'

'Grangé and the others?'

'You sent them back to Marienburg fortress before their training was over. Why? That's what I want to know.'

'Must we talk in front of him?' Massur had turned his shoulders on me.

'I'm afraid we must,' Lavedrine replied. 'Stiffeniis is investigating the murders with me. General Layard knows, and approves.'

When it served his purpose, Lavedrine treated me like a brother. If my presence made Massur uncomfortable, so much the better. It was the two of us against Massur. At the same time, I realised that a single word would reduce me in an instant to the ranks of a humble, conquered Prussian once again.

338

'What's a Prussian got to do with dead Frenchmen?' hissed Massur.

Lavedrine rubbed his nose. 'The dead in Marienburg are French officers. But other people have died in a similar manner in Lotingen, Prussian civilians. We believe that the killer is the same person, and we are looking for the motive.'

Massur's black eyes stared fixedly at Lavedrine. The sky above was cloudy now, but any source of light must have been painful for him. That was why he had constructed that covered dais, I imagined. It was a dark cavern from which he could observe his men. Why did he not wear coloured glasses? The answer was obvious. Would he hide those reptilian orbs from the men that he hypnotised and menaced with them? His power lay in the evidence of his mutilations. Would any soldier dare to disobey him?

'What connection can there be?' Massur murmured. His head shifted a fraction, his eyes fixed on me. 'What's your opinion, Prussian magistrate?'

I placed myself at Lavedrine's shoulder, advancing no further.

'In Lotingen, the Prussians blame the killings on a vampire,' I said. Like Lavedrine, I wanted to disconcert Massur.

'Vampire?' he said, breathing out the word in a sibilant hiss. 'I don't believe in those. Do you, Lavedrine? I've never worked out whether you do believe in the supernatural, or whether you use it to scandalise others. And what about you, Herr Procurator Stiffeniis?'

I was caught in the crossfire between the two of them.

'This is Prussia,' I said. 'The people here believe in vampires. I have seen the corpses in my hometown. Now, having seen a corpse in Marienburg, and spoken to a survivor, I know ...'

'What?' Massur's head jerked in my direction.

'That they were killed in the same manner,' I said emphatically. 'I know what happens in Prussia when there is an outbreak of vampirism, Monsieur le Colonel. But in Marienburg, inside a French fortress, when a French soldier's throat is ripped open, I am in … *terra incognita*.'

Lavedrine stepped up to Massur. 'Forget the vampires, Jacques,' he said. 'Let's talk about those three officers, instead. Why did you send them back early? What had they done?'

'Grangé, Gaspard, Lecompte.' Massur pronounced the names slowly. He might have been spitting shards of glass off his tongue. 'I heard what had happened to them. I cannot say that I am upset by the news.'

'What did they do?' Lavedrine insisted.

Massur looked down at the cobbles. 'They were everything that an officer shouldn't be,' he said. 'They were the dregs. Insubordinate, disrespectful, indolent. Cowardly hyenas ready to feed on what the lion leaves behind. A vile example to other men, officers of the worst sort. Do you need to hear more?'

'Did you follow them to Marienburg and punish them?'

Massur's lip curled. He let out a puff that may have been a laugh. 'I haven't been outside this house for the last three months. I did not murder them, if that is what you are thinking. I would have done, given half a chance. I could have run them ragged, or let the bayonet slip in combat, but they weren't game for risks. They covered for each other, lied for one another. They were Bretons, and rich enough. The French army stinks of preferment these days …' He shrugged his shoulders, and he glared at me. 'I bet the Prussian army's just the same. Ranks bought and sold like sausages and beer. Then, their masters wait for Jacques Massur to turn them into real

340

soldiers. A dead fop is no damned use to any man. Those three were too far gone. They'd sold their souls, left their boot-marks on the shoulders of their fellows.' He shook his head, and he spat. 'Things are changing, Lavedrine. For us, and for the Empire. The *Grande Armée* is getting set to face an enemy that fights according to a different set of rules. Accept those rules, or you'll go down. Spain was a lesson in pure terror, believe me. Lots of nations have learnt from them. No holds barred, that's the new motto. *Guerrilla* is a very different thing from *guerra*.' His gaze settled on me, then drifted back to Lavedrine. 'We don't need men to hold a square, or march in columns. We need to move like wolves in the woods at night. The Russian wolves are sharpening their claws out there on the steppe.'

His breathing came in fits, his one lung pumping like a bellows, as he gave emphasis to the words that poured from his mouth.

'What did they do, Massur?' Lavedrine's voice was soft and gentle, as if he wished to calm the other man down. 'You still haven't told me.'

'There was a Prussian family living here,' he said, and he hesitated for a moment. 'This house was theirs. We left them half of it, and I did my best to keep the two sides well apart. Most of the large houses have been requisitioned in this part of the country. Sometimes everyone manages to get along, but in other places there have been squabbles, problems. Deaths ... General Layard was insistent on that point. He didn't want any trouble. Only officers were sent to me for training. But then, those three arrived ... I always line them up the minute they come, and I tell them straight: leave the Prussians in peace. Minimum contact. None at all, if possible.'

'What happened, Massur?'

There was no mistaking Lavedrine's tone of voice. It was an order.

'Sebastien Grangé was fucking one of the Prussian women,' the colonel said, his voice tense with rage. 'I don't know how he met her, where, or when, but he managed to dodge the guards. On more than one occasion. He left his quarters after lights-out, and the other two covered up for him.'

Lavedrine was silent for a moment. 'Isn't it what soldiers do?' he said. 'Isn't it part of their informal training? They carry off the heart of one of the enemy, and even better if there's a baby left behind.'

Massur's eyes flashed with anger. Until that moment, he had seemed immune to Lavedrine's provocations. This time, I thought Massur might physically attack him.

'I am not here to teach men how to rape,' he snapped.

Different thoughts went flashing through my mind.

'Is rape what we are talking about?' I asked.

Massur spoke to Lavedrine, ignoring me. 'In a place like this, there isn't much room for Romeo and Juliet. In any case, the rest of the company soon heard about it. They saw the way those three behaved on exercises. Their hearts weren't it. They never listened. They didn't try. Then, the others started taking the piss. There were arguments, fights. Someone would have ended up getting killed. I was told that they'd been boasting about it.'

'About having a woman?'

Massur's lip curled up in a sneer. 'That was only half of it, Monsieur Procurator. Grangé claimed that he had found a way to lay his hands on cash by means of the girl. A fortune, it was said. Truth or lies, I've no idea.'

'What happened to this woman?' I asked. 'Where is she now?'

'She ran away. I cannot help you there,' he said. 'The serfs left soon afterwards, as well. There's no-one ...' He made a loud clicking sound with his tongue, then called for his adjutant, a lieutenant named Lebrun. 'There is one mad old hag who is still living down in the cellars in the west wing. God knows why! She won't be shifted. Not 'til we decide to throw her out ...'

My throat was dry, my voice cracked.

'This young woman,' I said. 'Do you know her name? Or the name of the family that was living here?'

Massur looked at Lavedrine, and he shook his head.

'It was not a good idea to bring a Prussian here,' he said.

He turned to face me once again. 'She was the only daughter of the owner of the Kirchenfeld estate. Her name was Emma Rimmele.'

Chapter 25

'We still call it the Prussian zone,' said Lieutenant Lebrun.

We were skirting the banks of the moat, going around the house towards the gate on the other side.

'Once the bedding arrives, we'll occupy that part of the building, as well.'

He hesitated for a moment, then offered an opinion.

'It's all very well for officers and men to drill together under Colonel Massur,' he said, 'but you can't mix ranks where lodgings are concerned. The troops are forced to sleep out under canvas. We need the space. We should have got rid of those Prussians from the start.'

The tents of the French soldiers were laid out to the south and east like a siege force. The French were closing in on the house from all sides. Beyond the encampment, at the foot of a slight rise cloaked in woods, I saw a cemetery and a chapel enclosed by an iron fence. I could see the damage that had been done there. Two or three crosses lacked their arms, a sculpted angel had lost its wings and head. I recalled what Emma had said, the anger in her voice.

Our family graveyard … Procurator Stiffeniis. They shoot at the crosses to calibrate their muskets.

I saw the proof of what she had told me. Emma had not lied to me. She had lived there, the French had come, and she had carried off her father and her mother's coffin to Lotingen.

With the family gone, there was no need to isolate the west wing. There was nothing to stop a lone French wolf going into the Prussian zone. All the lambs had fled. Indeed, I thought, the French had done what any man does when he takes possession of a house: they had crushed and killed every spider, mouse and rat. They had disinfested the house of Prussians, and driven off the Rimmele family like vermin. Only one Prussian remained. An *old* hag, as Massur had specified, a woman that no-one would care to rape.

I stopped walking, caught my breath, trying to control my anger. Lavedrine was walking ahead of me, but he stopped, turned to me, and asked, 'Are you all right?' He took a step or two in my direction, eyeing me as if he were a doctor, and I showed signs of some dangerous illness.

'Quite well,' I snapped, holding up my hand to keep him off.

'Let's speak with this witness, then get out of here,' he murmured. 'I dislike the place as much as you appear to do.'

After crossing a narrow wooden bridge, we entered by a low arch. The inner courtyard was dominated in the centre by a large stone well. Lebrun threw open a door on the left, and invited us to enter.

'This was the Rimmele kitchen. It will be our new mess-hall,' he announced.

I imagined taking his throat between my fingers and squeezing it until his face turned purple. Then, I looked around me. The room was large and almost bare. A long table beneath the windows, a wooden bench on either side of it. A stone sink, a water-jug and pump stood in the corner of the room. A small dresser was pushed up against the wall, a row of pewter beakers dangling from hooks. A huge stone fireplace occupied the entire end-wall.

It was similar in every respect to the Prior's House in Lotingen.

If the Schuettler brothers had appeared, I would not have been surprised. Indeed, had I seen that room without seeing anything else, I might have guessed the name of the owner. I could imagine Emma Rimmele moving around that room, opening the dresser, taking out a jug of wine and two beakers. I saw myself sitting on one of the benches, while she perched on the table-top beside me. I could smell her skin, feel her breath on my cheek as she bent close. I felt the pressure of her lips on mine, the gentle pinch of teeth against my flesh …

'There isn't much to see.'

Lavedrine's complaint echoed round the room.

The day the body of Angela Enke was found in the well, Emma had told me how she had come to Lotingen, and why she had rented the Prior's House under the watchful eyes of the Schuettler brothers. The house was large, unmanageable, almost bare. It was, she said, almost identical to the house that they had left behind, the house that belonged to her father and his ancestors. She had chosen the Prior's House to avoid pitching her father deeper into mental confusion.

Emma Rimmele had not lied to me.

'Where is this woman?' Lavedrine asked.

'Below, monsieur.' Lebrun pointed to a narrow door. 'She barricaded herself down there when the family left. We hardly see her. We call her the Ancestral Ghost …'

Lavedrine cut him off in mid-sentence. 'Has anyone questioned her?'

'You'd have to catch her first.'

Lavedrine opened the door that Lebrun had indicated. A window-slit lit a tiny landing and the beginning of a narrow, stone staircase which spiralled down into darkness. 'Is there no way of calling for her to come up?' he asked.

'We'd have to drag her up by force, monsieur. If that's what you want …'

'We'll go down together, Lavedrine,' I said, stepping through the doorway. 'The lieutenant can wait for us here.'

'I'd never go down there,' Lebrun replied. 'Except on the colonel's orders.'

'And Massur did not give that order,' Lavedrine growled back at him, and began to follow me down the stairs.

I thought I knew what was *down there*, as Lebrun had so mysteriously described it. These rooms are a common feature of many old Prussian country houses. There was such a place in my father's house on the family estate in Ruisling. My brother, Stephan, and I had gone there once, and once had been enough. There was an unforgettable smell, and I made it out the instant that I stepped into the stairwell.

The staircase was lit by slits which were covered with iron gratings. They were intended to let in air rather than light. As we went down, the air grew colder, and that, of course, was what it was supposed to do. At last we stepped into a room which had been hacked out from the solid rock on which the foundations of the house were laid. The floor was a crazy-paving of broken tiles of different sizes, shapes and colours. Three low arches gave strength to the structure, and they had been picked out in a curve of carefully aligned red bricks, like the ones from which the outer walls of the dwelling were made. A lighted lantern was hanging from a hook beneath the central archway. The stone walls had been recently whitewashed, a clear sign that the room had been in use and that it was regularly maintained.

'Is anyone there?' Lavedrine called out in German.

There was no echo, and no reply.

Beyond the arch to the right there was a bed, a table and chair, a brown ceramic stove. I walked across, touched it with my hand, and found that it was still hot. 'This is where she lives,' I said, noting a narrow cupboard and a small chest of drawers against the wall.

As I turned towards Lavedrine, who had gone to explore at the other end of the cellar, I stopped short, and caught my breath. Above the arch, there was a fresco. The painting was faded but still distinct. It represented a coat of arms – a central shield, a knight's helmet above, a laurel crown below. But it was the motif above it which held my gaze. I had seen it before – smaller, less precise, and in the form of a squiggle or a seal – on a document that I had found in the archive in Lotingen. There, it had been tiny, almost insignificant. Here, it was the single focal point of what I took to be the Rimmele coat of arms. It was the Greek letter *pi*, and, beneath the device, an elegant legend written in Italian ran from one end of the arch to the other: *Tre imperfettibile è degno archetipo di quella serie che svela, volgendo circolare, mirabile relazione*. It was, I guessed, one of those ancient conundrums, a mathematical puzzle referring to the perfect number, three. Precisely what it might have signified was beyond me. And the fact that I had seen the same symbol reproduced in Lotingen on the wedding contract confused me all the more. Was it Erwin Rimmele's personal cipher?

'By all the gods!' Lavedrine exclaimed from the far end of the room.

He was staring at three carcasses. Dangling on hooks suspended from the ceiling, the creatures were small and they had been expertly skinned. Two tiny tusks revealed that one was a young boar. In the middle was a more compact animal with short legs. The one on the right, judging from its long legs and graceful neck, was an immature deer. On the floor beneath each carcass was a pewter dish. Two of the bowls were full to the brim, while blood still dripped from the sliced throat of the deer.

Two more hooks hung empty, with waiting bowls beneath them.

'What place is this?' he whispered, touching the chain above the boar, which set the body spinning in the air.

'This is the Blood Room,' I said. 'That's what these cellars are called. In the country there's one on every estate. Game is brought here to be killed and drained. The blood is collected, and used in making sausages, black puddings, that sort of thing.' I pointed to a wooden trough containing large lumps of salt crystal. 'Sometimes, it is called the Salt Room. As the meat begins to turn, the carcasses will be cut into pieces and stored in salt and herbs inside those barrels.' A dozen barrels stood along the wall. 'Salted meat could be used in times of siege, or in the worst days of the winter. This room was the pulsing heart of the house; this was the place where blood flowed.'

'That one is a badger,' Lavedrine said, pointing to the creature in the middle. 'It reminds me of my home. Have you ever tasted *blarieur au sang*, Stiffeniis? The meat is surprisingly tasty.'

'It is not merely a matter of food,' I answered. 'These rooms were a reminder of ancient times. So long as game was killed, so long as the blood flowed, it meant that the house would prosper. That's why it is so cold and dry. To preserve the meat, but also to save the family living upstairs from the smell of it. Frederick the Great outlawed private slaughtering practices

349

in the interests of modernity and hygiene. He ordained that state abattoirs be opened on the outskirts of every town. The cottage where Grangé died near the Black Bull was a butcher's house.'

'For once I agree with your King Frederick,' Lavedrine muttered. 'I prefer not to see what I am about to put into my stomach.'

I sniffed the meat. 'These have been recently killed. Game takes on a stronger scent when it has been left for days or weeks.'

Lavedrine touched the edge of one of the bowls with his foot. The blood shifted as a solid lump, a sign that it had almost coagulated. 'Someone has been ignoring the edict of Frederick the Great, as well as failing to pay French taxes.'

'The more animal blood that flows, the more human life there will be,' I said, thinking back to my childhood in Ruisling. 'It means that the estate is thriving.'

'This is what the vampire seeks,' Lavedrine murmured. 'Blood. Life. Vitality.'

He lost no opportunity to make a connection with what had happened in Lotingen. Things which were commonplace and normal to a Prussian took on a different meaning in the eyes of a Frenchman.

'The person living in this cellar intends to keep the heart of the household pulsing,' he said, looking at me. 'Is that a fair assumption?'

I did not answer him. My thoughts flew off at a tangent.

'You knew who this estate belonged to, didn't you, Lavedrine? Before we even came here. Why else did you bring up the name of Emma Rimmele in the *longue paume* court this morning?'

He raised his hand and ran his fingers through his hair. 'I

had no idea at all when I mentioned it,' he replied. 'You can believe me or not, as you wish.'

'Were you not listening to Massur?' I said. 'Emma Rimmele is the victim in all of this. She was raped, and by a French officer ...'

'Raped?' he sneered. 'It is a word which covers a multitude of sins.'

'Massur chose the word, not I, Lavedrine. That's why Grangé came to this part of the house. That's why he was sent away. I see rough hands which tear at flimsy female clothing. I hear cries of protest, while the object of his lust struggles to resist, screams silenced by the threat of worse to come unless she surrenders.' I paused for a moment, holding his gaze. 'This is rape. As Massur said, this is no place for Romeo and Juliet.'

Lavedrine was staring at me as if he saw me truly for the very first time. 'God help you, Hanno Stiffeniis,' he hissed, narrowing his eyes. 'This is the fruit of *your* imagination. It is what you would have liked to ...'

A door slammed.

'What do you want?' a voice cried in alarm.

A woman had entered the room, while we had been engaged. She stared at us in amazement, her right hand on her heart, her left hanging down at her side, holding a wild hare by the ears. The animal kicked and struggled, but it could not shake free. 'Do you speak my language?' she asked, her voice trembling with some emotion.

'Speak to her, Stiffeniis,' said Lavedrine in French. He bowed his head in the direction of the woman, then went to sit on the stairs by which we had descended to the room.

I was free to play the magistrate, it seemed. I told the woman who we were, but not the reason for our being there.

'The Rimmeles sent you here, I suppose?' she said.

'The Rimmeles,' I repeated vaguely.

That name was an order. She began to speak. Her name was Adele Beckmann. She had been born on the estate sixty-five years before. There was nothing of the madwoman about her, as Lieutenant Lebrun had insisted. She was a Prussian serf, faithful and loyal. Though freed by the French, she did not thank them for it. She wore clothes that women of her kind have worn for centuries: a long brown skirt, a white blouse expertly embroidered with flowers of different colours, a blood-red apron. Her clothes were clean and crisp, except for traces of mud which clung to the hem of her skirt and to the wooden clogs on her feet.

'Frau …'

'I am a widow,' she corrected me.

'Widow Beckmann, you are the only …'

'Has something happened to the master, or to Emma?' she asked. She must have clutched more tightly at the ears of the hare, for it began to kick out viciously with its long hind legs.

'Nothing has happened to them,' I replied.

Adele Beckmann's green eyes studied me. Forty years ago, she had been beautiful. Now, her shapely face was wrinkled like a weathered rock.

'Why did Emma and her father leave the estate?' I asked.

She stared at me as if unable to believe what she had heard. 'Haven't you seen the soldiers, sir?'

'They stayed on for some time after the soldiers came,' I said. 'Did something happen which … which drove them away?'

It was like dropping a stone into a very deep well. I listened for the splash, then realised that I would probably wait forever. Did the Widow Beckmann know that her mistress had been raped? And would she tell me if she had heard cries, or seen Emma's reaction to the assault?

'Emma carried off her father and her mother,' she said at last.

I felt a surge of energy as I rushed over to the wall, grabbed a three-legged stool, and carried it back to where Adele Beckmann was standing.

'Sit down, Widow Beckmann …'

'Where are they?' she asked, ignoring the stool.

'In Lotingen,' I replied, as if I had travelled all that way to tell her the news.

'God be praised! My angel,' the old woman said, looking up to heaven. 'She took her mother home, then. The master will be better off for that. Here, there was only strife and commotion.'

I had to fight the temptation to look heavenwards, and repeat her words. Had Emma told me a single thing that was not confirmed by what I saw, or by what I heard from the lips of Adele Beckmann? I stole a glance at Lavedrine. He was on his feet now, legs apart, hands behind his back. His perplexed expression sent a shiver of satisfaction racing through my being. The servant's words had cancelled out his sarcasm and his doubts.

'Let me sort out *this*,' the woman said, 'and I'll tell you everything.'

She gave a rapid twist of her left wrist, spinning the captive hare around by its ears, then jerked very hard to one side. A high-pitched squeal was stifled as the animal's neck snapped with a loud crack. Adele Beckmann turned away and walked to the sink. As she returned, I saw that she was holding a rag in one hand, the dead hare in the other. She approached the hooks and the hanging meat, and fixed the hare by its bob-tail to one of the free hooks. In an instant, she raised the cloth to cover her blouse, whipped a small curved knife from beneath her apron, and slit the animal's throat with a single thrust.

Blood began to stream into the bowl below.

Adele Beckmann breathed out loudly, turned towards us, wiped the knife on the cloth, put it back beneath her apron, then sat down on the stool.

'When the master was young, there was no lack of game to bleed in this house. He was such a fine man, and powerful, too. The family was rich. But then ...' She clasped her hands, and shook her head. 'Things got worse, sir. His health collapsed. His mind, sir. He didn't recognise no-one. They had the farm, of course, but it wasn't the same. Emma tried to brave it out with just her mother, but then the fever came and carried off the mistress. And then, sir, the last nail in the coffin,' she said, uncaring of the pun, 'the French came shortly afterwards.'

Adele Beckmann looked up at me, and her eyes were as dead as those of the hare's.

'And how did Emma react?' I encouraged.

'She suffered, sir. Hid her beauty from the world. I did not see the colour of her flesh for weeks. Tied up like a black bundle, she was. Black veil, black gloves. 'Twas as if they'd buried *her* in the funeral vault, along with her mother.'

I had seen the bare shoulders and the olive skin of Emma Rimmele. I recalled the dress that she wore. It was black, as ritual prescribed, but it was short and skimpy, showing off her arms, breasts and ankles. Lotingen had been shocked by it. I had caught my breath more than once at the sight of her. There was nothing remotely 'buried' about Emma Rimmele! Then again, I thought, far from home, her greatest worries left behind, the death of her mother more remote in time, Emma might have found that a new life was possible.

'You mentioned the arrival of the French,' I said.

'That's right,' the woman replied. 'Herr Erwin didn't take it well. All those new faces to confuse him. But … well, it seemed to put a bit of life into Emma. She spoke French, of course. I suppose that was it. She seemed to find new reserves of strength.'

'In what respect?' I asked.

Adele Beckmann looked down at the rough red hands which were clasped in her lap. 'I thought … that is, I think she was in love, sir.'

Lavedrine appeared at her shoulder, leaning over, looking into her face.

'With one of the French officers?' he asked.

Widow Beckmann glanced at him, eyes wide with surprise. 'Oh no, sir. Not one of them. How could she? They were the enemy.'

Evidently, she thought that Lavedrine was Prussian, regardless of his accent.

'Who, then?' he asked.

'She had had to go to Marienburg, sir. She'd been there several times. Her father was sick, and there was business to attend to, things to do with the house. I suppose she must have met him there.'

'Who?' Lavedrine insisted.

The woman shrugged. 'Whoever he was, sir. She didn't say. She'd go to Marienburg for a day or two. And then, one day, she didn't come back. Two men came to the house with a cart that afternoon, and they brought a note from Emma. It seemed a strange request at the time …'

'What did she want?' I asked before Lavedrine could intervene.

'Her father was to go to Marienburg. She'd found a doctor who could treat him. The problem was that Herr Erwin would never have abandoned the Mistress. But Emma had thought of that. The men had been told to remove Frau Gisela's coffin from the family vault. Emma had found a safer place to lay her, she said, and she'd sent those men to do just that: to carry Herr Rimmele and her mother's coffin to Marienburg.'

'It seems odd that she did not come back herself,' Lavedrine interposed. 'And that she would entrust such a delicate task to strangers.'

'Come back here, sir?' Adele Beckmann appealed to him. 'It don't seem odd to me. The French would have tried to stop her leaving. She'd have had to ask permission, and she would never have done that, sir. She had taken flight. She wasn't coming back to ask no favours.'

'When did the men take the coffin?' I asked her.

''Twas after dark, sir. Our cemetery is close to the woods and the highroad, and the French had started drinking by then. While the men were opening up the vault, I dressed Herr Erwin and I walked him down the lane to the front gate. Those were Fraulein Emma's instructions, the men said. They would all be going home. Her very words, sir. That's what I was to tell Herr Erwin. Going home. He went as meek as a lamb.'

'Home?' I repeated.

Adele Beckmann wiped a tear from her cheek. 'Poor man! He didn't recognise this place no longer. Everywhere he looked there were Frenchmen. It drove him mad, sir. She had to take him away. You mentioned Lotingen before, sir. That's where Emma's mother came from.'

There was a question that I had to ask. I felt as if I were using that short curved knife of hers to cut her own throat as I asked it. 'Had Emma been raped by one of the French officers? Was that why she was afraid to return, do you think?'

Adele Beckmann smothered a cry with her hands.

'Is that what happened, sir?'

I heard a hiss from Lavedrine. 'Stiffeniis, this is not the way to go about it.'

'Would she have told you?' I insisted, ignoring his protest.

She raised her eyes to me in supplication. I could see how upset she was. 'But she … she was … I'd have sworn that she was in love. I thought she'd met a gentleman. She seemed so … so radiant. Her mother's death was painful … a terrible shock, but she was getting over it.'

She broke down, sobbing, thoughts and phrases spilling from her lips as quickly as the tears flowed. 'This house is cursed,' she said. 'Cursed forever. The blood of these small creatures is not enough to save them.'

'It's not your fault,' I murmured gently, trying to reassure her. 'There was nothing you could do. You did your best by him, and by her.'

As I spoke I thought that all the blood in Prussia could not have saved them.

'They'll not be coming back,' she cried, sobbing into her apron. 'Never more.'

There was no consoling her, nothing to be done.

We left by the narrow side door which Adele Beckmann had used to enter the Blood Room. Behind us, we could hear her voice, repeating the plaint over and over again to herself.

Never more, never more …

The woods on that side of the park were an impenetrable

357

thicket. It was there that Widow Beckmann went in search of animals to trap and slay. A herd of bulls would not have been sufficient, I thought, to assuage the gods who had brought down evil on the house of Erwin Rimmele.

Lavedrine was in a dark humour.

He had no wish to meet Massur again, he said, as we turned the corner of the house, and saw our carriage standing by the bridge where we had left it, the driver asleep on his box.

With a quick rap on the roof, Lavedrine jumped aboard and I followed him.

As we were driving down the avenue towards the gate, he turned to me and said: 'What really happened here, do you think? Why did Emma and her father abandon the house? If she had been raped by a Frenchman, wouldn't she have told you, a Prussian magistrate, of the injury that she had suffered?'

Rage choked me for some moments. Could he be so sceptical regarding all that he had seen and heard? 'Would a woman admit such a vile thing to a man?' I said angrily. 'She was in danger. She *is* in danger. The threat is still hanging over her. If you ask me, Lavedrine, *that* is the connection with the murders in Lotingen.'

'What are you thinking?' he asked.

It had come to me in a blinding flash.

'Sebastien Grangé boasted that he had found a treasure. He was speaking of the riches of the Rimmeles. He may have blackmailed Emma, threatening to tell the world what she had been subjected to. She suffered violence, and the shame which followed it. Let's say that she paid him off the first time. He and his friends may have become more pressing. The violence may have been repeated. Other officers may have learnt of it, and tried to press their own advantage. Either for sexual rewards,

358

or for a share in the profits of the extortion. Wasn't this what you suspected?'

Lavedrine held my gaze, but he did not reply.

'Emma Rimmele could be the next victim of the vampire,' I insisted.

An ironic smile appeared on Lavedrine's lips.

'If it was a rape,' he said. 'But what if she was moved by love? By passion? Adele Beckmann said that she was radiant, despite her mother's death and her father's decline. Is there any reason why a Prussian woman should not lose her heart to a Frenchman? Even if he has invaded her country, and her home?'

I clenched my fists until they hurt, but I did not answer him.

'Are you jealous at the thought that she might be enamoured of a Frenchman?'

'We must go to Lotingen,' I growled, ignoring his arrogance.

'Not yet,' he said. 'One thing remains to be done in Marienburg.'

Chapter 26

'He appeared out of nowhere the day that I arrived in town.'

Lavedrine stopped the coach before it could enter the city gates. 'It is quicker to walk from here, and twice as pleasant,' he said, climbing down into the road. 'On the way, I'll tell you what I know about the man.'

We went along a riverside lane which was not much more than a narrow gravel path. The red-brick walls of the castle loomed high above us on the left. Had anyone been looking down from the battlements, we would have seemed like tiny dots. It was chilly in the shadows, though the day was bright, even dazzling, as the afternoon sun flashed off the surface of the river.

'Is he Prussian?' I asked.

'Alexander Oleg Krebbe was born in Marienburg,' he said. 'When I say that he *appeared*, I mean exactly that. He is ghostly white, almost transparent. When I spotted him standing in the courtyard, I was tempted to believe that he had passed through the castle walls. No-one had tried to stop him at the gate. He simply walked into the guards' office and told the sergeant that he wished to see the colonel who was investigating the murders of the French officers.'

'Murders? Only Gaspard was known to be dead at that time.'

'Precisely! No-one knew that Lecompte had been wounded,

or that Grangé was still missing. Even so, he used the plural. Murders. And he had another surprise in store for me. Whatever was going on in Marienburg, he said, and he was most emphatic, *it had to be* connected with events in Lotingen. Well, until that moment I had heard no news of anything out of the ordinary in Lotingen. Imagine!'

I stared at him, puzzled.

'I must have looked as shocked as you do now,' he said. 'I thought that he was raving mad. There he was, standing in the castle courtyard, using that word as if it was quite normal, telling me what I ought to do about it.'

'Which word?' I interrupted.

Lavedrine raised his chin, and smiled. '*Vampire*. Krebbe was convinced that a vampire was responsible for all of the murders, both here and in Lotingen. And he was glad a Frenchman was conducting operations, he said. It was the only way to put an end to tales which had been circulating for centuries in Prussia. More deaths would certainly follow on, he predicted. Accurately, it should be added. He had come to offer me his help.'

'That was generous of him.'

Lavedrine smiled again. 'I did not take him up on the offer. Oh, I was not brutal with him, Hanno, if that's what you are thinking. He was very old, most dignified, and extremely polite. I found him altogether a most intriguing gentleman. I informed him that we French have no practical experience of vampires, and I warned him to be careful with the guards. They don't like it when someone pulls their pigtails. He took it all very calmly. He handed me a German-language newspaper, and asked if I'd be kind enough to read the front-page article at my leisure, and then, so to speak, he excused himself and …

well, *disappeared*. Like a ghost, as I said before. I went to my room and I read the piece – it was about the body of the girl found dead in the well in Lotingen, and it described the manner of her death. Two wounds to the neck, it said. Just like the officers who'd been attacked in Marienburg. Your name was mentioned, as was the news that vampire fever had broken out. Well, I saddled my horse and I rode at once to Lotingen, as you know.'

I thought it over for a moment. 'What we have heard today in Kirchenfeld suggests a better line of attack,' I said. 'Rivalry between French officer groups should convince us that the opinions expressed in Lotingen are the fruit of childish ignorance and fear. Equally, they show us that Prussians have a hard time explaining anything without inventing a sinister story.'

'Still, we must take Professor Krebbe's offer of help seriously,' he countered. 'His perspicacity merits our attention. Firstly, in spotting the similarities, and, in the second place, by attributing the crimes to a vampire. Aren't you curious to hear how he reached his conclusions?'

I was, of course, though I was careful not to say so.

'This is the very oldest part of town,' said Lavedrine, turning left and heading for a low bailey-gate which led into the district, making a quick demonstrative gesture with his hand as we came into the street.

It was a rank, unhealthy place, the roofs so close together that the sky was reduced to a narrow blue strip above our heads. The houses had once been rich. Now, the black timber frames leaned precariously like a row of drunks, crowding each other for space, all swaying in the direction of the river. Bottle-glass windows bulged into the street in the ancient style of bays, while the wooden shutters seemed to be in a state of universal decay.

'I traced his address in the Realm of Universal Intellect,' Lavedrine went on. 'He is classified as a "metaphysician". As they share the same initial letter, his file and Kant's were close together, and that is another interesting coincidence.'

Could the French use the same descriptive label for a serious philosopher like Immanuel Kant, and a man like Alexander Oleg Krebbe, who appeared to be a dabbler in vampire lore? I began to doubt the value – and the danger to Prussia – of the information which was being gathered in the intelligence room that General Olivier Layard held dear.

The street broadened out to form a bulge. There were six or seven stalls in this space, mostly selling vegetables, though one was offering fish none-too-recently arrived from the Baltic Sea, if the lustreless eyes of the halibut were anything to go by. An impressive brick tower stood on the corner.

'This should be his house,' said Lavedrine.

As he raised the heavy iron door-knocker, and let it rap, I hoped that the Realm of Universal Intellect might once again fall flat on its nose.

The studded black door swung open. A tiny lady of great age, and even greater dignity, looked out at us. She was wearing a severe black dress with a starched linen bib, and a stiff winged bonnet like a French nun. Lavedrine announced his name and his rank, and was about to do the same for me, when the lady clapped her hands, as if some long-awaited fortune had fallen on the house, and she answered his good German in perfect French.

'Monsieur le Colonel,' she said, waving him into the hall, 'I am certain that my husband will be delighted to receive you.'

My presence was superfluous, I gathered.

'The vampire scholar is expecting you,' I hissed as I followed him in.

The hall was bright and austere. Black and white tiles, a carved ebony chair with bits of mother-of-pearl set in the frame and legs, a matching mirror on the wall, nothing else. 'Welcome to heaven,' she said, her tiny wrinkled face and bright eyes crackling with humour, 'though I know you are more interested in hell.' She added snappishly: 'Hell is up the stairs in this house. I'll have none of it down here!'

She threw aside a dark red velvet curtain, pushed open a door, and shouted: 'Alexander Oleg!'

'Yes?' a gruff, distant voice replied.

'You have guests, Herr Professor!'

'Who is it, my dear?'

'A French colonel and another gentleman,' she called back.

'Well, send them up!'

She stepped aside. 'He's up there, messieurs.'

There sounded like a place that she avoided. As we began to climb the stairs, I wondered what I was letting myself in for. We seemed to have stepped into a different world. If heaven below was empty, hell above was full. The walls were covered with slips of paper – letters, notes, and annotations of every colour, shape and size. Some were sheaves of many leaves which had been tacked to the walls with pins, while others were skimpy notes scrawled in ink on torn scraps of paper and card. Frau Krebbe shut the hall-door abruptly at our backs, and the multitude of papers shifted and rustled in the sudden draught, like an army of crows rustling their dark finery.

'All the way to the top,' the voice boomed down.

Looking upwards, I saw that the stairwell rose three floors, and that it was illuminated by a skylight. The tower seemed to shimmer with the improvised wall-papering, as if it were going to crumble and collapse. And that was not the end of the chaos. From the first step at the bottom to the last step at the top, the wooden stairs were cluttered with boxes, three or four in height, all containing bundles of paper, each one marked with a letter of the alphabet and a number.

'What is this place?' I whispered to Lavedrine, as we turned on the first landing and began to climb to the next floor.

He looked at me, pursed his downturned mouth, and shook his head.

We must have mounted fifty stairs before we reached the summit and Professor Krebbe. He was closer to eighty years of age than seventy, yet his face was plump and pale – youthful, I would have said – his skin the consistency of dough which had risen, then slowly begun to gather dust. His hair was a wild white mane which framed a large mouth, large ears, a handsome nose, and two blue eyes which would have looked well on a man of twenty. His glance flashed from Lavedrine to me, then back again.

'You came at last, sir,' he said to the Frenchman, offering his hand. 'You, instead, are Prussian,' he said, turning to me. 'I heard your intonation, though you were speaking French.'

'I did not speak,' I said.

'You were whispering,' he replied with a smile. 'That stairwell is like an ear-trumpet, magnifying sounds. I could hear you breathing. I hear every word that my wife says to my detriment, too, but please don't tell her.'

I smiled and told him who I was.

His eyes lit up. 'Herr Procurator Stiffeniis, I had formed the impression that you were shorter and slighter from the newspaper report. One must always be careful of words. You'll have told the colonel that this is no ordinary investigation,' he said, and now he seemed to be more interested in me than in Lavedrine, as if, being Prussians, we shared some common ground which might exclude a Frenchman.

'I certainly have,' I said, for want of anything better.

'Come in, sirs.'

The room was square, large and high. Massive wooden beams as black as pitch revealed the sand-coloured tiles of the roof directly above our heads. Double windows gave a view of Marienburg Fortress, three castles sitting inside its curtain walls, each keep higher than the next, and the cathedral at the far end. More bewildering than the view was the state of the room. Boxes, boxes, and more boxes. Papers pinned to the walls, papers massed in heaps on tables, papers scattered on the floor in tottering piles. Everywhere, bits and scraps and pages of paper, and all written on.

'My dictionary,' Professor Krebbe explained. 'The roots and derivations of the Germanic language groups. First use, and all subsequent usages of a word or phrase,' he added in a modulated breath with all the passion of a believer. 'All subsequent modifications of its sound, tonal shifts and meanings.'

How many ducks had lost their quills in his service? How much ink gall had the oak trees of Prussia yielded up to him? The entire Black Forest must have been torn from the ground and pulped with rags to make up all the paper that he had used.

'My *magnum opus* will soon be finished,' he said, noting our amazement at the mess. 'I'm currently working on the letter O, enriching the *lemmata*. Fresh data comes in constantly, you see. Words and their meanings grow like trees. New leaves and branches sprout all the time, while others remain like the rings inside the trunk itself. A word is never fixed in meaning for very long. Each meaning has its history, and it tells us what was in the heads of the people who used, or continue to use, them ...'

'Give me an example, professor,' Lavedrine interrupted brusquely.

Krebbe chuckled to himself. 'My hobby-horse, forgive me. I so admire French thinking, it goes straight to the heart of the argument.' He raised his finger. 'So, where were we? Well, some words may seem basic and unchanging – mother, father, life and death, for example – yet it is not so. If these basic concepts were to stop expanding to accommodate the range of new everyday meanings, they would shortly die out and be replaced by something better.'

He hesitated, snapping his fingers.

'Take a word like ... like ...'

'Vampire,' Lavedrine suggested immediately. 'Isn't that why you came to see me at the fortress?'

Krebbe looked left and right, as if to be certain that we were alone.

'You are correct, monsieur. I have long collected folk tales which speak of the vampire, or blood-sucking witch. Here in Marienburg we call it the *Nachzehrer*, but there are a host of names for it. You would be surprised how many vampire tales still circulate in Germany. I have made it my business to speak with any academic or scholar who has ever mentioned such phenomena. Rasmus Christian Rask, librarian in Copenhagen, for example. Jakob Grimm, the court librarian in Westphalia, and his brother. Poets and seers, I have been in touch with them all, from Masäus to von Arnim, von Kleist, even Goethe himself. And every one of them reports at least one legend or story in which the vampire makes an appearance.'

'Let me ask you a question, sir,' Lavedrine cut in, arms folded, eyebrows raised, halfway between curiosity to hear more, and impatience with the old man's loquacity. 'How can you help us to find the killer?'

Professor Krebbe looked at him for a moment. 'You can only defeat an enemy that you know, monsieur. I am sure the French don't need lessons in military tactics from an old Prussian scholar like me?' Then, his glance fell on me. Surely he was asking himself what my position was. Did I collaborate with the French invaders, or did my duty oblige me to follow them around?

Lavedrine was not provoked.

'I am asking whether you believe in the existence of vampires, Professor Krebbe.'

Krebbe closed his eyes, and grimaced.

'Even the most practical of Frenchmen would agree, I hope, that there are many aspects to the concept of "existence"? Do I believe in supernatural creatures which refuse to die, which feed their immortality on the blood of the living? Frankly, I do not. Do I believe that there are mortals who kill by striking at the victim's neck and throat in the manner of the vampire? Certainly, I do. I believe that these *vampires* have appeared many times in the history of Prussia, and not here alone. The chronicles of northern and eastern Europe – from the most ancient to the most recent – provide detailed accounts from the mouths of reliable witnesses, regarding people who have been murdered in this specific fashion, the sequence of events repeating itself *ad infinitum*: a knock at the door, a familiar face, an invitation to enter, the fatal attack with the teeth, the sucking of blood. There! All this leads me to believe that vampires *do* exist, Colonel Lavedrine. And that the deaths that you are investigating here, and which Herr Stiffeniis is facing in Lotingen, are the work of vampires. The question is … Do you mind if we sit down and discuss this matter more calmly? I only have one chair, but …'

Krebbe indicated three piles of leather-bound books, taking the one in the centre for himself, inviting Lavedrine and me to sit on either side of him. Had our hair been as white, and had we been as old as he, we might have been the modern male equivalent of the ancient *Moirae*, the Three Fates who superintend the birth, life and death of all men.

'The question is?' I reminded him.

'Who is the vampire?'

'Who, indeed!' Lavedrine snapped.

'I have found many interesting treatises,' Krebbe continued. 'Would you believe me if I said that one of the most informative was published sixty years ago in southern Italy by a Catholic bishop? Giuseppe Davanzati of Trani was a most refined scholar. Having heard tales of vampires in Austria and Moldavia, he set out to demonstrate by logic that such fears were the fruit of credulity. "A myth based on ignorance", I quote him.' He turned to Lavedrine and smiled approvingly. 'In France you have Calmet's *Dissertation sur les apparitions des anges, des demons et des esprits, et sur le revenant et les vampires*, which records cases which occurred in Germany. These are scholarly studies, of course, yet, the very same elements are found in the folklore of the Grimms, and the poetry of von Kleist. Davanzati says: "We should never deny merely for the sake of denying." Like him, I began to ask myself whether there

369

might be any truth in these folk tales. In the details, most particularly.'

'Which details?' I asked.

Krebbe rubbed his hands together and smiled.

'Well, the vampire is not a monster, for example,' he said. 'No-one has ever spoken of them as being deformed. Monstrosity is the first mistake of the fantastic imagination. The vampire, on the other hand, retains the identity of the person who was living. Indeed, the people that he meets do not even realise that he is dead. The victims do not try to defend themselves. Historical reports reiterate the modality of attack. The victim is found alone. Generally there is an expression of surprise on his face. On his neck there is a bite mark, and death is the result of a severed artery.'

This was the news that Knutzen had sent to the villagers of Krupeken. If they saw Angela Enke, they should not be deceived into thinking that she was the same girl that they knew. They must run from her, keep her at a distance, avoid her at all costs.

'And there's more,' Krebbe continued. 'A decaying corpse – by its smell and its colour – warns us to keep well away. The vampire, instead, does not smell of death. Fresh blood invigorates it. It has heightened colour in the cheeks, its eyes may gleam, it appears to be invested with vital energy. Blood excites it, then nourishes it. There is no suggestion that it is not what it appears to be. There is no evident change in the physical aspect. Members of the family are easily taken in by this. Would a woman refuse to sleep with her spouse? Would a daughter deny a kiss to her father? The kiss becomes a suffocating weight, the embracing "lover" overwhelms the chosen victim with the indescribable physical force of the assault. The vampire does not aim to kill, but only to feed. The problem is, they feed until there is no blood left.'

'Blood,' I murmured.

The word seemed to inspire Krebbe to new heights. 'Ah, you cannot imagine the amount of material I have collected on the subject. Leviticus defined blood as "the juice of life", and Christ himself promised us new life by drinking His blood. The notion is that blood is life-giving. The vampire is irresistibly attracted by the smell of it. Then again, you'll recall the passage from the *Odyssey* when Ulysses speaks to Tiresias?'

Lavedrine and I shook our heads like students who had not prepared for the lesson.

Krebbe continued unperturbed: 'Ulysses descends into the Underworld in search of Tiresias, who is dead. He seeks information, but before Tiresias can speak, he needs to find energy. Life. Ulysses offers him a bowl of goat's blood, which the seer drinks to the very last drop, and all the while, Ulysses fights off the other dead souls who want to drink from the same bowl.' Herr Krebbe shivered visibly. 'It is a horrid scene. Only Homer could have described it with such dramatic power.'

'Marienburg and Lotingen?' Lavedrine reminded him.

Krebbe seemed pleased with the question. 'You are the living proof of what I have said, sir. Only the French can free us from a malediction which has cursed us for centuries. You do not take refuge in the supernatural. You want an explanation which resides in men.'

'Are you saying that vampires are human?' Lavedrine suggested.

Professor Krebbe nodded. 'As ferocious as human beings can be,' he said with gravity. 'It is not the blood that they are after, naturally. But what they can obtain by means of the terror which spilled blood unleashes. This is true in every instance of vampirism that I have been able to study. The terror that they create is real.'

'Real?' I challenged him. 'But you just said ...'

'That I believe in the power of the *legend*, Herr Stiffeniis. It leads unscrupulous men to do horrid things. You know of the edict of Empress Maria Theresa. Just try to imagine the problem that she had to face, continued and repeated outrages throughout her territories. The fact that the law is still in force is proof of the fact that "vampires" – I use quote marks! – still flourish.'

Krebbe took a deep breath.

'The vampire is as powerful today as ever,' he continued. 'It has often been recalled from myth to life for some specific purpose. Every time it happens, the same wild terror of the walking dead is revived, the blood of the living is spilled, and the so-called "vampire" achieves what it set out to achieve.'

'And what is that, sir?' asked Lavedrine.

'Strength. Influence. Riches. The elimination of a person, or many people, to obtain those things. Villages, towns and cities in thrall to lawlessness, the inhabitants reduced to the level of ravening beasts. Who looks for the true cause when a vampire is blamed for it? Logic gives way to ritual, sense to nonsense. The myth hides and covers every evil.'

'So, who should we be looking for, Professor Krebbe?' Lavedrine enquired. 'And why would this particular vampire attack Frenchmen here in Marienburg, and Prussians twenty miles away in Lotingen?'

Krebbe rubbed his hands, shrugged his shoulders. 'You must look for somebody who knows the terror that the word conjures up. Somebody who measures the effects that it has on the minds and hearts of simple people. Somebody who is trying to achieve something here, and something there. I know not what, precisely. At the end of his life, even the great Professor Kant addressed the problem.'

'Kant?' Lavedrine and I sang out in chorus.

Professor Krebbe regarded us with a show of amusement. 'Wait here a moment,' he said, standing up, making for a stack of boxes which lined one wall of his workshop. He worked his way like an adept through the papers in a box marked 'Letters: J–K', returning with a sheet of paper held between the thumb and forefinger of his right hand. 'This is one of my great treasures,' he said. 'A letter which I received from Immanuel Kant not long before he … Well, sirs, you may not know it, but his last years were … troubled. This may be one of the last lucid things that he ever wrote. It is dated 1793, and it was his … ah, *belated* response to a note of mine. Let me explain. The facts are as follows. In 1765, there was an outbreak of vampirism in a village near Königsberg. I was a student; I'd hardly begun to study the subject, but Professor Kant had a reputation as a man who was open to discussion on the most arcane and various of subjects. I had read a pamphlet written by him in reply to an enquiry from a young lady, asking for his opinion of Emanuel Swedenborg. You have probably never heard of him. He is long out of fashion. Swedenborg claimed to speak with souls of the dead. Well, Kant examined the matter, and he startled everyone by declaring an open mind on the subject: there was not sufficient evidence, he said, to allow a rational judgement. I wrote asking Kant for an opinion of vampires, but I did not get the answer that I was hoping for. He was too busy writing up his dissertation for the university – he had just applied for a post as magister – but he promised to reply when

373

he had the time. And so he did. Thirty years later! Thirty years, can you believe it? It was as if a day or two had passed, as you will see from his letter.'

I was paralysed by this news, unable to move, incapable of stretching out my hand to receive Kant's letter from the offering hand of Professor Krebbe.

Lavedrine was not so inhibited. 'May I see it?' he asked, taking the letter.

'Please, sir, read it aloud,' Krebbe enthused.

Lavedrine carried it over to the window, and did as he had been requested.

Dear Alexander Oleg Krebbe,

I have been pondering on your question concerning the nature of vampires. The data at my disposal is limited, except for the instances recorded in scientific journals and the newspapers, with which you are already certainly familiar. However, a recent encounter obliges me to think again on the question that you once asked me: <u>what is a vampire?</u>

Some time ago, I met a young man who revealed to me an aspect of human existence which I had never considered previously. He told me of a dark and terrible place in which, I admit, I would be curious to venture, though I fear I may not have much time left in which to do so. It is not a physical place, sir. It has no geographical location. It resides somewhere within the human soul, or, as I prefer to think of it, inside our True Self. If you ask me where the vampire may be found, I would say that it resides there. In all of us. At the dark heart of our hidden Self. Externally, it has our aspect. It may be amiable, intelligent, apparently normal.

374

And yet, suddenly, out springs the hideous hidden creature, and it is identical in every single case.

Having made its home in our blood, it dwells there like a rat in a drain.

If only I had the time, I would sit down this very day and revise to the roots my old 'Ich denke' concept. When 'I think', I no longer believe – as I once did – that I can be wholly conscious of what I am doing, nor can I be certain of the value which I ought to attach to my conclusions. The hidden creature is stronger than we are, you see. It wants what we do not. It acts as we would never do. There, <u>this</u> is the vampire. This is why the vampire plagues us still. The vampire expresses a predatory longing which is a part of us. It follows a primary instinct, and this makes it very dangerous.

Excuse the delay in replying, etc., etc....

Lavedrine finished reading.

Without shifting his eyes from the page, he said: 'Hanno, I don't suppose you have any idea who Professor Kant might have met in 1793, have you? I wonder what they may have discussed to alter his philosophical vision so radically?'

With an effort, I managed to shake my head. I had met Kant in 1793. I had told him of my experience in Paris that year, and of what I had felt as I stood beneath the guillotine and saw the ease with which a human life could be snuffed out.

At last, words began to issue from my mouth. I surprised myself by how calm I sounded. 'It does not greatly surprise me,' I said. 'Not really. I met Kant on a number of occasions. In the final years of his life, he spent a great deal of time in the dark place that he describes. Only he – and God, perhaps – knows what he saw there.'

I swallowed hard, and looked away.

At the dark heart of our hidden Self . . .

Shortly afterwards, we took leave of Professor Krebbe and 'hell' upstairs, and hurried down to 'heaven' below, where Frau Krebbe was holding the front door open in expectation of our immediate departure.

She seemed less friendly than when we had arrived. Indeed, she spoke German, and she sounded quite severe.

'I have my opinion of what you were discussing up there,' she said.

Clearly, she had been listening to our conversation with Professor Krebbe by means of the 'ear-trumpet' of the stairwell.

'And what is that, ma'am?' Lavedrine asked politely, humouring her.

She narrowed her eyes, and stared at him aggressively.

'I don't believe that words have only sound and meaning,' she said. 'Words wield power in this world. So long as the word continues to exist, so long as we repeat it, the vampire will come to answer the call. Strike it out of the dictionary, sirs! Dash it from your lips! That's what you should do!'

Chapter 27

We walked once more onto the riverbank.

Evening was coming on, the sun was very low and it was even brighter than before. The slanting rays cast a strange orange glow on the oily, slow-flowing surface of the water. The baked red bricks of the castle walls seemed to shimmer, as if they had just come fresh from the kiln. Window-panes glared like dancing flames. The roofs of the towers and bastions gleamed like burnished brass.

Lavedrine stood still for moment, observing the spectacle.

'It looks as if a shower of blood has fallen on the city,' he said.

I did not comment on his opinion. A greater sense of oppression weighed me down. There was more to it than the casual play of sunlight on bricks, blown glass and polished slate. The unnatural colours seemed to me to presage something ominous and menacing. I had to shade my eyes against the light, praying that the sun would quickly sink from sight, that night would come on soon, bringing darkness, restoring everything to dull normality.

'Layard has some excellent bottles of Mosel in his cellar. We'll ...'

'I am leaving, Lavedrine. I'm going home to Lotingen. Tonight,' I said flatly. 'I hope that you'll not try to prevent me.'

He pulled up sharply, forcing me to do the same. His

puzzled face loomed close to my own. 'Have you seen anything to convince you that the investigation in Marienburg is over, for I have not.'

'I should apologise,' I interrupted him. 'I was wrong, and you were right from the start. The murders in Lotingen *are* connected. The trail starts here in Marienburg, just as you said.'

He stared at me as if he wished to read my thoughts. 'Why leave, in that case? Explain it to me, Hanno, if you will. What did I grasp from the start, and what have you failed to see until now?'

'The killer is not one individual,' I replied. 'The cause of everything is the rivalry which exists between competing groups inside the French army. They are fighting over Emma Rimmele. *She* is the booty. With the help of his friends, Grangé believed that the prize was safe, but then a rival group decided to wrest it from them. They lured him out to that abandoned cottage on the other side of the river. There were no Frenchmen there, only Prussian smugglers and the like. It was the perfect spot for what they had in mind. Grangé was murdered, then the killers turned on his closest friends. Their group was soon wiped out.'

Lavedrine shook his head. 'You convince yourself too easily,' he said. 'Why, in your opinion, did the struggle then shift to Lotingen?'

'Isn't it obvious?' I protested. 'Emma Rimmele is there. They know where she is hiding. All the rest follows on from that plain fact. The hunt goes on. It is the identity of the hunters which has changed.'

'Is it really so simple?' he replied brusquely. 'Why kill the seamstress? Why murder the two men who worked in Lotingen cemetery? Why not go directly to Emma Rimmele and take whatever they were after? Why conjure up the myth of the vampire?'

He waved his hands in the air, gesticulating wildly, as if to convince me that what I was saying made no sense at all.

'I do not know,' I admitted. 'I only know that I must go to Lotingen. There, at least, a life may be saved.'

'Emma Rimmele,' he murmured, raising his chin to the heavens, blowing out his lips, as if he were sick of hearing her name. 'If she has been the victim of a rape, and if you are correct in believing her to be the obsession of a group of French officers, she'll not allow a Frenchman to approach the house where she is living. She'll be on her guard against them.'

'Massur has trained those men to kill,' I reminded him. Even so, there was some truth in what he had said. I recalled Emma's terror when she spoke of the French. When Lavedrine called at the Prior's House, she had been frightened at the thought of meeting him. That was why she had come to me, and appealed for my protection. That was why I had promised to help her.

'They may have wished to isolate her,' I said, 'striking at anyone who had had any sort of contact with her. Angela Enke was a suspicious Prussian peasant girl, yet they broke through her defences. The two gravediggers were big, strong men, well able to defend themselves. Even so, they were murdered, too.'

'How could any Frenchman get close without provoking suspicion?'

'Remember what Professor Krebbe says,' I replied. 'The vampire's face does not alarm the victim. It may be familiar, even reassuring. It may seem harmless ...'

We walked on in silence for some moments.

'What strange thoughts are buzzing in your head?' he asked me.

'There is something that I have not told you,' I admitted. 'If you are to remain here, then perhaps you should know it.'

'Tell me now,' he said quietly.

Did he feel as I did? We seemed to be advancing through an unknown land where nothing was quite what it seemed. As soon as we turned in any particular direction, as soon as the perspective was altered, all certainty seemed to slip away, like shifting sand beneath our feet.

'I spoke to the serving-girl at the Black Bull inn,' I said.

He frowned and looked at me. 'The girl who is in prison with her master?'

I nodded. 'Her name is Elspeth. Elsie. She is young, very impressionable. I thought that her imagination had run away with her. She told me something that I did not take very seriously at the time, but now, well, after speaking to Krebbe, and having heard Lecompte's account of the attack, I don't know what to think. She told me that she had seen … well, a strange female presence, that's how she described it. A shadow moving in the darkness down by the river. A woman or a girl near to the house where Grangé died. With blood on her hands. It reminded me … that is, it makes me think of the sketch Lecompte made on the wall of his room.'

'Why did you not tell me this before, Stiffeniis?'

I shrugged. 'The child was full of unbelievable stories. Wolves and snow, tales of … of people dying. Landlord Voigt dismissed every word she said as superstition. It was impossible to say what was real, he insisted, and what was not. I went there to see, of course, and the old slaughter-house made a dismal, sinister impression on me. But … well, that was not all. She told me that they still slaughter animals there.'

'I thought the place was closed,' he said.

'It is,' I replied. 'But local Prussians continue to use it. They sacrifice animals, spilling blood to placate the evil spirits and other demonic creatures which are thought to dwell there.'

'Evil spirits? Demonic creatures?' Lavedrine's lips rasped with exasperation. 'Perhaps we ought to start believing in these *creatures*, Stiffeniis. Everybody else in Prussia seems to do so. What did you actually see when you entered there?'

His eyes lit up with interest.

'It is a barn, more or less,' I said. 'There is an iron grille which covers a window, and from there I could see the cottage where the body of Grangé was found. On the ground beneath the window, there were footprints, and a bit of cloth. It was stained with blood, I think. There was even the rotting carcass of a dog …'

Lavedrine laughed aloud to himself. 'Do you now believe that this mysterious female – this *creature* of Elsie's imagination – is, somehow, real? Do you think that she was really hiding there, watching Grangé, waiting to take him by surprise? A woman? Have you changed your mind entirely? Not long ago, you seemed convinced of the guilt of French officers.'

I wiped my brow with my hand. I felt a sheen of sweat on my skin.

He stared into my face, while I looked fixedly at the river.

'Elspeth may be what she seems, and nothing more,' I conceded. 'A young girl with a wild imagination. The sinister nature of the slaughter-house may have done the rest.'

'Nevertheless, you heard Lecompte with your own ears,' he added sharply. 'He insisted that he had been attacked by a woman, the same odd creature he had drawn on the hospital wall, and which he attempted to describe for us.' He ran his hands through his curls, as if they were a nuisance and he

to root them out. 'You should have told me this, Hanno,'
 eproachfully. 'Every detail adds to what we know, even
tne most improbable.'

We walked on in silence for a minute or more.

'A mysterious female presence near the house,' he murmured.
'A mysterious female figure who attacked Lecompte.' He laid
his hand upon my arm. 'Is it possible that two such different
witnesses could imagine more or less the same thing?'

The sun burst over the turrets, sinking down behind the
castle, throwing the towers and battlements into stark, black
profile high above our heads, casting dark shadows on the
riverbank where we were walking.

'Layard has taken them all into custody,' he said, measuring
out his words. 'We should question those people from the inn
again, more carefully this time.'

'We, Lavedrine?' I said, turning off the river path towards
the castle gate. 'As I told you, I will be returning to Lotingen
tonight.'

'What about Elspeth?' he protested. 'Don't you want to know
about the dark female creature that she said she saw? Don't
you want to confront her story with what Lecompte has told
us? We could bring them face to face, and see what comes of it.'

I faced up to him then.

'I have a better idea,' I challenged, appealing to his sense of
irony. 'Just think! We could take a serious look at the feuding in
the ranks of the French army. We could play the rival officers
off against each other, and make them confess to all their sins.' I
slowly shook my head. 'Would Layard let you do it, Lavedrine?
Would he allow you to hang out the dirty washing of the *Grande
Armée* in public? Would he permit a Prussian magistrate to
keep you company while you did it? That's what you must do

in Marienburg. Alone and without my help, I'm afraid. I will be in Lotingen. As I said, I will be attempting to save a life.'

I walked rapidly on ahead, while Lavedrine still lingered there.

'Have you considered the other possibility?' he called after me.

I slowed down, letting him catch up with me.

'Which possibility are you talking of?' I asked.

'That Emma Rimmele came to Marienburg of her own free will to meet Sebastien Grangé. Adele Beckmann said that she was mourning for her mother. The French were already in the house. Yet Emma appeared to be happy. *Radiant* was the word that the serving-woman used. Whatever occurred between them, it had already taken place at Kirchenfeld. What if Emma Rimmele was in love with Sebastien Grangé? What if she followed him to Marienburg? Have you taken that possibility into consideration, Hanno Stiffeniis?'

I shook my head and walked on quickly, as if he were a bore and a nuisance from whom I wished to be free. I strode in through the castle gate, pointing over my shoulder with my thumb as one of the sentries stepped forward to prevent me from entering.

'I'm with Colonel Lavedrine,' I said, and I marched straight past the man.

'You cannot reject a hypothesis because it offends you, Stiffeniis,' I heard him calling at my back.

The sun sank entirely below the horizon in that instant.

I felt the towering heaviness of the fortress gate above my head, and I was relieved by the darkness of those walls. I hurried across the courtyard, making for the outside staircase which led up to the first floor where the officers were quartered.

I would collect my things from the room, then leave.

As I began to mount the steps, a soldier came running down.

'Monsieur, I've been looking for you,' he declared, stopping on the step above me. He glanced from me to Lavedrine, who was now on a slightly lower step. And there his gaze remained as if I had suddenly become transparent. 'Colonel Lavedrine?' he asked.

Lavedrine came bounding up the stairs, and stood at my side.

'What is it?' he asked, resting one hand on his thigh.

'A woman arrived some time ago, monsieur. She was asking for you. General Layard gave orders to put her in the room at the far end of the corridor upstairs, and to let her wait there until you came.'

'A woman? Did she give no name?' he asked.

'No, monsieur. She has come from Lotingen, it seems.'

I left them talking, climbing the steps two at a time in my hurry to reach the floor above. Was Emma Rimmele there alone, surrounded by French soldiers? Had she come to Marienburg alone, and without her father? The messenger had said nothing of an old man. Had she ventured unbidden into the wolf's lair? Only some greater danger than the ones she had already faced could have brought her to do such a thing.

I raced in through the open door.

Lavedrine was breathing down my neck. I heard his boots ringing on the tiles.

Emma would be forced to face him, she would be subjected to his questions. She would be inhibited by his presence. She would certainly be frightened. I turned on him, fists clenched, as if to meet an assailant.

'Let me talk to her first, Lavedrine. Alone.'

384

Lavedrine regarded me. His hands were on his hips, and he was shaking his head, looking at me as if I had lost my wits, a dangerous madman that it was better not to confront. Nevertheless, he tried.

'We need to talk, Stiffeniis. Before you meet … the lady.'

I stepped close to him.

'Wait here,' I said. 'I'll call for you to come when the time is right.'

My voice was hard, determined. There was nothing to discuss.

The expression on his face disturbed me. Was he amused by what he saw in me, or by the thought of finally meeting Emma Rimmele? There, I thought, that is what I must defend her from. The heartless irony of Serge Lavedrine was more devastating than any question he could throw at her.

I turned away, strode down the corridor, stood for an instant before the door and gently began to beat my knuckles against the wood. Without waiting to be called, I opened the door and stepped into the room.

It was larger than the one that I had been assigned, and more comfortable. A small fire had been lit. It was the only illumination in the chamber.

She was sitting on a chair, her feet resting on an iron bar which was set into the stone before the fire. Her pointed shoes were neatly aligned and close together, like those of an orderly, well-composed, self-possessed person. The play of the firelight made no impression at all on her black clothes, which were heavy, opaque. They held her body as tightly as a sheath, emphasising her slender arms, and the mass of her dark auburn curls, which fell like water from a fountain over her narrow shoulders. Pale hands were clasped in her lap, issuing from sleeves so tight they made her seem far thinner than she really was. As she turned to greet me, I saw the two red globes of coral dangling from the lobes of her ears like two bright cherries on either side of a dark leaf.

'Good evening, Hanno,' she said. 'Is Lavedrine here?'

Chapter 28

'Helena!'

I heard the surprise in Lavedrine's voice. He pushed past me, striding across the room in a fit of anxiety and concern. 'You are well, I hope?'

'Well enough,' she replied in measured tones. 'Edviga woke up in a foul mood this morning, otherwise I would have been here earlier. But once the baby was settled, what was there to stop me?' She smiled at him, then her glance washed over me. 'Lotte will be able to look after them for a day or so, I am sure. I caught the public coach from Lotingen after lunch. It isn't much of a journey.'

'Did you have any problems at the gate?'

Lavedrine seemed bogged down in practicalities, while one question loomed in my mind: *What was Helena doing in Marienburg?*

My wife shook her head. 'I told the officer of the guard that I had come to speak with Colonel Lavedrine on a matter of importance.' She smiled at him again, even more warmly than before. 'Your name works wonders, it seems. They brought me to this room, and they let me wait.' She pointed to the fireplace. 'They even lit the logs. They said that you were lodging in this part of the fortress. *Both* of you, I mean.'

She looked in my direction as she added this codicil.

I did not move. My hand had frozen on the cold metal

handle of the door. Until that moment, I thought, I might have been invisible to the pair of them. Lavedrine was standing beside Helena, and he was vibrant. She remained seated, looking calmly up at him, as if that room were her own front parlour. He laid his right hand gently on her left shoulder, leaning above her, kissing the air, his lips so close to the mass of curls that she had bundled up on her head with a whale-bone clasp that I recognised too well. Lavedrine had given it to her as a parting gift the day that he left Lotingen two years before. It was a favourite of hers. I had no doubt that she had chosen to wear it, knowing that she was going to meet him.

'You can't imagine the pleasure that it gives me,' he said. 'And such a surprise! Hanno ran on ahead, while the messenger was informing me that a Prussian lady was waiting for us to return.'

'I'm sure it was a great surprise for Hanno, too,' my wife said, her fingers playing with her hair, pushing the curls behind her ears to display the coral earrings dangling from her lobes. 'Then again,' she added, gazing into the fire, 'a Prussian lady? Indeed, I wonder whether *I* am a … disappointment.' She softened the acidity of this comment with a darting smile in my direction, her eyes bold and challenging.

'What brings you here?' I asked, taking three steps into the room. It sounded ruder than I had intended, but there was no helping it.

Helena studied my face, as if deciding how to answer me.

'Necessity,' she said at last.

'What do you mean by that?' I snapped.

Lavedrine took a step forward, as if he meant to defend her. They might have been a married couple confronting an intruder. A pained smile pulled at Lavedrine's lips, while my wife's expression was as calm and impenetrable as the Baltic Sea on one of those rare days when there is no wind to ruffle it.

'I had no alternative,' she said. 'I have learnt something which I think that you should know. Both of you. It concerns Emma Rimmele.'

Did the floor shift beneath my feet? I veered to the right and sat down on the edge of the bed. Had I fallen all the way to the centre of the Earth, I would still have been robbed of the power of speech.

'Emma Rimmele?' Lavedrine repeated, as if he, too, was unsure of what he had just heard. 'Have you found out something about Emma Rimmele?'

'Helena is not a magistrate,' I opposed. I did not wish to see my wife drawn into the case. 'Whatever gossip she may have stumbled on in Lotingen, it cannot change what we know concerning Emma Rimmele in Kirchenfeld.'

I looked at my wife as I spoke, but I could not see her face. The fire in the grate seemed to require all of her attention in that moment.

'Are you sure of that, Hanno?' Lavedrine asked, pointing his finger at me like a loaded pistol. 'Have you forgotten the help which Helena provided during the Gottewald case two years ago? Without her, we would never have got to the bottom of the affair. If Helena has taken the trouble to come here, we must hear her out.'

'Giving evidence,' I murmured unhappily.

'Helena's name will not appear in any report,' he said. 'This will be a quiet, informal chat amongst ourselves, and nothing more.'

Helena never took her eyes from the fire. Her composure

surprised me somewhat, but I could raise no objection. Not that Lavedrine would have given way, in any case.

'Excellent!' he cried, holding out his hands to her, pulling her to her feet as if the band had started up and he had invited her to dance. 'Come, Helena,' he encouraged, leading her around the chair, as if they were taking the first walk of the quadrille before he handed her over to me. Though she presented herself before me, she did not curtsey.

Instead, she looked down at the tiled floor.

'I think that I would prefer to sit,' she said.

With an able flick of the wrist, Lavedrine turned the chair around and placed it at her back. Thus, as she sat down again, I found myself looking directly into the face of my wife. Lavedrine rested his hand and weight upon the back-rest of the chair. Had it happened accidentally, or had he engineered it? Helena and I would be obliged to look into each other's eyes; any attempt to avoid doing so would be immediately evident.

Helena looked up at him, and flashed a smile. 'I am ready,' she said, the smile fading away as she looked back at me. 'Hanno and I are eager to hear what you have to say.'

Suddenly, I was reminded of evenings at home, when Lotte came to sit with us in the parlour and the children demanded a story before going up to bed. Helena looked no different than usual, while I was in a far more agitated state.

'I saw Emma Rimmele,' she began. 'It was the day after … the day after Angela Enke's body had been found. She was coming down the lane which leads towards the Cut and the Prior's House, while I was going to the cemetery. It did not take very much to see … That is, to understand …'

'To understand what?' Lavedrine helped her.

'That any man who sees her cannot remain … immune.'

'Immune to *what*, Helena?'

I asked this question. I had no choice. If we were to hear more superstition, I wanted to get it out of the way, and quickly. I studied her hands as I waited for her answer. They were bunched in tight fists upon her knees. I could see the tension in the whiteness of her knuckles, made all the whiter by the black cuffs of her dress, and the red marks left on her wrist where she had tied the bows of the sleeves too tightly. I clutched my hands together, fighting the impulse to lean across, release the bows, and tie them up again more loosely. It seemed to me to be a small, unnecessary torment which Helena had inflicted on herself.

I glanced at her, but she did not look up.

'Immune to what she is,' Helena said quietly. 'There is something so … so unsettling about her. Even the way she dresses, though it is not a question of her clothes. Is it a mourning dress she wears? Transparent tulle and flimsy muslin show more than they can hide. She has such striking hair …'

She closed her eyes, raised her hand to cover her lips. A wave of suppressed emotion sent a shudder through her body. 'When I saw her, I understood the effect that she must have upon men. All men. She swept through the town like the fever epidemic. Every man who sees her is struck by her, and he is helpless to defend himself. It is another sort of … fever.'

I listened to what she said, and I did not reply. I recalled, instead, a juridical text which I had recently read. It described the state of mind of a man who cannot defend himself against an accusation which is evidently true. Denial gives way to resignation, dull acceptance of an inevitable fate. That was how I felt.

'Have you seen her again?' Lavedrine asked quietly. 'Since that day, I mean.'

Helena slowly shook her head. 'No,' she said, looking up at Lavedrine. 'But I … Well, I made enquiries while Hanno was here with you in Marienburg. I had to know more about her. To satisfy my own curiosity. And now, I know a great deal more than either of you do. Certainly more than Hanno managed to discover on her account.'

'What *are* you insinuating, Helena?'

The question exploded from my lips.

My wife was accusing me of failing to conduct the investigation as I ought to have done. Was Lavedrine pleased to hear his doubts expressed by my wife? Was he trying to set us at each other's throats, acting as the wedge to prise us apart and divide us, one from the other?

'I went to the Prior's House in the afternoon,' she said, ignoring my question. 'She was not there. She has disappeared, it seems.'

I made to stand, but Lavedrine caught my wrist and held me fast.

'There may be many explanations, Hanno. Not the one that you fear,' he hissed. He turned once more to Helena. 'Had something happened at the Prior's House?'

Helena shook her head. 'She left there shortly after you and Hanno departed for Marienburg. Within an hour or two, a carriage was being loaded at the gate.'

Helena's voice was even, unemotional. As sharp as a surgeon's knife.

In my head, I heard a different voice. A passionate, persuasive voice. *If anyone must hunt for me, Herr Procurator, I hope it will be you.*

Helena had gone in pursuit of Emma Rimmele, instead.

'Who told you this?'

Although I tried, I could not make this question sound less accusatory.

Helena rested her elbows on her knees, cradling her face in her hands. She stared into my eyes. 'Who are you defending, Hanno? Yourself? Emma Rimmele? She has fled. Do you understand me? She has gone. Forever. Herr Schuettler was amazed by the speed with which she left. She had always told him that the Prior's House was the only place where her father would find peace. The next instant, she abandoned it. She is no longer in Lotingen. She took the old man with her.'

'The Schuettlers wanted money,' I countered. 'Emma had nothing more to give them. And she had no authority to gain access to her father's deposits in the bank. Herr Rimmele was rich, but they might as well have been as poor as mice. He recognises no-one. Not even his own daughter ...'

Helena shook her head. 'I do not think they asked for money. Gurt Schuettler said that he had offered to repay a part of the rent that she had paid already.'

'The Schuettlers had threatened to throw the Rimmeles out ...'

'Is that what she told you, Hanno?'

Helena turned her face towards the window, as if she could not bear to look at me.

Lavedrine stretched out his hand, and patted my shoulder, shaking his head, warning me to say no more. 'There is one thing I do not comprehend,' he said to Helena. 'You went to the house where Emma Rimmele ought to have been. You did not tell us why you went there.'

'Curiosity,' she replied quite calmly. 'I had learnt something on her account. I had seen the effect that she had had upon my husband. I wanted to know how far she had bewitched him.'

I brushed Lavedrine's hand aside.

'What conclusion did you reach?' I challenged her.

Helena looked at me as she replied. Her stare was so intense, I hardly dared to breathe. I saw no anger in her eyes, yet her lips were trembling. I saw pain, an infinity of pain.

'I realised how easily she had distracted you, Hanno. You were so partial in your concern for her that you failed in your duty. I am not talking of your duty to your wife and family, I am talking of your duty as a magistrate. You failed to do what was in your power to protect the people in the town. I got my first intuition of it when Serge came to Lotingen. He asked you questions that you could not answer, things you had apparently avoided, things you had purposely set aside, ignoring what you knew, dismissing what you had been told …'

'What else was there to know?'

She did not answer. She breathed in deeply, and shook her head resignedly.

'What could *you* find that I did not, Helena?'

She breathed out slowly, audibly, expelling every ounce of air like the final wheeze of an empty bellows. 'It happened by chance,' she said. 'Luck, I suppose you would call it. I had been to see Herr Froberger at the Office of Public Works …'

'Whatever for?' I asked her.

Anger blazed up in her eyes. 'You told me that Anders' gravestone was ready, that Ulrich Meyer had cut it and taken it to the cemetery. That the stone was there … I wanted to know when it would be erected. And who would do the work. You know how long I've waited! I went to insist that it should be done at once. But with Merson dead, and Ludo dead, and you involved in other things, Hanno, I was afraid that it would never be done. I prayed that Froberger would speak with Ulrich Meyer.'

She bowed her head.

'What did Froberger say?'

'He nearly had a fit,' she said. 'The cemetery is in the hands of the French, and until a new gravedigger could be appointed nothing can be done. He showed me a stack of papers, Hanno. Orders waiting to be carried out. Not just the stone for Anders. He was so insistent, thrusting the documents into my hand. There are priorities, he said. Work is done in order of urgency. Perhaps he feared that I would take my complaint to the mayor. And while he was explaining this, he kept piling papers up in front of me. That was when I saw the name.'

She pressed her right hand to her mouth, crushing her lips with her knuckles.

'Which name, Helena?' Lavedrine's voice was little more than a whisper.

As he spoke, he reached out and laid his hand on hers. I would have liked to do the same thing, to comfort her the way that he was trying to do. But would she have accepted it from me?

'Gisela Kassel ... An order to remove her coffin from the Kassel vault. Merson had placed the body there, while waiting for Emma Rimmele to provide the documents regarding its removal from Marienburg. There was no legal proof that the coffin contained a member of the Kassel family. Merson had pinned a note to the page, saying that he was worried about a coffin being left inside a vault unless it had a right to be there. He used the word *intruder* ...' Helena halted for a second. 'That is how he spoke of whoever lies inside that coffin, Hanno. He called her an *intruder*. They use the word in Lotingen to speak of vampires. According to Lars Merson, Emma's mother was an intruder in the cemetery.'

The she-devil, Lars Merson muttered when he saw Emma Rimmele entering the cemetery. Was this the reason for his resentment? Ludo Mittner had told me that Merson had done as Emma had asked. Had Merson then gone searching in the Lotingen archive for the documents that she had been unable to provide?

'Merson wanted to remove the coffin,' Helena concluded. 'With Merson dead, that job was left for Ludo Mittner to do.'

Was it all a question of the disputed right to use a vault?

I jumped up. This time Lavedrine's hand could not restrain me.

'How could she produce such documents?' I challenged Helena. 'They told us in Kirchenfeld that she ran away, leaving everything behind her.'

'If Emma's mother was a Kassel,' Lavedrine encouraged my wife, patting her hand, ignoring my protest, 'why did Merson think that the body did not belong in the Kassel vault?'

'In Merson's opinion, the documents proved the illegitimacy of the burial ...'

'I examined the file myself,' I contended.

'Lars Merson had been there before you, Hanno,' Helena replied quietly. 'He did not believe what Emma Rimmele told him. And clearly, it cost him his life.'

'What could it be? What could Merson have found?' I asked her crossly. I had never spoken to my wife that way before. Nor had I ever seen her react to me in such a determined manner.

She straightened her back, squared her shoulders, looked me in the eye in silence. She might have been daring me to go on, but Lavedrine stood suddenly between us.

'What did Merson discover?' he asked, holding both of her hands, looking into her eyes. This gesture of intimacy seemed to say: speak to *me*, Helena, tell *me* what Hanno does not wish to hear.

I studied Helena's profile as she stared back at him. Her lower lip trembled visibly. And when she spoke again, her voice was laboured, as if it cost her a great deal. 'Rupert Kassel, Marquis von Trauss, Emma Rimmele's grandfather on her mother's side, learnt something about his future son-in-law which frightened him. Indeed, he tried to stop the marriage which had been contracted between his only daughter and the young Erwin Rimmele.'

'What was the accusation?' Lavedrine persisted.

Helena clasped his hands more tightly. 'Erwin Rimmele had been a wild young man, a fervid nationalist, it seems. He had conspired against the king, who embraced the Enlightenment and French ideas. Erwin was a founder member of a secret society, a sort of aristocratic cult, which idolised the power of Prussian blood. When the bride-to-be's father found out, he opposed the marriage. The rebels ritualised their meetings with the sacrifice of animals ...'

Helena's words froze the blood in my veins. Adele Beckmann had told me that animals had always been slaughtered in the Blood Room at Kirchenfeld, though the law prohibited it. Even in his dotage, Erwin Rimmele had continued to re-enact the rituals of his youth, a violent cult, dedicated to blood, energy, the life force. My eyes met those of Lavedrine, a signal flashed between us. I feared he might tell Helena what we had seen in

Kirchenfeld to demonstrate that he believed the truth of what she was saying.

He held my gaze for a moment, then nodded imperceptibly.

'Prussia is full of legends regarding blood-letting,' I began to say.

'Rimmele was suspected of something worse,' Helena insisted.

'What?'

She looked down at her hands again. 'I do not know,' she admitted.

'Whatever the objection may have been,' I said, 'it was soon overcome. Erwin Rimmele married Gisela Kassel, they had a daughter, and he lived out his life in peace on the estate in Kirchenfeld until the French arrived and drove them off.'

My head was spinning. Helena had picked up Merson's malevolence towards Erwin Rimmele and his daughter. Was it not the same sort of prejudice that I had encountered in Lotingen from everyone who had met Emma? Everything that she had said and done had been interpreted in negative terms. Helena had stumbled onto the same downward path. I had still not heard a word which denied what Emma Rimmele had told me.

'The fact remains that Rupert Kassel *did* refuse his daughter's hand in marriage,' she insisted, 'even though the legal contract had been signed.'

'If Erwin Rimmele was as powerful as it appears,' said Lavedrine, letting go of Helena's hands, running his hand through his hair, 'would Rupert Kassel have dared to say no?' He shook his head and breathed out noisily. 'Is it possible that the colour of blood is always stronger in Prussia than the pale, untinted truth?'

I might have thanked Lavedrine for what he had just said. Helena's imagination needed to be curbed, not encouraged. It would not be easy for her to accept the truth. It had cost her a lot to come to Marienburg and throw these fantasies in my face. Her credibility was now in question. She had brought herself to that pass.

But she was not defeated.

'I wondered about that,' she said, looking up at Lavedrine. 'And Merson took it very seriously. To exhume a coffin and refuse a Christian burial is not a question to be treated lightly. Merson believed that Gisela Kassel had married Erwin Rimmele against the will of her father. In his opinion, she was no longer a member of the family. Indeed, he had found a document to that effect in the archives, and he had removed it ...'

'Preventing you from finding it,' Lavedrine put in, glancing at me.

Helena turned to me, her face set grimly. 'You convinced yourself that there was nothing more to be said on Emma Rimmele's account, Hanno. You never considered the possibility that she might lie to you, as well.'

She bowed her head, and crossed her arms, like a lawyer who has finished making his appeal to the court, and turns towards the judge, waiting patiently for the sentence to be pronounced.

'How does this relate to what has happened in Marienburg?' I asked Lavedrine, ignoring Helena. 'We are talking about five murders. Six, if we include the failed attempt on Lecompte. I do not see what Emma Rimmele stands accused of.'

Helena did not look up.

'I have not come here to accuse Emma Rimmele. Nor do I accuse you, Hanno. Still you fail to understand me. I came to

399

Marienburg hoping to put an end to an epidemic. An epidemic, I would say, more terrible than the fever which carried off our little son.' She stared at me. I had seen that look a thousand times before. Her eyes were alive. They were gleaming bright with passion and with love.

For me.

'I know that the vampire really does exist, Hanno,' she said, her eyes not leaving mine for an instant. 'This creature is possessed of vast and terrible powers. All of us in Lotingen have fallen victim to her in some way or other. Only the truth can save us.'

I had no answer, and Helena had no more to say.

Lavedrine stepped into the silent space between us. Suddenly, the room seemed very small indeed.

'It is time for us to rest,' he said, wagging his forefinger at my wife. 'You, above all, Helena Stiffeniis. The instant I saw you here, I knew that you had come to save us from ourselves. Hanno and I are like two bulls locked horn to horn. You have done much to unlock us, I think.'

He glanced at me, and a smile lit up his face.

Whether in complicity or embarrassment, Helena smiled at him.

'There!' he declared. 'That's what I wanted to see. We've been short on pretty smiles in Marienburg for quite some time. Can you make yourself comfortable in this room for tonight? It is too late to send you home again.'

Helena looked around her, taking in the narrow single bed, as if seeing the place for the very first time.

'Thank you, it will do perfectly well,' she said.

'Excellent. I'll give orders for food, hot water and some towels to be brought.'

He hooked his arm in mine. 'Hanno, you'll be in your old room just across the corridor. Sleep well, Helena!'

'Good night,' I said, and Helena returned it.

Outside in the corridor, Lavedrine was not so tender with me. 'Can't you understand that her heart is torn apart by jealousy and fear? She really thought that she had lost you to that woman. She is telling the truth when she says that she has come to help you. Hold tightly to her hand and seize the olive branch that she is offering you.'

'I don't know what you want from me,' I said. 'I don't know what either of you expects. I only wish that my wife had never become involved in this affair.'

He bared his teeth and smiled in my face. 'You dragged her into this mess, Hanno, and you must never forget it.' He stood aside, made a flourish of a bow, and let me pass. 'I'll have food and hot water sent up for you, as well.'

'Thank you kindly,' I replied, turning away towards my room, then turning back to face him. 'If you need to enter my room for any reason, Lavedrine, I'd be grateful if you knock. I prefer to wash in private.'

I thought he was about to throw a punch at me. He raised his fist, and took aim at my nose. An instant later, the punch fell gently on my upper arm, and his face relaxed into a smile.

'I'll try to resist the temptation that those doors represent for me. Both doors!'

Chapter 29

'I smell the stink of Massur in all of this.'

We huddled together in the corridor – Lavedrine, Helena and myself – talking in whispers, looking all around, like prisoners who had just escaped from captivity, and who feared being taken into custody again. Lavedrine glanced again at the contents of the note, shaking it angrily in his fist.

General Layard refused to allow me into the prison where the Prussians from the Black Bull inn were being held. 'The fact that you have questioned them already counts for nothing,' Lavedrine snarled. 'I should have guessed! Massur is behind it, advising Layard to rid himself of you, and to keep me on a very tight chain. The general wants me to go there alone and interrogate them all again!'

'Are Helena and I supposed to disappear?'

'He wants you both to go home,' he said, staring beyond my shoulder, his face twisted with rage. 'What a waste of my time! What will they tell me, a Frenchman, that they have not told you already? If they told you little, will they tell me more? If the girl pulls out that tale of a mysterious female, I'll force the details from her ...' He stopped in mid-sentence, a puzzled expression frozen on his face, as if to ask us both what was wrong. A moment later, he smiled. 'Nothing physical, I promise you. I'll bring French rationalism to bear on wild Prussian fantasy. Lecompte has been infected by the same disease since coming here to Marienburg. He and the girl appear to share the same set of sinister impressions. I'll have them bring up a carriage for you. You'll be in Lotingen in a couple of hours.'

'I am not leaving,' I said defiantly.

Lavedrine peered hard at me. 'Layard will send someone to throw you out of the fortress. Don't even dream of trying to enter the prison. They will not let you out again. His word is law in both those places.'

'I want to take another look at the cottage where Sebastien Grangé was killed,' I said. 'Over there, the general commands no-one. It happens to be the scene of a murder. I can go there if I wish to.'

'What is there to see?' he protested. 'Grangé's body—'

'Has been removed,' I said. 'I know all that. I'm interested in the place itself. Puzzled, rather. Do you recall our conversation last night? How was it possible to creep up on the victim, a trained French soldier, a man of considerable experience, catch him off his guard, and do away with him? Didn't he try to defend himself? And if not, why not?'

He listened to me, a familiar ironic smile playing about his lips.

'You want to know what danger threatens Emma Rimmele,' he said quietly. 'And discover how the attack might be arranged. You are still convinced that she will be the next victim, aren't you, Hanno?'

'The danger may have reached her door already,' I said, thinking of the news that Helena had brought. 'Emma Rimmele may have tried to run away, but it does not mean that she escaped them.'

Lavedrine did not reply immediately. Whatever he was thinking, it made him smile. 'I'll go at once to the prison, get it over with, then write up my report for General Layard,' he said. 'It will give me the greatest pleasure to do so. Jacques Massur will get much more than he bargained for.'

'Massur?' I asked, perplexed.

Lavedrine's eyes were cold and distant. 'This story begins in Kirchenfeld, Stiffeniis. Those three lieutenants were serving there under his command. If he had done *his* job, none of this might have happened.'

He intended to denounce his rival, it seemed.

'I'll have the carriage brought for you, then, Helena.'

She stepped up to him, those red coral earrings dancing wildly. 'I won't be needing one, thank you,' she said, 'I will be with Hanno.'

If she surprised me, she certainly surprised him. He opened his mouth to say something, then closed it wordlessly again, thrusting his hands into the pockets of his leather coat, staring down at the points of his Italian riding-boots.

Helena watched him steadily, a fixed smile on her lips.

'I've come between the two of you enough as it is,' he said at last. 'You must decide for yourselves who stays, who goes, and where and when and how.'

Helena lifted her hands, pushing vagrant curls behind her ears with trembling fingers, exposing the earrings more markedly. There was something defiant in the way that she did it. 'It has nothing to do with Hanno,' she said. 'I am capable of making my own decisions, Monsieur le Colonel.' She looked at me, and her gaze was penetrating. 'I wish to see the house,' she said. 'I wish to see it with you, Hanno.'

What more was there to say?

Five minutes later, standing by the main gate, we parted from Lavedrine. Five minutes more, and Helena and I were seated side by side on the bench seat of a rowing boat, as it pushed off from the bank. The wherry-man had agreed to carry us across the river in the direction of the Black Bull inn. Ten minutes more, a steady breeze in our faces, we had landed on the other bank, and begun to walk in the direction of the slaughter-house, and the cottage beyond it.

We had not exchanged a word since leaving Lavedrine.

'Soldiers,' she said, looking to the right.

Two French sentries were standing guard outside the closed door of the tavern. If that side of the river had been a Prussian domain the day before, the French were out in force there now. And even if Lavedrine persuaded General Layard to free the landlord, I could not avoid thinking that Wilhelm Voigt's alehouse might remain forever empty, his beer turning sour in untapped barrels. Would he ever claim again that only German was spoken over there?

The slaughter-house seemed more forlorn than I remembered it. A large empty shed, and nothing more. If Voigt and Elspeth had told the truth when they spoke of animals being butchered there, fresh blood to assuage the 'creatures of the night', then the French had put them all to flight: Prussians, butchers, beasts, and creatures. The vampires had been driven off, at least for the moment. No blood would be spilled while the French were there, unless it were Prussian.

As we entered the yard of the cottage, heads looked over the balustrade which gave access to the upper floor of the dwelling. Two French soldiers had been lounging on the wooden steps. They jumped up, shouting, muskets in hand, pointing them at us. One man came running down the stairs, levelling his firearm at my stomach.

'This place is off-limits,' he shouted in French, as if it were a *lingua franca* known to every man who walked upon the earth. 'There's a murder enquiry going on.'

The other soldier came down to join him. He stood there, smiling sullenly, ogling Helena, jibbing the firing-end of his musket up and down. 'What's the judy doing here, then? And what are *you* up to, my friend?'

There was no mistaking his meaning. I realised the danger we had walked into. Helena, most particularly. I had never seen those men before. The guard had changed; Sergeant Coin and his soldiers had gone, and Lavedrine was not there to protect us. These Frenchmen understood that I was a Prussian, nothing more. And at my side there was a Prussian woman.

'The "judy" is my wife,' I corrected him. 'And I am the magistrate who must investigate the murder.'

'Wife?' the soldier snorted sarcastically.

'Magistrate?' the other one said.

I saw the scene as it might unfold. One man would hold me at gunpoint, while the other had his way with Helena. She would resist, of course, and I would try to save her. Would they shoot me first, or make me watch, before they shot the pair of us? Something of the sort had happened to Emma Rimmele, after all.

A look passed between those men.

They were weighing up the risks.

I glanced at Helena. Did she see fright in my eyes? When she spoke up, I thought I was imagining it. Her French is quite as good as mine. 'My husband and I were asked to come here by a French officer, Colonel Lavedrine,' she said boldly. 'Serge invited us to look inside the cottage where the murder had taken place. He'll be here very shortly. Now, you,' she pointed at the bolder of the men, 'what is your name?'

The two men exchanged another look.

'We'll give our names to the colonel when he turns up,' the first man said, lowering his musket, stepping aside.

'We'll wait for him upstairs,' I managed to add.

'*Comme vous voudrez, monsieur,*' the soldier replied, and this time he saluted. He turned away, put his fingers to his lips and let out two sharp whistle blasts, calling to another sentry who was upstairs on the balcony leaning out to watch the scene. 'Let them in, Louis,' he shouted. 'Colonel Lavedrine will be here any minute.'

We climbed the stairs, Helena going first.

The third man pressed himself against the rough daub wall to let us pass.

'*Bonjour, madame,*' he said with a rapid nod of his red-capped head to Helena. And then, to me: '*Bonjour, monsieur.*'

Helena stopped in front of the door. 'Is this the place?'

I nodded, though it was nothing like the gloomy murder house that I had entered with Lavedrine two nights before. Bright sunlight lit the balcony, bouncing off the wall, the door and the window. By lantern-light it had seemed dark and sinister. Now, it was nothing more than rough plaster, wooden joists, and a steep sloping roof of ancient tiles. Helena laid her hand on the door, a panel of which was split where the French soldiers had broken in. I felt no great anxiety about letting her go in there. The corpse had been removed and buried. And yet, she did not enter at once.

'What are we doing here, Hanno?'

I was surprised at how calm she sounded.

'This is where Sebastien Grangé was found,' I said, telling her quickly who he was, mentioning the condition in which his body had been discovered.

407

Helena listened in silence. Then, she looked out over the balcony and into the small enclosed courtyard. 'Who was living here before he came?'

'Nobody,' I replied, explaining that the house had been abandoned when the French closed down the abattoir. I was careful not to repeat what the chambermaid had said about the continuing illicit use of the slaughter-house, nor about the people who were supposed to go there, and what they did with the blood of the animals that they butchered. I did not wish to frighten her. 'There is no good reason for anyone to come here,' I said. 'Nevertheless, this is where Grangé was murdered.'

'Did he know that the place was deserted?' she whispered, leaning close to me.

'Probably. That's why he came here,' I said. 'He certainly knew that there were no Frenchmen on this side of the river.'

'Why would a French officer wish to avoid people who spoke his language?' she asked, stretching up on her toes, leaning out over the balustrade, looking in the direction of the slaughter-house, which was fifty paces or so beyond the gate and the yard. 'And why, having seized the place, do the French not use that building?'

'They have built their own abattoir on the downwind side of town.'

'Wherever they go, they must have abattoirs and cemeteries which are to their liking,' Helena murmured. 'Don't you think that's odd, Hanno?'

'What?'

'Animals must not be killed where the stench of blood might give them offence. The dead must not be buried anywhere near the living. They make such sharp divisions between life and death.'

She was looking at me as she spoke, but she did not seem to see me. Her eyes were hooded, blank, expressionless.

'I like to think that we, and they, are not so very far apart …'

I was perplexed, lost. 'What are you saying, Helena?'

She was silent for some moments. 'Anders is very close,' she whispered. 'I can almost see him … just there beyond my reach, but I … I cannot touch him. And yet it is just a tiny step …'

Suddenly, whatever she had seen was gone.

'Have you no idea what Grangé was doing in this place? Alone among Prussians?'

'No-one knows, or will say. The Prussians deny having seen him …'

'So, what was his connection with Emma Rimmele?'

I took a deep breath, then told her what had happened on the Rimmele estate in Kirchenfeld. I kept nothing back. The rivalry between the officers, the groups that formed, the loyalties that were made and broken, the duelling and deaths. Then I spoke to her of Emma Rimmele, saying that she had become the object of Grangé and his friends, and of other groups, too.

'Nobody remains untouched by her presence,' she said quietly.

'They hoped to lay their hands upon her father's wealth,' I said, as if that were the prime consideration, as if to remove myself from Emma Rimmele's sphere of influence. 'We believe … that is, Lavedrine and I think that she may have been … raped.'

'Raped?'

I saw the look of distress on her face. Having risked a similar fate herself at the hands of the French soldiers, I hoped that Helena would understand the situation in which Emma

Rimmele had found herself. Alone, undefended. Without a Prussian magistrate, or the name of a French colonel to protect her.

'She is still their object, their prey, though she managed to escape them here,' I continued quickly. 'That's why she came to Lotingen. Wherever she goes, they go, too, scattering death around her, isolating her, driving her to submit ...'

'You and Lavedrine believe that Grangé was killed by a rival group of officers that was chasing her?'

I nodded, surprised at the ease with which Helena managed to comprehend the complexity of what had taken place. 'That's the way it seems,' I said. 'A second officer was murdered in town in the same fashion. A third man barely escaped with his life. They were both close friends of the first.' I told her what we thought had happened, and how Grangé had been killed. 'Two wounds to the neck, puncturing a vital artery. The victim quickly bleeds to death.'

Helena looked at me, her head on one side. 'That is the way the vampire kills,' she hissed between her teeth, her voice so low that I was not certain whether I had heard it, or imagined it. 'That's why Lavedrine was drawn to Lotingen. He was following hard on the vampire's trail.'

She placed her hand upon the door, which swung back gently on its hinges.

We stepped inside.

Everything was more or less the same, though it looked very different in the daylight. The body was gone, of course. They had wrapped it up in the bed-sheets before they carried it off. The rest of the bedding had been burnt or thrown away, presumably. The wooden floor was old and worn, the planks hewn from knotted pine. There was a large dark stain close beneath the window, where Lavedrine and I had found the body. There was more blood on the wall and a cluster of spots on the low ceiling, but those stains did not seem so stark as they had seemed that night.

I took a deep breath. The air was fresher, too. The stench of decomposition had almost dispersed. The air inside the building was not much different from that outside in the yard. It was sweet, and only slightly tainted, a trifle more powerful than the smells of the river and the farmland which stretched away in three directions, together with the blood of years spilled in the nearby slaughter-house. The essence of living things lingers longer than any other smell.

I looked more carefully at the furniture.

Two kitchen chairs with wicker seats, a square table, a single chest of drawers. Old and scuffed, not particularly well cared for. Not worth caring for, perhaps, but practical and utilitarian. A little labour with a bucket, mop and dusters would make the place liveable, and even comfortable in a sober sort of way. I was disconcerted to discover that the little house was pleasant, even homely. It was in the country, a short walk from a river. I could hear the singing of birds. Chopped logs had been stacked in the fireplace. A kettle was resting on a low ledge of the hob, waiting only to be filled and put on the fire. The table and chairs were coated with a film of dust, but that could easily be swept away. And above the table – the only decorative thing in the room – was a small watercolour picture in a frame.

Helena was staring hard at it, her chin cradled in her fist.

'What are you peering at?' I asked, going towards her.

She did not answer me directly.

'This is a home,' she said some moments later.

I looked over her shoulder at the sketch. 'A pretty one, too.'

'Not the picture,' she said. 'I am talking about this house.'

'Before the slaughter-house was closed ...'

'It is *still* a home,' she said, raising her finger, touching the corner of the picture-frame, setting it swinging on its nail. 'Otherwise, why would anyone bother to hang up such a nice little picture here?'

If only Lavedrine and I had done the same thing the first time that we entered the place. If only we had looked beyond the horror of the decomposing body on the bed. Had either of us directed his lantern towards the picture on the wall, we might have noticed what Helena had just seen.

I leant closer, staring at the picture, wondering exactly what she had seen.

A thatched cottage, a hedge and garden, flowers ...

I placed my finger on the corner of the picture, as she had done, moving it on the axis of the nail on which it hung. The wall beneath the picture was a uniform dark grey, the same dust-ingrained tint as the rest of the wall. Hanging nearby was a pierced metal plate with a wooden handle, the sort of implement we use for roasting chestnuts. I shifted that, and I saw the outline of its form – light grey against the darker background of the uncovered wall. The chestnut-roaster had been hanging there so long, it had left its impression on the surface like a silhouette.

'This view was put up very recently,' Helena said slowly. 'But why would an officer hang a picture up if he was on the run, or if he was using this house to ... to do what? Why do you think he was here, Hanno?'

'Lavedrine and I believe that he probably used the house as a meeting-place. They might, for example, have been smuggling amber ...'

'Why meet here?' she asked. 'They could have met more easily down by the river. The reeds are thick. No-one would have seen them there at night. Why come *here* at all?'

She plucked the picture from the wall, examined the frame for a moment, then handed it to me.

'Do you see what the hanging loop is made from?' she asked.

I did not need to touch it, but I did so. Hair had been neatly woven together like a tiny rope. The hairs were blond. Two distinct shades of blond, I corrected myself, that is, hair belonging to two *different* people. Sebastien Grangé's hair was blond. So, who did the other shade of hair belong to?

Emma Rimmele's hair was dark brown …

'It is a love token,' Helena continued. 'Perhaps Lieutenant Grangé was not here on some sordid business, such as you have described. He might have come to meet a lover. Indeed, I think he did. And she came willingly to meet him. I would say that this was their home. That is, the home that they were dreaming of, perhaps.'

Helena placed her hand on mine.

'Are you certain that Emma was raped by Grangé, Hanno?'

The smell of blood swept over me like a monster wave. I tasted it in my throat and nose, suffocating and horrible. I put the picture back in its hook, made my way quickly to the door, stepping out onto the balcony, into the light and the fresh air. I rested my hands on the wooden rail, steadying myself, looking down into the yard below. I felt as if I were about to lose my senses.

I felt Helena's hand rest lightly on my shoulder. Her hand caressed my shoulder, then came to rest upon the back of my neck. 'Something has upset you,' she said. 'Was it that picture? The loop of hair? Or something I have said?'

How could I answer? Could I tell her that her reading of the signs had probably been correct? That Grangé had almost certainly met a woman there, and more than once? Would she believe me if I told her that it was the memory of the blood that had upset me, the sheer quantity of blood that Lavedrine and I had uncovered beneath the bedding two nights before? And what was I to say of those interlacing strands of blond hair?

I breathed in deeply, felt the rhythm of my heart slowing down.

I told Helena what Elspeth, the little chambermaid from the Black Bull, had told me.

'A dark creature,' Helena murmured. 'A mysterious female presence. Spying on them, perhaps. I wonder …'

I waited, wondering too, but she did not go on. She was waiting for me, perhaps, but I could tell her no more. I stared towards the iron grating of the far-off window of the slaughter-house, as if, by looking, I might clarify the troubled thoughts which raced in a jumble through my mind.

'It looks like a cage to contain a wild beast,' she whispered.

Her hand came to rest on my arm, catching at my wrist, holding it tightly.

'Please, take me home,' she said, her voice fearful, low.

We returned to the riverbank, skirting around the slaughter-house, so far as the narrow path would allow. The French soldiers had apparently abandoned the place. No-one stopped us as we left the house and the yard. Nor did we meet them again as we took the path towards the river. But as we stepped up onto the raised embankment which contained the river's flood, I was not surprised to see them standing to attention, shoulder to shoulder, muskets at their shoulders. Nor to see an officer towering over them, as if he were inspecting them.

Only the fact that the officer was Lavedrine surprised me.

One of the men must have warned him of our presence, for he turned to meet us. His expression was darker than a starless winter night.

'What brings you here?' I gasped. 'Has something happened at the prison?'

Anything could have emerged from his interrogation. Elspeth might have told her tale again. Wilhelm Voigt might even have confessed to the murder if they had used the irons on him. It would all depend on Layard's desire to close the case and send Lavedrine packing.

He shook his head. 'Not there,' he said.

Even so, the dark clouds did not shift from his face.

Helena let go of my arm and took a step towards him. 'Serge, what is wrong?'

Lavedrine held her gaze for a moment, then he looked at me.

'You must go home at once, Herr Procurator. What you feared,' he said, 'has happened in Lotingen.'

Chapter 30

'I never saw the like of it, monsieur.'

The sergeant wiped dripping snot from his nose on the silver stripes of his lower sleeve, and glanced back over his shoulder. 'I fought in the Vendée back in '93,' he said, his eyes wide with revulsion at the memory. 'Them Tawny Owls didn't dare do nothing to equal this lot. Nor the *sans-culottes* in Paris. I was there during the worst days of the Terror. But this … uh … it's ferocious …'

The hiss of this word shifted into a guttural rasp of impending vomit. He turned away, hacking, coughing, his revulsion almost certainly justified by the horror of what he had seen inside the cemetery walls.

He turned again to face me, ducking his head apologetically to my wife.

'Wasn't there a guard?' I asked him. 'There've been two murders in as many days.' I pointed across the lane to the copse where the crucified body of Ludo Mittner had been savaged by dogs. 'One of the bodies was found just there.'

The man snarled in what was, I realised, a bitter laugh. 'There were sentries posted, all right, monsieur.'

'And yet they did nothing to stop it.'

He looked me squarely in the eye. 'What could two men do against a pack of beasts, monsieur? They saw them coming down the lane, they tried to hold them back, but it didn't work. Like fools they fired off their muskets, and then they were fucked. A bayonet wasn't going to stop that lot. Not in those circumstances. We are skirmishers, monsieur, we fight, and then we run.'

I nodded.

'They were lucky to get away with their lives, I reckon. They gave an account of what they'd seen, and all the officers were in a tizz. They wanted to send out the heavy brigade.'

'Colonel Claudet issued orders, I imagine?'

'His orders were to send for you, Monsieur Procurator,' the man erupted. 'And here you are. He thought that you might be able to stop them. Unfortunately, you did not come to work your magic on your countrymen.'

'I was out of town last night …'

'And isn't that a pity, monsieur,' he said dismissively. 'I doubt you could have done much, in any case.'

I stepped beyond him, and passed through the large ornamental iron gates, one of which had been torn from its hinges, and thrown to the ground. Helena had been standing forlornly at my elbow while I spoke to the French sergeant. Now, she clung onto my arm, and I could feel her trembling. I knew what was going through her mind.

Anders.

To the left of the gate, Lars Merson's cemetery was what it had always been: a haven of peace where the dead had been laid out in orderly ranks to wait for the final trumpet. Some of the stones marking the graves and the vaults in that section were two or three hundred years old, covered in moss, darkened by weathering, the names no longer legible. Nothing had happened to disturb the rest of those who slept on that side of the burial ground.

417

But on the right, it was a different story.

There had been rain in Lotingen the night before, it seemed. What had once been grass was now churned mud, hardening in the sun, ploughed up by many boots and shoes. Flowers had been crushed beneath the heedless feet of those who had devastated the place. Glass vases in which the flowers had once been standing were broken into shards. Sunlight speckled on the broken fragments, which shone like a thousand diamonds cast upon the earth. A drunken army might have swept through the cemetery. Many gravestones and markers had been rooted up, thrown aside, some broken, others shifted. And there were gaping holes in the ground, as if the cemetery had been subjected to a massive bombardment. The field of Jena must have looked like this as our troops took flight, abandoning their positions and their equipment, leaping out of shattered trenches and collapsed earthworks, leaving their useless cannon behind them as they followed in the wake of the broken infantry squares and scattering cavalry. And as they fled, they left behind the corpses of their fallen comrades.

Wherever I looked, I saw fragments of wood, tilted statues, shattered crosses, fencing torn up, trampled down, any obstacle carelessly pushed or pulled aside. There were bodies, too, as if a massive explosion had uprooted them. Bare skulls stared up at the heavens from empty sockets. Other skulls had been pressed down into the soft soil by heavy feet. They looked as if they meant to eat their way to the centre of the Earth. Hands – fingers bent and twisted – sat on top of clods of earth like large black spiders. Arms and legs lay twisted and stretching, as if they had been frozen in the act of rising from the dead.

How many bodies had been disinterred?

'Anders?'

Helena's voice was a pitiful pleading sob. There was no way to hide from her what I was seeing, nor to protect her from what I still feared. I took her hand in mine, leading her like a child along the path towards the forgotten corner of the cemetery where my own son, and Angela Enke, had both been secretly laid to rest.

'Close your eyes,' I urged her. 'Trust in me.'

And for my own part, I prayed. *Yea, though I walk through the valley of the shadow of death, I will fear no evil: for Thou art with me; Thy rod and Thy staff they comfort me.*

As we passed through the ravished graves, we might have been traversing Hell.

'Don't look, Helena,' I whispered, guiding her carefully around a twisted corpse which lay directly in our path. It was the body of a woman. Her diminutive size and the discoloured shroud in which she had been buried told me so. Skeletal hands stretched stiffly from the sleeves of her eternal nightdress. A tiny skull with tatters of blackened skin was still attached to the skeleton, while a cluttered skein of long grey hair wafted gently in the breeze. The body had been tipped from its coffin, then left behind as if the Day of Judgement had come and gone.

In this, the newest section of the cemetery, the area where they might expect to find what they were looking for, they had dug up grave after grave. I counted nine deep holes in all. Each body had been torn from its coffin, examined, dismissed, discounted, the skeletons mixed and scattered by their rough handling. Who could hope to re-compose them? Bones, skulls, funeral clothes, everything had been thrown aside as the rampage moved on to the next, and the next, and the next.

My voice rose into my throat, but my cry died there.

I turned to Helena, placing my hand upon her shoulder, shaking her.

'Helena.'

It was the only word that I could manage to pronounce at first.

'Look!'

We stood together, holding hands, looking towards the plot where Merson and I had buried the child. There was nothing to mark the place, nothing to distinguish it as a grave. The tiny wooden cross had been trampled underfoot. Having come to me in Marienburg, Helena had placed no fresh flowers on the plot. The withered blooms had been carried off by the rushing tide of marauders. She fell down on her knees on the grass, clasping her hands together, her voice a babbling brook of disconnected wails and half-formed words. I heard the name of God and His son in the midst of them.

I looked beyond the plot of grass, and there was Angela Enke.

Her corpse had stopped them short. She had brought the desecration to an end. She had, in a sense, saved Anders. They had found her body, and there the hunt had ended. Five days and nights had not yet passed, but her corpse was riddled with corruption and decay. She was hardly recognisable as the girl that I had brought up from the bottom of the well. If the hunters were looking for a vampire that they believed was Angela Enke, they had been disappointed. The infidels had pulled her out of the pit, examined her for signs of vitality, then pushed her out of the way. Of life, there was no hint remaining. Her skin had turned black, it had swelled, split and burst, exploding outwards, revealing more than I desired to see. The trailing worms and slugs were enough for me.

'The true horror is down that way, monsieur.'

The French sergeant was standing at my shoulder, his flat face grimmer, and even less expressive, than before, his finger pointing further down the path

'In town they are saying that they found what they were looking for.'

I left Helena on her knees, lost in communion with her infant son, while I followed the sergeant, turning away from the desecrated part of the cemetery down by the river, taking a gently rising path which leads towards the ancient vaults of the noble families on the slight knoll on the eastern boundary. My heart was thudding painfully in my chest.

I knew where he was taking me.

'Here we are, monsieur.'

The tomb might have been a pagan temple on the Palatine hill in ancient Rome. It was made of local sandstone. No longer red, the stone was stark black, as if the edifice had been baked in a sooty oven. The problem with sandstone is that it erodes, and this particular vault was in a very bad state, as if it had not been attended to in many, many years. The family name was inscribed above the door.

I had been there before, but on that occasion, I had not had time to look at it.

KASSEL.

The letters were worn, but they had been deeply cut, and were still legible.

'What did they find here?' I asked the sergeant, and my voice sounded strange to my own ears.

'Come and see for yourself, monsieur,' he replied.

I followed the Frenchman into the Kassel funeral vault.

The iron gates which sealed the tomb had been rudely

ripped from their hinges. As I waited for my eyes to adjust to the gloom, my nose was assaulted by the mould of ages. Bones had been scattered over the stone floor. I counted six skulls, then I spotted another one in the darkest corner. But it was the coffin in the middle of the room on newly-made trestles which immediately won my attention. It seemed to glow in the twilight. The wood was relatively clean and new. The lid had been unscrewed, removed and cast aside. I stepped up to the coffin, my legs barely able to hold me up.

I knew what I would find in there.

It was two or three feet long, made of ash, poking vertically into the air.

I heard the French sergeant speaking at my back.

'You are Prussian, monsieur. Can you explain these things?'

I did not try. I was robbed of speech.

I knew what that coffin ought to have contained. Emma Rimmele had told me. She had brought it all the way from Kirchenfeld. Her mother had died some months ago of the nervous fever, she said. Having seen the state of Angela Enke, who had been dead but a few days, I had prepared myself to stare into a face which was marked by advanced age, the ravages of a mortal illness, and the greater ravages of *post mortem* decay. I had prepared myself for horror.

But that was not what I saw.

I do not know how long I stood there, staring down into the coffin.

Nor do I know how Helena arrived there. But suddenly, she was standing by my side. 'Is this the vampire they were looking for?' she murmured, holding onto my arm, leaning forward, peering into the coffin. 'Who is she, Hanno?'

There were signs of imminent decay on the forehead, dark

spots, staining. Even so, the skin of the cheeks was the purest white of unsullied eggshell. The well-formed mouth was a round black hole, the white teeth framed by shapely lips of ghostly grey. The half-closed eyes had sunk into their dark sockets, the eyelids parted. And yet, I could see that she had once been very beautiful. Her long hair was laid out on her shoulders, and it was blonde. As bright and golden as it had been when she was living.

... woven together like a tiny rope. Two shades of blond ...

'She is not wearing a shroud,' Helena murmured.

The girl's fine figure was encased in a long pink dress. Her legs below the hem were covered by pale silk stockings. And on her feet she wore an elegant pair of calfskin slippers which matched the colour of her dress. The upper half of the dress was covered by a massive dark brown stain of dried blood. Not blood spilled recently. Not caused by the ash spike which had been driven through her heart. The death-wound was on the left side of her slender neck, and it was unmistakable. Two round black holes, ripped skin, the haemorrhaged artery.

I heard the sergeant click his tongue. Her beauty was so evident that it could still provoke lascivious thoughts in the mind of a soldier. Clearly, this was *not* the aged mother of Emma Rimmele. Nor was it the corpse of the Emma Rimmele that I knew, though they looked to be about the same age, more or less.

'Who is she, Hanno?' Helena whispered.

I cannot say how long I held my breath. It burst from me in a sudden gasp. 'She is Emma Rimmele,' I said. 'The *real* Emma Rimmele.'

Helena did not speak at once. She huddled close by my side,

slipping her arm through mine. 'You know where she has gone to,' she said very quietly. 'You know where she is hiding.'

The silence inside the tomb was unbearable.

I felt my wife's weight pulling on my arm. Her mouth pressed close to my ear. Her voice was the merest murmur.

'You have to stop her, Hanno.'

Chapter 31

Commissariat de Police.

Fresh black letters on a cream ground.

An older German script was just discernible beneath it.

The city had finally fallen to the French after an extended siege by General Lefebvre in May 1807. Elsewhere in Prussia, it would have been a cause for civic dismay. But this was Danzig. The inhabitants had never liked being Prussian, though their city had long been the capital of West Prussia. Now, thanks to Bonaparte, they could call themselves free citizens of the Republic of Danzig, a semi-independent state under slack French dominion. The city had become a pirate colony once again, as it had been in the good old Hanseatic days.

Would they find the time to waste on a Prussian magistrate, I asked myself.

My fears were realised as soon as I entered the building, gave my name to the clerk who was sitting at a desk beside the door, and told him why I had come.

'Looking for a woman? Do you know how many of those we've got in Danzig?'

The clerk's sharp voice echoed off the walls, ran round the large empty hall, and came back to him.

'This one is suspected of thieving in Lotingen,' I specified.

'Our book of light-fingered wenches is thicker than the Bible,' the clerk replied, and he sounded very proud of the fact, as if no other town could contain so many thieves, nor such proficient female ones, as Danzig. 'Are you sure she is here?'

'She arrived three days ago,' I said.

I did not mention that I had visited the Merchants' Bank in town that morning. She had withdrawn a considerable sum of money there just two days before. In fact, she had emptied the account in her father's name, and was now a very rich woman.

'We'll need to check whether she registered,' the clerk said, giving me a sly look. 'She might have dropped a false name at the customs gate. Thieves often do, you know.'

'She'll have used her own name,' I assured him.

Without a registration slip, no-one could enter the city. The toll for strangers – persons intending to do business there, or sail off on the Baltic Sea – was five florins, the officer at the gate had told me, which would allow them to stay for up to a week. My fear was that she had already left the town.

'Can you check arrivals and departures?' I asked. 'I want to know where she was lodging.'

The clerk stopped fiddling with his pen. He glanced around the empty hall, then placed his white hands flat on the desk, leaned forward and said in a low voice: 'Consulting official documents in Danzig has its price, sir.'

I brought my face close to his. 'How much?'

'A florin each, in and out.'

'Two florins?' I repeated.

His tired black eyes peered into mine. 'Do you want the information, or not?'

I searched in my pocket and found a thaler coin, which I placed on the table.

His hand shot out and covered it. 'This is Prussian money,' he hissed.

'And worth two Danzig florins,' I replied. 'Prussia will still be here when Danzig sinks beneath the sea.'

He lifted up his hands in surrender, and the coin had disappeared.

'What is the name of this female thief that you are looking for?'

'Emma Rimmele,' I said. 'She is here in the company of her father, I think.'

'A thief with a father? That's a turn-up. What is his name?'

'Erwin Rimmele. He is old, sick. His mind has gone. He may not know who he is.'

The clerk pinched his thin lips together, nodding towards a long wooden bench by the far wall. 'Sit over there, if you will, Herr Procurator. I won't be gone more than a few minutes.'

I sat down, watching as he shuffled away down the hall. He looked no more than forty years old, though he moved like a man who was twice that age, and would probably take twice as long as he had promised.

Instead, my coin appeared to have given wings to his uncertain steps.

'Herr Procurator Stiffeniis,' his voice boomed from beneath an arch a minute later. 'Come here, sir. Come quickly.'

As I passed beneath the arch, I saw a taller figure at the end of a corridor talking with the clerk. The two men were starkly outlined against a large window at their backs.

'We may have what you're looking for, sir,' the second man announced, coming towards me, leaving the clerk in his wake, presenting himself with a welcoming smile on his face. Such smiles, as a rule, light up the eyes of children who expect a treat. I was not surprised by the open hand which accompanied

427

this smile, as another one of my despised Prussian thalers disappeared from view.

'You may just be doing us a favour,' the man went on, and I was tempted to hold out my hand and ask for my money back. 'An old man was found down by the port last night, wandering around in a state of evident confusion. Unable, or unwilling, to say who, or what, he was, they brought him here. As nobody has come today to claim him back, I was on the point of consigning him to the lock-up for the poor and the insane, for such he appears. I can get no sense out of him, and we cannot keep him here in cells intended for whores and their pimps. So, let us hope you are able to identify him. By the way, sir, I am Georg Kaplan, captain of the watch.'

'I would like to speak with the man,' I said.

If he were Erwin Rimmele, I had the feeling that Captain Kaplan would be walking him down to the hospice for the insane that day, in any case. I was glad that I had found him, obviously, though I had little hope of getting anything useful out of such a witness. He was lost in a mental fog, as Emma had never failed to tell me.

'Follow me,' Herr Kaplan said, turning away, leading me along the corridor towards a ramp of stairs which went down into the basement.

'I'd like to speak with him alone,' I said, as Georg Kaplan palmed another thaler.

'I have to lock you in,' he said. 'I'll give you twenty minutes, right?'

I turned away and took a lamp from the wall. I did not offer to pay.

'Right,' I said.

Kaplan opened the door, and I stepped inside, the key

turning immediately in the lock behind me. The lamp flared like coal-gas in a mine; it took some moments for my eyes to get accustomed to the gloom. The stench was as dense as a Baltic fog. Black mould scarred the blistering walls like leprosy. The tiny room appeared to be empty except for a heap of rags on a pallet.

Something shifted, and the pile moved.

A hand emerged and began to scratch what was, I realised, a matted mop of uncombed hair. Erwin Rimmele was curled up like an egg, pressing his knees against his chin, his face buried in a grey mattress which was spewing forth straw. The straw was rotted, black, creeping with lice.

'Herr Rimmele, I am Hanno Stiffeniis, the magistrate from …'

'I know who you are,' he said, looking up at me, his voice harsh, strained. 'I know why you're here. You could have stopped her. You had your chance. I told you! She was not what she appeared to be.'

He was not incoherent, as Kaplan had reported. Nor as his erstwhile keeper had always insisted. Not then, at least. I stretched out my right hand, laying it gently on his shoulder. I could feel him trembling beneath my fingers. I squeezed gently, feeling his bones, hoping to reassure him by my presence, and gain his confidence.

'We met that day in the cemetery …'

'You should have taken her then,' he snapped.

His eyes held mine, gleaming like silver coins from the bottom of a dark pit.

He swung his legs towards me, heaving up his body, sitting on the edge of the pallet, leaning forward. The smell of him caused my tongue to catch in my throat. How long had it been

429

since he had seen soap and water? His once-white hair was matted with dirt. His bony hands were blacker than his face.

'Where is she?' I asked.

He raised his hand, combing out his knotted hair. His fingers quivered and shook, barely within his control, as his hand moved jerkily back and forth, rearranging his hair. There was a stately earnestness about it, as if he had something important to say, but would not say it until he had spruced himself up.

'How do I look?' he asked, dropping his hands into his lap.

I pretended to examine his face. 'Much better,' I lied.

'The bird has flown,' he said.

I was amazed by his lucidity. Had everything been exaggerated and distorted to manipulate *me*?

'I had no idea,' I admitted. 'I did not realise what was going on.'

He nodded slowly, frowning, raising his hand, passing his fingers through his hair again. I watched and waited, then began to fear that he would never speak again.

'Where has she gone?' I prompted him.

He stopped his combing, his hand poised above his head, staring at me with a look of the greatest intensity. He pushed an imaginary curl behind his ear, shifting others off his forehead.

'They came for her,' he murmured.

'They?' I repeated. 'Who, sir?'

His eyes blazed open. 'Those who wake the living dead,' he hissed. 'You know how they do it, don't you? Everyone in Prussia does.'

I looked into his eyes and shook my head. 'Tell me, sir,' I invited him.

He smiled to himself before he spoke. 'You have to wake the creature up before you can kill it forever,' he whispered, leaning close to me. 'The eyes must be wide open, or it will come back. It will return to haunt us all.'

I have questioned people of every sort – prisoners, witnesses, anyone who can add to what I know. In Erwin Rimmele's case, I lacked a compass. What was madness, what was truth? Regarding what I knew already, this posed no problem. Regarding all the rest, I would have to take his hand and walk with him along the same dark path.

'When did they come for her?'

'Why did you come to the house?' he fired back.

'A girl had been murdered …'

'The first time,' he said, and laughed. 'But you returned.'

'I had to ask questions. The killers …'

He began to chew on a fingernail, ignoring me. 'She knew the killers,' he said at last. 'She knew what they could do. The threat was clear to her.'

I hunched forward, very close, looking into his mild grey eyes. 'How did they manage to threaten Emma?'

He shuddered violently. 'Emma? *Her?*'

I held up my hands to pacify him. 'That woman,' I corrected myself. 'The young woman who was at the house with you. The one who claimed to be your daughter. How did they frighten her?'

'They left a sign. They always do. We're watching you, it said.'

'A sign, Herr Rimmele? Which sign are you talking of?'

'The tooth,' he said. 'They yanked it out before they threw the body into the pit.'

I did not need to ask of whom he was speaking. 'Why do such a thing?'

'It was a message. She could not escape from them. They had placed a corpse where she was hiding. You saw the wounds

431

yourself. The sign of the vampire. People would blame her, kill her. Unless she did as she had been told.'

He knew what had happened at the Prior's House. He knew the details concerning Angela Enke's death, as well as the accusations which had followed on from it. But how had he known? There was no way that he could have known, unless she had described it to him. He lived in total isolation, seeing no-one but her. Clearly, she had told him what had happened: the body in the well, the tooth in the bucket, the fact that somebody was menacing her.

Why would she tell him?

'You knew what the tooth meant, didn't you?'

Erwin Rimmele nodded his head. 'It's a sign of treachery, a promise that treachery will be avenged. Your tooth is next, it says. She could not escape from them. Whatever she was doing, it was not what she'd been told to do.'

'You guessed what she was up to, didn't you?'

'Wasn't it obvious? She wanted what belonged to me, and she ...'

He stopped in mid-sentence, caught hold of my hand.

'Give me the piss-pot,' he said. There was something in his voice which told me that he was used to giving orders, used to being obeyed. 'Give it here,' he snapped.

I resented the distraction. What he had been saying was beginning to make a kind of sense. How much longer would his clarity last? Emma had told me of the sudden swings to which his mind was subject, and she might have been telling the truth.

'The pot,' he said again, more urgently.

I reached down and picked it up, holding my breath to avoid the sickly stink. As I stood up again, Rimmele stretched out his right hand, his left hand burrowing among the rags, searching for an opening. He jolted upright, throwing back what passed for a shirt across his shoulder, his trousers slipping down around his knees. He stood before me, catching at his trousers by the waistband, his member held in the other hand.

I took a step back, holding out the chamber-pot.

'Who were they, Rimmele? Who was threatening her?'

He stared at me defiantly. His legs were as white as chalk in contrast with his black face, neck and hands. His sex poked out from the bush of long white hairs at the base of his stomach like a slice of blackened, desiccated fruit.

'Were they French soldiers?' I demanded.

I thought that he might spit in my face. 'They were Prussians. Nationalists. Patriots. Men of honour. Our history is long and glorious. A group of knights, followers of the late Franz von Sickingen, began it all in 1525. Before the battle of Frankenhausen. Two and a half centuries later, I became the Grand Knight. Our meetings were held in Kirchenfeld. In the Blood Room. Far from prying eyes. We swore allegiance to our German brothers. We vowed to fight for a German nation. We sealed an oath in blood!'

He closed his eyes, and seemed to sway.

'Have you ever tasted blood?' he went on quietly. 'Strength surges from the dead corpse to the living body. It made us strong. It made us dangerous.'

'Dangerous to whom?' I prodded gently.

'The enemies of Germany,' he replied with great deliberation. 'Even a Prussian king can be one of those. They called him the "Great", but Frederick's soul was French. He spoke their language, played French music, drank French wine, invited

Frenchmen to *Sans Souci* at our expense. Voltaire was his chosen guest.'

'You tried to kill the king, didn't you?' I said, recalling the note in the Lotingen archive. That was why Kassel had opposed the marriage contract. That was the news which Merson had discovered, and that Helena had brought to Marienburg. Erwin Rimmele had deflowered Gisela Kassel, and forced the marriage on her father.

'Tried, and failed,' he murmured.

I held the chamber-pot a trifle closer.

Rimmele's eyes fixed upon it. Sweat broke out in pearls on his forehead.

'Give it here, be quick!' he demanded.

'Kassel had discovered your plot,' I said, still holding back.

'He did not want to give his daughter to me. But that was easily overcome. He could not refuse me once he learnt that I was one of them.'

'One of whom?' I probed.

'The vampires,' he said, and all the breath hissed out of him. 'I recruited them. I was their point of reference. Young men, patriots, ready for anything. Ready to feed on my blood when greed got the better of them. They wanted what was mine.'

'How did the vampires kill, Erwin?'

He seemed perplexed by such sudden intimacy, hearing his name on my lips.

'How?'

'How was the death blow delivered?' I insisted.

He let go of his trousers, which cascaded down around his ankles.

'A single bite,' he said with a sickly smile. 'A wound to the neck

434

like two sharp, pointed teeth. The instrument was made to my design. The symbol of our brotherhood. The Greek letter, *pi*. Two sharp prongs. One jab, the job was done. The chosen one was gone, along with his blood. We had his strength, his riches. His family shunned him. His energy was ours. The others were too terrified to ask what had happened.'

How many people had he killed? How many more had been murdered by the younger members of his fraternity? How many slaughtering bands like his had sprung to life in Prussia over the centuries? How many bloodthirsty vampires had they invented? How many of them still survived?

'Kassel wished to save his daughter from the likes of you,' I said.

'Too late,' the old man said. 'I had made my way into his family by then.'

'A familiar face,' I murmured. 'His daughter's espoused. A vampire …'

Rimmele stared down his nose at me. 'Gisela loved me. Passion makes the blood flow quick,' he sneered. 'You've never tasted victory, Herr Stiffeniis. That is what we have lost. A taste for blood, a delight in conquest. Important decisions are never made on the field of battle. Delicate strategies require closed rooms, deep thought. What were von Trauss's scruples to me? I had his daughter; his daughter had my Emma. Then, a vampire took her place.'

He sat down on the bed as if his legs had been whipped from under him.

'Tell me about the vampire who got her teeth into you, Herr Rimmele.'

He raised his head, and looked at me in a state of evident confusion. Was he searching for an excuse, an explanation,

435

something to confound me? Or was the darkness closing in on him again?

'The woman who took your daughter's place,' I spelled it out for him.

'She … she wanted …' He seemed to choke on the words. 'She wanted everything. She brought that girl to me at the house, the one who was murdered, hoping to seduce me. And when that failed, she … she came naked to my bed. My own daughter …' He stifled a cry. 'No, *not* my daughter. No woman, either. A demon. A demon had taken Emma's place.'

My gaze fell on his shrivelled sex.

In the same instant, she appeared before my eyes. The creature I had known as Emma Rimmele. She might have been there in that room, enjoying his shame and my humiliation. Her lips so eager to feed on the flesh of others, so knowledgeable in the ways of pleasure, so ready to suck what she craved from those that she had chosen.

'My daughter went to Marienburg,' he said unprompted. 'There were things to do, she had to go. I could not manage the estate, and Emma seemed pleased to help me. She had not smiled since the day her mother died. She did everything that a daughter should. But one day she did not return from town. Nor the day after.'

'And so you went to Marienburg,' I concluded.

Herr Rimmele nodded. 'A carriage came to carry me off. Emma had sent it, the driver said. Gisela's coffin had been removed from the vault. We would all be together again in a better place. It … was … a … lie!'

I watched him sob, but felt no compassion for him.

'Emma was dead,' I said. His daughter had been murdered in the cottage with Grangé. The Frenchman's body had been left there, while the corpse of the girl had been carried off to Lotingen inside her mother's coffin. 'Did she take your daughter's place so easily?'

'It was dark. Her clothes were black, she wore a hood. She did not speak. I could smell that she was … different, though I could not see her face. That vixen sat beside me in the carriage. I felt her lips against my neck, breathing into my ear. "Emma is dead," she whispered. "You will live, or die, Erwin Rimmele, when I decide it."'

I saw the scene like a silhouette theatre on a wall. A beautiful young woman, a helpless old man. Lips pulled back, sharp teeth edging down towards the pulsing vein in his neck. The odour of the woods and fresh-turned earth, the perfumes that had entranced me that day at the Prior's House. I was sickened by it. And suddenly, the lantern-slide clicked, and changed. The man was younger, equally in her thrall. Was it myself? Another? I knew she would not hesitate to use her charms on any man.

'Find her, Stiffeniis. Throw her back into the hell-fire pit from which she crawled. Quiet her forever! Make the world safe …'

The sound of hissing distracted me.

I looked down.

Erwin Rimmele was urinating onto the trousers at his ankles.

No sooner finished, he began to scream, and he gave no sign of stopping.

Ever.

Chapter 32

'Face down, sir. Make her gnaw the earth.'

Georg Kaplan, commander of the town watch, was convinced that there was nothing human about the corpse. 'Heaven forbid! We don't want her waking up again in Danzig,' he exhorted.

'Face down,' I conceded, ashamed of what I had just said, ashamed of what we were about to do.

Kaplan had sent the other two policemen to wait for us by the coach. The corpse had been rolled up in a canvas sheet to avoid exciting curiosity as they carried it away from the riverside warehouse. One or two of the lodgers had watched the proceedings, but they showed little real interest. Then again, to see the police removing a corpse from such a place must have been the order of the day.

'I will write the report,' I insisted, as we reached a wood outside the town which Kaplan declared a suitable spot for the burial. 'This location must remain a secret.'

'Don't worry about that, Herr Stiffeniis. What happened in Lotingen cemetery will not be allowed to happen here in Danzig.'

The concern on his face surely matched my own. We intended to do what Merson and I had done the week before with the corpse of Angela Enke. A clandestine burial. It was becoming a ritual. It seemed to me as if the seamstress from

Krupeken were taking posthumous revenge on the woman who had been the cause of her death. The murderess would lie in unhallowed ground without a name, or any symbol of Christian pity to mark the place.

'No-one heard or saw a thing,' Kaplan murmured. 'I cannot figure it.'

The warren in which the body had been discovered might have been built to contain and suppress every sound, voice and smell. And every vice, too.

I planted the shovel in the loose, sandy soil and began to dig.

I remembered going up the narrow staircase, following Georg Kaplan, then passing through a sort of tunnel – the walls, ceiling and floor were all the nameless shade of filth and careless abandon. The tenement was on the waterfront in the poorest part of the town. Light filtered through a distant window frame with no glass, or from the open doors of tiny rooms where eight, nine, ten pairs of eyes glanced up at us. We had burst into rooms on either side of the one where the body had been found, asking the paupers huddling there if they could help us.

Some seemed not to understand the words.

Others turned away, or shook their heads, their eyes blank, uncaring.

The building smelled like a shed where herring are pickled in salt, then hung on lines to desiccate, or be smoked. At some point, though, the drying-rooms had been divided into living-spaces. The poor had taken the place of the fish, hanging over flop-house ropes, seeking oblivion in standing sleep. It was a vision of hell that Dante might have recognised. A corpse could rot in there every day of the week, and no-one would have noticed.

She had been there for a night, perhaps two. And yet, there was no trace of the corruption that one might have expected in such damp air, so close to the water's edge. Her skin was just as I remembered it. Smooth, flawless, with a point of bright colour in the cheeks. Full red lips, white teeth. Physical perfection. The appearance of the corpse convinced Herr Kaplan of the danger. He took one look, and said to me, 'We must get rid of her before the terror spreads.'

I rested on my shovel, watching Kaplan dig. His frenzy seemed to be growing.

She had come to Danzig, obtained the money, then found a place to hide for the night. And that had been her fatal mistake. If she was invisible, so was her killer. Before she could cry out, she was dead, and no-one knew, or cared. The warehouse owner had seen them, of course. He had noticed her anxiety to conclude the business and get in off the street. 'She didn't quibble about the price,' he said, as if it was the least a customer could do. 'The pretty lady', he called her. 'The old man could barely stand up. He didn't know what day was what, if you ask me.' To clarify the concept, he tapped his finger against the side of his temple. The following day, he had seen Erwin Rimmele wandering off alone, like a man who was lost.

She was dead by then, I supposed.

I asked him if he had seen anyone else leave the building.

He shrugged his shoulders, shook his head.

It took an hour to dig a hole, ten minutes more to fill it in again.

Back in town, Kaplan took me to his office. He poured us both a glass of schnapps, while I sat down at his desk intending to write immediately to Lavedrine. First, I told him what Helena had discovered in the cottage near the slaughter-house.

You guessed correctly, Lavedrine. It was not a rape. It was passion, love. It was in that cottage that the lovers met after Massur had sent the insubordinate officers packing from Kirchenfeld. Emma Rimmele must have followed in the wake of Grangé. They had probably arranged it. But somebody was following them. A 'strange female', as Elspeth, the serving-girl from the Black Bull tavern, reported. The same 'mysterious presence' that Lecompte insisted had attacked him. A female killer. They let her enter the love-nest for some reason.

There were <u>two</u> victims that night – too much blood, as you suspected.

Grangé was left to rot, but the corpse of Emma Rimmele was carried off to a place where no-one would have thought to look for it: inside the coffin of her mother, which was brought from Kirchenfeld, and was soon to be placed inside the Kassel family vault in Lotingen cemetery. Lecompte and Gaspard were next on the list. They must have known about Grangé and Emma. They had seen her, or they had met her. They had to die, as well.

At that point, this 'mysterious female' took possession of Erwin Rimmele.

She became Emma Rimmele, and in Lotingen the river of blood continued to flow.

I drained the schnapps, then began to tell him what I had seen that day in Danzig. While I was writing this account, I prayed to God that I would never be obliged to report such a story again.

The body was stretched out in the centre of the room.

441

Like an island in a sea of blood. The gown had been ripped away from her body. Her breasts were naked. She lay flat on her back. A wooden pole had been driven deep into her left breast, and it had found its way to her heart. Her lips were white, utterly drained of blood. The face was a pale, fixed shadow of its former self. The eyes were bloodshot, as if the shock had caused the veins to haemorrhage. A metal clip – an oval hair-pin with the beaten image of the Medusa – had been pressed down hard into the right side of her neck. It lay almost flat against her skin, like the metal plaque that a manufacturer might use to indicate the name of his company.

I prised the hair-clip brooch away, though I did not remove it entirely. There were two round holes in the jugular artery which matched the wounds – the vampire's teeth, let's call them – that I had observed on the necks of the corpses of Angela Enke and Lars Merson in Lotingen, and which we saw together in Marienburg on the neck of Grangé. You had seen the same wound in the necks of Lecompte and Gaspard.

I do not know who killed her. Nor can I say who, in truth, she may have been.

She has been buried in an unmarked grave.

I sent the despatch by messenger to Lavedrine in Marienburg, and then I waited, expecting him to arrive before the day was out. I ate a little lunch, then walked out along the quays, watching the ships, the bustle of the harbour, the simple straightforwardness of it all. I spent a good part of the afternoon sitting on a bench in the square where Georg Kaplan's office was situated. I had given that address as the place where Lavedrine and I might meet. As the day moved on, I went over the entire story in my head, trying to clarify those points which seemed less certain in my understanding of the affair, knowing that Lavedrine on his arrival would ask me to explain it all to him from beginning to end.

Lavedrine did not arrive. Nor did any message. I could not understand it.

What had happened to prevent his coming to Danzig?

First thing the following morning, I set out for Lotingen and home.

Two hours later, as I jumped down from the saddle outside my office, a group of townspeople gathered around me. Some of them asked after my health. Others were more concerned about the recent events in the town.

I could tell them very little, except to say that I believed the French soldiers would remain on guard at the cemetery. At least, until a new sexton had been appointed, and the damage had been set to rights.

And yet, where there is a crowd, there is always a troubling voice in the middle of it. A man stepped forward, his eyes bright with fright, or excitement. 'That vampire got what was coming to her. Isn't that right, Herr Procurator? The vixen what was living out at the Schuettlers' brought the seeds of evil in that coffin of hers. They flowered, an' all! Turned an old hag into a fresh young girl. Lord have mercy on us! Them are the most dangerous, sir. Young and pretty. Who would dream of being bitten by such a sweet thing? Who'd have the courage to say no to her!'

I picked up my bag and walked into the office without saying a word.

443

Chapter 33

I heard the door in the outer office.

It opened, then closed, and silence followed on.

Knutzen.

The first thing that my secretary did each morning was tend his vegetables and feed his pigs. Arriving afterwards at the office, he would put aside the filthy smock that he always wore, replacing it with the threadbare black jacket which he invariably donned for work.

I let out a sigh.

Every time that the door opened in the last few days, I had been straining to hear the voice of Serge Lavedrine, fully expecting the Frenchman to come barging into my room, upsetting my plans for the day. The official report had still to be written up; I was waiting anxiously on his news from Marienburg regarding the fate of the Prussian prisoners.

I would have suffered the Frenchman gladly, but Gudjøn Knutzen was the last thing that I needed. He would harp on endlessly about what had happened in Lotingen the week before, explaining for the umpteenth time why he had been obliged to tell Selleck, the saddler from Krupeken, about the finding of the body of Angela Enke, and how, in doing so, *he* had saved the village burial ground from the desecration which had ravaged the cemetery here in town. With each repetition of these themes, the suggestion that I had not done my duty seemed to swell and grow.

I rose from my desk instinctively, meaning to send him home for the day.

I threw the door open, and found Helena standing on the threshold.

'Hanno …'

She was very pale, her eyes huge and restless. Her dress and bonnet might have been hewn from black granite, they seemed so stiff and heavy. A stray curl had escaped from her bonnet. It was the only point of colour about her.

'What brings you here?' I asked, my voice gruffer than I intended it to be. Helena made a point of never coming to the procurator's office. Only a matter of the greatest urgency would drive her to do so. 'Is something wrong?'

'It's Lavedrine,' she said in a rush. 'He was at the house an hour ago.'

'The house?'

'On his way to Königsberg. Under military escort, Hanno. Four armed soldiers, a sergeant …' Helena laid her hand on my chest, and pushed me backwards. 'Let me in,' she gasped. 'I must sit down. I'm out of breath.'

I stood aside, watching and waiting in great confusion, while she sank down on the visitor's chair which stands in front of my desk. For an instant, the figure of my wife was cancelled out by a memory of a wild mass of auburn hair, the Medusa clip holding it in place, the face and perfume of another. My head was filled with the essence of the person that I was trying to forget. Emma Rimmele. The things that we had said and done.

Not Emma, I corrected myself. The woman who had murdered her.

445

'What's all this about?' I asked, sitting down on the far side of the desk.

Helena took off her bonnet, and her hair fell free. As she pushed it back behind her ears, I saw the red coral droplets hanging from her lobes. Sharp needles coursed through my veins in the place of blood. Lavedrine had been to the house unexpectedly, taking Helena by surprise. He would certainly have noticed the earrings. He must have realised that she wore them always, and that she held them very dear.

'General Malaport has sent for him,' she said. 'There is to be an inquiry of some sort. He would say no more.'

I collapsed back in my seat.

'Why did he not tell me this himself?'

Helena stared into my face. 'He wasn't sure that he would find you in the office. The soldiers were impatient to be gone. He knew, instead, that I would be at home. He asked me to deliver this note to you without delay.'

She put her hand in her pocket, and brought out a folded sheet of paper.

'You must add the details to your report, he said. And sign it in your name only.'

I took the crumpled paper from her outstretched hand. There was no wax, no seal.

'Have you read it?' I asked her.

Helena shook her head.

I opened the paper, glancing quickly at the contents. It was an informal letter, a hastily written note. He signed himself familiarly, Serge Lavedrine, without mentioning his rank in the French army.

I read aloud:

Dear Hanno,

In Kirchenfeld, I should have realised that a battle was about to begin. Jacques Massur has accused me of bringing the 'enemy' into his camp. He was speaking of you, of course. You've seen enough to understand the nature of our relationship. It is a question of giving blows, and taking them. I have responded, accusing him of failing to discipline the officers from Marienburg who were under his command in Kirchenfeld.

The dispute will be heard by General Malaport, and I must go to Königsberg.

At the same time, I do not want this feud to compromise our investigation.

We cannot allow the Prussians in Lotingen to live in fear of vampires and the disturbances which terror brings. Nor can I allow the rivalry between officer groups within our ranks to persist. Everyone must know – French and Prussians alike – that the killing is over, and that the murderers have been identified.

I trust you to do that, and ask you to submit a full report.

Strange as it may seem, Jacques Massur has done us one good turn.

As you know, he was about to take possession of the estate in Kirchenfeld. No sooner had we left the house than he arrested Adele Beckmann, the last remaining one of the Rimmeles' servants. He had her sent to Marienburg where she was imprisoned with the Prussians from the Black Bull inn. You will recall that General Layard had ordered me to question them again. Adele was among the prisoners. She had seen us together, you and I, and she seemed disposed to answer my questions. I did not ask about the house, her

447

master, or the master's daughter. I said nothing of blood rituals, or esoteric practices. I asked her for names, and nothing more. The names of the men who frequented the Rimmele household.

The following details should be included in your report.

First, the conspirators.

Three young Prussians have been taken into custody, and they have confessed their crimes. These terrorists once courted Erwin Rimmele as the high priest of their patriotic order. In truth, they wanted his money to finance their own rebellious adventures. They saw the declining state of his body and mind, and they determined to relieve him of his riches. Their scheme was hampered by the fact that Erwin had a faithful daughter. A daughter, I should add, who showed no interest in her father's adepts and their attempts to court her. Emma Rimmele's heart was pledged elsewhere. She had fallen in love with a French officer, Sebastien Grangé. The conspirators decided to replace the daughter with a female guardian who would answer only to them. This was their scheme: to persuade Erwin to allow her access to his bank and funds.

Second, the creature herself.

Her real name is a mystery. Where she may have come from is more mysterious still. Some Eastern tribe, perhaps, which trains its children in the arts of assassination. On no account would they admit – not even under the threat of torture – to having any precise knowledge of the woman. It was sufficient for them that she was a murderess, and that she served their purposes. She murdered Grangé and Emma, then she turned on Lieutenants Gaspard and Lecompte. However, she served her masters only up to a point! If

they were greedy, she was greedier still. She tried to outwit
them, intending to carry off Rimmele's riches for herself.
The conspirators hounded her to Lotingen, threatening to
expose her as a fraud and a killer. When she ran away, they
followed her, and murdered her in Danzig with the very
same instrument she had used to visit death on anyone who
opposed her plans: a metal brooch with two sharp prongs.

Their description of her murder matches yours in every
detail, except one …

I stopped reading.

'This may be gruesome,' I warned, looking at my wife.

Helena stared boldly back at me. 'I am not afraid,' she said,
and I took up where I had left.

… in every detail, except one. The most hideous of all.
You report that a wooden spike had been driven through
the killer's heart. They swear to heaven that they did not
do it. Having admitted everything else, I wonder why they
baulk before that accusation? I don't know what to make of
it, except to say that we are in Prussia. In this strange land
of yours, some things will always remain in the shadows, I
suppose …

My mind was in Danzig in that dark room. I could not shake
that image from my thoughts: the naked breast, the wooden
stake, the lake of blood. Erwin Rimmele had been alone with
the corpse. Did he have the strength to cleave the usurper's
heart? Or had he watched as the deed was done by someone
else?

Helena stood up.

'Lavedrine said something else before he left.'

She was, I realised, waving a piece of paper in the air in front of my nose, as if to wake me from some spell which had possessed my senses. 'It is a *laissez-passer*,' she said, 'made out in your name, and in mine. We can go to the cemetery whenever we wish. Come with me, Hanno. There's something there that we must see. Both of us. Lavedrine was most insistent about it.'

I stood up, barely taking in the news, hardly hearing her voice. My head was still thumping with that unanswered question, which bounced around the walls of my brain like a fly trapped inside a bottle.

Who had quieted the vampire in Danzig?

'Let me put this note in a safe place,' I murmured, reaching for the *nécessaire* which Helena had given me for my birthday, untying the knot, rolling out the leather pad and the sheet of un-sized paper which I used for drying the ink.

I had brought the *nécessaire* to work with me, having carelessly left it on the table in the entrance-hall at home when Lavedrine had whisked me off to Marienburg. Before I took my leave of Helena that morning, I had made a great show of picking it up, shaking it in my fist.

'My baton of office,' I proclaimed, wanting Helena to see that I was home, intent on taking up my life again where I had left it off. I wanted my wife to understand how much I valued it, and her. I wanted to put the recent past behind me.

As I rolled it out on the desk-top, I recalled the last time that I had used it. The day that the impostor came to my office, asking me to write a note which would testify to her father's precarious mental health, and verify her identity as his one and only lawful heir. 'What a pretty object!' she had remarked, watching as I pressed the affidavit down to dry the ink, then taking the *nécessaire* from my hands, rolling it tightly up again, knotting the ribbon, where I would have tied a bow.

Knot or bow?

I could not remember how the ribbon had been when I unloosed it just moments before.

As I placed Lavedrine's letter inside the *nécessaire*, I felt a shock go through my body, robbing me of breath. My eyes were fixed on the white sheet of blotting-paper. The letters were blurred, though the words were clear enough. Impressed in reverse on the blotter, I saw my own signature, and the words, *I, Hanno Stiffeniis, Magistrate of Lotingen, affirm as follows: that the bearer of this document is Emma Rimmele.*

Below this declaration was the name of the merchants' bank in Danzig.

I might have been at sea in a squall. I felt the roll of the waves beneath the keel, I gripped the edge of the table to steady myself.

Helena was standing at my shoulder, staring fixedly at the blotter.

'That paper absorbs everything, doesn't it, Hanno? There is something almost magical about it.' More quietly she added: 'The vampire left her mark, I see. She told you where she was going. You were the only person who could stop her.'

I had never seen such an expression on her face.

Had Helena opened the *nécessaire* in my absence? Had she seen what I had written? Had she known of my involvement with that woman, the extent to which my judgement had been swept aside by the force of my emotions?

Lavedrine had dismissed the wooden stake through the vampire's heart in Danzig as a matter of no great importance. Would Helena see it in the same light, knowing what she knew?

Would she suspect me of a hideous crime against the dead? Would she think that I had quieted the vampire, freeing myself forever of that creature?

'Helena, I …'

Her hand fell gently on my own.

'Take me to the cemetery,' she said.

We stood in silence before the grave for quite some time.

Then, Helena read the inscription out loud.

ANDERS STIFFENIIS

FEBRUARY, 1810–JULY, 1810.

HE SLEEPS IN THE ARMS OF THE LORD BEFORE HIS TIME.

Lavedrine had ordered the French soldiers guarding the cemetery to erect the headstone and place the curb-stones around the grave. They could not refuse to obey a colonel, I suppose. Helena had what she had wanted since the day that our little boy passed away.

I felt her hand searching for mine.

I caught her fingers, squeezed them gently, carried them to my lips.

'I'll go to Königsberg tomorrow,' I said. 'I'll take my report, and testify in his favour before General Malaport. The French will learn of the debt that Prussia owes him.'

'Lavedrine has freed us of our vampires,' she said.

'They must never be allowed to rise again.'

'Amen,' Helena intoned.

Chapter 34

That night there was a full moon.

There were dogs in the front garden. I heard them howling for some minutes.

Then, I heard them no more.

At first light, I set out for Königsberg.

Acknowledgements

We are indebted to Paul Barber's marvellous *Vampires, Burial and Death – Folklore & Reality* (Yale University Press, 1988) in deciding what was feasible, and what was not.

Dissertazione Sopra I Vampiri, first published in 1741 by Archbishop Giuseppe Davanzati of Trani (Besa, 1998, a cura di G. Annibaldis), was equally valuable.

Special thanks to our agent, Leslie Gardner, our editor, Walter Donohue, our project editor, Katherine Armstrong and everybody at Faber & Faber for their continuing support.